THE RIPPER'S WIFE

If these wild, wicked words were true . . . Jack the Ripper was no longer a faceless fiend stalking the streets of Whitechapel and my own bad dreams. He had another name, an ordinary mundane man's name, James Maybrick, and he was my very own husband, the father of my children.

As I lifted the diary from my lap a brass key fell from its binding. I was catapulted at once back through time to the morning I had sat as a young, naïve bride at my husband's desk and rattled the locked drawers. My life had indeed turned out to be a fairy tale after all, only not one of the pretty, happily ever after stories, but the most sinister one of all—I was indeed Bluebeard's bride, Jack the Ripper's wife. And amongst the many secrets my husband was harboring was a cachet of murdered, butchered women, like the dead wives in Bluebeard's secret chamber. When I had opened the cover of that diary I had peeked into that secret room, and now, now I held in my hand the key. . . .

God help me, I prayed as I walked into my husband's study.

Books by Brandy Purdy

THE BOLEYN WIFE

THE TUDOR THRONE

THE QUEEN'S PLEASURE

THE QUEEN'S RIVALS

THE BOLEYN BRIDE

THE RIPPER'S WIFE

Published by Kensington Publishing Corporation

THE
RIPPER'S
WIFE

BRANDY PURDY

KENSINGTON BOOKS
www.kensingtonbooks.com

KENSINGTON BOOKS are published by

Kensington Publishing Corp.
119 West 40th Street
New York, NY 10018

All Kensington titles, imprints, and distributed lines are available at special quantity discounts for bulk purchases for sales promotion, premiums, fund-raising, and educational or institutional use.

Special book excerpts or customized printings can also be created to fit
specific needs. For details, write or phone the office of the Kensington
Special Sales Manager: Kensington Publishing Corp., 119 West 40th
Street, New York, NY 10018. Attn. Special Sales Department. Phone:
1-800-221-2647.

Kensington and the K logo Reg. U.S. Pat. & TM Off.

eISBN-13: 978-0-7582-8890-5
eISBN-10: 0-7582-8890-5
First Kensington Electronic Edition: November 2014

ISBN-13: 978-0-7582-8889-9
ISBN-10: 0-7582-8889-1

First Kensington Trade Paperback Printing: November 2014

10 9 8 7 6 5 4 3 2 1

Printed in the United States of America

AUTHOR'S NOTE

This is a work of fiction inspired by the controversial document known as the Ripper Diary, and the lives of James and Florence Maybrick, Jack the Ripper, and his unfortunate victims. Creative liberties have been taken with all—certain characters and events have been altered, eliminated, embellished, or condensed.

The heart is deceitful above all things,
and desperately wicked: who can know it?

—Jeremiah 17:9

She was the most beautiful young lady
I ever saw, and the most amiable. . . .
And she was the most innocent.

—*Daisy Miller* by Henry James

She is more to be pitied than censured,
She is more to be helped than despised.
She is only a lassie who ventured
On life's stormy path ill-advised.
Do not scorn her with words fierce and bitter,
Do not laugh at her shame and downfall.
For a moment, just stop and consider
That a man was the cause of it all.

—a popular ballad of the 1890s by William B. Gray

PROLOGUE

*Love makes sane men mad
and can turn a gentle man into a fiend.*

On the outside it looks so innocent, just an old battered book, musty and dusty, nothing special at all. An ordinary diary bound in cardboard covered in rusty black cloth, corners bent and bumped like a quartet of bruised and broken noses, a tad frayed in places like curmudgeonly eyebrows grown wildly awry, chipped and fading gilt accents. Seven lucky gold bands adorn the spine. I chose it for that reason, because *he,* because *we,* believed in luck. You could walk into any stationery shop in the civilized world and find one just like it. I know: I'm the one who bought it.

When you open the cover, that's when the horrors begin. Your skin begins to crawl and your blood begins to chill, and you discover that this battered old diary is anything but ordinary. No dreaded dentist appointments, tedious afternoon teas with a vicar avariciously fond of cucumber sandwiches and saving cannibals' souls, quarrels with the giddy young wife about her ludicrous, exorbitantly priced bonnets—*silly* things sprouting stuffed canaries and spinach! However can she keep a straight face and wear them?—and her abominable, troublemaking mother, or taking the children to a Saturday matinée for an afternoon's flight of fantasy to see *Peter Pan.* Oh no, nothing like that! It's like walking into the parlor and seeing blood dripped across a cream-colored carpet in a trail leading straight to a torn and bloody corpse. A most unexpected sight when all you're expecting is the calm and mundane, orderly ordinary. You've come to have tea after all, not to scream and fall fainting over a corpse.

It begins with the words I've quoted above, scribbled in a scrawl of ragged red, big, bold, bright jagged letters and blobs of ink like spattered blood, garish and vulgar as a gin-soaked harlot's lip rouge, sloppily sprawling across the page like a wanton body on a rumpled bed, written as though by a drunkard in the grip of the tremors or someone with palsy who cannot quite command the pen, yet with such *force,* such *rage,* the words at times nearly cut, like a knife, right through the page. A murderer's words, it's easy to imagine them written in blood with the weapon that took so many lives, including, in a sense, my own.

I was the first or, perhaps, the final, victim. Maybe I was neither. Maybe I was both. Maybe the man who wrote this diary didn't destroy me at all. Maybe *I* destroyed myself. Maybe in the end all it amounts to is one weak woman's desperate attempts to justify all the things that went wrong in her life. You, dear reader, will have to decide. I've faced a judge and jury before. I've already experienced the worst and lost everything that matters. This time I'm not afraid. If you condemn me, there's nothing left that I hold dear that you can take from me now, not even my life.

Those vicious red words were written by my husband. The man I spent fifteen years in prison for murdering, the man whose death exiled me permanently from my children's lives and hearts. This is his diary, the one that I, as a blissful young bride, bought for him. It was a different century, sixty years ago, but it might have been only yesterday. I remember it so well—that bright blue sky day when I, so light of step in my pearl-buttoned boots of white kid, so sweetly ignorant and only eighteen, with a garden of silk daisies, cherry-red poppies, bluebells, and black-eyed Susans blooming on my straw hat and a rainbow of ribbons bouncing down my back to tickle the big, floppy lemon chiffon bow on my bustle, skipped into the shop and plucked it off the shelf. With a radiant smile, I announced to the clerk that it was "a gift for my husband" as I plopped it down upon the counter and told him, rather grandly, to charge it to my husband's account and wrap it in such a way as would appeal to a gentleman of the most refined and elegant taste, in striped paper perhaps—burgundy and forest green or navy blue and cream? I tapped my chin and pondered—and there simply *must* be a bow, a very neat, tidy, *masculine* bow, not a big, flowing, feminine thing, oh no, that would *never* do for Jim!

Those with a thirst for sensation, those who avidly peruse the penny illustrated papers, following divorce dramas and murder trials like bloodhounds, the kind of ladies and gentlemen of leisure who take their opera glasses and a boxed lunch to spend the day sitting in a crowded courtroom; cotton brokers; learned doctors; lawyers; politicians; sanctimonious moralizers; and the self-important, supercilious members of what we from the American South would call "the highfalutin" Currant Jelly Set, will know his name quite well—Mr. James Maybrick of Liverpool. But the rest of the world knows him by another name, one written in blood—Jack the Ripper.

Every love has its own peculiar story tied up with disparate, desperate bows of melodrama, madness, romance, tragedy, passion, pain, and farce, sacrifice and gluttony, tenderness and grace, honor and deceit, punishment and pleasure, sanctity and sin, the bland, ho-hum ordinary and penny-dreadful thrills, where vengeance and bliss sometimes sleep side by side in the same bed. Pure or profane, every love exacts a beautiful or bitter price. It *always* takes some toll, whether it be a pittance or a fortune, like a tax upon the hearts of those who tender, reject, or receive it. Love *always* leaves a mark: a scar, a smudge, a stain. Even those who long for love but lack it cannot escape unmarked.

It's been on my mind so much these last few days, tugging at me so urgently, shaking me, whenever I try to rest or sit idle for too long, with a cat on my lap, dreaming over faded photographs and movie magazines, making me feel like I'm waking up with the house on fire when all I want to do is sleep, to go on waltzing with the ghosts in my dreams. Dreaming of what was and what might have been . . .

I've been thinking about forgiveness, forgetting, and living with, and living without, monsters masquerading as mild-mannered men and the strange angels the Lord sometimes sends, even to those who seem, at first glance, the most unworthy of them, and all the strange, terrible, and beautiful creatures that lie in between the blackest black and the whitest white, and all the many shades of gray that bridge the gulf in between, tattered yellow newspapers, faded photographs of the dead, those who are gone and lost forever, and flickering images, larger than life and platinum precious, projected, like magic, on a screen.

My name is Florence Elizabeth Chandler Maybrick. My family and friends called me Florie, but, when he loved me he called me Bunny. I was Jack the Ripper's wife, maybe even the reason, as a clever rhymester once wrote, a man who was society's pillar became a killer. This is our own peculiar story.

Florence Maybrick

Gaylordsville, Connecticut

October 7, 1941—may this be a lucky day for beginning this endeavor. God give me the strength and courage to see it through!

❧ 1 ❧

It began with a shipboard romance, the sort of thing you might find in any romantic novel, play, or film. From time immemorial it always seems to have been the rule that when presenting romance to the masses, the hero and heroine must meet in a memorable manner, something amusing, adorable, or antagonistic, that will spawn an entertaining anecdote they can regale their friends and relations with for years to come. But happily ever after really depends upon where you end your story.

Did you ever sit and wonder what happens to the lovers locked in a passionate embrace after the gilt-fringed curtain goes down or the words *The End* appear upon the silver screen? Does Prince Charming *really* love and adore his Cinderella forevermore, forsaking all others as long as they both shall live, till death they do part? Or does he, sooner or later, exert his royal and manly prerogative and take a mistress, an ambitious lady-in-waiting, a buxom, bawdy laundress, or a pretty little actress perhaps? Are we really expected to believe that the noble bluebloods of the court accept a former servant girl as their queen? The young and naïve never think or worry about such things; when you're only eighteen it's easy to believe in love lasting "forever" and "happily ever after."

The setting was picture-postcard perfect—a spick-and-span

new steamship, part of the prestigious White Star Line, all fresh paint, varnish, and high-gloss polish, a veritable floating palace, with a buff-colored funnel belching steam high above our heads, regally bearing us across the ocean from New York to Liverpool. The SS *Baltic* might have steamed right off one of those popular souvenir postcards almost everyone in those days collected. It was all *that* perfect—*gilt-edged perfect!* It was the perfect place to fall in love!

Looking back now, in hindsight after six decades, if I were to cast the movie of my life, I might have been pert, blond, and vivacious Carole Lombard, champagne bubbly in a bustle and ringlets with an Alabama belle's molasses accent, dense and sweet, and he might have been dignified and debonair, sedately suave William Powell, a little staid and stodgy perhaps—some might even have gone so far as to call him "pompous"—but with a ready smile, a wry sense of humor, and a twinkle in his eye. He made my heart flutter and skip like a schoolgirl! With a tall silk hat and a diamond horseshoe sparkling in his silk cravat, dapper in a dark suit straight from Savile Row, patent-leather boots, and immaculate dove-gray gloves and matching spats, he was every inch a gentleman.

I suppose I must sound awfully silly, but every time he looked at me it was like receiving a valentine. Pictures of hearts, Cupids, cooing doves, clasping hands, and bouquets of flowers and boxes of chocolates tied up with red and pink satin bows filled my head like a bewildering array of pretty cards on display in a stationer's shop, and I just didn't know which one to choose, and in truth I didn't want to. I wanted them *all.* I wanted *him!* He was *everything* I had ever dreamed of. Or perhaps the sadder and wiser and much older me of today should correct the gauche green girl of yesteryear and say that he *represented* everything I had ever wanted. In those days, it was *all* about appearances. In society, style trumped substance every time.

It was March 11, 1880. Like the date inside a wedding ring, it is engraved upon my memory and heart. How could I *ever* forget? It was the day my life changed forever.

I was eighteen, bubbling over with high castle in the clouds, hopes and champagne dreams—intoxicating, sensuous, thrilling, and sweet. A living doll—I think at almost eighty I'm old enough to say that now without seeming vain—who always saw the world through rose-colored glasses. I was a dainty little thing, with a curvaceous corseted hourglass figure, tiny waist bracketed by generous bosom and hips, dressed in the latest Parisian fashions, with gleaming golden ringlets, violet-blue eyes that provoked my many beaus to say that they would make forget-me-nots droop and weep with envy, sugar-pink rosebud lips just *longing* to be kissed, the white magnolia blossom skin we women of the South prized so, and ankles and wrists so tiny and trim. I was a delicious little dish!

It seemed as though I had spent my entire life hiding under shady hats and veils to keep the sun from singeing me with its hot, crisp, baking kiss, and being scrubbed down vigorously with buttermilk and lemon juice in a never-ending crusade against freckles. And for the blemishes that seemed to erupt whenever I was overly excited or anxious Dr. Greggs prescribed a face wash of elderflower water, tincture of benzoin, and *just a little* arsenic. Not enough to hurt, he assured me in his kind, grandfatherly way when I shrank back and fearfully demurred when he handed me the prescription, remembering a play I had seen about an evil, scheming woman who had put arsenic in her boring old fuddy-duddy husband's soup so she would be free to abscond with her lover, a worthless but *excruciatingly* handsome lounge lizard with hair like black patent leather who danced like a dream and never threw away the love letters foolish women sent him lest he have to do something so menial and mundane as work for a living. I *relished* every thrilling, wicked moment of it and had sat through it *five* times, in wide-eyed wonderment, leaning forward in my seat, even though it made my stays pinch, anxiously nibbling my nails and a bag of toffee.

Despite being a seasoned traveler, a habitué of sophisticated Parisian salons and worldly European circles, and a rather sporadic attendance at a deluxe Swiss school for affluent young ladies in Vevey where I did little more than sit in the garden, eat chocolates, dabble in watercolors, devour romance novels, and gaze at the breathtaking vista of blue lakes and snowcapped mountains and dream until I graduated at sixteen, I was never blasé or jaded. In those days, I exuded a bewitching, bewildering blend of innocence and confidence, shyness and sophistication. I wore them like a halo that protected me like Saint Michael's shield. I glided through life endowed with the sweet certainty that nothing bad could possibly ever happen to me. I believed in the innate goodness of people; I trusted in the kindness of strangers and was eager to like everyone and wanted them to like me. I gladly proffered my trust until I was given reason to withdraw it. But even then I never stopped believing that most people truly are good at heart, though they might sometimes behave badly because they were hurting inside or driven by some dark or desperate compulsion or circumstances I was not privy to. I wished them well and accepted their failings and flaws as endearing little foibles and went on believing that good would eventually triumph over whatever darkness assailed their poor souls. I didn't believe in evil then; to me the Devil was just another storybook villain; I never thought I'd end up dancing, or sleeping, with him.

I was traveling with Mama, the bountiful-hearted and -bosomed, white-blond, violet-blue-eyed Baroness Caroline von Roques, a worldly-wise Alabama-born beauty whose numerous admirers always poetically declared that her hair was like a field of our Southern cotton silvered under a full moon, and my brother, the handsome gilt-haired "Alabama Adonis," Dr. Holbrook St. John Chandler.

We had just left New York, where we had been spending time with dear old friends and making new ones, adding to our collection of admirers, the candy boxes, bouquets, and books of sonnets they sent us with declarations of undying devotion piling up high in our hotel sitting room, and just having a grand giddy ol' time. It had been a whirlwind visit filled with lavish luncheons, society teas, and dinner parties, fancy dress balls, the theater and opera, daily shopping excursions, tailors and dressmakers appointments, brisk canters in the park on proud, high-stepping steeds that would have delighted my cavalry officer stepfather if he had been with us, and *thrilling* race meets where we all wagered recklessly on the ponies and gave our handkerchiefs and little charms for good luck to the handsomest of the jockeys. All Mama had to do was smile and mention our cousins the Vanderbilts and all doors instantly opened for us and credit was graciously and generously extended at all the best stores.

We planned to do much the same thing in London before we returned to Paris, which we worldly wanderers were pleased to call our home, though more for stylistic reasons than any fixed address, and where "Handsome Holbrook" had his medical practice, his waiting room packed with excited and excitable females all suffering from some form of womanly or nervous complaint.

Just like one might expect in a play or a film, James Maybrick literally swept me off my dainty little feet. It was our first night out to sea. I was *so* excited. I *loved* ocean travel. It *never* made me ill. I had already lost count of the number of times I had crossed. Though I had a fine collection of postcards, souvenirs of all the ships I had sailed upon, I had never bothered to count them. I was eager to purchase one of the SS *Baltic* to paste into my album and explore every splendid inch of this magnificent 420-foot ship; Captain Parsnell had already promised me a personal tour. He commended my daring and adventurous spirit. I wasn't even afraid to venture down into the belly of the beast to see the boiler room manned by sweaty bare-chested stokers black faced with coal dust and rippling with hard muscles.

In a new gown of Wedgwood-blue satin with a wide white embroidered chinoiserie border edging the full, draped skirt, and a waterfall of white silk roses, blue ribbon streamers, and cascades of snowy lace falling from my bustle, I was hurrying from my stateroom. I had dallied too long over dressing, fussing and fidgeting, dancing around the room, humming love songs, and making sure I was perfect in every way.

The leather soles of my blue satin slippers pattered and my taffeta petticoats rustled like a flock of bellicose doves as I raced to the dining saloon.

On the companionway there was a moment of sheer panic when all of a sudden I seemed to go from stairs to air. I felt myself falling, and then, just as suddenly, I was safe, my quivering body cradled in a pair of strong masculine arms.

When I dared open my eyes, a diamond horseshoe was winking at me from a gentleman's black silk tie. *He's caught me in his arms like he has his luck in that glittering U,* I thought. Slowly, I raised my eyes to see a pink mouth smiling at me from beneath a dapper mustache, so deep a brown it was deceptively black, carefully formed and waxed beneath a fine patrician nose, and then I was staring into a pair of intense dark eyes, *sharp and sure as a surgeon's knife,* I vividly recall thinking. My unknown savior held me like a bride about to be carried over the threshold of her new home. My bosom heaved, but I couldn't breathe. I felt all aflame, as though I'd just emerged from a visit to the boiler room. I felt the perspiration pool between my breasts and a flaming blush dye my cheeks a pepper-hot red. I couldn't speak. My tongue felt like a clumsy knot of wet pink ribbons. *I must be scarlet as a lobster and seem about as dumb as one!* I thought. Where, oh where was that coy, flirtatious, smiling miss I had always been with my beaus? *I needed her!*

Before the gentleman and I could exchange a single word— surely I would have said something soon!—General Hazard and his wife were upon us, reaching out to me with the most tender concern. Exclaiming that they had seen the whole thing and watched in heart-stopping horror as I began to plummet but hadn't been able to reach me in time.

The Hazards were like an uncle and aunt to me; they kept homes in New Orleans and Liverpool on account of the General's dealings in the cotton trade, and we had often visited and traveled with them. The General and Mrs. Hazard both suffered from rheumatism and other age-related infirmities and loved to go anywhere they might enjoy the baths, luxuriating in the hot, sulfurous waters and sipping mineral-rich tonics, being pampered by nice doctors, who brought sweet dreams instead of nightmares to one's bedside and never prescribed nasty medicines, pretty, smiling nurses in starched white caps and uniforms that rustled like angels' wings, and sure-fingered muscular masseurs with faces fit for magazine covers but bodies that looked poised to enter the boxing ring. Mama and I had accompanied the Hazards to several fashionable spas and sampled such delights for ourselves, though neither one of us was ailing and we were both in the bright bloom of health. But it was always fun to be petted and pampered, especially by such nice, attractive people.

"Florie! Oh my dear, I'm trembling still! When I saw you start to fall my heart stopped!" Mrs. Hazard exclaimed, patting her heart through her black bombazine bodice.

"Thank heaven you were here, Jim, to save our Florie," General Hazard was saying to my gallant savior, mopping his worried brow and frowning beneath the upside-down horseshoe of his droopy pewter mustache. "If it hadn't been for my gout, my heels would have spouted wings and I would've caught you myself, my dear!"

I felt my slippers touch solid ground again. I was on my feet, and *still* flustered and speechless. *What was wrong with me?* Mrs. Hazard's arm was around my waist, and I was leaning weakly against her, ever so grateful for her support, as I didn't quite trust my feet, and introductions were being made.

His name was James Maybrick; he was a wealthy cotton broker with offices in Norfolk, Virginia, and England's prosperous port city of Liverpool, where he was born and still made his home. The Hazards had known him for years. The General had often done business with him and enjoyed his hospitality at the Liverpool Cricket Club, and Mrs. Hazard had lost count of all the times he'd shared their table. They were clearly very impressed with him. "Solid as a rock, my dear! You need have no fears about James Maybrick!" Mrs. Hazard assured Mama when she took her aside and asked for his particulars.

After that, we were almost constantly together, sitting in the deck chairs, wrapped in warm tartan flannel blankets, deep in conversation over steaming cups of tea or beef broth, or just leaning back, resting and enjoying the salty sea air; strolling the promenade deck, a proud pair of seasoned travelers, smilingly reassuring those of our fellow passengers who were nervous and green; playing cards; dining and dancing; sitting beside each other, our fingers sometimes discreetly, daringly, entwining, at the ship's concerts; or with our two heads bowed over a single hymnal during religious services. Every evening Mr. Maybrick would call for me at my stateroom and escort me in to supper and then, afterward, to the ladies saloon for coffee and conversation, while he retired to the smoking room for brandy and cigars with the other gentlemen. Then he would retrieve me for a moonlit stroll before seeing me safely back to my stateroom.

The attraction was instantaneous; we were like two moths drawn to the same flame. But no one seemed to understand; they all accounted it some great mystery, like some dime museum oddity in which some element of chicanery might be commingled with the wonderment it inspired. All were in agreement as to why Mr. Maybrick should be so smitten with a ravishing young belle like me, but when they looked at him all they could see was a portly, paunchy, pasty, middle-aged Englishman who talked a great deal about cotton and horse racing. Were they all blind and deaf? Why couldn't they hear his enthusiasm and see how when he smiled he lit up like a jack-o'-lantern? He was like a great big overgrown boy, and my heart just wanted to reach out and hug him. I couldn't help but love him. Their confusion was the conundrum, not my feelings!

They made so much of the fact that he was forty-two and I a mere eighteen. I didn't understand all those frowns and behind our backs whispers that had a way of always reaching my ears, all those muffled murmurs about pretty babies being snatched from cradles. In the South where I was born and spent my early childhood, husbands were often considerably older than their wives, and in the sophisticated European society I had grown accustomed to in my teens this was also commonplace; I had met men in their seventies with wives my age.

I only ever worried about Mr. Maybrick's age upon those occasions when I noticed that his pallor seemed much more pronounced and his eyes appeared bloodshot, like the dark pupils were snared in a scarlet spiderweb, and I detected a slight tremor and cold clamminess in his hands. Sometimes they appeared so pasty white and limp that I actually shrank from touching them. There were times when he would rub them vigorously, complaining of numbness.

Many times he would take from his pocket a beautiful wrought-silver box with a rather charmingly risqué bas-relief design on the lid of Nelson's notorious mistress, Lady Hamilton, as a scantily draped "nymph of health," more bare than bedecked, and put a pinch of the white powder it contained into his tea, soup, or wine. But I was too well-bred to ask what it was.

I was sorely afraid some illness might swoop down and carry my Mr. Maybrick away from me on the Wings of Death. But whenever I tentatively expressed my concern he would smile, call me his dear "Bunny," and say, "I'm afraid I'm not as good a traveler as I like to pretend," and, with a sweet shamefacedness, blame it all on a slight touch of mal de mer.

I believed him because I wanted to believe him. And why should

I have doubted him? In those days, it was "the demon rum" the do-gooders crusaded against, not the contents of the medicine cabinet.

Gullible and innocent, I had no way of knowing that some gentlemen, especially those of middle or advancing age and those of weak constitution or insecure nature, routinely took "virility powders" or a "pick-me-up" tonic containing such dangerous, potentially deadly, ingredients as arsenic and strychnine to stimulate their masculine powers. Certainly no gentleman of my acquaintance would ever have been so boldly indelicate as to discuss impotency and aphrodisiacs with a well-bred virgin like me. Not even my doctor brother would have dared broach the subject. And if Mama, who was the wisest and most worldly woman I had ever met, knew about this peculiar manly indulgence she never saw fit to enlighten me.

Why could all those naysayers and frowning faces not see all the *wonderful* things Mr. Maybrick and I saw in each other? We both loved travel, good food, and books, keeping au courant with the fashions, and the heart-pounding excitement of the green table and turf; we were both spellbound by the roulette wheel and avidly courted Lady Luck.

He was no callow youth bent only on getting my bloomers off. I could talk to him and learn from him. He even made speculating on cotton seem exciting as a game of chance when he told me all about "bear sales" wherein cotton one doesn't actually possess is sold in the hope of being able to cover the obligation by buying at a lower price later and thus making a profit of thousands of dollars. I was utterly fascinated. He was the *first* man who had ever made me feel like I was more than a living doll.

Why couldn't they understand? How could I *not* love him? And what he could give me—a solid, steady, and respectable English home, *real* roots, a foundation, the chance to build a life and, God willing, grow a family. Though none would ever have guessed it to see the giddy girl caught up in the social whirl I was then, I was bone weary of wandering, of living out of a trunk, in luxurious hotels or the chateaux of the aristocrats and millionaires Mama sometimes intimately befriended. I didn't want to stop dancing or for the excitement to ever end, but I wanted to settle down, to go home after the dancing was done to a place that really was home, to my own fireside, familiar and dear, not just another house or hotel in which I was merely a guest.

But they didn't understand. Whenever Jim and I strolled past on the promenade deck, people would whisper and shake their heads. Dour old dowagers and iron-gray spinsters, who had long since given up all hope of marrying, would turn and stare or *glare* after us, branding our backs, *determined* to make their disapproval felt. They whispered about indiscretions, making our courtship sound so sordid, speaking in hushed, appalled tones about how late I stayed out, "*after dark,* my dear, and *without* a chaperone!,'" and our lingering on the deck, watching the moon and the stars mirrored in the glass-smooth sea with his arms about me, his breath warming my skin, and my soul, as he called me his darling "Bunny," and how when he brought me back to my stateroom he tarried overlong in the sitting room saying good night to me.

Mama thought Jim would make a *grand* husband for me. So what if he was older? He was respectable and rich, "solid and dependable as the Bank of England." I imagined his face as an engraving surrounded by dictionary entries for words like *Strength, Stability,* and *Security.* Mama and I were from the South, where cotton was king, and knew enough cotton brokers to know that Jim's boast that "trade is enthroned in Liverpool with cotton as prime minister" was absolute truth.

Jim was equally impressed with my pedigree. I feared Mama would drive him mad with all her chatter about the important men nesting like fat partridges in our family tree, friends and relations of royalty and founding fathers, like Napoleon and Benjamin Franklin, high-ranking clergymen, Harvard graduates, bankers, founders of schools and railways, real estate barons, the first Episcopal bishop of Illinois, a Secretary of the Treasury, and a Chief Justice of the Supreme Court. My grandfather had founded the town of Cairo, Illinois, and been caricatured by Dickens in *Martin Chuzzlewit,* and my father had sat on the Supreme Court and served as Assistant Secretary of State for the Confederacy. And, of course, there were our cousins the Vanderbilts.

Though I wished she wouldn't, Mama made me sound like some kind of heiress, one of those wealthy American girls the newspapers had dubbed "Dollar Princesses," girls who traveled to Europe on fishing expeditions to catch a title to put the crowning touch on their millions. My stomach was all queasy and I felt like a fraud, a sham heiress, when she dropped hints about the two and a half million acres of land in Virginia and Kentucky that I might one day inherit, conveniently neglecting to mention that it was all swampland and there was some complicated legal tangle about just who in our family actually owned it. It was all a great muddle that would have cost too much to unravel, the lawyers would have gotten richer and us only poorer, and the land would have just sat there stagnating without a buyer, so we just left it be; no one really thought it was worth all the bother.

She also glossed over the scandals of her own past, the label of "adventuress" many affixed to her name along with words like *conniving, duplicitous, ingratiating, sychophantic,* and *scheming;* the two dead husbands whose deaths the gossips claimed too conveniently coincided with Mama's desire to change partners; her numerous love affairs—they said she went through men like handkerchiefs—and her amicable separation from my worldly and debonair Prussian stepfather, Baron Adolf von Roques. She deftly deflected attention away from his absence with nigh constant reminders that he was attached to the embassy in St. Petersburg and thus of necessity spent much of his time in Russia away from the bosom of his loving family. Glowing with wifely pride, she described his service under Crown Prince Frederick as a cavalry officer in the Eighth Cuirassier Regiment. His troupe of ballet girl mistresses and handsome male secretaries, always tall and candlestick slim, with hair slick and shiny as black patent leather, his hot and hasty temper fueled by a taste for vodka in vast quantities, and his penchant for dueling over the slightest perceived insult were of course never mentioned. Mama was always a practical woman who preferred to accentuate the positive and ignore the negative like dust swept under the carpet.

Their arrangement was entirely amicable. It was not by any means an unhappy marriage; on the contrary, it was all very sophisticated and civilized. But Mama was prepared to admit that it might seem distressingly bohemian and unconventional to the typically traditional, and narrow, English mind. So why risk muddying the waters by talking about it? After all, what had their marriage to do with mine? At the time, I thought it made perfect sense. It was not, of course, the kind of marriage I wanted for myself; I wanted the whole beautiful fairy tale of everlasting love and happily ever after. I wanted no storm clouds to mar my perfect blue sky, so I kept smiling and silent and let Mama do all the talking. She said she knew best, and I believed her. I didn't want to make a single frown or worry line crease my beloved's brow. I really was the sweet, old-fashioned girl he thought I was, not some wild bohemian child of the demimondaine, so why give him any cause to doubt me?

I loved Jim and truly I did not want to mislead him, but when I voiced my concerns to Mama she insisted that I keep silent. I would *never* be able to forget or forgive myself, she said, if such an overt display of honesty dashed my hopes entirely.

"Darlin' "—she clasped my face between her hands—"your face is your heart, you are incapable of lyin', but you've yet to learn that honesty can cost a woman dearly. You will blame yourself every day o' your life, an' quite rightly too, for costin' yourself that which would have brought you perfect happiness. In this world, a woman must be cunnin', not naïve an' timid, or else she loses out to another, a rival, who is not afraid to be clever an' take chances. Listen to your mother. *I know;* I have *vast* experience in these matters."

She was adamant that I must leave *everything* to her; besides, it was unbecoming for a young girl to talk of business and financial matters. "If you're goin' to do that, Florie, you might as well put on some blue stockin's an' spectacles and scrape your hair back into a bun an' give up *all* hope of a husband, for you'll certainly *never* get one by talkin' o' those matters!

"After you're married you'll fall to quarrelin' an' quibblin' about finances soon enough; every couple does." She sighed, reminding me that as a third-time wife she was in a position to know. "Enjoy the bliss o' ignorance an' freedom from bein' tied down by facts an' figures while it lasts, darlin'. The honeymoon'll be over soon enough; it *always* is."

What could I do? She was my mother and a wise and worldly woman who "knew how the game is played an', more important, how to win it." I loved her, and I knew she loved me and always had my best interests at heart, so, as always, I nodded and said, "Yes, Mama." Some might say that was a mistake, that any marriage begun in deception is doomed. All I can say is that she was my mother. All little girls are brought up being told to listen to their mothers and that they'll be sorry if they don't, and I didn't want to be sorry and looking back years later, still nursing a broken heart and longing for Jim and what might have been. I wanted to be Mrs. James Maybrick with all my heart and Mama was *determined* to make my dreams come true. "The heart doesn't lie, but sometimes the tongue has to," she said, "an' which would you rather have, a whole honest tongue or a broken heart?" Of course, I chose my heart; I always did.

The last night of the voyage, our last chance to dine amidst the shining silverware, white linen, and cut-crystal splendor of the first-class dining saloon before we docked in Liverpool, Captain Parsnell stood to make the customary announcement.

"Ladies and gentlemen," he began, "it is my pleasure to inform you that we have made the Atlantic crossing in the usual excellent time upon which the White Star Line prides itself. We have moved at a steady sixteen knots and shall dock in Liverpool in the morning. It has been, I think, as quick a crossing as can be managed by any steamer currently in Her Majesty's service. Customarily, at this time, I would propose a toast to Her Majesty, Queen Victoria, but this evening I wish to first offer another toast. I think perhaps you can guess to what, or should I say, rather, to *whom,* I refer. . . ."

He paused to allow some polite chuckles and to give the disapproving dowagers a moment more to glower through their lorgnettes and frown at us. But Jim and I just smiled into each other's eyes and clasped hands across the table.

"I raise my glass to the health of two who met aboard this ship only seven days ago. They embarked as strangers, but found romance upon the high seas. This very afternoon they informed me of their intention to wed this summer. A toast, ladies and gentlemen, to the long lives and good health of Miss Florence Chandler and Mr. James Maybrick! A toast to the happy couple—to these two who shall soon become one!"

Everyone, even those who disapproved most vehemently of our romance, raised their voices and glasses to wish us well. It would have been the epitome of discourtesy to do anything else.

That night my whole world was rosy and filled with delight. The wine was sweet as nectar and I'm afraid I might have drunk a little too much.

Long after most of the lights had gone out, Jim and I lingered up on deck, wrapped in black velvet darkness and each other's arms.

"I never want this night to end!" I whispered, safe and contented in his embrace. "If I go to bed, I'm afraid when I wake up in the morning it will turn out to have all been just a dream."

We watched the golden sun rise over the deep blue sea. When a dolphin broke the surface Jim rubbed his diamond horseshoe and guided my fingers to do the same. Seeing a dolphin meant certain luck. "We're on a winning streak," Jim said. "With you at my side I'll *never* lose."

When he escorted me to my stateroom, lingering for one last long kiss before he let me go, he boldly whispered into my ear, "I dream of the time when I need not leave your side when we say good night, though, in this instance, it is in fact good morning."

I was the happiest girl in the world, and I *knew* Lady Luck was smiling down on me, blessing this venture.

❧ 2 ❧

Jim and I were married on July 27, 1880, at the most elegant church in London, St. James's in Piccadilly. *All* the most fashionable people had their weddings there. Members of the Currant Jelly Set, Jim told me, would never even *think* of being married anywhere else.

The society columns, to my secret shame, all described me as "an American heiress" and on my wedding day I looked like one, but that did not dispel my fear that someone would come charging up the aisle in the midst of the ceremony, yank my veil off, and denounce me as a fraud. Time and again I wanted to go to Jim, to kneel at his feet and tell him the truth about those two and a half million acres, but the fear of losing him was so great it made my stomach ache. I'd throw down my diamonds on the gaming table but *never* my heart.

My gown was from the House of Worth. Nothing less would do, Mama said, and Jim agreed, "It *must* be Worth, by all means!" in a tone that implied being wed in a gown designed by any other would be the equivalent of being married barefoot in a burlap sack.

"You shimmer like an angel's wing!" Mama sighed, wiping a tear from her eye, the first time she saw me in it.

It was ice-white glacé satin that shimmered just like ice under the sun, embroidered with delicate silvery-white roses and lilies, hundreds of seed pearls and tiny crystals. Embellished lace stretched across my breasts and fell from my shoulders in demure little cape sleeves. The skirt cascaded voluminously over my bustle and flowed out behind me in a raging river of embroidered and beaded satin and lace ruffles, forming a train that four little girls in pink and blue dresses with silk rosebud wreaths on their curly heads would carry.

This was yet another indulgence my husband-to-be had granted me—blue and pink were my two favorite colors, and I had gone back and forth endlessly trying to decide which color my bridal attendants should wear, provoking the dressmaker at times to hair tearing and tears. Then Jim had come along and dispensed with the dilemma altogether by saying I should divide the attendants in two and have half wear pink and the others wear blue. In the end, I had *twelve* bridesmaids, half of them gowned in chiffon-draped silks and rose-laden hats in shades ranging from the palest baby's blush to the most delicious, decadent rich raspberry pink and the other six in hues of blue from delicate aqua to the midnight perfection of the world's finest sapphires.

When Mama stepped forward in her dusky-blue lace and satin to drape her very own pearls, a triple strand with a diamond-encrusted gold fleur-de-lis clasp, around my neck there were tears in her eyes even though she was smiling. I had never seen my mother cry, and I fell weeping into her arms. All morning I had felt like my life was only just beginning, but now, like a hammer's blow from out of the blue, it came crashing down upon me that life as I had always known it was actually *ending*. My days of roaming the world with Mama were over. I would be saying good-bye to her and Holbrook. Though he would be "just a brief jaunt away" across the Channel in Paris, busy with his medical practice, and whenever the wanderlust did not seize her Mama would be there too, all of a sudden the Channel seemed as gigantic as the Atlantic.

Mama smiled and dried my tears and chased all my fears away. She made that grossly swollen Channel shrink right back down to size. "A mere pond," she called it, assuring me that she would *always* be there whenever I needed her. We had always been not only mother and daughter but dearest friends also, and *nothing*, not

even marriage, could change that, she said, reminding me that I
had been with her through three marriages. "We've always been together, but now it's time for you to take center stage, darlin'. It's
time for you to play the wife, an', in time, someone else will come
along to play daughter, an' you'll be the mother. But"—she took
my face in her hands and gazed deep into my eyes—"no matter
what happens, you will *always* be my daughter."

A knock on the door told us it was time. My knees buckled beneath my gown. Suddenly I wanted to sit down on the floor and
bawl like a baby. But Mama was there, bearing me up, giving me
strength.

"Just think of it, Florie. You an' Jim are embarkin' on a *grand*
adventure!"

I took a deep breath and stood up straight and Mama walked
around me, arranging my veil. Silver and white mingled so closely
in its fine mesh I could never decide if it was more silver or white,
and little embroidered silver flowers, seed pearls, and crystals encrusted its edges. The mirrors and my mother's eyes told me that I
looked like a princess, and now, I knew, I must behave like one.

With a nod of approval Mama pressed a bouquet of white lilies
and roses framed by scalloped silver-veined lace into my hands, and
I walked forward to confidently embrace my destiny.

"Everythin' will be all right," Mama whispered in my ear as she
relinquished my arm to Holbrook, to walk me down the aisle, and
with all my heart and soul I believed her. Like a sudden summer
storm, all my fears had passed.

The smiling faces of our guests passed by me in a blur. The
women's gowns and feathered hats were like sherbet-colored clouds.
Ever afterward whenever someone told me they were at my wedding,
I would just nod and smile; I had to take their word for it. Those
pink fairy floss clouds my head was wrapped in kept me from even
remembering meeting Jim's brothers, Michael and Edwin, though
it was little more than a hasty smile, a "how d'you do?," and a peck
upon the cheek. I couldn't have described those fellows fifteen
minutes later if the police had asked me to. All I saw was the shining bright dream of the future and Jim, standing at the altar, waiting for me in his new suit with a white satin waistcoat embroidered

with the same pattern of silver roses and lilies as my gown, and his lucky diamond horseshoe winking at me from his silver silk cravat. I was blind to everything and everyone else.

When I took my place at his side I smiled and spontaneously reached out and took his hand. "This is the start of a *grand* adventure!" I whispered.

"Indeed it is!" Jim agreed with a smile as bright as my own, and squeezed my hand tight.

As one, we faced forward, toward the future, together, and became man and wife. We never looked back.

We sped across the Channel. The wind and the tide were with us, like dear old friends wishing us well, hurrying us on to happiness; even the gulls seemed to shout, *Godspeed!* We made the crossing in four hours and were at the hotel and in our evening clothes just in time to sit down to supper, our first as man and wife.

I'll never forget that first meal: rosemary chicken, tender green asparagus, buttery new potatoes rolled in herbs, and a lemon custard cake, a golden marvel of a cake, with custard and lemon jelly between each sumptuous spongy-gold layer, the top drizzled with rich ribbons of the most decadent dark chocolate I had ever tasted. I vowed from the very first bite that every year on our anniversary and whenever we had something special to celebrate this would be our dinner.

The next eight weeks were heavenly, all kisses and bliss. Every night I fell asleep with my head on my husband's chest, listening to his heartbeat, soothing and steady, with his arms holding me. Every morning I awakened to a room filled with roses, thinking I had died and gone to Heaven and a perfumed cloud was now my bed. I was in my husband's arms, and that *was* heaven to me. The initial pain, the "necessary unpleasantness" Mama had mentioned, was past so quickly it was *nothing*—Mama had been right; "one faces worse ordeals at the dentist"—and I experienced only pleasure. I recall it all now only in a series of pretty pictures, like an album filled with postcards from days gone by, pictures of a rosy past that may or may not have been real. I don't know anymore; I just can't remember it without that soft, romantic, rosy golden glow. Maybe the truth is I don't want to.

Though Mama and Holbrook were also in Paris, Jim and I didn't see them or anyone else we knew. We shunned all society save our own, wanting no one but each other.

"This," Jim said, "is *our* time."

"Ours alone," I agreed.

Jim took me to Versailles, to view the gilded remains of a vanished world burned and blown away on the hot and violent winds of revolution. I was elated yet, at the same time, so terribly sad when I traversed the Hall of Mirrors, supremely conscious of my shoes echoing upon the marble floor as I followed in the ghostly footsteps of Marie Antoinette.

To cheer me out of my sudden blue doldrums, Jim pulled me into his arms and began to waltz with me. Seeing my reflection in my sky-blue linen suit and hat, rakishly tilted and crowned with a bevy of weeping blue ostrich plumes, passing in a whirl of swirling skirts and swaying feathers, I forgot—just for a moment—that I was a grown-up married lady and, like a little girl, imagined that I was Marie Antoinette and the belle of the ball all blurred into one.

Later, I stood outside the Petit Trianon and tried to envision Marie Antoinette in one of her white shepherdess dresses with adoring courtiers surrounding her like a flock of sheep. From the time I was a little girl I had been fascinated by tales of the tragic queen. I had several postcards with her likeness and others evocative of the times in which she had lived pasted in my album. I loved the splendid panniered gowns with their ladders of bows climbing the bodices, billows of lace at the sleeves, like bridal veils for the elbows, and the towering befeathered and bejeweled powdered coiffures. "Dresses decorated like birthday cakes and hair like wedding cakes with sugar roses and swags of candy pearls," I said to Jim's amusement as we stood before a wall of gilt-framed portraits. I *loved* to hear his hearty chuckle, to know that he was laughing *with* me, not *at* me.

I wouldn't know till afterward, but, as a surprise for me, Jim ordered pretty porcelain plates, figurines, vases, and paintings, charming bric-a-brac, to adorn my bedroom and had it all shipped back to England. He asked an old friend, Mrs. Matilda Briggs, whom he had described as "a marvel of efficiency" and was trusting to oversee the furnishing and decoration of our house, to transform my suite into a little eighteenth-century wonderland for me where I could reign like Marie Antoinette over my own little kingdom.

In a quaint little antique shop Jim and I found a miniature of a handsome dark-haired man with a haunting, melancholy visage. The shopkeeper said it was Count Axel Fersen, the Queen's gallant lover, her own dear Swedish Sir Galahad, chivalrous and loyal to the last breath. Jim bought it for me along with a miniature of Marie Antoinette so that these two star-crossed lovers might be reunited to gaze into each other's eyes from across my crowded whatnot shelf. "You are so good to me!" I cried, and threw my arms around his neck and kissed him right there in front of the shopkeeper.

In the elegant emporiums, Jim sat proudly, every inch the elegant English gentleman, occupying a gilt chair as though it were a king's throne. Sometimes there was a glass of wine or a fine cigar in his hand; other times he fiddled idly with his favorite walking stick, the ebony one topped with a substantial golden knob made in the shape of a miniature bust of a rather grim-faced Queen Victoria, his thumb boldly caressing "the old girl's bosom," and watched as I paraded past him in the latest Parisian fashions.

There were gowns for every season and situation. Light and airy sprigged floral and pastel confections trimmed with ruffles, smart suits of soft velvet, raw silk, or crisp linen, afternoon, walking, at home, evening dresses, and riding togs. No plain, boring broadcloth for me, Jim said; I must have violet-blue velvet to match my eyes, with a jabot of lace at my throat and ostrich plumes on my hat. Satins, silks, brocades, damasks, taffetas, chiffons, and velvets in a variety of colors. Jim's favorite was a gold-lace-festooned ball gown, with a bouquet of red velvet roses on the bustle cascading down onto the train, in his favorite color, arsenic green, against which, he said, my beauty seemed especially strong and vibrant. "The sight of you in that color is like a tonic to me," he said as I twirled and danced before him.

He chose a bathing costume of bright coral pink edged in black for me instead of the traditional reserved and respectable white-bordered nautical blue or black. We spent hours selecting marvelous hats, each one as decadent as a dessert, trimmed with feathers, wax fruit, silk flowers, or stuffed birds; high-heeled shoes with almond-point toes; leather boots and boudoir slippers; silk stockings, handbags, gloves, paisley shawls, and parasols; capes, coats, and muffs, sables and ermine; necklaces, brooches, and bracelets; rings for my fingers and bobbing jewels for my ears; ornaments for my hair; lace-trimmed undergarments; silk and lace nightgowns, negligees, and dressing gowns. My favorite was a pale blue peignoir trimmed with wispy, tickling feathers that made me giggle. There was even a gay and daring red and white candy-striped corset with red satin suspenders to hold my stockings up.

While I laughed and spun before him like a little girl playing dress-up, worry secretly gnawed at the back of my mind. Could we *really* afford all this? I wanted to ask Jim, but I remembered Mama's advice about discussing finances, so I bit my tongue. Jim seemed happy; buying me things seemed to give him as much pleasure as it did me, and I didn't want to spoil it for either of us. *If money* must *be worried about, time enough for that later,* I decided. *Tomorrow shouldn't be allowed to spoil today. Right now we're still dancing; the fiddler can wait to be paid!*

Back at the hotel, with my hair unbound, in a boudoir gown of lavender silk overlaid with sheer white net embroidered with a swarm of shimmering, iridescent pearly-winged butterflies, I sat on Jim's lap and grew blissfully giddy and dizzy from his countless kisses and the bubbly gold champagne from the glass he held to my lips. He fastened a necklace of amethysts framed by golden flowers and opal-winged butterflies around my throat and slid a luscious lavender and creamy mint jade-winged butterfly comb into the "molten gold waves" of my hair and told me how much he loved and adored me before he lowered me onto the polar bear rug before the fire and made love to me until we fell into an exhausted slumber.

The next day he took me to a photographer's studio and, holding a pink rose and wearing the cerulean-blue satin and silver lace gown he had bought me and the pearls Mama had given me, I imitated Madame Vigée-Lebrun's famous portrait of Marie Antoinette. Afterward, an artist would carefully apply colors to tint it. It would always be Jim's favorite picture of me. He would even take it with him when he traveled without me; it would proudly adorn his desk in a beautiful silver frame until the day he died.

At the races and gambling tables I stood beside him, breasts heaving, lips parted, with ecstatic excitement, eyes bright and intent upon the horses, cards, ebony-eyed dice, piles of clacking chips as sweet and enticing as candy, or the spinning black and red wheel that could make or break fortunes. Sometimes he won, sometimes he lost, but Jim said that like the diamond horseshoe he felt naked without, I *always* brought him luck. He had even taken to kissing my hand after I had stroked the horseshoe before he placed his bets.

We both believed that games of chance were the most fascinating, exciting thing in the world; *nothing* surpassed the thrill that took possession of us when we played, not even the passion we found together in bed. We reveled in Lady Luck's fickle and flighty embrace, constantly trying to coax, court, and woo her. She was aloof and cool one moment, passionate and all-embracing the next. Beautiful and pitiless, sometimes she hurt us, but we *always* came back for more. Many years later, when Lady Luck had long since spurned and turned her back on me, I would see a most delightful film, full of dancing, fun, farce, and mistaken identities, *The Gay Divorcee,* in which the debonair Fred Astaire loftily spoke the words "Chance is the Fool's name for Fate." I wish those words had come to me in those heady, halcyon days with Jim; I would have embroidered them on samplers to deck the walls and handkerchiefs for both of us, and even on the hems of my petticoats, they so perfectly expressed how we felt.

On our last day in Paris Jim woke me with a kiss, then hurried me into the frothy white muslin frock with the pearl buttons and straw hat he had laid out for me. He took me back to Versailles, to picnic at the Petit Trianon. We fed the swans and golden carp bits of bread and cake and lay back in each other's arms, filled with contentment, lazy as two cats who had supped their fill on cream, and kissed and dreamed. Life could not have been more perfect or exquisite!

Then came Florence, Rome, and Venice. The Grand Canal, like a picture on a postcard: a starless black night lit by torches. A golden-haired girl in a golden gown and a shawl of beaded black lace. Black plumes in the rich gleaming coils of her high-piled hair. A mask twirled idly on a long gilded stem, playing a coy game of peekaboo with her face. She reclined languidly in a gondola, leaning back against her husband's chest, watching in breath-stealing wonder as the golden sparks of fireworks showered down into the glassy black waters that mirrored them. The gondolier sang in a velvety tenor voice, magical as the night itself. They kissed as they glided beneath the graceful arch of the Rialto Bridge. Joy everywhere, love everywhere—crowding the landing stages, filling the surrounding squares, leaning from balconies and windows, skipping and frolicking over the bridge. Everyone in love, with each other, the night, or just in love with love.

Cream linen suits and sensible straw hats, museums, coffee in quaint cafés, feeding pigeons in the square, masterpieces of Renaissance art, classical statuary, and Baedeker by day. Churches whose gilded spires soared up so high they seemed to puncture Heaven. Kisses stolen in fields of scarlet poppies and golden wheat. Roman ruins and romance by moonlight. Sipping sparkling wine and dancing beneath the starry brilliance. Cool silk gowns of white, ice blue, or mint green, ardent hands, and red-hot kisses. Cold, unyielding white marble statues staring with blind eyes at soft, pliant, living pink skin.

Our last night in Rome, we waltzed in the moonlit arena of the Colosseum, humming our own music, beneath the shadow of the cross where Christian martyrs had been thrown to the lions.

More beautiful picture postcards to paste in the album of my memory, to remind me that it wasn't all just a dream, that, for a time at least, my life really was picture-postcard perfect.

❧ 3 ❧

When we returned to Liverpool and drove past a high ivy-clad stone wall along Riverdale Road, turning in at No. 7—*our lucky number!*—and I saw Battlecrease House for the first time I nearly died of rapture. I couldn't speak. I didn't know whether to laugh or weep. I was falling in love again, this time not with a man but with a house—the house that would be our home. I would be the living, beating heart of these twenty rooms, the one who made sure it really was a home, not just a stately three-story pile of pale-champagne gold bricks held together by mortar.

Silly as it sounds, I wanted to lie down on the lawn, to roll, wallow, and sprawl on the grass as though it were a green velvet bedspread. I wanted to cup each flower in the garden gently in my hand and caress its petals as I bent to breathe in its sweet fragrance. I wanted to sit in blissful idleness on each stone bench, feed the fish in the pond, pet and feed carrots to the horses in the stable, bones to the hunting hounds kept in the adjoining kennel, hug the statuary and dance round the trees like an adoring pagan acolyte, and tame the proud pair of peafowl that roamed the palatial gardens to eat from my hands. There was even a wishing well I wanted to throw my whole purse into just to say, *Thank you!* I wanted to invite the whole world to a croquet party straightaway and say warmly to each and every person, *Welcome to our home!* as I served them tea and tiny sandwiches and dainty cakes with blue and pink frosting. It was all I could do not to dash across the street to the Liverpool Cricket Club and invite the men in spotless white flannel playing on the green beneath the blinding blaze of the sun and the ladies lazily watching them from beneath their shady hat brims and drooping parasols to come over right away. Like the Pied Piper, I wanted to lead them all back, skipping and prancing, singing and dancing, to our home, Battlecrease House, No. 7—*lucky number seven!*—Riverdale Road. *Home! My home!* my heart kept singing. *Home sweet home!*

Chuckling with delight, Jim swept me up into his arms, playfully comparing my ice-lemon silk gown, so creamy and cool, over crisp layers of ruffled white organdy, to a beautiful lemon meringue confection, and carried me up the front steps to a door set with the Maybrick coat of arms, the haughty hawk, perched on a gold brick with a sprig of flowering may in his beak, over the boldly written banner TEMPUS OMNIA REVELAT—TIME REVEALS ALL.

The white tulle atop my hat was tickling Jim's chin and he tilted his head, angling to avoid it, but it was just too much.

"Although that hat frames a face as pretty as a picture, would you mind taking it off, my dear? The tulle is rather ticklish," he said.

I laughed in sheer delight and instantly complied.

"Daisies." Jim smiled at the silk flowers tumbling haphazardly over the brim. "You remind me of Mr. James's *Daisy Miller.* 'She was the most beautiful young lady I ever saw, and the most amiable. . . . She was also the most innocent.' "

I smiled and sighed, "Oh, Jim!" as though it were the first time I had received this pretty compliment when in truth it must have been the thousandth; my beaus were always comparing me to the impetuous and innocent madcap Miss Miller, the free, frank, and unfettered American girl traipsing across Europe with her mother and brother in tow.

The door opened before us and I found myself staring into a face rigid as a marble soldier's, so frigidly strict and superior beneath its tight, smooth-lacquered mahogany-red coiffure that I felt instantly inferior, as though I had just been found guilty of the most grievous offense and was about to be stood up against a wall and shot. I blinked and blinked again, then sighed with relief. The face I now saw before me was smiling, gracious, and inviting. I *must* have been more tired than I realized. Or it was just a trick of the light.

"Welcome," she said, stepping back and ushering us into the oak-paneled entrance hall. "Welcome to Battlecrease House!"

"Didn't I tell you Matilda was a marvel?" Jim smiled as he set me down.

I couldn't answer him; the sedate opulence that surrounded me had quite stolen my voice away. I was standing on a Turkish carpet, an oriental fantasy worked in deep red and antique gold, and right beside me, within fainting distance, was a beautiful oak sofa carved with an intricate pattern of clinging vines and flowers, upholstered in deep crimson, echoing the leaf pattern of the paneling and the crimson damask covering the walls.

In those, my first moments inside Battlecrease House, a sort of magic was at work. This was my home and I *never* wanted to leave it. I felt the most enchanting, wonderful contentment falling like fairy dust from the ceiling onto me, seeping through my skin straight into my soul. If a fairy had emerged from the woodwork right then and asked me my wish I would have instantly replied, *To live and love here forever with Jim.* No girl had ever been as lucky as me.

Like a child on a treasure hunt, I wanted to explore every nook and cranny, but Jim's hand was gently cupping my elbow, guiding me into the parlor.

Here all was royal-blue and white damask rococo splendor, as though Jim and I were a pair of lovers walking right into the Blue Willow pattern. There were sofas and chairs and footstools with ball and claw feet, all upholstered with blue and white damask, rich royal-blue velvet curtains trimmed with silk bobbles, tables and cabinets of gleaming dark mahogany, and an impressive array of gold-rimmed Blue Willow china pieces on display. Presiding regally over the mantel of a fireplace set with porcelain tiles illustrating the ancient love story that had inspired the famous pattern was a beautiful statue of the Chinese Goddess of Mercy mantled in rich blue and gowned in white with a fat black-haired almond-eyed baby in her arms. And a big blue and white Buddha sat cross-legged with a lotus blossom blooming out of his outstretched palms on the tea table.

I stood there awestruck, no doubt giving a fine imitation of a slack-jawed country yokel who had never seen the inside of a fine house before. It wasn't that I was unaccustomed to such opulence. Far from it, I had never known anything but the finest things in life, in the various plantations, town houses, mansions, chateaux, country estates, seaside castles, baronial manors, and hotels I had stayed at throughout the years. It was simply that this time I was not a guest; this was *my home!* I had never felt such an instant connection to a place, as though the walls had a life of their own and were reaching out with invisible hands to welcome me. I wouldn't be packing up and leaving when boredom set in or a new sensation beckoned. Jim and I would live, love, and grow old here together. This wasn't fleeting; this was *forever!* Everything here that was new now would become old, familiar, and dear, timeworn, and even more wonderful. I would give birth to our children in one of the beds upstairs, play with them in the nursery, celebrate their birthdays, and someday toast their engagements in the dining room. And if Heaven blessed me with a daughter, when she turned sixteen I would host a ball here in her honor.

Mrs. Briggs cleared her throat and Jim gently nudged me forward.

A man with a big black walrus mustache and fast-retreating hairline was seated at the piano, idly tricking out a tune. Abruptly he stopped and with the cold and distinctly superior air of a Prussian general stood up and came to bow stiffly over my hand.

This was my husband's famous brother, Michael, better known and beloved by the British public as Stephen Adams, the composer and singer of popular songs. Jim had told me all about him. Michael, whose brilliance had first been remarked when, as a boy, he sang in the church choir, was the darling of the music halls. He had toured the world, given concerts at Covent Garden and command performances for crowned heads. His fine baritone voice, equally adept at grand opera and popular ditties, everything from stirring sea chanteys to sentimental ballads, had been heard soaring in Mendelssohn's *Elijah* and Wagner's *Lohengrin*. I had seen him in the latter myself during my travels with Mama and had even thrown a red rose at his feet when he took his bow. But, of course, he hadn't noticed me. Why ever would he? I was just one amongst the admiring throng. I had even heard that when he played the music halls, where the atmosphere was wont to be rowdy, some—I hesitate to call them ladies—had even been so brazen as to throw their drawers onto the stage. Some even attached little notes giving an address where he might meet them for some amorous disport if it pleased him.

Michael's talent had afforded him two fine homes—a London mansion overlooking Regent's Park and a summerhouse on the Isle of Wight—and a reputation as one of London's most desirable bachelors, rendered even more irresistible to covetous females because he appeared entirely impervious to their charms. Some whispered that he and his songwriting partner, Frederick Weatherly, were partners in an even more intimate manner. But I never knew Michael well enough to ascertain whether there was any truth to those rumors. He would later, albeit in the aftermath of the Oscar Wilde scandal, suddenly marry his housekeeper, the aptly named Laura Withers, a butcher's forty-year-old icebox-cold spinster daughter with a face like a meat cleaver who was happy to be married in name only to a famous man if it meant she could gad about town in feathered hats and fine dresses in a black japanned carriage and lord it over all the shopkeepers who had once looked down upon her as a servant.

When he spoke to me, Michael's words were cold and precise, like daggers of ice, and his eyes were no warmer. After meeting him, I could never again quite convince myself that I had actually seen this man bounding across a stage with a big, cheerful smile plastered across his face, joyously belting out song after song for his adoring public. Surely the footlights had played a trick upon my eyes and it was only a man who resembled my brother-in-law. This arrogantly sneering cold and condescending man standing in my parlor and that hale and hearty, bubbly and bouncy, singing and dancing fellow couldn't possibly be one and the same man!

Whenever Michael looked at me, his eyes seemed filled with

hostility. Perhaps he thought I wasn't good enough for Jim? Or, being an astute businessman with powerful and widespread connections in artistic, business, and social circles, possibly Michael had made inquiries about my family and discovered just how much had been exaggerated. Or he might have been one of those chilly Englishmen who deplored all Americans, holding each one he met personally responsible for hosting the Boston Tea Party and igniting the spark of rebellion in the Thirteen Colonies. I never could figure out quite why he so vehemently disliked me and disdained my every overture of friendship.

Edwin, however, was an absolute delight, affable and sweet, full of gossip and glee. Jim's nominal partner in the firm of Maybrick & Company, Edwin had lived with Jim and would continue to do so here at Battlecrease House with us, when he was not visiting Michael as an excuse to enjoy himself in London. The youngest Maybrick brother and, honesty compels me to admit, the handsomest one was twenty-eight, tall, sun kissed, and slender, unlike his paunchy, pasty siblings, with his dark hair still luxuriant and thick, and lively brown eyes lit up with a devilish twinkle. He cultivated a pencil-thin mustache and had a taste for loud checkered and striped suits, garish neckties, waistcoats, and dressing gowns that looked like the bold, bright patterns were the work of color-blind lunatics. He was as avid for penny-dreadful novels as any twelve-year-old boy; that day in the parlor there was a copy of *Varney, the Vampire* peeping from his pocket. And he loved dime museums and melodramas and liked to boast that he had not only seen the Elephant Man but also shaken his hand. There was a warmth and sense of fun about Edwin that set me instantly at ease, and I liked him from the first moment.

While my eyes were still being dazzled by his forest-green waistcoat with a bold pattern of gaudy, bright yellow lemons, green-and-yellow-checkered suit, and striped tie he took my arm and led me away from the grim and glowering Michael to sit upon the sofa.

"Don't mind Michael. He can't help being a cold fish; it's just his way. I keep telling him he should dress up as an old woman with gray hair and spectacles, a cane, ear trumpet, and shawl, and do a song and dance about the agonies of old age and rheumatism; don't you know, they'd love that in the halls," Edwin added with the most infectious grin. I already knew it was going to be fun having him for a brother.

Still holding my arm, Edwin leaned even closer and discreetly jerked his chin in the direction of Mrs. Briggs.

"Don't be fooled by that iced-lemon exterior, so cool and poised. She'll scratch your eyes out—in a perfectly nice way of course—and *kill* you with kindness if you let her," he whispered. "Hell hath no fury like a woman scorned. Didn't anyone tell you?" He drew back and searched my baffled face for some sign of comprehension. "No, I can see they didn't! Oh dear, oh dear, oh dear! Well . . . better that you should hear it from me . . ." He dived right in with all the relish of a glutton into a vat of chocolate sauce. "Jim jilted dear old Mattie over there to marry you, my darling Florie— I may call you Florie, mayn't I? Formality really has no place in the bosom of the family," he added with a lingering glance down at my own. "To save face, she rushed Horace Briggs to the altar so she wouldn't have to force a smile and welcome her erstwhile betrothed's radiant young bride home, to the house *she* decorated and always thought would be hers someday, as an old maid. Poor old Horace." He gave a wicked chuckle. "He stood at the altar looking like a cow on the tracks struck dumb with fright at the sight of an approaching locomotive! A locomotive covered in white satin and orange blossoms! It was so sudden I didn't even have time to buy a new tie," he pronounced as though this were some great tragedy.

I giggled and slapped Edwin playfully upon the knee. "I do declare, *Brother* Edwin," I said, my voice full of syrupy sweet Southern charm, "you're as gossipy as an old woman!"

"*Brother* Edwin." He pursed his lips and shook his head dolefully. "You make me sound like a monk, though if any woman could drive a man to such despair he would contemplate entering a monastery I daresay it's you. Oh, Florie"—he gripped my hand hard and stared deep into my eyes—"if only I had met you first!"

This was no joke or frivolous, flirty banter; he was *serious!* There was such an intensity in his eyes, and the way I felt his thigh burning mine through my skirt I was afraid he would forget I was his brother's wife and pounce upon me right there in the parlor in front of everybody. I squirmed, trying to fight the vivid picture that suddenly filled my mind of Edwin on top of me, kissing me.

I suddenly felt very hot, flushed and flustered, and guilty, even though I hadn't actually done anything. I loved my husband! How could I be entertaining such thoughts about his brother? I bolted up quickly and went to join Jim, linking my arm possessively through his and darting a warning glance back at Edwin, who merely smiled at me and pulled a big bright yellow silk handkerchief out of his pocket and began toying with it, forming the folds into a shape with a pair of ears that very much suggested—if I am not mistaken, and I don't think I am—a bunny.

I tried to engage Mrs. Briggs in conversation about how beautiful the house was, but she simply stood there stiff backed and stared at me, and I soon felt like a perfect fool standing there babbling. I might as well have been talking to a statue. Mercifully, I was able to catch Jim's eye and he smiled and came to my rescue. He might not have been a knight in shining armor, only a middle-aged Englishman in a black broadcloth suit, with the buttons on his waistcoat straining from all the rich, decadent dishes we had enjoyed in France and Italy, but he was my hero and, best of all, *mine*. In that moment, I fell in love with him all over again.

I wished he would banish them all, so that we might be alone on this, our first night in our very own home. But, of course, that was impossible and would have been awfully impolite, since Mrs. Briggs had taken such pains over the house and Edwin and Michael were, after all, family and it was Edwin's home too, so I could hardly turn him out; I just hoped he wasn't going to be difficult.

Jim kissed my brow and said I looked weary and asked if I wouldn't like to have "a little lie-down before supper." I was on the verge of uttering a grateful, heartfelt *yes* when Mrs. Briggs insinuated herself between us, prying my arm, with a grip like a wrestler's, away from Jim's. Before I even thought about going upstairs, she said I simply *must* meet the staff. There was steel beneath the silk of her voice that made me fear the consequences of refusing. After all, this *was* England and she knew how things were done here better than me, so I nodded, smiled, and said I would be delighted and let her lead me to the kitchen.

It was spacious and well ordered, everything polished, bright, shiny, and new, white tiles, black iron, and brilliant copper, delicious aromas emanating from inside the mammoth black stove and the pots on top, the women all clad in black dresses with spotless white linen collars and cuffs, frilled caps and aprons, and the men in immaculate black suits and white gloves.

When we came in they all stopped what they were doing and lined up like soldiers for inspection. There was a housekeeper, Mrs. Grant, who was also the gardener's wife; Mrs. Humphreys, the cook; Bessie and May, the downstairs and upstairs maids; Jeffrey the coachman; and Mr. Grant, the gardener, who also looked after the horses and dogs.

I smiled and spoke a few words to each of them, finding some little compliment to bestow or a question to ask, addressing them all warmly and by name, a little trick I had learned to help commit new names to memory, but their faces were as stiff as their backs. They were so stingy with their words, answering me with as few as possible, that I felt self-conscious about how generous I was being with my own. I found no answering warmth in any of them. No welcoming smiles. *It will take time,* I tried to tell myself. *I'm new to them, and all this is new to me. None of us knows quite what to expect from the other.* Yet I couldn't help feeling the sharp twin bites of jealousy and resentment when I told them they might return to their duties and every last one of them turned and looked at Mrs. Briggs and only dispersed at her nod. *I* was the lady of the house and they should look to no other but me to give the orders!

I started back to the parlor. I wanted Jim to be the one to show me my room for the first time, but Mrs. Briggs caught hold of my arm with fingers like steel. My word, but she was a deceptively delicate woman!

"*This* way, my dear." She drew me toward the stairs, and I had no choice but to follow her up them. I knew it would be bad form to make a scene. She didn't even give me time to pause and admire the stained glass in the stairwell; I only caught a fleeting glimpse of reeds, water birds, and my husband's coat of arms in passing.

It was the most beautiful room I had ever seen, spacious and sky blue, combining bed and sitting room. Just knowing it had been created for *me* brought tears to my eyes.

Carved gilt Cupids smiled down at me from every corner of the ceiling and leaned with knowing smiles on pudgy little arms from the tops of the mirrors, picture frames, chair backs, and bedposts. There was even one set as a medallion above the fireplace. I rushed to caress this cameo Cupid's chubby cheeks and dainty wings; I just *knew* he would bring me luck and ensure that this room was always filled with love.

Above the mantel, upon which was arranged a series of gilt-embellished blue and white porcelain plates painted with the portraits of famous eighteenth-century beauties such as Marie Antoinette, Madame Pompadour, and the scandalous and tragic Du Barry, hung a splendid reproduction of the famous Fragonard of a woman in a swing kicking off one shoe as a handsome young man crouches hidden in the bushes to peep up her billowing peach skirt to catch a glimpse of plump, bare thighs above her garters. Jim had laughed when we saw it together in Paris and said he hoped for her sake she was wearing drawers and for Peeping Tom's sake that she wasn't. I had no idea Jim planned to buy it for me.

The windows were hung with sky-blue silk figured with delicate pale-gold flowers, and the canopied and curtained four-poster bed, sofa, and chairs were also done in the same beautiful blue. The carpet was a garden of pastel flowers and the tables and whatnot shelves were crowded with the most marvelous clutter, charming figurines, gilt-framed miniatures, little Dresden ladies in lacy porcelain skirts, antique fans spread out on gilt stands, plates, and bud vases, that Jim had bought for me in Paris.

"It's all *so* beautiful! I can never thank you enough!" I turned to Mrs. Briggs with gratitude shining in my eyes only to see hatred *blazing* in hers.

Tentatively, I put out a hand. "Please . . . Don't hate me! I didn't know!"

"Well . . . you do now," she said with all the feigned smiling civility of a Borgia proffering a poisoned cup of wine, and, with a frigid nod and frozen smile, went out the door. And I was left alone, knowing that I had made an enemy and with no earthly idea what to do about it. It wasn't my fault!

*   *   *

I don't know how I got through the rest of that evening. I was like a graciously smiling automaton sitting in the palatial faux medieval splendor of the dining room with suits of armor, standing like sentries, flanking each door, surrounded by high walls papered in bloodred damask. We dined at a long table with the most beastly uncomfortable gilded chairs upholstered in the same bloody red, reminiscent of royal thrones, all regal lions, unicorns, and ball and claw feet, so that each guest who sat at our table would feel like a monarch.

I pretended to listen to the conversation around me, somehow managing to smile and laugh at all the appropriate moments and evade Edwin's foot trying to entice my own to mischievous play beneath the table, while my head throbbed and the light of the crystal chandeliers catching the wineglasses and silverware made my eyes ache.

I even felt caged by my clothes. I could not wait to return to my room, to kick off my onyx and silver filigree buckled pink satin French heels, pluck all the pins and silk roses from my hair, and shake down my high-piled golden pompadour and gratefully shed my black lace–overlaid mauve satin gown, whalebone corset, steel and horsehair-cushioned bustle, ruffled petticoats and drawers, and black silk stockings, leaving them all littering the carpet for the maid to pick up in the morning. All I wanted to do was sink down into my bed, free and unfettered in my peach silk nightgown, and seek refuge in the sweet oblivion of sleep, after first guiltily crying my eyes out because suddenly I wasn't as happy as I thought I should be.

Michael was *so cold,* Edwin I feared was *too* hot, Mrs. Briggs hated me, and the servants were so aloof they might as well have been on top of Mount Everest. What if I encountered the same chilly disdain when Jim and I went out in society? What if I always found myself up against an icy wall of feigned and frigid politeness? Was there anyone in England, except Jim, I could trust? Whom could I turn to? A time was certain to come when I would need someone besides my husband, an understanding friend to unburden my heart to and ask for advice.

I felt so alone and helpless. I was used to being liked, even adored; I had never had to work to win people over before. I was tempted to rise from my bed, despite the abominable ache in my eyes and head, and dash off a frantic letter to Mama. But pride held me back. I was a grown woman now and married. I should be mistress of my own mind, affairs, and house, not behave like a little girl running crying to Mama every time life was cruel or hurled some unexpected obstacle in my path.

Then Jim was there in his fawn velvet dressing gown, leaning over me, stretching the length of his body ardently over mine, kissing my fluttering lids and throbbing temples, letting me feel his love, and all my fears, along with my headache, at least for the moment, fled as I surrendered myself body and soul to love, sweet love.

I awoke too late to breakfast with Jim before he left for the office. *Tomorrow,* I pouted, and scolded myself, as I arose, with a renewed sense of confidence and purpose, and reached for my cream lace peignoir trimmed with peach satin ribbons and stepped into my satin slippers. *Tomorrow,* I promised as I yawned and shook back the golden weight of my hair, I would be there, smiling across the breakfast table in one of the pretty new dresses Jim bought me, to greet him, ready to hand him the marmalade and refill his teacup. I was *not* going to be one of those lazy, slugabed wives who thanklessly sent their husbands off to work without a kiss and a smile and making sure they've had a good breakfast first. *Jim will leave this house every morning knowing how much I love him!*

Rather than ring for a maid, I impulsively decided to postpone my breakfast and go exploring while the house was still quiet and it was too early for callers. I had no idea if any of Jim's friends or any of mine and Mama's, like General and Mrs. Hazard, would come calling so soon, but I had a feeling Mrs. Briggs would not make herself a stranger no matter how much I might wish it.

Standing in the midst of my beautiful bedroom, I hesitated. My suite was nestled between two very dear rooms I was most eager to see. The nursery was to the left and Jim's suite was on the right. This was *exactly* what I wanted, to keep my loved ones close to me, so that we might always be together. I wanted to be there for my husband whenever he might desire or have need of me, and for my children to be able to climb into bed and snuggle up to me if they had a bad dream and wake me eagerly on the morning of a special day we planned to spend together.

Unable to decide, I closed my eyes and spun around, stopped on the count of ten and opened them, and went to the door nearest me—the nursery. I gasped when I flung the door wide and found myself staring at an entirely empty room. Naked white walls, not the whimsical Mother Goose wallpaper I had envisioned, faced me on four sides, a blank white ceiling above my head and bare floorboards beneath my feet. There was not one stick of furniture. Even the windows I had pictured wearing sunny yellow and white gingham curtains trimmed with white eyelet lace and silk ribbons were naked.

Why had Mrs. Briggs left it barren? I was a young woman, and as passionate as these early days of my marriage had been, I felt it was a sure bet that I would soon be expecting. Or was I being unfair? Perhaps she thought that furnishing this particular room would be trespassing *too* far? Maybe she meant to be kind and leave me *one* room to decorate myself, to respect a mother's right to choose the colors and toys and furniture her babies would see every day?

I decided to be charitable, and, with a smile, I spun gaily around and skipped back across the sky-blue expanse of my bedroom and into Jim's suite. Here all was deep crimson plush, heavy red-tinged brown satin the color of dried blood, and dark mahogany with the muted shimmer of antiqued gilt. It was a dark, somber chamber, stifling and oppressive, with the curtains drawn tight, the kind that would make one prone to tiptoe and whisper. As I peeped through the velvet curtains at the perfectly made bed within, I sincerely hoped that whenever he felt amorous Jim would always come to me; I didn't think I would like sleeping in his bed.

In the dressing room, I caressed and admired his clothes, watered and embroidered silk and brocaded waistcoats, silk and velvet neckties, shirts of the softest snow-white handkerchief linen, and nothing but the finest coats and suits Paris and Mayfair's Savile Row had to offer. Impulsively, I wiggled out of my robe and bundled myself into one of his coats, though it was far too big for me and the sleeves flopped over my hands like a pair of black broadcloth puppets. Smiling, I playfully batted them against each other like Punch and Judy. I reached up to the top shelf, where Jim's hats were kept, and plopped a shiny black silk topper onto my head, laughing when it sank down over my eyes and bumped the bridge of my nose. I hugged myself tightly, closed my eyes, and breathed deeply, trying to catch his scent. When I heard footsteps out in the hall I started guiltily, fearing one of the servants might be looking for me, and quickly put everything back where it belonged, though I would have liked nothing better than to go on wearing my husband's coat all day long so that I might feel embraced by him in his absence.

In the masculine haven of his study, adjoining the bedroom, I found walls of watered champagne silk, oak paneling, discreet touches of antique gold, and heavy oak tables and chairs upholstered in cognac-colored leather with brass studs. There were shelves filled with gilt-embellished leather books, including works by Shakespeare and Dickens, a great globe of the world I delighted in spinning, glass cases filled with fascinating fossils, and cut-crystal decanters that shimmered like diamonds against the rich, warm golden and smoky topaz colors of the fine aged whiskey and brandy inside. The walls were decorated with ancient maps with unexplored territories marked "Here be Monsters," with drawings of dragons and sea serpents, and a fine selection of gilt-framed Landseers depicting magnificent stags and heroic Newfoundland dogs rescuing drowning children.

I sat back in the big, comfortable chair behind Jim's desk and smiled across its wide oaken expanse at my framed photograph and sniffed his cigars and dared take a tiny sip of his very strong brandy as I rattled the heavy brass knocker knobs on his desk, each one fashioned like the hideous snake-haired head of Medusa. To my dismay, I found them locked, to protect petty cash from pilfering servants and vital business records no doubt, not any dire, dramatic secrets like in a novel or play. *This is my life,* I told myself, *my real, wonderful life, not a stage melodrama, after all, and things like that don't happen, not to happy people like us!*

I ventured next into his bathroom, a rather Spartan and severe room done all in black and white with shining silver pipes and fixtures, and white tiles with an elegant black starburst pattern. It was dominated by two tall ebony cabinets with frosted-glass doors that flanked the sink like a pair of the Queen's tall, unsmiling guardsmen. Filled, no doubt, with towels, bottles of cologne, bars of soap, razors and toothbrushes, and other essential and luxurious items of refined masculine grooming. Suddenly I wanted very much to touch them, all these dear, familiar objects he handled every day, to inhale their fragrance, to smell his soap and cologne, to daub it on my wrists and behind my ears. Today was the first day since we were married that we had been apart and I missed Jim terribly.

When I opened the first cabinet I was completely unprepared for what I discovered. All four shelves were *crammed* front to back with glass bottles and vials, clear, blue, amber, green, brown, and milky of varying shapes and sizes, pasted with grandiose and gaudy labels or capital letters embossed into the glass. Some were filled with liquids, others with pills, powders, or creams, and there were metal tins, cardboard boxes, porcelain canisters, bags, pouches, and packets of assorted sizes, some bearing bold words such as *POISON!* and *DANGER!*, dire warnings, and death's-heads. There was even a sizable store of bone-black charcoal, with instructions written on the labels on how to administer it in case of an overdose or the accidental ingestion of poison. Spilled along the edge of the shelf there was a dusting of white powder. The same, I suspected, as Jim routinely spooned into his food and drink.

This cabinet was an apothecary's shop in miniature. The closest thing I saw to a harmless toiletry article was a goodly supply of an American concoction I had often seen advertised called Indian Princess Hair Blacking and some equally absurd preparation with a garish label depicting an unshorn Samson in a typical strongman's pose and leopard-skin loincloth posing for a curvaceous Delilah lounging beneath the red and gold inscription SAMSON'S BEST HAIR-DRESSING COCAINE: IT KILLS DANDRUFF, PROMOTES GROWTH, STRENGTHENS HAIR, VANQUISHES GRAY HAIRS & CURES ALL IRRITATIONS & DISEASES OF THE SCALP! I didn't know whether to laugh or cry. When I spied a box of Chinese Hair Tea with a bevy of kimono-clad women clustered around a goldfish pond combing out ink-black hair hanging down to the ground I found myself doing both.

My mind began to spin, like in a game of blindman's buff, frantically grasping and groping for a reasonable explanation. Did Jim plan a business venture in the apothecary trade? Were these perhaps samples given by the manufacturers? Did he have a kinsman or friend, or even a business associate, who had lately been in that profession and been forced to close up shop unexpectedly and Jim had generously offered to store his remaining stock here while he was away on his honeymoon? Or was my tenderhearted husband taking a collection to donate to a charity hospital, to ease the aches and pains of the less fortunate? But no, as much as I wanted to believe that, a closer look revealed that all these curatives had been opened and consumed to some degree. But perhaps that wouldn't matter to a charity hospital; the suffering poor would be grateful to receive whatever they could get—*No, Florie, no! Stop it; you're being a fool!*

I picked up a large amber bottle with a gold and green label boldly emblazoned *Du Barry's Invalid Food,* promising to cure *indigestion, flatulency, dyspepsia, constipation, all nervous, bilious, and liver complaints, dysentery, diarrhea, stomach acidity, heart palpitations, heartburn, hemorrhoids, headaches, debility, despondency, cramps, spasms, seizures, nausea, shaking fits, sinking fits, coughs, catarrh, asthma, bronchitis, consumption, snake and animal bites, and all male, female, and children's complaints,* all in one bottle, if you were fool enough to believe it.

A new fear suddenly caught hold of me. Was my husband deathly ill and keeping it a secret from me? Had he married me for one last, desperate grasp at happiness, to experience the pleasures of the marriage bed before the cold, cold grave? Was I to become a widow when I was barely a wife?

If I knew what was wrong perhaps I could help, or—my hopes soared—my brother Holbrook was a doctor! I would write to him, or, if it was something particularly dire, one of those ailments where time is of the essence, we could hasten back across the Channel and consult him in person. Or maybe Jim wasn't sick at all and he was merely being a tad *too* zealous about the preservation of his health? There was a name for such people, though I could not, for the life of me, think of it at the time, the kind of folk who fancied stepping in a puddle of cold rainwater would send them to death's door or that every disease they ever heard of would soon be visiting them. But taking all these medicines couldn't possibly be good for Jim and might even kill him. Arsenic and strychnine were deadly, dangerous poisons, and many of these medicines mentioned one or the other upon the label, like the several bottles of lavender-tinted Fowler's Solution, staring at me with a label describing it as *a delicate and delectable mixture of white arsenic and lavender water.* The cabinet seemed to contain a vast store of arsenic in powdered form; one particularly large sack was labeled *Industrial Arsenic.* I supposed that meant it must be even more powerful than that routinely dispensed by druggists. And my husband seemed to have invested in bulk in strychnine tablets. I would have to write Holbrook and ask his advice on how to wean Jim.

I knew Jim had brushed shoulders with death a few years back when he caught malaria on a business trip to Virginia. Maybe that had scared him and sent him running to the doctor or drugstore for every ache and sniffle? Or—a new horror dawned on me—had he been putting on a brave face when the truth was that his illness had fatally crippled his constitution? *No!* I refused to believe that! He was *so* vigorous and vital, younger and handsomer than his years. Alexander the Great had had malaria; I read that once in a magazine somewhere. It was the kind of thing only weak, puny people died of, not robust and virile men like my Jim.

I put down the amber glass bottle I had been holding, something from America called Dismal Swamp Tonic. My hand was shaking badly and it rattled against bottles of Kilmer's Swamp Root and some mysterious concoction called Kickapoo Indian Sagwa, with a proud Indian chief's stalwart, noble profile printed upon the label, vowing that this *Great Indian Remedy will cure rheumatism, chills and fever, loss of appetite, scrofula, and any disease arising from impure blood or a deranged liver.* A cowboy grinned back at me from the bottle beside it: *Doc Lone Star's Genuine Snake Oil Rendered from REAL Texas Rattlesnakes for the Guaranteed Cure of ALL Aches, Pains & Diseases! This is NOT an INTOXICATING BEVERAGE but a REAL MEDICINE of REAL MERIT and PLEASANT to the TASTE! ONLY $1 a bottle!*

One might as well use dollar bills for matches! I slammed the bottle down in disgust.

In my Alabama childhood, I had seen the traveling medicine shows and been entertained by them, the singers and dancers, faux Indian chiefs, and the bombastic spiels proclaimed by charlatans who were no more doctors than I, a little girl in pigtails, was. I had laughed, clapped, and sung along with the rest of the audience. But now, for the first time, I saw the danger in these potions. They weren't just harmless sugar-water the gullible downed in the hopes of living forever, turning a puny milquetoast into a Hercules, or growing a new head of hair on a scalp bald as a billiard ball. That which promised to cure could actually *kill!*

And my husband was poised to become one of their victims!

Jim was a businessman and one of the most intelligent, well-read men I had ever met; surely he couldn't believe all this! There *had* to be some rational explanation!

My poor head felt like it was swimming in syrup and my eyes were drowning in tears. As I tried to steady my breathing, my eyes fixed upon the bough of sunny yellow lemons decorating the label of Lymon's Lemon Cough Curative ~ *90% alcohol derived from the oil and peel of GOD'S GOLDEN FRUIT—the Marvelous, Miraculous Lemon! For the cure of consumption, dyspepsia, neuralgia, and all complaints of the stomach, liver, bladder, kidneys, bowels, and organs of generation, pains of the teeth, ears, back, and extremities. A soothing topical for burns, cuts, abrasions, and animal bites. Also a fine flavoring for ice cream, jellies, custards, puddings, and pastries!*

There was actually an address housewives could write to in order to obtain recipes!

"Merciful heaven!" I cried, wondering who would be fool enough to spoon cough syrup onto their ice cream or actually make dessert with it. I held on to that cabinet for dear life when all I wanted to do was push it over and smash every last bottle inside it. The trembling of my hands shook a bright red tin from the shelf and I bent to retrieve it.

Quinn's Cocaine Tablets: The ONLY Sugar-Coated Cocaine Tablets! Ask for Them by Name! Take them for Coughs & Colds, Sore Throats, Catarrh, Neuralgia, Nervousness, Headaches, Singing in the Ears, Depression of Spirits, Sleeplessness, Heart Palpitations, Fever, Gout, Rheumatism, Waning Vigor, Female Complaints,

Toothaches, Painful Skin Lesions, Warts, Animal Bites, and Syphilis. The #1 Preferred Remedy of Vocalists & Actors!

This was *too* much! I slammed it down in disgust, so hard I dented it, but I didn't care. Inside my head I was *screaming*. I couldn't stand looking at this smorgasbord of snake oil! I slammed the cabinet door shut and sagged weakly against it, sliding to the floor. I felt like Bluebeard's innocent young bride, the happy girl in the fairy tale whose dream come true turned to one of horror almost overnight. He gave her *everything*—the keys to his castle, all the rooms filled with riches and pretty things. He asked only *one* thing of her—that she not enter one dismal little room in the cellar. But stay away from it was the *one* thing she could not do. She couldn't enjoy the treasures and pleasures; she couldn't stop wondering what secret was hidden inside that forbidden room. When she finally unlocked the door she found the floor awash with blood and the murdered, mutilated bodies of her husband's previous brides, women just like her who also could not resist the lure of that forbidden chamber. Though Jim had forbidden me nothing, I had presumptuously rattled drawers and opened doors and I had discovered something I wished I had not, something far worse than a cache of naughty nude French postcards hidden in a drawer beneath my husband's underclothes.

I slumped down upon that cold, hard floor and cried my heart out. I cannot tell you how much time passed before I finally forced myself up and slunk back to my room. All of a sudden I was unbearably weary. I hardly had the strength to move my feet. I walked straight past the maid gathering up my clothes from the floor where I had left them the night before, and crawled onto my bed. I just wanted to sleep. It was the only way I could think of to escape. I wanted to believe it was all a nightmare that I could, and would, wake up from. Downstairs, no doubt, the servants would be gossiping about "what a slugabed the mistress is" and ruminating on the slack and lazy ways of American girls. But I didn't care. I just wanted to be left alone.

I prayed for sleep, but it wouldn't come. I couldn't stop thinking about the contents of that cabinet wreaking their horrible destruction upon my husband's vulnerable innards. Whenever I closed my eyes I saw dead rats, the still tiny black bodies of house-flies done to death by arsenic flypapers, and Jim taking out his little silver box, sprinkling the white powder onto his porridge. My mind whirled with melodramas I had seen in which arsenic played a prominent part and accounts of murder trials I had shuddered over before quickly turning to the next page in the penny papers. But those people were bent upon working malice upon another, killing annoying pests, relatives, husbands, and rivals, not destroy-ing their own stomachs!

When Jim came home I was still lying there in my rumpled nightgown and lace peignoir, one satin slipper on, the other fallen to the floor beside the bed, my eyes bloodshot and swollen red with tears. He ran to me and caught me up in his arms and began stroking the golden mess of my hair, his voice frantic with concern.

"Bunny, what's wrong? Are you ill? Shall I call a doctor? Can I get you something . . . ?"

"From your medicine cabinet?" I blurted out, violet accusation blazing from my eyes. "I'm sure there's nothing a doctor can give me that you don't already have to cure me of everything from singing ears to snakebite!"

Jim abruptly let go of me, recoiling as though I had slapped him. He stood beside the bed, staring down at me as though he had never seen me before. For a moment, I didn't recognize my own husband; he had suddenly become a stranger, a chilly, dangerous stranger who made the hairs on the back of my neck stand up.

"*That* is none of your business," he said. "It is something you are too young and inexperienced to understand."

"It *is* my business!" I shouted.

Kneeling on the bed, I reached out for him, trying to draw him close, to relax that sudden steeliness of manner and spine. All I wanted to do was banish that cold stranger and bring my beloved back to me. "And I'm not too young. I'm your wife, Jim, I love you, and you're doing yourself no good taking all that poison. I'm afraid you'll end by *killing* yourself! You *must* wean yourself off it at once! I'll help you! I'll write to my brother; I'm sure he'll kn—"

I didn't get to finish. Jim hit me. The honeymoon was over. I didn't even see the blow coming. It was one more thing I had never expected from him. First, a cabinet full of poison, then, an even crueler blow. *Oh God, don't let there be any more horrors lurking undisclosed!* One moment I was sitting up on my knees hugging my husband, *pleading* with him to save himself, the person I loved best; the next I was lying sprawled across the bed, with my head dangling over the side, bleeding from my nose and lips. My ears were ringing, and I was seeing what I thought for a moment was fireworks erupting against the ceiling. I heard a woman crying. It took me several moments to realize that it was me.

"*Bunny!* God help me, what have I done?" Jim rushed to gather me in his arms. He cradled me against his chest. "I'm *so* sorry! I didn't mean to. I swear, I don't know what came over me. I've never raised my hand against a woman before! My brothers will tell you I am the gentlest man God ever made! Edwin jokes that I won't even suffer the servants to use flypapers! It will *never* happen again, I swear, as God is my witness! *Please,* Bunny, *forgive me!*"

I heard his voice as though I were underwater even though his lips were right against my face. I cringed and winced away from the thousand kisses he seemed intent on giving me to atone for that one blow.

I closed my eyes and told myself it was all a bad dream and when I opened them my world would be all right. *Tomorrow will be better,* I chanted inside my head, over and over again, like a prayer.

Like a possum playing dead, I pretended to swoon. I was glad when Jim laid me back against the pillows and, after a few lingering caresses to my hair, covered me and quietly left. I didn't know what else to do. There was nowhere, and no one, to run to. I couldn't go dashing off to Paris at the first sign of matrimonial discord and throw myself weeping into Mama's arms. I couldn't let all those people who had disapproved of our marrying nod and say, *I told you so!* My pride couldn't bear it. And maybe it really was the first and last time it would ever happen. Lots of people make a mistake and never repeat it; they learn from it and turn out the better for it. Time would tell, I assured myself, and if it *ever* happened again I could always swallow my pride, pack my bags, and go back to Mama. But that *wouldn't* happen; everything *would* be all right! Tomorrow really would be better; I just had to get through tonight!

And somehow I did. Jim left me alone. A maid brought me my supper on a tray, but I didn't eat a bite. For the first time since we had been married we slept apart, only I couldn't sleep. I wondered if Jim was suffering as much as I was. We were meant to be happy *together,* not remorseful and regretting apart. Countless times I quietly rose and crept to his door, I cupped the bronze knob in my hand, I caressed it longingly, the way Jim always did my breast, but I couldn't bring myself to turn it. As much as I wanted to, I just couldn't turn that knob. Each time, with tears in my eyes, I returned to my lonely bed.

The next morning I rose early and morosely endured the maid May's ministrations, performed with all the diligence and precision of a military exercise. She didn't utter a single friendly word as she yanked my corset strings so hard it made my waist feel like a chicken having its neck wrung. It didn't really matter, I told myself. I was in no mood for conversation anyway. So I stood in gloomy, self-conscious silence and let her lace me into a flowing morning gown of lilac chiffon with lavender satin ribbon trim that flowed beautifully over my bustle and crown my coiled and braided hair with a pretty frilled white breakfast cap with a spray of silk violets and dangling loops of ribbon. Neither of us mentioned my bruised and swollen face, not even when she stood directly in front of me pinning a corsage of silk violets to my breast.

With a stalwart air, I descended the stairs, bravely determined to ignore the stares and whispers of the servants, and took my place at the breakfast table in the conservatory, surrounded by leafy palms and gilt pagoda birdcages filled with canaries and finches. I had no choice but to show my naked face. I had never had cause to paint my face before. I still had the lustrous glow of youth about me, so I hadn't yet acquired the accoutrements, much less learned what creams, rouges, and powders to buy to best hide the bruises, or how to apply them, and I couldn't quite bring myself to send May out to buy them, then devote a hasty half hour to attempting to master the art. I could just imagine myself descending the stairs, head held high, face painted like an inept circus clown's, and the servants tittering that only harlots, actresses, and fast American girls painted their faces; my stomach turned somersaults at the very idea. Having Bessie stare so that she almost overflowed my teacup was better than suffering through that.

Jim came in whistling one of Michael's nautical ditties and lightly kissed my cheek. Feigning blindness to the livid purple-red plum of a bruise blooming there, ignoring how even the featherlight touch of his lips made me wince, he told me how beautiful I looked. I smiled bravely at him across the breakfast table and watched as he took the familiar silver box from his breast pocket and liberally sprinkled the white powder I now knew was arsenic onto his porridge and into his tea.

Jim smiled and reached for my hand. "I daresay you would be horrified, my darling Bunny, if you knew that right now I am taking enough arsenic to kill you."

He was right. I couldn't hide it; I was *horrified*. I wanted to leap up and overturn the breakfast table. Death was floating in his teacup, dangling from his spoon; how could he make a jest of it?

He took a sip of his tea and smiled at me. "Yes, I can see by your face you are." He took a heaping spoonful of his porridge. "But you mustn't worry; I know what I am doing, better, I daresay, than most doctors. My medicine makes me stronger, and I am a better man for it."

I nodded wanly and forced a fragile smile and, like a dutiful wife, offered my husband some marmalade for his toast, while expecting that at any moment he would gasp, clutch his chest, and fall over dead before I could even scream for help. But I was afraid to speak up. I couldn't shake the memory of the blow he had struck me. Privately I didn't think anything used to poison rats could be good for a human being to ingest, but I bit my tongue and strained my trembling lips into what I hoped was a convincing smile. The truth was I wanted the fairy tale back, to don a smiling mask and dance through the days as if in a giddy masquerade. I didn't want the ugly truth to write his name on my dance card. I had already begun running. I disliked confrontations. I didn't know how to be brave. I was never what you would call an assertive person; my spine was more like a licorice whip than a steel rod.

After Jim had gone I sat down at my lovely little Louis XV writing desk, with its drawers inlaid with sky-blue-stained mother-of-pearl, and wrote a long letter to Mama. When I was finished, I rang for the maid and gave it to her to mail.

A few moments later Mrs. Grant, the housekeeper, returned with my letter. It was then that I discovered that before departing for his office Jim had instructed that no letter of mine was to be dispatched without his first having read it. It was for my own good, Mrs. Grant explained, lest I write anything hasty I might regret in the heated aftermath of a marital spat. I was a young bride, and a highly emotional one at that, and might not realize how easily these things were blown out of all proportion.

"All couples quarrel, and the first tiff feels like the end of the world, if I may take the liberty of saying so, ma'am," Mrs. Grant, cool as a cucumber and sour as a pickle, volunteered.

Fighting to hold back my anger, I snatched my letter and dismissed her.

With furious fingers I shredded it, ripping it until not even one word could be read, before tossing the fragments like snowflakes onto the fire; the flames, it seemed, were the only ones I could confide in and trust to keep my secrets safe and private.

I was trapped, like a wild animal caged in a zoo, and I didn't like it. I kept to my room all day, pacing, imagining the walls closing in on me, and feeling like I couldn't breathe. I'm afraid I spoke rather sharply to the maid when she knocked and offered luncheon.

When Jim came home he had a surprise for me. He was carrying an object draped in a sky-blue blanket. He sat it on the floor and, like a magician, whisked off the blanket to reveal a basket in which a fluffy white kitten with a blue satin bow tied around her neck lay curled in a nervous little ball. I squealed with delight. I had always *adored* cats, and now I had a little beauty of my very own.

"Oh, Jim!" I cried as I knelt and gathered her tenderly against my breast as Jim explained, in words similar to Mrs. Grant's, why he had felt compelled to *temporarily*—how curious that Mrs. Grant had left that word out!—censor my correspondence.

"Of course you may write to your mother, my angel," he said. "I only wanted to prevent your dashing off something in haste that you might later regret, words that might lead to this unfortunate, ugly incident being endlessly dredged up instead of being laid to rest and buried as it deserves."

The way he explained it made perfect sense. I felt my anger evaporating. Here was my own dear, kind, sweet, gentle Jim; how could I *ever* have been frightened of him? Last night suddenly seemed all a bad dream. I was ever so glad I hadn't sent that letter; it might have changed forever how Mama regarded Jim. My hasty words had painted him as a monster. I had actually called him "a great bully" and "a brute," it shamed me now to remember. And if Mama had carelessly left the letter lying about and someone else had read it . . . Oh! I shuddered as I realized the horrific consequences that might have resulted from one impetuous letter! No wonder people spoke about the pen being mightier than the sword; for the first time in my life I actually understood what they meant. Jim had been so right and I so wrong! I *must* learn to think before I acted. I really was an impulsive, emotional creature, all heart, no head, sometimes, and I *needed* a husband like Jim to be the voice of reason and keep my head out of the clouds and my feet on the ground.

"All is forgiven?" Jim asked as he knelt beside me.

"All is forgiven." I smiled up at him.

He gathered me in his arms, and while I cradled my kitten he gently, patiently, explained that the way I had blurted out my reference to his medicine cabinet, in such an accusing manner, had wounded him to the core and he had struck out blindly. He had been unforgivably hasty with his fists when he should have used words, and *only* words, patient, gentle, loving words like he was using now. He had been raised to always consider appearances and how others might perceive things, so he knew quite well what his cluttered medicine cabinet might suggest. The way I had spoken and looked at him had struck a nerve, like sugar on a bad tooth. I had made him feel like some degenerate opium fiend, lazing his life away with a pipe in some smoke-hazy den, instead of a respectable, upstanding English businessman who had been "perhaps a tad overzealous" about the preservation of his health since his bout with malaria.

"I almost died, Bunny." He shuddered at the memory. I put my kitten down and took my husband in my arms and kissed him and stroked the hair I now knew owed its darkness to Indian Princess Hair Blacking.

"I cannot tell you how awful it was, or how afraid I was," he continued. "It is an illness I would not wish upon my worst enemy. When the quinine failed to work, I felt certain my hours were numbered. I could *feel* my time on this earth slipping away, minute by precious minute, but I was in such agony I almost didn't care; my body and soul were worn-out from fighting the disease. You cannot even imagine unless you have gone through it yourself, and I pray you never do, my angel. Malaria is a disease that leaves a permanent mark upon a man. Though he may seem to recover, he never truly does, and is forever afterward vulnerable, and that is a way no man likes to feel, much less appear. It shows a strong man just how weak he really is. Some say it is God's way of reminding a man that he isn't invincible, some even call it an antidote to hubris, and I cannot but agree. It certainly shakes all the strength and pride right out of you. It was the arsenic and strychnine that saved me, and I take them still to give me strength. Without them . . . I feel weak, but they make me strong—"

"Oh, Jim, forgive me! I didn't know! I didn't mean . . ." I began to weep and burrowed against his chest. "I never want you to be anything but well, and when I saw all those medicines . . . I was so afraid you would die and leave me . . . that you would harm yourself. . . . After all, it *is* poison you're taking!"

"We all take some poison or another." Jim shrugged. "But my darling Bunny, you *must* trust me. I am your husband and I love you, and I would *never* do anything that would take me from your side. I have made myself an expert in these matters; I know just how much I can take. I am not so reckless as to gamble with my life, only my money." He smiled and stroked his diamond horseshoe.

So I let myself be comforted. He was my husband; I loved and trusted him. And I was, as he said, young and inexperienced; I should not have presumed to judge when I myself knew nothing and had no personal experience of arsenic beyond the little hint in the face wash Dr. Greggs prescribed for me, and I had even been timid and afraid of that, my mind chock-full of murderous melodramas and poisoned rats.

What a silly little fool you are, Florie, I scolded myself as I relaxed in my husband's loving arms and listened to my kitten purring contentedly against my breast. *You behave more like the heroine of some silly blood and thunder melodrama than a real flesh and blood wife! You really* must *acquire some sense before you make a fool of yourself out where all the world can see; you* know *the Currant Jelly Set won't be half so forgiving as Jim!*

❧ 4 ❧

Jim threw a ball at Battlecrease House to introduce me to the Currant Jelly Set. I should have felt right at home, I'd moved in such elite circles all my life, but here I felt like I was standing in the middle of the ballroom on a sinking ship with no hope of salvation.

Their eyes scorched and froze me at the same time, and their nostrils curled like someone was holding a tray of steaming manure right under them. Every time they mentioned the fact that I was *American* one might easily have imagined them substituting the word *half-witted* instead.

They were the most patronizing and condescending set of people I had ever met. Even those who were shorter or of a height with me looked down upon me like Zeus and Hera from the lofty top of Mount Olympus. They would cut you dead over round-toed shoes if almond-shaped ones were all the fashion. Lemonade spilled on a white glove, limp frills on a linen shirt, and a slip of the tongue or a word stuttered or mispronounced were the social equivalents of suicide, and sins *exposed, not* sins *committed,* were the greatest offense in their eyes. It didn't matter one whit to them if a man slept with his neighbor's wife, only if it ended up in the divorce court or the penny papers; you could rack up all the debts you pleased as long as you didn't end up being publicly declared a bankrupt and having your possessions sold at public auction. If you weren't equal to or better than the person next to you, you were *nothing*. They presented what appeared to be a wall of cold British solidarity—they did after all refer to themselves as a *set*—but they would turn on one of their own without hesitation, like wolves on the weakest in the pack. Smiles hid daggers, and compliments concealed contempt. There was no such thing as sincerity in the Currant Jelly Set.

I couldn't *stand* a single one of them! The feeling was overwhelmingly mutual. They might embrace Jim as one of their own, but I would be tolerated only on sufferance; I would *never* be one of their exalted number.

But God would grant me a reprieve and, for a brief, blessed little while, make the cold waters closing in on me recede.

As I stood stunned in the midst of the gold and champagne brilliance of the ballroom, chandeliers blazing over my head, I suddenly felt dizzy and weak. The next thing I knew I was lying limply on one of the champagne and gold brocade sofas.

Edwin was leaning over me, nonchalantly sipping champagne while fanning me with my own gold lace fan and urging the immediate loosening of my stays as his eyes devoured the décolletage of my arsenic-green bodice. Jim knelt anxiously beside me, kissing and rubbing my hands, mumbling a jumble of words that seemed to be a litany of diseases; I think I heard "scarlet fever" and "diphtheria" amongst them. A rather prominent doctor was amongst the guests, and he insisted that the crowd of frowning faces forming a tight circle around us retreat and give me air. After whispering a few discreet questions into my ear, he ascertained the cause of my malaise was quite natural and proffered Jim his heartiest congratulations.

"My angel, I am *so* proud of you!" Jim said as he carefully carried me upstairs as though I were as delicate as one of the Dresden shepherdesses on my whatnot shelf and laid me on my bed where cherubs smiled down at me from all four posters.

"A baby," I kept whispering and stroking my stomach. "I'm going to have a baby!" When I looked in the hand mirror Jim obligingly fetched for me my formerly wan face was truly glowing.

*   *   *

For the next several months I lived quietly. I had a *wonderful* doctor, Dr. Arthur Hopper, whom I chose myself, because of his kind, friendly manner and the fact that he was *not* a member of the Currant Jelly Set and did not equate my being American with being uncivilized and simpleminded. He advised me to curtail my social activities when I tearfully confided how lonely and outcast I felt. I'd been visiting in England many times in my life, though mostly in London and at the country estates of Mama's friends, but now that I was to make my home here I felt for the first time like a pariah, about as welcome as a leper at a royal garden party. Even my own brother-in-law despised me. I'd overheard Michael scornfully describing me to Jim as "a featherbrained adventuress out to feather her nest with pound notes" and "a vain, superficial coquette concerned only with clothes and hats." To his credit, Jim refused to hear anything against me and walked out, and I hastily withdrew to the foot of the stairs, pretending I was just then descending, so he wouldn't know I had heard.

So on Dr. Hopper's advice and with Jim's blessing I restricted my socializing to weekly at-home dinner and card parties with a few carefully chosen guests and an occasional night out at the theater or opera. The dreaded making and receiving of calls I could easily avoid by claiming, often quite truthfully, that my condition made me woefully unwell.

The rest of the time I sat in the sweet solitude of my beautiful blue bedroom or the parlor with my kitten, reading the latest novels and magazines. I even read some of the delightfully awful penny dreadfuls, like *Varney, the Vampire* and *Sweeney Todd, the Demon Barber of Fleet Street,* that Edwin always left lying about like a tomcat marking his progress through the house. And I had my nursery to decorate! At last I had the Mother Goose wallpaper and yellow gingham curtains I had been dreaming about!

I spent many happy hours crocheting dainty baby booties and coats trimmed with silk ribbons in various pastel shades so they would be suitable for either sex. I wanted to make all the clothes my baby would wear, so he, or she, would feel my love in every stitch. I did have some skill with a needle after all, and I *loved* doing delicate and elegant fancywork like this, but Jim insisted that our son—he was certain our firstborn would be a boy—be completely outfitted with nothing but the finest from the best department stores and Mama deluged us with baby clothes from Paris and little lace-trimmed gowns made by nuns in secluded Swiss convents perched high in the Alps. She even sent us a suite of Black Forest Furniture carved from heavy dark walnut, in which playful bears climbed and hugged the legs of the various pieces.

And throughout every day I was constantly caressing the beautiful imperial-green jade ring encircled by emeralds and diamonds that Jim had given me. As soon as he knew I was expecting he had commissioned it specially from the jeweler. Always a believer in luck, and charms to lure it, Jim had heard or read somewhere that expectant mothers in China wore rings set with a great big jade cabochon mimicking the shape of a pregnant belly, which they stroked continuously for luck. Even before that, he had given me a charm bracelet with two dozen beautiful dangling gold, silver, jeweled, and enameled lucky charms from all around the world. There was even a silver dolphin to remind me of the one we had seen that beautiful dawn aboard the *Baltic*. Truly, with my big jade ring on my finger, my luck-laden bracelet on my wrist, Jim at my side, and his baby in my belly, I felt like I really must be the luckiest woman in the world.

Every afternoon I liked to go out for a walk, but as my condition became more prominent Mrs. Briggs took it upon herself to take me aside and explain to me, in slow, carefully chosen words better suited to a simpleton, that in England expectant ladies did not show themselves in public.

I resented her interference. I was fully mindful of the proprieties and had already equipped myself with the best set of maternity stays money could buy and I had had several lovely loose silk wrapper-style or Watteau draped dresses made, a smart green and white tartan skirt and jacket for afternoon calls and shopping, and a beautiful black satin empire-waisted evening gown draped from the collar down with black lace to wear on those increasingly rare evenings out. Dearest Mama had also sent me a similar frock of midnight-blue satin veiled with a fine, sheer black netting embellished all over with faceted jet beads and pastel-rainbow-flashing black peacock pearls. And whenever I went out for my afternoon walk I always wore my coat-cloak, which covered me like a tent. It was made of mauve merino trimmed with a bold broad turquoise border along the wide bell sleeves and voluminous hem and had a row of carved turquoise rose buttons down the front. Though Mrs. Briggs deplored it as "too flamboyant," it always made me smile and feel good to wear it. Jim loved the way my walks and my joy in my coat-cloak put the pink back into my cheeks and every day had a messenger boy from a flower shop deliver a cheery corsage for me to wear upon the lapel.

After the initial sickness had passed, it was, overall, a calm and joyful pregnancy. The only sad moment came when we received word from Paris that my brother, Holbrook, had died suddenly. He had kept his illness secret, even from Mama. He was only twenty-five. Dr. Hopper and Jim concurred it would be unwise for me to travel, so Jim attended the funeral service for both of us. The day of the funeral I sat alone in my bedroom all day with Holbrook's picture beside me, holding the black-bordered card inscribed *Fell Asleep in God* beneath an engraving of a slumbering angel. I smiled through my tears remembering all the happy times I had spent with Holbrook. I was very lucky to have had such a kind and gentle, fun-loving brother. We'd been friends as well as siblings. Despite being called the "Alabama Adonis," Holbrook didn't have a vain or arrogant bone in his body, and by that time I had known enough handsome men to know just how rare and special he truly was.

My son was born on March 24, 1882. I remember vividly even after all these years the searing, flesh-tearing red pain. My sense of decorum entirely deserted me. I screamed and screamed. I writhed, twisted, contorted, and exposed myself shamefully, willingly assuming the most undignified and embarrassing positions when Dr. Hopper asked me to, *anything* to end my agony. My body disgraced me in every way imaginable. I thought I was going to die. When Mrs. Briggs came in to warn me that the neighbors would hear me, I threw my chamber pot right at her head. I am both sorry and glad to say I missed her, though the flying splatter quite ruined her dress.

Then it was over. One last push, and he slithered out of me, and I fell back exhausted and immensely relieved to find that after all that I was still alive.

Jim and I named our son James Chandler Maybrick, but that seemed such a big name for such a little boy, we always called him "Bobo." He was the most *beautiful* child I had ever seen.

"No boy has a right to be that beautiful," Mama would say when she arrived posthaste from Paris and saw my son sleeping angelically in my arms, smelling of rosewater and milk, and wearing a dainty white linen smock I had embroidered with red roses.

His hair was the same deceptively black-brown as his father's, thick but straight when I had been hoping so for curls, and his brows were "like two black caterpillars kissin'," Mama said, pointing out how they almost met above his perfect little nose that turned up just a tiny bit at the tip. I *dreaded* the day when I would have to pluck them. He was certain to cry; then so would I. But oh, the magnificence of his eyelashes! He was born with a double row of them, licorice black, luxuriant, thick, and looking ludicrously long on such a tiny baby. They actually cast shadows on his cheeks.

Jim jiggled the little gold Egyptian eye dangling from my charm bracelet and smiled and said that double row was certain to bring our boy luck. From the day he was born whenever my son lost a lash and I could find it I always kept it in a gold locket set with an aquamarine heart. Later, when he was older, he would bring them to me himself, presenting each fallen lash to me with a theatrical bow, saying, "Here's another lash for your locket, Mama; may it bring you the *best* of luck!" He was *so* adorable! More beautiful than any angel!

"Sure enough, he'll be a charmer," Mama said. "He's already got bedroom eyes. Look at 'em, Florie, like pools o' melted chocolate!"

"Oh dear!" I sighed, then laughed until I cried. After all, such worries were *years and years* away! "As long as he never breaks *my* heart, Mama, I shall be content!" I said, and covered my sweet angel with kisses. I had never loved anyone so much.

❧ 5 ❧

Bobo's birth changed *everything*. Mama summed it up nicely when I tried, in my own muddled, befuddled way, to explain, "You've stopped bein' a bride an' started bein' a wife now, darlin'."

She was right. That blissful sense of expectancy, of opening my eyes every day to some new, joyous wonder, just wasn't quite there anymore. In fact, I feared I felt it dying a little more each day. No matter how hard I tried to hold on to it, it was slippery as an eel. I still loved my husband as much as ever, and the beautiful home he had given me, and I wouldn't have traded my precious baby boy for all the jewels in the world. But . . . It just wasn't the same anymore. . . .

Jim had his business, important people to see, meetings to attend, his friends and men he was trying to make deals with to wine and dine and socialize with at strictly masculine domains like the Liverpool Cricket Club and the Turkish baths. Sometimes, seeing how tired I was, he even accepted invitations without me. There were many nights when he went out alone and didn't come home until long after I was asleep. I was busy with the baby, and I was somewhat laggard in recovering from his birth. My energy seemed to flow out with my milk. Dr. Hopper admitted the birth was one of the most difficult he'd ever attended and he had been in some despair for my life, though he'd kept it so well hidden I advised him if he didn't already play cards he should start right away; with a poker face like that he'd soon amass a fortune.

After Bobo's birth, I just didn't bounce back the way I expected I would. Everything seemed to leave me exhausted no matter how much I rested. For the first time in my life I found myself looking forward to stealing afternoon naps. While May laced me into my clothes I'd find myself darting longing looks back at my bed, going through the day counting the hours until I could return to it. Most mornings I couldn't even rise and have breakfast with Jim no matter how much I chastised myself for not being the wife I had always wanted, and intended, to be. But whenever I spoke to Jim about it, he always smiled and kissed me and told me not to worry my pretty head about it. He'd rather see me smiling and well rested when he came home in the afternoon than yawning, with dark circles round my eyes like a raccoon, offering him his marmalade in the morning. So I took him at his word and started having my breakfast in bed at whatever hour I happened to wake up. Often I remained in my wrapper with my hair in curl rags until half past noon.

And what good would my rising at the crack of dawn have done anyway? Even if I'd been there, smiling across the breakfast table, to greet Jim, would it have *really* made any difference? The servants still looked to Mrs. Briggs for their orders. They treated me like I was a little girl playing at house and not the *real* lady of it.

That woman contradicted me every chance she got! Time and again I'd plan a special menu for a dinner party only to sit down and find something completely different being laid upon the table. Whenever I dared question the cook about it she'd get all haughty and say, "Well, Mrs. Briggs said . . ." And when Jim and I threw a ball, I'd sit down with the conductor and plan the music the orchestra would play, only to find, when it began, that the program had been changed entirely. Once I bought a lovely vase only to discover, when I went to fill it with a specially ordered bouquet from the florist, that Mrs. Briggs had taken it upon herself to return it and exchange it for another. When I confronted her, she didn't deny it. She said my taste was "a tad too flamboyant," so she had changed it for "something more suitable." Then, she actually turned to *my* husband, touched his arm, and asked, "Don't you agree, Jim?" And he did!

It was even worse after Bobo was born. While I was confined to bed recovering Mrs. Briggs took full charge, and after I was up she was ill inclined to step aside. I dearly wanted to bar all the doors to that woman, but I didn't have the power. Indeed, it seemed like everyone but Edwin was mystified as to why I disliked her. Even Jim deferred to her. She was always saying, "Jim, I suggest . . . ," "Jim, I really think . . . ," "Jim, you should . . . ," or "Don't you agree, Jim?" Of course, he *always* did. It was as though I, his wife and the mother of his son, counted for *nothing* in that house!

Whenever I tried to talk to him about it, Jim would laugh it off and suggest that perhaps I might be being "just a tad ungrateful" to someone who was only trying to help me. Or he would laugh and ask "But, darling, don't you prefer being a lady of leisure?" Only Edwin truly grasped what was happening, but having him lean over my shoulder, give a witchy cackle into my ear, and whisper in a wicked, raspy voice, "Double, double, toil and trouble; fire, burn; and, cauldron bubble," whenever he saw Mrs. Briggs working against me really didn't help rectify the situation any.

No matter how many times I showed my husband in the dark that I was indeed a woman, by day- or gaslight he treated me like a little girl. He and Mrs. Briggs foiled my every attempt to grow up. It didn't matter how many nights I took off every stitch and let my hair down and rode him like a thoroughbred; morning always came and I was reduced to feeling like a little girl in pigtails, short skirts, and pinafores again, playing at house and hosting pretend tea parties with her dollies. Is it any wonder that there were days when I just didn't feel like trying anymore?

Jim's frequent business trips only added to my woes. He often traveled to London, Manchester, and even across the ocean to New Orleans and Virginia. I hated being parted from him for so long. The days and weeks would *drag* by. To my surprise, I found myself missing my old roving life. Maybe I truly did have the wanderlust in my blood like Mama? I would have loved to have gone with him. But I had a baby now. I wasn't a bride anymore; I was a wife and mother. The home and the hearth were my place now, not ocean liners, luxury hotels, and casinos. No honeymoon lasts forever. Maybe later, when Bobo was older and away at school, Jim would take me with him and it would be like another honeymoon. I hoped so; I hated to think that the grand adventure of life was over and all I really had to look forward to was sitting by the fire with my knitting and the vicarious thrill of romance novels.

Of course, I had Bobo to console me. Dressing him was my favorite pastime. I didn't let his little phallus stop me; I simply covered it up with layers of lace, ruffles, embroidery, and ribbons. I was *determined* to enjoy myself while I had time; he'd be a big boy wanting short hair and trousers soon enough. As his hair grew, I put him down to sleep in curl rags every night and soon he had a fine head of satiny brown-black corkscrews. I played with him every day as though he were a living doll, changing his little outfits half a dozen times or more, leaving them all scattered on the floor for May to pick up. I bathed him in rosewater and made such terrible messes feeding him that Jim began to wonder if I didn't need glasses to help me find the baby's mouth. Was there something about holding a spoonful of porridge that rendered me blind? Jim wondered.

But, in those early days, I discovered that babies sleep a great deal and there were only so many hours in which I could indulge in such play. It's hard to dress a grumpy, shrieking, squirming baby the way one would a doll.

I don't mean to imply that life was entirely without diversion, only that it had lost some of its vibrancy and luster. To put it bluntly, I was bored. Genteel games of whist with other members of the Currant Jelly Set, the usual dinner parties, society balls, the opera and theater, obligatory afternoon calls, ladies' luncheons and tea parties—there was a sedateness about it all that bored me to tears. It had all become so stale and predictable.

There were so many nights when I'd find myself standing in a crowded room, smiling and chattering away as though I hadn't a care in the world, and I'd still feel all alone. I'd be all too aware of the forced smiles and the coldness hiding behind them. I was in this world but not truly *of* it, and believe me, there *is* a difference. Sometimes I'd forget myself and launch into an anecdote from my carefree Southern youth, recollecting all-night riverboat parties on the Mississippi, floating balls, with the scent of honeysuckle, jasmine, and roses borne upon the river breeze, delightful times when I'd drunk rum punch and danced till dawn with handsome young bucks and flirty-eyed belles just like me, then slept the day away, rising in time to have supper for breakfast, only to suddenly become aware of silence so profound you could have heard a pin drop. I'd stop and look around and see them all struck dumb and scandalized as though I'd just admitted to opening the door to the postman stark naked. The rest of the evening they would be darting glances at me and whispering behind their fans or in little huddles that dispersed as soon as I drew near and I'd overhear snatches of conversation like "not just fast—*swift,* my dear, *swift!*" I just knew they were talking about me.

I was crestfallen. I knew I had been careless, but I couldn't help it; I was just being me, and, sometimes, I forgot that wasn't acceptable anymore. But, to my mind, I wasn't an actress, and I didn't think it was fair that I should have to spend my life playing a part for a hard-to-please audience hell-bent on disliking me. If I had to pretend to be someone else in order for them to like me, then they didn't really like *me.* I just didn't see the sense of it.

Sometimes I felt like Edwin was my only friend, and having lost my own brother, I valued him all the more. We spent a great deal of time together, probably, in hindsight, more than was wise.

I never knew when he'd burst in on me, shake me out of my doldrums, shouting, "Devil take the office!" when I asked why he was not at work, and slap a hat on my head and a cloak around my shoulders and drag me off to the dime museum or an afternoon matinée. "Nothing's better than a penny dreadful brought to life!" he always said. Any sideshow featuring freaks or magicians was sure to attract Edwin. He'd readily volunteer to let the strongman lift him over his head or to step forward and tug the bearded lady's whiskers, daring to let his eyes drift down to her bosom as he did so, and he'd pay to kiss the fat lady, and he never tired of telling about the day he had shaken the Elephant Man's hand. The instant any magician asked for a volunteer from the audience Edwin was on his feet with his hands waving.

He was forever trying to perform magic tricks, dreaming of the day when he could abandon the office forever, he hated cotton and bookkeeping so, and take to the stage as "Edwin the Extraordinary." But he was the most inept magician I ever saw. His tricks *always* went hilariously wrong.

I remember once when I was hosting a ladies' luncheon and he attempted to entertain us with a trick involving a handkerchief and the contents of a pepper shaker; poor Edwin made the mistake of standing next to an open window on a windy day and pepper went flying *everywhere.* We were convulsed with sneezes and our eyes were streaming and stinging, and one poor lady's sneezing brought about similar eruptions from the other end that mortified her so completely that she would never come to our house again.

Another time Edwin lost the tame white dove he had been practicing with for months and thought it had landed on Mrs. Hammersmith's hat, but when he went to catch it he discovered it was only a stuffed bird nesting amidst the silk cabbage roses and he had quite ruined her new hat, mangling it with his big, clumsy man's hands when he snatched the dove off. She sobbed hysterically when Edwin offered her a handkerchief only to have a dozen rainbow-colored ones all sewn together come rushing out of his pocket and proceeded to beat him about the head with her handbag several times, all the while calling him a dunce, a mutton-headed dolt, a nincompoop, and an absolute fiend—I personally thought the last was rather strong. After all it was only a hat, and not a very pretty one at that. Afterward, when I put a piece of steak on the swollen lump on his forehead, he tried to make a joke of it, wondering if the brick she was carrying in her purse was solid gold.

A month rarely passed without him dragging me off to the Anatomy Museum, which I daresay sounds a tad improper, on the select afternoons when ladies were admitted. They boasted over 750 wax models that were authentic replicas of all the human organs and even had displays depicting the birthing process and various surgical procedures to "advance science and learning," and Edwin insisted we had to see them all. He'd stand before the exhibit about "self-pollution" eating his toffee corn and joke that the placard that described it as "the most pernicious evil practiced by man upon himself" contradicted the sign over the front door that shouted in huge gilt-edged black letters: MAN KNOW THYSELF! and have me laughing so hard I almost burst my stays.

Sometimes we even attended séances together, which were then still quite fashionable. We'd sit in the darkness, part of a circle of joined hands, while the medium went into her trance. Spirit hands rattled tambourines, tilted the table, and wrote messages on sealed slates. Cloaked by darkness, Edwin would sometimes lean over and let his lips graze my neck or cheek, nip my ear, or blow on my face, and beneath the table his thigh always pressed against mine, and I could not evade these attentions without breaking the circle. I tried not to let it trouble me *too* much. We were having so much fun; I was *never* bored with Edwin, and I didn't want to spoil it.

Worst of all were the days I spent alone. I'd get so bored I could scream. Bobo would be napping, I couldn't abide Mrs. Briggs, my friendly overtures only made the servants colder, no book or fancy-work could hold my attention, and I would just sit there feeling sorry for myself. So I'd dress myself up in a fine frock and feathered hat, intending just to go for a walk, and find myself drawn like iron filings to a magnet straight to Woollright's Department Store.

It was the *grandest* store in Liverpool, a great big glossy new de-partment store crammed with every conceivable luxury. I'd buy ready-made dresses, or fine fabrics I'd send straight to Mrs. Osborne, my dressmaker, furs, shoes, handbags, hats, fans, gloves, and jewelry, corsets and other undergarments, silk stockings, robes and night-gowns, parasols, perfumes, scented soaps, pretty little knickknacks like china pug dogs and soapstone Chinese dragons, vases, books, candy, pastries, sheet music, furniture, curtains, carpets, lamps, pic-ture frames, fine china, crystal, newfangled gadgets for the kitchen to bewilder the cook, and clothes and toys for Bobo, even when he was far too young for them. I would find myself buying him mar-bles when I knew perfectly well that a baby that age would surely swallow them, and hoops to run after when he was barely walking, hobbyhorses he couldn't yet straddle, and plaid knickerbocker, Zouave, and velvet suits à la Little Lord Fauntleroy, and wide-brimmed straw hats with grosgrain streamers to set off the long curls I planned to cultivate like prize-winning roses on his dear lit-tle head when he was still in the cradle. And, if that doesn't beat all, one day I even bought a fully equipped dollhouse and not one but *three* gilt-edged porcelain tea sets painted with cabbage roses—the toy department had it with the roses done in pink, blue, or yellow and I just couldn't decide which—for a daughter I didn't even have and, as far as I knew then, might never have. I bought silk and velvet neckties and dressing gowns for Jim and Edwin, and even Michael in my never-ending quest to make him like me. Once I even bought him an elephant foot umbrella stand and a stuffed aardvark (I was trying to make him smile).

I'd end up spending the best part of the day shopping, so I'd have to rush to get home in time to welcome Jim. When I unpacked all my parcels my bedroom was awash with so much tissue paper and boxes you could hardly see the carpet.

Deep in my heart, it worried me. Shopping was becoming like a drug I reached for at the least little twinge of boredom or loneliness. I was as dependent on it as Jim was on his arsenic. It filled and gave me something to show for all the empty hours. The smiling faces of the salesclerks were such a welcome change from all the disapproving frowns of the people who filled my life now. I often sat, chin in hands, on the side of my bed, staring down at my purchases spread out on the floor before me. Sometimes I'd feel *so disgusted* with myself I'd vow that tomorrow I would take them *all* back and *never* do this again. I had my books, and my embroidery, to occupy me, and I might even take up china painting again, or maybe I could find some sort of ladies charitable society that would truly welcome my help. But somehow, no matter how good my intentions were, my resolve always crumpled and I managed to talk myself out of it. I *always* found a reason to keep everything I bought; I never returned a single thing.

Every month the bills got higher and I'd find myself a nervous wreck, prostrate with worry, sick headaches, and a sour stomach, worrying what Jim would say, but he never said a word about any of it except to comment on how pretty I looked in my new finery or how thoughtful a gift I'd chosen. He even said the elephant foot umbrella stand I'd given Michael was "charmingly exotic as well as utilitarian" and the stuffed aardvark was "the perfect conversation piece every parlor requires" and that he was the luckiest man in the world, to have such a beautiful wife who always chose such nice things for him, his family, and friends.

I loved him so, and every day I kept vowing I would do better, that I would make myself into a wife worthy of him. I kept promising "tomorrow" and every day when that tomorrow actually came I said "tomorrow" again and went on just the same, wallowing in bed until half past noon and spending money like it was water and gallivanting around to dime museums, freak and magic shows, and melodramas with the irresponsible, irresistibly charming Edwin. My metamorphosis into that perfect wife was as much a failure as one of my brother-in-law's magic tricks.

$\mathcal{P}$ 6 $\mathcal{P}$

Bobo was just taking his first steps when I found myself pregnant again. One moment I was standing there with my arms outstretched, my son toddling toward me in a rose satin gown trimmed with blue rosettes. The next I was flat on my back, staring dizzily up at the spinning ceiling, trying to see it through a starry haze.

Jim was adamant. I'd dallied too long and we simply *must* engage a nanny. Now that I was expecting again I couldn't possibly take care of myself and Bobo too.

The sickness that had dogged me in the early days of my first pregnancy, usually passing by mid-afternoon, this time was unrelenting. I couldn't keep a thing down and began to lose flesh. Dr. Hopper ordered me to bed, and I rarely left it, rising only sometimes, for a few hours, in the late afternoon or evening.

Once again, Mrs. Briggs reigned supreme at Battlecrease House. Jim entrusted her with finding us the perfect nanny. Mrs. Briggs was to handle the whole thing; I wasn't even permitted to sit in when she was interviewing the applicants. *She* was to have *first and final* say about the woman who would take care of *my* children! No matter how much I wept and raged about it, Jim stubbornly refused to see it my way. "Children need discipline, Florie, not sugarplums ten times a day," he said.

The nanny Mrs. Briggs chose for us was Alice Yapp, an innkeeper's horsey-faced spinster daughter from the aptly named Nag's Head. She *still* figures in my nightmares, staring at me with big fishy eyes swimming behind the thick lenses of her steel-rimmed spectacles, hair the color of horse chestnuts scraped back in a severe bun to fully reveal a face as friendly as a hatchet. I wouldn't have been surprised to awaken in the night and find her standing over my bed with an ax. We *hated* each other at first sight. I *begged* Jim to dismiss her, to find someone sweet to look after our children, but he and Mrs. Briggs were in complete accord that "children need structure and discipline, and that's what nannies are for." The moment Nanny Yapp took Bobo in her arms, I started to lose him. She contradicted me at every turn, pouring her always politely worded grievances into Mrs. Briggs's all too willing ear and worming her way into the good graces of the whole household staff; she was after all one of them and I was the outsider. We were like chess players trying to outmaneuver each other, and the children—*my* children— were the poor little pawns.

Why does the miracle of birth have to be so horrid? I felt so ugly and ungainly as I tottered around, swollen, half-sick, fearing I'd spew all the time, embarrassed by the blemishes erupting on my face, feeling like the pimple on my nose was drawing stares like a big pink and red bull's-eye, and hating the way my clothes chafed but feeling slatternly whenever I dared flout propriety and venture out of my room in my robe. Even though the spring weather was quite mild, I felt stiflingly hot. I was sweating like a field hand, even though I'd done absolutely nothing. I'd lie in bed in my chemise, sucking on hard ginger candies to quell the nausea and plying a palmetto fan, feeling unable to breathe with fear whenever I thought about the ordeal that awaited me. I was *terrified* of the pain to come, afraid that this time I might not survive it.

Sometimes I'd force myself to rise and put on one of my silk Watteau dresses and go to the nursery to see Bobo. I'd go in, with a book in hand, ready to read to him, only to find Nanny Yapp already sitting beside him with a book that she had chosen herself, always something serious and morally edifying, with not a bit of fun in it. She disdained the picture books I bought for him as "frivolous" and was equally disapproving of *Little Lord Fauntleroy,* which I just *loved* reading to him, especially when he was old enough to wear the suits it inspired.

With his long ebony curls and white lace collars set against velvets in shades of garnet, cinnamon, licorice, plum, tawny, and chocolate to set off his coffee-bean-brown eyes, he was downright breathtaking. You never saw a child more beautiful, he could melt *any* heart, he was *so sweet,* and he just *loved* to cuddle and kiss.

The trouble was Nanny Yapp had no sense of fun and not one nurturing bone in her body.

On the rare days when I felt well enough to sit on the floor with Bobo and spread his little dresses out, getting ready to play dress-up with my beautiful living doll, Nanny Yapp would stop me as soon as I'd put the first one on him. "*Now* that the business of dressing is *done,* it's time to move on to other things," she'd decisively declare, and pick him up and take him away from me. When I tried to insist I wanted to change his clothes, she'd give me a withering stare and say, "We must learn to make up our minds, to make a decision and stick to it. We must remember that we lead by example, and we don't want this young man to grow up to be a vain, changeable, and indecisive clotheshorse who will be late to the office every morning because of the time he wastes dithering over which necktie to wear, now do we?"

Ribbons and roses and lace also had a way of disappearing from Bobo's little dresses; Nanny Yapp didn't deny she cut them off, as she was of the firm opinion that his wardrobe was "unsuitably ornate for his gender now that he is getting older, madame. If you persist in dressing him in this manner, when he is old enough to walk in the park and play with the other boys they will be certain to tease him."

I thought it very mean-spirited of her to spoil my pleasure. If she caught me giving Bobo bonbons, or the sugar cubes I used to slip into his little mouth every time I saw him, she'd scold *me,* saying children should not have sweets between meals, desserts were for afterward, and that "dietary discipline" was "essential to a child's healthy and proper upbringing." She accused *me* of teaching him unhealthy habits and said if I kept on he'd grow up to be one of those languid persons who thought nothing of lounging around all day with a box of bonbons. He would ruin his teeth, his figure, and eventually his health, she insisted, if I persisted in encouraging this bad habit. She gave me such a scalding look I half-suspected she thought I'd be sneaking him brandy and cigars next or taking him off to opium dens when we were supposed to be visiting the zoological gardens!

If I dallied overlong bathing Bobo, loving the feel of his smooth, baby-soft skin, marveling that this gorgeous creature had actually come out of my body, that Jim and I had made this little angel, she'd stand at my shoulder and stare at me as though I were a criminal.

"You will encourage him to evil tendencies, ma'am," she'd say, and briskly roll up her sleeves and take the washcloth away from me and proceed to scrub Bobo as though he were a greasy skillet in the kitchen sink instead of a beautiful little being with angel-soft skin and feelings. She was equally disapproving when, after his bath, I wanted to rub my pink rose-scented lotion into his skin, to ensure it would stay sweet smelling and soft. But Nanny Yapp thought this would breed "indolent and effete habits" in him.

The lovely pastel-colored perfumed soaps I always bought for Bobo also had a way of disappearing. I was certain that woman took them for her own use; when I got close to her my nostrils often caught an expensive whiff of roses and lavender not in keeping with her salary. I had already noticed that there was lace and ribbons trimming her petticoats beneath her plain uniforms and aprons, snipped, I suspected, from my son's wardrobe. But Jim refused to be drawn into it. He was seemingly deaf to my every complaint about that wretched woman.

I almost died bringing my daughter, Gladys Evelyn, into the world. Outside it was the most beautiful July day you ever saw, all blue skies and butterball-yellow sun, but it was absolute *Hell* inside my bedroom. I could *feel* the demons' claws tearing at my innards. I felt like my spread legs were each tied to a wild horse and I was being torn apart by them. I bled and bled and screamed and screamed. When I felt my flesh burning and tearing, I wished I were dead; it seemed the *only* way to escape the agony. Every time I felt the child writhe inside me, I thought my last breath was going out with my scream.

This time Mrs. Briggs didn't dare come in, only stuck her head around the door to tell me that such carrying on was unseemly; after all, women had babies every day. Suffice it to say the names I called her were unmentionable then and still are now in polite society. I think we were both surprised; I never even realized I knew such words. The crude brutality of childbirth must have dredged them up out of some long-forgotten memory of when I'd overheard the conversation of sailors. Then it was all over. I fainted with relief. Everything went black for me before I could even hold my daughter in my arms. Dr. Hopper had to stab a lancet into the sole of my foot to shock me back to my senses. I still shudder and feel sick and light-headed at the memory of that terrible remorseless pain. No one should ever have to suffer so!

Afterward, I developed such a fear of childbirth I could hardly bear for Jim to touch me. Terror flooded every part of me when, smiling over Bobo's and Gladys's dark heads, he jokingly declared that now all we needed was a pair of golden ones to match mine and our little family would be complete.

Like some poor shell-shocked solider boy, I'd find myself reliving the worst agonies of childbirth in moments when I should have been experiencing only the most exquisite pleasure. I consulted with Mama and began to make some discreet attempts at contraception, experimenting with different methods, praying each time I would not bungle it and find myself expecting again.

The fear was *so* great, I had trouble relaxing; I was tense and awkward where I had once been so fun loving and free. I no longer initiated our love play; most of the time I just lay there and left it all to Jim, and I know he missed the naked adventuress who loved to let down her golden hair and cast off her inhibitions with her clothes, and the naughty banter that always accompanied our mutual explorations. I would have complained of headaches, only he always had some remedy ready to dose me.

When we made love, if I'd managed to discreetly slip into my bathroom before I'd always be worrying that the little sponge or one of the French womb veils Mama sent me from Paris I'd inserted might slip or that Jim's nose might catch a suspicious whiff of lemon juice or vinegar or the little string meant to make retrieval easier might dangle or catch on his finger and give me away. On the nights when I'd been unable to prepare myself, I worried that the cuddling afterward, which I adored so, would delay me from douching with the mixture of warm water, lemon juice, vinegar, and carbolic acid I always used and give Jim's seed a better chance to take root. A couple of times I was so tired, and the warm weight of Jim's body so comforting and sweet, that I was lulled off into sleep and missed my chance and was in absolute terror until my courses came. Once, when they were late and I was terrified of what that might mean, I tried to bring them on with a foaming douche of nitric acid while Jim was at work. I don't know how I got through that without screaming the house down. I nearly bit my lip clean through and had to make up a tale about tripping on the stairs to explain the bloody marks my teeth left.

I felt doubly bad for deceiving Jim, for not openly telling him what I was doing and why. But men so seldom understand these things. They take that verse in the Bible to heart about women being meant to bring forth offspring in pain, without being able to fathom just how bad that pain actually is. They think we weak, delicate things make overmuch of it, that we, wanting sympathy and presents, and to loll around in bed afterward being waited on hand and foot for a fortnight, greatly exaggerate. I wanted to tell him the truth, but I was so afraid of how he'd react. I wanted to believe he would understand and be content with the two children we had, but another part of me was afraid of the anger I knew lurked inside him, that my confession might bring the violence out. He might even forbid me privacy in my bathroom to make sure I never attempted the like again, and I just couldn't bear the thought of May, Mrs. Briggs, or—God forbid!—Nanny Yapp standing there scrutinizing me at moments that should have been absolutely private.

It was such a difficult position to be in; I loved my husband and for him to hold and kiss and touch and caress me all over, his lips and fingers bringing me to the pinnacle of pleasure, but inviting him to do so only opened the door to more. Every time I opened my legs to him, I felt more and more fear and less and less pleasure. I wanted to hold on, I wanted it to stay, I didn't want to lose the intimate joys of our marriage, but the fear was ripping it all away. I just could *not* forget the pain, and that it had almost killed me, and that this pleasure was the prelude to that pain. Jim and I were always superstitious about threes, the third time being the charm, and I was certain that if I was brought to childbed again it would be the end of me.

The horrors of her birth seemed to also have left a mark on Gladys. She was a sickly little mite and gave Dr. Hopper a deal of trouble trying to coax her into staying in this world where she belonged. Dark-haired like Bobo, but with my violet-blue eyes, poor little Gladys wasn't blessed with even a smidgen of her brother's beauty. She was a plain, poorly little thing. I dearly hoped Mama would be proven right when she predicted that Gladys was probably just a late bloomer: "No daughter o' yours could *ever* be anythin' but beautiful, Florie!"

Nanny Yapp seemed to take the same instant dislike to my daughter as she had to me and was apt to neglect her in the nursery. Time and again, I'd hear my daughter *screaming* at night and rush in only to find her unattended, in a pitch-dark room. I'd turn on the light, take my daughter in my arms, comfort her, then roust that woman out of bed, rip the covers off her, and demand to know what she was about ignoring my child, leaving her to scream her throat raw in the dark. The poor little mite couldn't speak yet; crying was the *only* way she had to make herself heard and let us know if anything was wrong.

But Nanny Yapp always faced me, cool and indomitable as an iceberg in her white nightgown and cap, and said that Gladys already had all the earmarks of a nervous child and if I wanted her to grow up to be a timid, frightened woman, leaping out of bed and running to her and coddling her every time she cried was exactly the right way to ensure that unhappy outcome. Gladys, Nanny Yapp said, must learn that crying wasn't the way to woo attention or win affection, and once she understood that she would sleep through the night without a single whimper.

I wanted to kick that awful, cold and unfeeling woman right down the stairs, but Nanny Yapp went running to Mrs. Briggs, just like she always did. Then they both went and had a talk with Jim.

My husband called me into his study like he was the headmaster and I some troublemaking student and said mother love must be blinding me because Nanny Yapp was "quite right," and had once again proven herself "an exemplary nanny any household would be blessed to employ" and that I should consider myself lucky to have her. "We would not be so fortunate to find her like again." My first instinct was to shout, *Well, hallelujah, I sincerely hope God did break the mold after He made her!*, but I knew better.

"We do things differently here in England than you do in America, Bunny dear," Jim said, kissing my check. "You'll see. Nanny Yapp knows her business, and everything will turn out right in the end; isn't that right, Matilda?"

"*Quite right,* Jim." She nodded and moved to stand beside him, as if *she* were his wife and I was the enemy they were closing ranks against. "I took great pains to find you the perfect nanny, Florie. I've never seen such splendid references in my life, and I went over them *most* carefully; I was *determined* that you should have the best. So why *you,* a woman with no experience with children beyond the act of giving birth, feel the need to question and cast doubt upon her judgment at every turn . . . I cannot fathom. But, I do know this. If you are not careful, she'll leave you and go to another family that will appreciate her. I suggest you apologize soon. . . ."

To my horror, Jim concurred. "The sooner the better, my dear."

For the first time, I wanted to kick my husband down the stairs too. But I just nodded and forced a smile. What else could I do? I knew I couldn't win, and, to my everlasting shame, I didn't have the gumption to even try. I was just too tired.

❧ 7 ❧

The years passed, each marked by a new dress, a champagne toast, and a kiss shared with Jim at midnight. It was 1884, then 1885, 1886, 1887, and that curious year of the three eights that will never come again—thank heaven!

I was twenty-six. Outwardly, I possessed everything a well-bred young woman could want or wish for. I had a wonderful, loving, and attentive husband, handsome and well preserved for his forty-nine years; maybe there's something to be said after all for arsenic as an embalming agent? I was a mother twice over, to a boy so beautiful the angels up in heaven must weep for missing him, and a little girl who was fast coming into her own fragile beauty. We were all dressed perfectly as Paris fashion plates, like we'd stepped straight out of the pages of *La Mode Illustrèe,* hand in hand, a smiling, happy family. We lived in one of the most beautiful houses in Liverpool. We were members of the Currant Jelly Set, leading a charmed life that revolved around society balls, dinners, race meets, card parties, and nights out at the theater. I had one brother-in-law who was world famous and cordially detested me, and another who was a charming wastrel, a loafer, who was my best friend and loved me more than he should have.

But it was all just a façade, like the sets for a stage play, just pretty, flat painted pictures, with no real substance behind, just a few sticks of lumber shoring it all up. The big bad wolf could have blown it all down in a single breath without even really exerting himself. At the slightest gust it would have all come down easier than the little pig's house of straw.

There had been a drastic dip in the cotton market that forced Jim to close his offices in America and cease his travels across the sea. I didn't rightly understand it; after all, didn't the world need cotton just as much as ever? People weren't wearing less clothes or using fewer handkerchiefs, or tablecloths and napkins. But I didn't try too hard to; I was happy to have my husband home with me instead of gadding about Norfolk and New Orleans without me. I even told Jim I wouldn't mind if we had to move into a smaller house with fewer servants; we could start implementing some measure of domestic economy right away by dismissing Nanny Yapp. Jim reacted to that as though I had poured a flagon of syrup over his head right in front of the Prince of Wales. He was *horrified* that I would even suggest it!

"Have you gone mad?" he demanded. "We would be *ruined* outright! All our creditors would see that we were in trouble and close in on us like sharks, each wanting the first bite, and that would be the end of us as far as the Currant Jelly Set is concerned. The most important thing we can do now is continue to keep up appearances. If we must retrench, we must make cuts *only* where it will not show."

Jim started by drastically cutting my household budget. Oddly, that was the very thing to make Mrs. Briggs decide it was high time for me to take a more active role in managing my own household. She'd been neglecting her own far too long on my account. I discovered then that apparently my husband expected me to be some kind of miracle worker, able to wave a magic wand and conjure up money or stretch a pound note like taffy and make it go further than anyone else could.

I *tried* to keep a budget, but it was simply impossible. Jim said I mustn't even *think* of cutting the servants' wages or reducing the size of the staff; servants being such a gossipy sort, word would be sure to get out and we would be ruined in no time. But out of the new allowance he allotted me there just wasn't enough left over to buy the usual provisions after their wages had been paid. And, as any housewife knows, little emergencies crop up all the time and they have a habit of doing so at the least convenient moments. The stove needed repairing, I cracked a tooth on a horehound drop, there was a leak in the roof, Bobo broke a finger, Bessie saw a spider and dropped a whole stack of our best china plates, one of the carriage horses tore a tendon, a pipe burst, and little Gladys was sick so often. Jim and I had to keep up with the Currant Jelly Set and be seen at all the most fashionable places, like balls at the Wellington Rooms, and keep boxes at the opera, theater, and races, and, of course, we had to keep up with the fashions. It all cost money, money we didn't have. For all the good it was doing me, I might as well have been using my household ledger to press flowers. I soon exhausted my supply of red ink and had to buy more from the stationer's shop—on credit.

I began buying more and more goods on credit and borrowing money from anyone who would lend it, even one hundred pounds from Mrs. Briggs, and then borrowing more from others to settle those little debts. Then I found myself making excuses, going up to London to visit an old friend or a maiden aunt who was stopping there, and taking pieces of jewelry I rarely wore to pawnshops where no one knew me, things Jim's sharp eye would never notice missing. But it was only a matter of time before I ran through all those, then I began consorting with professional moneylenders, ruthless men with eyes like sharks, agreeing, in desperation, to exorbitant rates of interest. I was playing for time, just trying to keep our heads above the fast-rising water.

Soon I was writing, pouring out my anguished heart, to Mama:

> *I am utterly worn out and in such a state of*
> *overstrained nervousness I am hardly fit for*
> *anything. Whenever the doorbell rings I feel ready to*
> *faint for fear it is someone coming to have an*
> *account paid, and when Jim comes home it is with*
> *fear and trembling that I look into his face to see*
> *whether anyone has been to his office about my bills.*
> *My life is a continual state of fear. There is no way of*
> *stemming the current.*

*Sometimes I wonder: Is life worth living? I would
gladly give up the house tomorrow and move
elsewhere, but Jim says it would ruin him outright.
We must keep up appearances until he has more
capital to fall back on, to meet our liabilities, since a
suspicion aroused would open the floodgates and all
claims upon us would come pouring in all at once
and Jim couldn't possibly settle even half of it with
what he has now.*

Here I have to admit one of my great faults. When it all became
too much, even though I knew I was only increasing our woes, I did
what I'd been doing for so long—I went shopping. A new handbag
with a cameo on the clasp or a pair of yellow satin high heels with
diamanté buckles was to me like one of Jim's arsenical "pick-me-
up" tonics was to him. And, after all, Jim said we must act as
though nothing had changed, so that meant continuing my sprees
at Woollright's; otherwise, people would talk.

Jim was now, I knew, stopping by the druggist for one of those
tonics every morning on his way to his office, then three more times
throughout the day, before having the fifth and final one on his way
home, and he'd increased the dosage from five to seven drops of
the arsenical solution. He'd actually boasted to me about that, as
though it were something to be proud of, and that in addition to
the white powder in his little silver box and the strychnine tablets
he was popping into his mouth like peppermints.

Every time I saw my husband I was afraid it would be the last
time. Every time the doorbell rang I was afraid it was either a bill
collector or someone come to tell me that Jim had dropped dead
on the Cotton Exchange floor after taking one strychnine tablet or
pinch of arsenic too many. I'd tried talking to Dr. Hopper about it,
and he said he'd make a note that we had had some conversation
about it in case my husband should die suddenly. Frankly, I didn't
find that at all comforting and *begged* him to talk to Jim about it.
Afterward, I wished I hadn't. Jim's anger was like that serpent
slumbering in Cleopatra's basket of figs. It was a week before I
could show my face in public again. By that time, I'd already mas-
tered the art of powdering and rouging over the worst of the

bruises. I no longer believed him afterward when he wept, cradled and kissed me, and promised "never again."

A day finally came when the doorbell *did* ring and I discovered a debt I never knew about, one that had nothing to do with hats and handbags. In fact, it wasn't mine at all. It was a debt my husband had hidden from me, a debt dating back to before I was even born.

A blowsy fat woman with hair hennaed redder than a smallpox pustule was standing there, picking with gnawed-to-the-quick fingernails at a striped satin skirt that had clearly not known a laundress's touch in some time. She stood there, fidgeting and hiccupping, fussing with her feathered hat's drooping brim, and smelling like a saloon, excusing herself by saying she'd been drinking to get her courage up.

She said her name was *Mrs.* Sarah Maybrick and she'd come to see her husband—Mr. James Maybrick—to remind him that she and the children, all *five* of them, had not fallen off the face of the earth, they were still alive, in Whitechapel, where they had always been, and were in dire want of money and wanting to know what had become of the allowance he was accustomed to send. "You must excuse me for comin' to your door like this," she said. "I would've written 'im a letter, only I can't write an' I was too ashamed to ask anyone else to do it for me."

That was the moment my world fell apart. As darkness engulfed me and I fell I saw it all break apart in myriad flying shards that could never be glued back together again. *This time,* I knew, when I opened my eyes again my world would *not* be all right. I'd not only lost my place in the world; I'd had it snatched right out from under my feet like a prankster had pulled a rug out from under me. I'd fallen hard and had all the breath knocked out of me and I lay there gasping and shattered. If that henna-haired slattern was Jim's rightful wife, then who and *what* was I? *A kept woman, his mistress, his whore?*

Unbeknownst to me, when I had been trying on my wedding gown there had already been a Mrs. Maybrick, hidden away in Whitechapel, the worst slum in London, sniveling over a soupbone simmering in a dented pot in a room over a watchmaker's shop, trying to stretch it enough to feed herself and her children, who then numbered three. They'd come so late in her and Jim's marriage she said she'd quite given up hope, but once she started she took to it like a rabbit and was popping them out right regular like, and, she patted her belly, she suspected she was expecting a sixth even now. The fourth and fifth, I would later discover, when my senses were restored enough for me to sit down and examine the dates, had been born *after* Jim married me—a boy two months before Bobo and a girl six months after Gladys.

I came to with my head cradled in the lap of that gaudy, grimy gown with those stubby pink fingers stroking my hair. She was saying that she could tell just by looking at me that I was "a good lady, a nice lady," and begging me to, out of the goodness of my heart, intercede with my brother on her behalf, as he was apt to be forgetful and neglect them all from time to time, he was such a busy man with his cotton business and all, but that didn't stop the children from growing or their bellies from grumbling. *My brother!* Jim had told her he was living in Liverpool with his sister! *He didn't even have a sister!* They'd been married some thirty years, since 1858, *four years* before I was born! Our marriage was a sham! A lie! A sin! Jim was a bigamist and our children, our precious children, a pair of bast—all these years later I *still* cannot bring myself to write that foul and ugly word!

I don't know how I got through it—I think I must have said something about feeling quite poorly—but I sent Mrs. Maybrick on her way, to catch the train back to London, promising I would indeed speak to Jim about her. I was still standing there reeling amidst the debris of my shattered marriage and life as I had known it up until the moment Sarah Maybrick knocked upon my door, when Edwin found me.

He crept up behind me and kissed the back of my neck. I didn't resist him. I didn't encourage him. But I didn't *dis*courage him either. Edwin's hands crept around to cup my breasts through my bottle-green bodice. The next thing I knew we were in the parlor and he was bending me over the back of a Chippendale chair. I heard my skirts rustling, layers of white ruffles and green damask shading my head like a parasol as he pushed them up and pulled my drawers down. He filled me at the moment in my life when I was feeling most empty. But I can't even pretend to be grateful. The truth is, I didn't feel a thing. I numbly, dumbly let something happen that never should. I stood there soulless as a dressmaker's wooden dummy. My first act of adultery was devoid of passion. Edwin took advantage of the situation—choosing a moment of dumb, numb weakness when I felt like I had lost everything and was still too stunned to react. He was my best friend; he *must* have known something had to have happened to leave me in this stricken state, so utterly unlike my usual self. My eyes were vacant, I didn't say one word, and my face must have been drained bloodless as one of Varney's victims. But did Edwin ask me what was wrong or try to comfort me the way a *real* friend would? No, he did not. How could he even think that was the *right* method or moment to start a love affair?

Looking back now, I have to wonder: Did a little part of me—the angry heart of me—decide if I was indeed a whore then I was going to act like one, right there in my keeper's parlor, and pay him back in kind? If so, I didn't play the part very well. I didn't squirm with delight or return Edwin's kisses. I took no pleasure, feigned or actual, in our intercourse. I just stood there, silently slumped over the chair, with my skirts up over my head. I'd be the Dollar Princess I never really was today if I had a dime for every time I've asked myself that question, then shied away from it because I was afraid of the answer. After all, I had always liked Edwin immensely. Maybe I'm being too hard on myself, or maybe the opposite is true. You, dear reader, will have to decide, but first take a moment to consider. Put on my shoes, if you will, and imagine that you lost everything you believed in and cherished in a single afternoon. Then, while you were still standing there, dazed and reeling, an amorously inclined man you'd always liked walked in and took you by the hand. What would *you* do?

In the end, all I know is that *if* it *was* revenge, it was *not* sweet. It cost me something very dear. By succumbing that once, I forever forfeited the pleasure I had formerly found in my brother-in-law's sweet and silly company. Edwin thought it gave him the right to possess me whenever an opportune moment arose. It ruined our friendship and I *dreaded* finding myself alone with him because I always knew where it was leading to.

Instead of sitting and chatting or going out like old dear friends the way we used to, after that fateful afternoon Edwin was more likely to chase me around the room, try to pin me down on the sofa, bend me over any convenient table or chair, or back me into a corner where my skirts would quickly come up and my drawers down. He'd paw and kiss me as I wept and implored, "Can't we be the way we were before?," though in my heart I already knew the answer.

But Edwin would merely bury his face in my perfumed neck and push my hand down where he wanted it to be and murmur that this way was much better, "the way it was meant to be, the way it would have been if only we'd met each other first . . . but . . . since we didn't . . . we might as well make the best of things. . . ."

He never once looked at my face, he never saw the way I'd wince and weep, though I doubt it would have made any difference anyway. Maybe that's why he preferred to take me from behind? It allowed him to feign blindness and pretend I enjoyed it.

I still mourn and miss the friend I lost that afternoon. It was as though the Edwin I knew and liked best had died and left behind a single-minded amorous identical twin to accost and bedevil me. And there was no one I could turn to for help. I couldn't very well confide in Jim or Mrs. Briggs. With Edwin living right there in the house it was simply impossible to avoid him; to snub and cold-shoulder him in any noticeable fashion would only invite awkward questions. I lost so many things that day—the sanctity of my marriage, all the trust and love I had poured into it and thought I had been given in return, my children's legitimacy, my self-respect, and my own respectability, the right to say with pride that I had always been a faithful wife. Then, as if that were not enough to lose all in one afternoon, I lost my best friend too. And the worst part is, if I had met him first, instead of Jim, I might have loved Edwin. I *had* loved him. And, by letting him have me, I had lost him forever.

Bent over the back of that chair, stifled by my tight-laced stays, blood rushing to my skirt-shrouded head, I felt as though I were sinking like a stone, drowning, like salt water was searing my nose, throat, and lungs. I felt that horrid heart-about-to-burst pounding. Then, all of a sudden, it was as though my head broke the surface, and I came up, gasping for air. I shoved Edwin away. Before I could say a word or slap his smiling face, the front door opened and I heard voices, Jim's amongst them. I froze. Edwin turned his back and nimbly did up his trousers and slicked back his hair. I stumbled over my drawers, down around my ankles, and almost fell. I heard them rip, but I hadn't time to fuss with hitching up all my many layers of skirts trying to pull them back up, so I snatched them off and stuffed them into the nearest vase and ran to the mirror above the mantel to put right my hair.

With all that had happened, I had quite forgotten that we were expecting guests for cards and dinner. Mr. and Mrs. Samuelson, the Carters, the Radcliffes, Dr. and Mrs. Drysdale, the Hammersmiths, the Dashmores, and, of course, Mrs. Briggs, and the poor man who had the misfortune to call himself her husband. It would be *hours* before I could talk to Jim in private. *Hours* in which I would have to smile and pretend and sit there in the parlor playing whist, stark naked under my skirts, aware every moment of the shameful wet heat between my thighs, with Edwin darting secret smiles across the table at me as though we really were lovers and what had passed between us actually meant something more than the end of our friendship.

I did it, but for the life of me I cannot tell you how. If you know the scandal that surrounds my name and are reading this hoping for a guidebook for discreet deceit within a marriage, to learn how a smart, sophisticated woman manages her secret amours, I'm sorry to disappoint you, but that was never who I *really* was or ever wanted to be and I bungled it all *so badly*. Whatever you do, dear reader, *do not* pattern yourself after me! The only thing I can offer by way of instruction is my many mistakes, and you're welcome to take what lessons you can from them.

I smiled and laughed, flirted and chattered like my old frivolous self, but I can't recollect a single word I said or that was spoken to me. I only know it seems like I spent the entire miserable evening trying not to look at that Blue Willow vase into which I'd thrust my drawers but feeling my eyes drawn inexorably toward it, fearing that the others would notice and someone would rise to admire it, or the flowers within, and discover my guilty secret. I felt like the lovers of the Blue Willow legend, whom the gods had taken pity on and transformed into doves, were laughing at me, mocking my misery with every flap of their happy wings. Love, *real* love, just isn't like a fable or a fairy story; the truth intrudes and makes it ugly every time.

Jim, calm and regal as a king in his red velvet dressing gown, with a glass of brandy and a cigar in hand, came in while I was sitting at my dressing table, brushing my hair. I instinctively pulled the gold-crusted bodice of my amethyst velvet dressing gown together over my breasts, the way I would if any man who was not my husband suddenly walked into my room while I was in a state of dishabille. My fingers fumbled over the gold buttons and I stumbled over the voluminous velvet folds pooled around my feet as I stood up and swung round to face him. My dressing gown was cut in a faux medieval style, with slashed-open sleeves hanging down long enough to trail the floor. I was always stumbling over it, but I loved wearing it. Jim said it was "a robe fit for a queen" when I modeled it for him, so he wouldn't complain when the bill came. I needed all its majesty now to shore me up. I needed a queen's cast-iron petticoat strength now more than ever before. My bare arms trembled, goose pimples rising, as I stood, braced against my dressing table, staring at Jim as though he were a snake.

He came toward me with a smile and bent to kiss me.

I pulled away. "Your wife came to see me today," I said.

"My wife is right here," Jim said, turning me around to face the mirror. He brushed the thick golden curtain of my hair aside, baring my neck, and pressed his lips hungrily to the pulse beating there. His fingers deftly undid my buttons and, in spite of my resolve to be strong, my nipples puckered. He lifted my breast out of my lilac silk nightgown and held it, cupped tenderly in his palm, caressing the nipple with his thumb, making my knees tremble.

Somehow I found the strength and shoved him away. "Don't touch me! I don't know who you are anymore!"

"*Bunny!*" Jim frowned and reached for me again, but I slapped his hands down.

"I'm talking about your *other* wife, your *first* wife!" I said as he stumbled back, staring at me with wide, astonished eyes. "Or have you forgotten all about Sarah Maybrick, the mother of your *five* other children? Don't tell me falling in love with me erased *thirty years* from your mind just like that!" I snapped my fingers in his face. "And two of those babies born *after* you made your vows to me, and another on the way now by the look of things!"

"Florie!" Jim cried, and came at me again. To my astonishment, he was *laughing,* there was a smile on his lips, and his arms were open wide. "Do you mean to tell me that Mad Sarah has been *here?* To *this* house? I can't believe it! I didn't think she had it in her; she's always been deathly afraid of trains."

"This very afternoon." I nodded.

Still laughing, Jim sank down onto the quilted velvet bench of my dressing table and pulled me onto his lap. "Don't fight," he admonished, playfully waggling a finger at me, when I resisted. "Sit down and *your husband* will tell you *all* about it. . . ."

I was a woman grasping at straws, wanting *desperately* to believe that there really was some rational explanation, that the shattered fragments of my world could be put back together again. So I sat there stiffly, not nestling into him the way I always used to do, and listened, my arms folded across my chest, giving him a furious, stubborn stare in the mirror.

He spun me a tale about Sarah Robertson, a buxom red-haired beauty who had roused his young lust when he was an apprentice boy, working at a London shipping office and living in a single rented room in Whitechapel above her uncle's watchmaking shop. Jim had dallied with her as young men are wont to do.

"You're a woman, Bunny, not a little girl anymore, so you know something now of the ways of the world. I was a young man, and my flesh was not only willing but weak, and I succumbed."

He had toyed with the notion of marrying her, but Michael, always the soul of sense, had talked him out of it, advising Jim to ask himself seriously if this was a woman he would be pleased to present as his wife to the Currant Jelly Set. The voice of reason had, of course, prevailed. But before Jim could let her down gently, Sarah had suffered a fall down the stairs, cracked her head open wide, lost a bucket of blood, and it was only by some miracle that she survived.

Her body recovered, but her poor battered brain did not. She began to imagine that Jim was her husband, and it became dangerous to leave her unattended where any man might get at her, for the part of her brain that governed morality was fatally damaged and she would welcome any man eager to embrace her as her "husband," Jim.

"The world is unfortunately full of many men who would take advantage of a woman, especially one as beautiful as Sarah was then, and say, 'Aye, Wife, here's your Jim!' " He shook his head and sighed over the perfidy of his gender.

She conceived three bastards that way while Jim was still in lodgings there. "None of them mine," he insisted. "I never laid a finger on her after the accident." That another two had come after our marriage and she might now be expecting a sixth was news to him.

Moved to pity by her plight and harboring fond memories of the family who had made him feel like one of their own when he was a lonely lad making his way alone in London, he had made a point of sending a sum of money to Sarah and her bastard brood each month, but circumstances had forced him to neglect this act of charity for the past several months.

"My own family must come first," he said, caressing my cheek. "I cannot think of clothing and feeding her children before my own. There are charities she can turn to if the situation is indeed as dire as she claims."

Tears pouring down my face, I wilted against his chest. I put my arms around his neck. I let him kiss me. He carried me to the bed and would have made the most tender love to me, but I wouldn't let him. I pushed him away and buried my face in the pillows and cried. He sat for a long time beside me, stroking my sob-shaking back, assuring me that Mad Sarah and her bastard brood would trouble me no more and the best thing I could do was forget. But I wouldn't, I couldn't, stop weeping or roll over and face him, and, after some time, I heard the door close behind him.

I cried because, even though I pretended to—and would go on pretending for the sake of my children and my own selfish self to avoid facing disgrace and hold on to the life to which we had all become accustomed—I didn't believe him. I wanted to, but the seed of suspicion had been sown and I just *couldn't* uproot it. I, who had so desperately craved a rational explanation, rejected it at the very moment when my prayers were seemingly answered with a story that might have sprung straight from the pen of Charles Dickens. And I cried for another reason—I cried because *if* it were indeed,

God help me, the truth Jim was telling me, then *I* was the one who had been untrue. *I* had betrayed our marriage that afternoon in the parlor with Edwin. I just couldn't face the truth or the lies anymore, so I pushed my husband away and hid my face in the pillows and cried.

There was no use pretending. I just didn't have the iron petticoats or steel backbone of Queen Victoria. I crumbled and fell to pieces where she and a woman more like her would have stood strong. All the pieces lay scattered around my feet and I didn't know what to do with them, where to begin, or how to pick them all up and put them back together again. I was doomed to failure, and I knew it. Maybe that's why I didn't even bother to try. I just left them where they lay, a mess to rot or be swept under the carpet, and went on, running from the truth and rushing headlong into the arms of the next disaster.

ఈ 8 ఈ

It was the Friday afternoon the striped foulard was ruined. That day is forever fixed in my memory as the one when I not only rushed headlong into the arms of Disaster but also *stayed* there, kissed him, and surrendered to him body and soul.

I was sitting in the parlor crying, as I so often did those days. The romance novels I was accustomed to wiling away the afternoons with now seemed trite and unbelievable, full of silly unrealizable dreams, and the bonbons had lost all their flavor. Not even the sweet velvet smoothness of chocolate could soothe me now, and a caramel or strawberry cream center no longer brought a smile to my lips. I was sitting there just staring at the syrupy red stain spreading over my purple-and-white-striped skirt and the pink speckled ruin of the pretty lace.

My head was aching like an ax had split it in twain, my ribs practically screaming beneath my stays every time I drew a breath, making me wonder whether I would have to invent a story we would both only pretend to believe and send for Dr. Hopper. I sincerely hoped not. I didn't want anyone to see me. My left eye looked like it was blooming out of a violet, the tears having washed away most of the powder I'd carefully applied that morning after spending half the night lying flat on my back with a slab of raw steak on it.

Jim and I had been fighting again. He'd banged and battered me all about the bedroom, kicked me when I was down, and pulled my hair until I cried. Then had come the familiar kisses and unbelievable promises that he would *never* hurt me again, followed by the long, tearful hours alone with cold raw meat over my eye, arguing with my proud, stubborn self, tallying up all the reasons why I couldn't just walk out. I just could not bring myself to accept that the dream of a happy home and hearth was well and truly dead and that it might be, at least partly, my fault. And the resulting scandal that would surely cling like tar and feathers to my children; divorce was such an ugly, bitter thing and the woman was usually blamed. *Men will be men; she should have just turned a blind eye,* the reasoning generally went.

Right on cue, at half past noon, a messenger boy from Woollright's Department Store had brought a sable cape lined with periwinkle-blue satin to the front door with a box of imported French bonbons and a perfumed pink card signed: "With loving regards from your most repentant husband." But at that moment the cape still lay snug in its nest of pink tissue paper, tossed carelessly onto my bed, and I'd sent the fancy French chocolates to the kitchen for the maids to gossip over; I just didn't have the stomach for them.

I was sorely worried about my little girl, Gladys. She was the reason Jim and I had gotten into that awful fight. I lost my temper and flat out accused him of trying to turn our daughter into a drug fiend just like him. She was five years old and still distressingly susceptible to every cough and sniffle, and starting to enjoy the attention sickness brought her, like extra ice cream to ease a sore throat. I'd caught her batting her little lashes and trying to flirt with Dr. Hopper while he was taking her pulse. Once I'd even overheard her telling Mrs. Hammersmith that she wanted to be an invalid like Elizabeth Barrett Browning when she grew up and wear pretty dresses and lie around on a couch all day and have the maid bring her medicines on a silver tray. Not a famous lady-poet, mind you, or the female half of one of the world's great love stories, but an *invalid!* I didn't like it the least little bit, this romanticizing of sickness, and I'd told Jim so several times, but he always chuckled and said it was a phase she would grow out of soon enough. But when my daughter started tearing advertisements for medicines out of magazines and asking if she could have them, I *had* to put my foot down. "She's becoming just like you!" I screamed at Jim. But Jim just laughed at me until he got mad enough to hit me.

That afternoon weeping in the parlor I was at my wit's end. Gladys had been crying all day for her Cherry Pectoral. It was a popular cough syrup for children. Jim said it was the most pleasant-tasting one on the market—and he should know. It *frightened* me the way she cried for it. She used to be just like Bobo, who stoically endured every vile spoonful, and not without tears and complaint, for the sake of the toffee or licorice drop that always followed to chase the nasty taste away, but not since the advent of the Cherry Pectoral. That blasted bottle had changed everything! Now Gladys couldn't wait for her dose. She watched the clock and would be tugging at my skirt or Nanny Yapp's if we weren't there with the spoon and the bottle right on the dot.

Gladys had even asked if she couldn't have it on top of her ice cream instead of chocolate sauce last night, then started to cry and kick her chair and pound her fists when I said no, indeed she most certainly could not, and snapped at Jim to sit back down when he said he didn't see why not and started up to get it. That was what had precipitated our quarrel, which continued later in the privacy of my bedroom.

Gladys and I had gotten into a terrible tug-of-war over the bottle while Bobo galloped around us in circles astride his dappled-gray hobbyhorse shouting, "Tallyho!" and pretending to be hot on the heels of a fox. I'd sorely underestimated the strength of an angry and determined five-year-old, and we'd ended by spilling the better half of the bottle all over my dress, and with Gladys flinging herself down on the floor to pound it with her fists and scream at the top of her lungs and bring all the servants running. Bessie, downstairs dusting in the parlor, had even dropped a vase, thinking someone must surely be being murdered upstairs. But Nanny Yapp had strode right in and snatched Gladys up and *slapped* her, stunning the poor little thing into sudden silence. Then I lost what fragile hold I still had on my own temper and almost slapped Nanny Yapp. The housekeeper and the cook had to actually get between us and escort me, with hands like steel clamps upon my arms, back downstairs to the parlor to calm myself, as though *I* were the one who was at fault when that awful woman had actually struck my child!

"You're all against me!" I cried, and not a soul in that house denied it.

I was still trying to compose myself an hour later when the doorbell rang. Then Bessie was showing in Mr. Alfred Brierley, a handsome young copper-haired gentleman who often did business with Jim on the Cotton Exchange. They had offices around the corner from each other and frequently met for lunch or at the Liverpool Cricket Club and Turkish baths. Apparently Jim was not in his office, he'd gone up to London on some sudden and important business, without even bothering to send a note home to tell me, and Mr. Brierley had some papers he'd rather Jim looked over this evening instead of waiting until he was in his office again on Monday morning. Therefore, Mr. Brierley had taken the liberty of bringing them around. He smelled of spices and Turkish cigarettes.

My cheeks began to burn. I turned away in shame; I didn't want him to see me this way—with my soiled dress and black eye. Before I knew it, I had begun to cry again, burying my face in my hands.

He sat down on the sofa beside me, put his hand on my shoulder, and in the kindest, gentlest voice said, "Please don't cry."

Ever so gently, he turned me around, and suddenly my head was on his shoulder. My breasts, quaking with sobs, were crushed against his chest as he held me, stroking my back in the most comforting manner.

"Oh! What am I doing?" Common sense pulled the reins on me and I sat up straight and tended to my own tears as best I could, noting with dismay that the last of the powder came away on my handkerchief. My eye was now naked as a blueberry. I must look a perfect horror. Crying certainly didn't improve my appearance any; no woman wants to receive visitors with a red, runny nose and eyes bloodshot and swollen from tears as well as a husband's angry fist.

Through my stained skirt, my thigh trembled against Mr. Brierley's green-and-tan-checkered trousers. I pulled away, startled by the welcoming warmth of him. Something about him just made me shiver and set me on fire all at the same time. I was startled to realize that I wanted to pull him closer even though I *knew* I should push him away. I was *appalled* at myself—I wanted to *kiss* him! I wanted him to kiss me! I would have stood up, moved to a chair, where I could sit solitary without the hot press of his thigh tempting me to unladylike thoughts, but I didn't trust my knees; I knew even without trying them that they had already turned to jelly.

I just couldn't understand it! I had met Mr. Brierley *many* times before. Besides being a friend and business associate of Jim's, Mr. Brierley was the bachelor all the belles in the Currant Jelly Set were casting their lines for. Bets were always being laid on who would be the lucky one to land him. He was a fixture at all the best balls, dinner parties, race meets, and first nights at the theater and opera, and I couldn't even begin to count the number of times he'd been to dine at Battlecrease House. So *why* was he having this strange effect upon me *now?* I'd even played croquet and cards with him without feeling anything out of the ordinary, not even the tiniest twinge of excitement, much less weakness and wobbly knees.

"Mr. Brierley, I do apologize! What must you think of me?" I said, lowering my head and giving a discreet tug to the wide lace ruffles on my cap, pulling them down as far as I could, and avoiding looking him in the face.

"That such a beautiful lady should never be anything but happy," he said, taking my hand in his, gliding his thumb over my skin in a way that made me shudder and think of more intimate caresses. Though it was just the back of my hand he was touching, the fact that it was bare skin filled my head with wanton thoughts of nakedness. Suddenly I wanted to be naked as Eve in the Garden of Eden, right there in our best parlor with Alfred Brierley.

"I've always said that Mrs. Maybrick has the *most* beautiful smile," he continued, his voice like pink silk on bare skin. "And no lady with a smile like that should *ever* be given cause to even *think* of frowning."

I looked at him then, full in the face, then, remembering my eye, wished I hadn't and tried to turn away again, but he wouldn't let me. He caught my chin in his hand and bent and kissed first my brow, then each of my eyes. "Your eyes are like wet violets," he said, before his lips traveled down to the tip of my nose then found my mouth, "sweeter than sugar candy." His red-gold mustache tickled my face, making me smile. "That's it!" He smiled. "Just what I wanted to see—the beautiful Mrs. Maybrick smiling at me!"

" 'Florie,' " I whispered tremulously as my arms went round his neck.

"Florie," he said, his voice a warm caress, as his lips found mine again.

I looked into his crystal-blue eyes, so cool and inviting I wanted to dive right in. It had been months since I'd let my husband make love to me. I missed his touch terribly, but every time I was tempted to give in the memory of Sarah came between us, her presence so palpable it was like she was right there in the bed with us, and I just *had* to turn away, presenting my back like a brick wall to Jim. I couldn't bear for him to touch me. But I was not made of ice or stone. I was a woman, flesh and blood, and I missed being loved. Desire overcame Reason; Temptation kicked Common Sense right out of the parlor. I lay back on the sofa and drew Alfred Brierley down on top of me.

All I can say in my defense is that he was kind to me.

❧ 9 ❧

For my daughter's sixth birthday I was *determined* to make a fresh start. I sat Jim down on the sofa beside me and though he didn't—*he couldn't!*—know *everything* I meant by it, I took both his hands in mine and said I wanted to wipe the slate clean and start *all* over again and make *everything* right between us. Jim smiled, drew me into his arms, onto his lap, and kissed me.

"My darling Bunny," he said, "*nothing* could give me more pleasure!"

For the first time since Sarah had come calling, I let him make love to me. I spent the rest of that night floating on warm, blissful waves of love. In my ecstasy and contentment I forgot all about sponges, womb veils, and douches. I just loved my husband and let him love me.

I had not seen Alfred Brierley privately since that one weak and foolish afternoon and I did not intend to.

"I love my husband and children," I told him discreetly from behind my fan when we met at a ball.

"Of course you do," he said, "but your heart is *so big,* Florie, is there *really* no room for another?"

"For a friend, there is *always* room," I said, and quickly left him. Mr. Brierley was temptation personified, and resisting him was powerfully hard. My knees were already weak and I feared my resolve would soon be too if I lingered.

I'd also been doing my earnest best to avoid being alone with Edwin without arousing suspicion. I'd told him softly under cover of Gladys's piano lesson that I wanted us to be friends as we were before, "nothing less or more." Before he could answer, I went to stand beside the piano, where Gladys and her teacher sat side by side on the bench, and private, indiscreet conversation was impossible even if he had dared to follow me.

After that, when he couldn't catch or keep me alone the impetuous fool began writing me letters, pages and pages filled with amorous nonsense. He kept begging for just one hour alone with me, to prove that he could please me in *every* way, promising that if I would come back to him we would be "jolly companions again, just like before, and share additional pleasures even more stimulating and sweeter," then went on to spend the next six pages enumerating them. But I never answered his letters. When he asked if I had received them I laughed and told him he should try his hand at writing romances; it was something he could do right there at his desk in the office to relieve his boredom.

The morning of Gladys's birthday, July 20, 1888, I awoke, after a most passionate night in Jim's arms, with roses in my cheeks, a song on my lips, my nightgown on the floor, and not a bruise upon my body. Jim had declared Gladys's birthday a holiday and promised to forsake the office altogether and leave it all to Edwin, even if that meant he would spend the day pulling doves and pennies out of cotton brokers' noses and ears or tearing up important notarized contracts he would promise but ultimately fail to magically restore to pristine condition, causing the poor clerks no end of bother.

Jim and I were having the most absurdly extravagant birthday party a six-year-old could possibly have, a costume party with over sixty Currant Jelly children invited. Our ballroom had been transformed into a magical fairyland with colored lanterns, silk flowers, and green gauze draperies, to create little bowers, and all kinds of little trinkets and treasures, coins, and brightly wrapped candies had been hidden throughout. For the children's entertainment there would be a puppet show, a clown, a magician—*not* Edwin the Extraordinary, thank God!—a storyteller, a fire-eater, a troupe of acrobats, a dancing girl dressed as a fairy queen, and a wonderful silver-haired man who was *so good* with children, dressed in a fool's bright motley and tinkling bells, a sort of summertime Lord of Misrule or Pied Piper, to lead the little ones in games like blindman's buff, Pin the Tail on the Donkey, Squeak, Piggy, Squeak, Hunt the Slipper, and to hand out prizes in guessing games and riddles.

I'd hired in half a dozen waitresses just for the occasion. I told that dragon-faced harridan at the employment agency, who kept raising her eyebrows so high at me I thought surely they would disappear into her hair and crawl all the way to the back of her head, to send only young and pretty ones who liked and were accustomed to being around children. I didn't want any sour-faced meanies scowling at or scolding the kiddies and making them cry. I planned to dress them all in sparkly pastel tulle and silk frocks, with silver paper wings on their backs and stars in their hair, and have them serve trays of tiny sandwiches and jam puffs, and to fill little crystal cups shaped like flowers with punch. I'd made a point of ordering *five* different kinds; the bright colors—red, green, yellow, orange, and purple—would look so pretty in the big crystal punch bowls I'd bought at Woollright's.

I'd gone back to the agency a day or so later and requested two nice young men to dress up as pink bunnies to hand my daughter her presents when the time came to unwrap them and to serve the ice cream. Being served a dish of cool vanilla with chocolate or strawberry sauce ladled on by a giant pink bunny was surely a memory every child would cherish. "We'll supply the costumes, of course," I assured the harridan. "Just choose a couple of nice young fellows who are fond of the little ones and send round their measurements to my dressmaker, Mrs. Osborne on Paradise Street."

Her eyebrows rising until I thought surely they would strike the ceiling, that humorless shrew frostily suggested that I petition a theatrical agency instead, that such an establishment would be better equipped to meet my requirements. Of course, I told her I would do nothing of the kind, it was waiters I wanted and her agency advertised that they supplied them, and if she didn't supply me she'd most assuredly be hearing from my husband and perhaps his legal representative. After all, a waiter was *still* a waiter, whether he was dressed as a pink bunny or in black broadcloth and white gloves; I didn't see what difference the costume could possibly make. I was hiring the lads to ladle out ice cream, not dance and sing!

"Mrs. Maybrick, you're a thoroughly silly woman!" she said, and I still can't quite believe it. Jim actually *laughed* when I told him! But I got my pink bunnies just the same.

My dressmaker had made Gladys a fairy princess costume in three shades of purple, her favorite color, with enormous puffed sleeves and silver stars and crystal beads sewn all over the big, frothy tulle crinoline skirt, and silver lace wings in back. I had given her an amethyst heart on a silver chain to wear with it, but Nanny Yapp pursed her lips, shook her head, and said Gladys was much too young for jewelry, that such ornamentation at her age would appear "vulgar and ostentatious," and suggested that Sir Jim—"Sir Jim" was what she had taken to calling my husband; she'd given him that name when he and Bobo were playing at knights rescuing the fair Princess Gladys, grabbing a toy sword and tapping him on the shoulder and solemnly intoning, "I dub thee Sir Jim of Battlecrease House!"—put it in his safe until she was sixteen.

"Stuff and nonsense!" I retorted. "She'll wear it to the party, and any other suitable occasion, and I don't want to hear another word about it!"

With her hair arranged in a mass of gleaming licorice-black ringlets framing the pale heart of her face and her violet-blue eyes drinking in all that purple, Gladys was a lovely little princess, and I just *knew* Mama had been right. Despite Gladys's puny plainness at birth, she was well on her way to blossoming into a beautiful woman. I was thinking I should start offering both my children's services as models to some of the more respectable artists for sentimental postcards and calendars and such, but Mrs. Briggs and Nanny Yapp were aghast at the idea and it was their opinion that counted with Jim, though I hadn't entirely given up on trying to talk him around.

I don't think a child ever lived who had such a magnificent behemoth of a birthday cake. It was an *enormous* thing, six tiers high—one sweet, sumptuous chocolate layer for each year of Gladys's life—*covered* with so many purple, lavender, and lilac icing roses you could barely see the white buttercream beneath, so that *every* child would be sure to get at least one, and there were exquisitely sculpted sugar fairies stuck on long, thin pins hovering like hummingbirds over the whole thing that would be given as prizes by the drawing of lots to twenty lucky children. I remembered being six years old myself and weeping at a friend's birthday party because her cake only had three roses and that greedy little vixen and her two sisters got them all. Well, no child would have cause to cry over icing roses at this party if *I* could help it!

When Jim and I finally left my bedroom, we went at once to the nursery. We wanted to spend some time alone with the children before the party began. Both of them came running, flying into our arms. Nanny Yapp protested that it was *most* indecorous for the children to be running about and receiving guests, even their parents, in their underclothes and curl rags, but Jim and I were in mutual accord and elected to ignore her.

Gladys settled herself on Jim's knee, in her chemise and bloomers, both threaded with purple silk ribbon and embroidered, by my own loving hand, with a border of violets, and Bobo, still in his angelic white nightgown, claimed my lap as his throne.

In honor of Gladys's birthday, Jim had bought them a new storybook, *The Happy Prince and Other Tales,* by Oscar Wilde, that contained five of the most beautiful stories I had ever read; I couldn't get through half of them without weeping. The author's words just seemed to *leap* right off the page and touch my heart every time.

Though stories were usually reserved for bedtime, "today," Jim said, "warrants a very special story that cannot wait until bed." He opened the green pebbled leather cover and began to read us the tale of the Happy Prince.

It was the story of the statue of an angel-beautiful boy mounted atop a tall pillar, his slim body encased in gold leaf, with sapphires for his eyes and a ruby in the hilt of his sword. When he was alive the Prince lived only for pleasure and was protected by the high palace walls from all the ugliness, meanness, and misery of the world, but in death, as a statue perched high above the city, he saw it all. So greatly did he feel the weight of the world's sorrows that he wept. But there was nothing he could give to alleviate it except himself. A sympathetic swallow postponed flying away to the warmth of Egypt for the winter to become the Prince's emissary; he stripped the Prince of his jewels and gold leaf to help the shivering, hungry poor. The swallow delayed his departure too long, too loyal to forsake the now blind prince, and died of the cold. At that moment the Prince's lead heart broke. The Town Councillors, so upset at how ugly and shabby the statue had become, ordered it melted down to salvage the lead, bickering all the while about which one of them most deserved a statue of himself. Curiously, the Prince's broken heart would not melt, so they threw it, and the poor little dead bird, upon the rubbish heap.

Tears poured down my face, and Bobo's cheek, against my own, was just as wet, as my husband read the story's bittersweet ending:

" 'Bring me the two most precious things in the city,' said God to one of His Angels; and the Angel brought him the leaden heart and the dead bird.

" 'You have rightly chosen,' said God, 'for in my garden of Paradise this little bird shall sing for evermore, and in my city of gold the Happy Prince shall praise me.' "

As Jim closed the book, Bobo used the sleeve of his nightgown to wipe my tears away.

"Mama's a silly goose." I laughed. "She always cries over that story!"

"You see, my dears"—Jim took his handkerchief and gently dried Gladys's eyes, then passed it to me, to dry Bobo's and mine—"you must *always* remember that no matter how beautiful you are on the outside, and you are both as beautiful as angels, it is the beauty *inside* that matters far more. Even when stripped of all his gold and jewels, the Happy Prince was still beautiful, more beautiful, in fact, in his shabbiness than he was in his splendor. Outer beauty withers and fades, but internal beauty lasts forever. You must always endeavor to be kind, thoughtful, and generous. Whenever you feel spite or selfishness encroaching, you must always stop and remember the story of the Happy Prince; it holds the key to *true* happiness. Remember how the little swallow was warmed by his good deeds and you shall *never* be cold inside." He kissed Gladys's brow, then reached over to caress Bobo's cheek.

"Come, my dear." Jim took my hand. "We will leave these young people to Nanny Yapp now. I shouldn't have made you cry." He traced the curve of my damp cheek. "But I thought this a very important lesson for our little princess, and prince, to learn before this ostentatious to-do we're about to have. I want them to behave with the same nobility of spirit as the Happy Prince, not like his conceited and selfish courtiers, when the house is filled with their little guests. I should like very much to hear tomorrow what a gracious little hostess our Gladys is, that she behaved with all the nobility of a princess and none of the haughtiness."

"You are *so good* to me!" I threw my arms around his neck and kissed him. "To all of us! Oh, Jim, I love you so! *We* love you so!" I cried as the children, echoing my sentiments, flung their arms around his legs and hugged him fiercely.

Jim had just finished fastening the delicate necklace of pink diamond flowers around my neck and admiring my new dress of lilac velvet with a sumptuous beribboned pile of pale pink silk roses on the bustle when a scream sent us scurrying back to the nursery.

I flung open the door and looked where Gladys was pointing. Bobo was sitting cross-legged on the floor, still in his little nightgown, with *The Happy Prince* open before him to the picture of the Prince in his gilt armor with the swallow perched upon his shoulder. My darling's beautiful long black ringlets lay scattered on the floor all around him. He'd cut them off in imitation of the Prince's medieval bob. Bobo was just snipping off the last one when I ran in.

"*What have you done?*" I screamed, and Jim had to catch me before I fell.

Bobo's face wore such a gleeful expression as he shook his head vigorously, like a dog after a bath, and he leapt up and ran to me.

"Don't cry, Mama," he said. "I'm seven years old—too big for curls! I have to tuck them up under my hat to keep the big boys in the park from pulling them and calling me a sissy. They make fun of my clothes too; they chase after me pointing and shouting, 'Little Lord Fauntleroy!,' and if they catch me they knock my hat off and hold me down and stretch my curls out and let them spring back while they laugh and call me names. Once they even made me pull my pants down to prove I wasn't a girl. I *hate* it, Mama. I *hate* the way I look! And as angry as I am, I can't shout at them or hit them, because inside I'm laughing at me too. Sometimes I have nightmares—I see myself going off to university in a Little Lord Fauntleroy suit with my hair in long curls and everybody pointing and laughing at me, or I see myself going to work at Papa's office, a grown man but still in those silly suits and curls, or getting married, standing at the altar with the bride with my hair in ringlets just like hers, the people in the pews pointing and jeering that the groom looks prettier than the bride in his lace and velvet! Oh, Mama!" He grasped my hand and gazed up at me with those beautiful melted-chocolate eyes framed by the longest lashes I'd ever seen in my life. "I don't want to be Little Lord Fauntleroy, I just want to be *me,* and I *can't* with those long girly curls and sissy suits!"

"It's true, ma'am," Nanny Yapp placidly volunteered. "The older boys have been tormenting him for quite some time and he has shown remarkable fortitude and restraint in dealing with them. You should be proud of him."

"You!" I rounded on her. "You mean to tell me you just *stood there* twiddling your thumbs and *let* him do *this* to himself?" I brandished a hand at Bobo's new bob. *"Why didn't you stop him?* He could have hurt himself with those scissors! He might have cut his ear off or put his eye out!"

"It was time, ma'am. He'd already kept his curls longer than most boys do; they are customarily cropped at five," Nanny Yapp said, then turned to my husband for affirmation. "Don't you agree, Sir Jim?"

To my horror, Jim agreed wholeheartedly, then turned to me, saying gently, "Like it or not, those curls *had* to go, my dear. I was planning to talk to you about it. I was going to take Bobo to my barber, but . . ." He knelt down and, like one gentleman to another, offered Bobo his hand to shake. "That's a fine job you've done, Son; I daresay no barber could have done better. You look wonderfully grown-up; Mama shall have to get you some new clothes. Won't that be fun, Bunny? You can take Bobo to Woollright's tomorrow for a whole new wardrobe more befitting of his maturity!"

I burst into tears and ran from the room and flung myself face-down on my bed, the big mound of pink roses on my bustle shaking with every sob.

Jim came and sat on the bed beside me and stroked my back. "Do pull yourself together, Bunny dear," he said gently, "for the children's sake as well as yours; if you keep on like this you'll make yourself sick. You mustn't let this spoil Gladys's birthday. Come now, sit up and dry your eyes, dear, you'll make your face all red and you won't look a bit pretty, and everyone will know you've been crying, and you *know* how people talk. Come on now," he coaxed, and when I did he daubed at my wet eyes with his own handkerchief. "That's my girl!" He smiled. "My Bunny is *so* brave!" He kissed me. "And you must be braver still—Bobo thinks you are mad at him, that you won't love him anymore without his curls. You must go and reassure him that that isn't so."

And that's just what I did. I sent down to the kitchen for three of the little pastel-iced dainty cakes I had ordered and three little cups of grape punch and went back to my children. I knelt before my son and looked him straight in the eye and told him, "You *know* Mama would love you just the same if you were bald as an egg and ugly as a gargoyle!" I stroked his shorn head. "It was just a surprise, that's all; I'd thought to have more time to become accustomed to the idea. We foolish mothers sometimes try to keep our sons little boys instead of letting them grow up as we should. Will you forgive your poor, silly mama?"

With a radiant smile Bobo instantly flung his arms around my neck and covered my face with kisses, giving me every assurance that all was indeed forgiven.

All smiles again, we sat on the floor and had a private birthday celebration all our own even with Nanny Yapp hovering over us like a black thundercloud warning this would spoil the children's appetites and they wouldn't enjoy the party as much if they couldn't join their little friends for cake and ice cream.

"Well, if it does, it'll spare you from having to worry that they'll forget their manners and gobble like hogs!" I shot back at her. I smiled and snapped my fingers in her face and sang the verse from that song Edwin was always singing about a lady's bird-tiny appetite when in public. Recognizing it, the children gleefully joined in:

"When with swells I'm out to dine,
All my hunger I resign;
Taste the food, and sip the wine—
No such daintiness as mine!
But when I am all alone,
For shortcomings I atone!
No old frumps to stare like stone—
Chops and chicken on my own!

"Ta-ra-ra Boom-de-ay!
Ta-ra-ra Boom-de-ay!
Ta-ra-ra Boom-de-ay!
Ta-ra-ra Boom-de-ay!
Ta-ra-ra Boom-Boom-Boom-de-ay!"

Nanny Yapp just glared at me as though it were my own manners that needed reproving and she wished she had the authority to do so, and said it might even make them feel compelled to try to keep up with their friends, who had not come to the party with their stomachs stuffed. Bobo and Gladys would surely overindulge and then be up all night with bellyaches, and if that happened we'd all know who was to blame. But I just smiled and sang that verse again. Bobo and Gladys cackled with delight, snapped their fingers at Nanny Yapp, and sang along.

After our cakes and punch, I helped Gladys into her fairy princess gown and fastened the amethyst heart around her neck.

"You look just heavenly, honey!" I said as I set the glittering crown atop her curls and handed her her silver wand. "You'll be the belle of the ball!" I smiled and fluffed her big puffy sleeves and crinoline skirt.

Bobo was going to be my little maharajah. I'd had a sumptuous tunic made for him of gold-flowered red brocade, red silk trousers, and little golden slippers with turned-up toes. I hung ropes of glass pearls and big paste rubies around his neck and crowned his cropped curls with a golden turban covered with paste gems and a tall white feather rising like a plume of smoke from the top of his head. I knelt before him and playfully called him "Your Highness" as I slipped rings set with immense faux gems onto his fingers and buckled a bejeweled belt around his waist to hold a little saber. "Look." I pointed. "It's got a ruby on the hilt just like the Happy Prince's! I hope you can walk," I teased, "you've got so many jewels on you. Don't you go outside and be falling in the pond now, darling, or you'll sink right to the bottom and drown!"

Bobo giggled. "I promise I won't, Mama," he said, and hugged me again. I buried my face in his little shoulder, ignoring the rough gilt threads scratching my face, and shed another tear or two, not over his curls this time but because my boy was growing up. He was such a loving little thing, so affectionate, I *dreaded* the day that would most surely come when he no longer wanted to hug and cuddle and kiss and would declare such things foolish and unmanly. Rare are the ones who truly keep that sweetness all their lives and do not turn on sentimentality like prizefighters or learn to use affection, kisses, and kind words as bait to lure women into even greater intimacies.

Live only for today, I kept telling myself. *Don't even think about tomorrow. . . .*

The children all seemed to enjoy the party. That should have been enough for me. After all, every detail was planned for their pleasure. But their parents quite spoiled it for me; after I saw their frowns and heard the whispers they fully intended for me to hear I just couldn't see it all in the same happy glow anymore. I walked alone, with no friend at my side, through the crowded ballroom, forcing myself to go on nodding and smiling when inside I felt like crying. I heard the whispers—they wanted me to—about the vulgar American, the Dollar Princess, how everything was ostentatious and overdone, especially that "monstrosity of a cake." I heard them mocking my Southern accent, turning my explanation about wanting every child to have a rose into a joke.

I needed a quiet moment alone to collect myself; my head was throbbing and the tears I was trying so hard to hold back were fighting for their right to flow. I made my way to the second parlor, thinking I would just sit down there and rest for a while. When my hand was on the knob and the door open no wider than an inch, I heard murmured voices, a man and a woman, and the rustle of skirts. A pair of lovers? I should have shut the door and disappeared, but I couldn't resist peeking, to see who it was.

Leaning in the window embrasure, framed by sunlight and roses, a couple stood embracing, a redheaded woman in peach satin trimmed with gold and white point lace, Christina Samuelson, and a dark-haired man in a dark suit, ardently smothering her mouth with his own, his hand greedily grasping her breast, which had sprung free from her tightly laced bodice. A smile danced across my lips. The Samuelsons were a young married couple and their union was said to be quite passionate; they had a habit of sneaking away together when evenings out grew too long and tedious, and also of leaving early to hurry home to their happy bed.

I started to back away from the door, praying it wouldn't squeak and my skirts wouldn't rustle. The kiss ended and the smile fell from my lips as the man lifted his head and the sun fully illuminated his face. That wasn't Charles Samuelson kissing Christina; it was *my husband!* I shut the door as quietly as I could, feeling like I was slamming it on my own heart. So much for new beginnings. . . .

This is the last *time; you are* not *going to break my heart anymore!* I silently raged at Jim as I slapped on a smile as false as the ones most of our guests were wearing. I returned to the party, smiling and graciously nodding as though nothing were wrong. As I walked by Alfred Brierley I discreetly put out my fingers to brush his in passing. I met his eyes, just for an instant, with an invitation in my own.

"Mr. Brierley." I nodded politely.

"Mrs. Maybrick." He smiled and nodded back.

When Jim came to my bed that night the back I turned on him was as chilly as ice. I didn't deign to explain. Let him figure it out or let the mystery linger, I didn't care. I had my pride. I never said a word about Christina Samuelson. What good would it have done? He would have only told me more lies, like all that rot about Mad Sarah, probably that Christina had thrown herself at him, and I would have grasped at them, like a drowning woman, so desperate to believe and keep hope and happiness alive and afloat.

* * *

The next morning when a messenger boy from the photographer's studio delivered the beautifully hand-tinted family portrait we'd posed for prior to Gladys's party I sat staring at it for a long time until tears blurred my eyes and I could no longer see it.

There we were, Gladys and me in lacy white dresses with sashes of violet-blue satin, an enormous satin hair bow for her and a fine feathered hat for me. We were sitting on a bench with Jim standing behind us smiling broadly with his hands on our shoulders, the very picture of a proud and happy husband and father. Bobo was leaning against my knee in a blue velvet Little Lord Fauntleroy suit and Alençon lace collar, captured by the camera, for the very last time, with curls flowing past his shoulders. How the camera *loved* him, his perfect angel face and long lashes. His face should be gracing calendars and candy boxes; he was just *so beautiful* it seemed a crime to deprive the world of the chance to adore him.

We looked every inch the happy family. *It's all an illusion,* I said to myself, *a lovely illusion.* Then I cast the picture aside, flung myself facedown on the sofa, and cried and cried as though my heart were breaking for the very first time.

❧ 10 ❧

Trying desperately "to melt this puzzling wall of ice" that had sprung up between us since our daughter's birthday party, Jim decided to treat me to a trip up to London for some shopping and to see that play everyone was raving about, *Dr. Jekyll and Mr. Hyde,* marveling about how the star, Richard Mansfield, effected the ghastly transformation from gentleman to madman right there on the stage in full view of the audience. It was the sensation of London, playing every night to sold-out houses. It had women screaming and fainting in the aisles. Pregnant women were afraid to go see it lest it leave so great and evil an impression upon their womb that they gave birth to a monster. Edwin had already seen it six times and could talk of nothing else. Every time someone mentioned it he went into rhapsodies. Regardless of where he was, he would leap up and act out scenes; a passing doctor once stopped on a street corner to make sure Edwin was all right and not in need of an immediate escort to the nearest insane asylum.

Still trying to entice me, Jim said we could stay at Flatman's Hotel, right in the elegant heart of Covent Garden, where all the cotton brokers stopped when they were in London, and I could go shopping and buy whatever I pleased while he attended to "some necessary business."

This "business" I knew, though her name never crossed either of our lips anymore, involved a visit to Sarah—Mad Sarah or the *real* Mrs. Maybrick, call her what you will; I was tired of the whole maddening muddle. Sometimes it didn't seem to even matter anymore; I already knew our marriage was a sham. I couldn't trust Jim anymore. I had tried, with the best intentions, to start anew, and I thought Jim had wanted that too . . . until I saw him with Christina Samuelson.

Jim also wanted to consult a new doctor, a specialist recommended by Michael, about his hands. I should have known it. This wasn't just a treat for me. Jim shopped for doctors like I did for dresses.

I'd thought at first this thing with his hands was just a nervous habit. Jim was forever fidgeting and rubbing them, complaining about how cold and numb they were. Sometimes the skin sloughed off like a snake's in long, ugly, flaky yellowish-white strips, and he took to slathering his hands with lotions until he had more bottles lined up in his bathroom than the vainest coquette. Sometimes he actually tried to engage me in conversation, like we were a pair of gossipy girls instead of husband and wife, about the merits of various lotions, soaps, and cold creams.

"Well, Bunny," he'd begin, "I've tried Whitworth and Son's Blue Lilies Lotion and Laird's Bloom of Youth White Lilac Cream, and I really must say . . ." After comparing and contrasting those two, he'd be on about Hinds' Honey and Almond Cream and Halloran's Milk of Honey until I wanted to smash every bottle of lotion in the house, preferably right over his Indian Princess–blackened head.

He'd seen an advertisement of a giant frog springing out of some river reeds advising a startled baby to take a certain kind of nerve pills—as though the sight of a giant talking frog walking upright on its hind legs going around dispensing medical advice weren't enough to unnerve anybody, let alone a toddler—and was now popping those like peppermints. He even had a poster of that silly frog hanging up in his study as though it were a Rembrandt.

Jim had confided to me several times that he had a deep abiding fear of paralysis and was afraid this numbness afflicting his hands might be the first sign of its encroachment. Sometimes his hands shook a little, sometimes they shook a lot, and I wondered, as drink will make a drunkard tremble and induce peculiar dreams and fancies, if it might not be due to all the drugs churning around in Jim's belly and swimming through his veins. He'd made a perfect one-man walking drugstore of himself and it just *couldn't* be good mixing it all up like that. He'd even started injecting himself; I'd seen the marks. He was actually quite proud of the nimble touch he'd acquired with the syringe, often bragging, "I daresay no doctor could have done better!" Jim had even shown me the beautiful syringe and needle set he'd bought and kept in an elegant silver case with his initials engraved upon it, accented by a dozen dainty diamonds. I feared my husband was courting disaster. And I was too, in my own fashion.

When I mentioned our plans for a London sojourn to Alfred Brierley he smiled and said what a coincidence it was; he was planning a trip up to London himself. He prevailed upon me to meet him, "for a discreet afternoon of delight." I said yes without a moment's hesitation. Sarah and Whitechapel were on my mind, and I just couldn't stop seeing Jim's hand cupping Christina Samuelson's peachy-pink breast. Sometimes it felt like it was painted on the undersides of my eyelids, there to torment me every time I closed my eyes. So I proposed Whitechapel as the spot for our tryst. *This time,* I vowed, revenge, if it ever really could be, really would be sweet.

When I stepped out of the cab, I entered an alien world, one where sorrow towered over me like a giant and pressed its great weight down fully upon my shoulders. It staggered me. Tears pricked my eyes and caught in my throat. Everywhere I looked there was ugliness and squalor. I took it into my lungs every time I drew breath—raw sewage, rank flesh, rotten vegetables. Dirty, raggedy, stick-skinny children with hands outstretched and eyes full of need, and women with haunted eyes and haggard faces, some with blackened eyes or toting baskets full of sad, pathetic flowers or matchboxes they were hoping to sell, instantly surrounded me, hands thrust out, begging. I'd never known the world could be like this—so ugly and full of hunger and naked need for just the bare necessities. I couldn't even imagine Jim living and loving here. How could he, how could *anyone,* bear it?

A shower of pennies hit the ground and they all dived down just as a hand closed around my arm, yanking me from their yearning midst, and I found myself walking hurriedly away beside Alfred Brierley. We fell seamlessly into step together, as though we had been walking together all our lives. To my shame, I instantly forgot all about those sad, hungry-eyed people.

He took me to a hotel, a drab little place, with a man who looked at us with knowing eyes as he snatched the coins up with fingers greasy from the fish-and-chips that he was loath to relinquish even long enough to pocket his fee. The smell of the grease and fish and his unwashed body almost made me gag. I hung back, feeling hot with shame, like I was glowing like a red-hot coal through my black veil as Alfred arranged about the room. I glanced down at my black silk dress, appliquéd and embroidered with scarlet silk poppies, and feared I had chosen rather brazenly, unwisely, and all too well. *Jezebel! Harlot!* I fancied those poppies screaming, pointing their embroidered foliage, which suddenly seemed to look, from this angle, more like Hell flames, up at me like accusing fingers. Some of the poppies on my bodice seemed to form themselves into the letter *A* like Hester Prynne's elaborately embroidered badge of shame. *Stop it, stop it* now, *Florie!* I wanted to slap myself. *You're imagining things! It's like seeing shapes in the clouds, nothing more!*

I trembled and, suddenly shy, I hesitated, as Alfred led me up the well-worn, rickety stairs. I suddenly felt like I was mounting the steps of a scaffold. I kept thinking about Hester Prynne, standing in the marketplace, the scarlet letter flaming on her bodice, proclaiming her sin to all.

"Darling—" Just that one tender word and a gentle tug at my hand was enough to get my feet moving again. In that moment, I would have followed him anywhere.

He opened a door. We didn't stop to look around or make small talk. He led me straight to the bed. He lifted my veil. I flinched and lowered my eyes, so ashamed I couldn't even look at him. I was half-afraid I'd never be able to face myself in the mirror again, that this burning shame would never leave me. But then I felt his fingers beneath my chin, so lovingly, so gently, tilting it up, to make me look at him.

"Darling"—there was that sweet, sweet word again, and I was

drowning in those crystal-blue eyes, hot and cold all at the same time, my heart dancing madly, whirling like a dervish inside my breast— "must you tantalize me so?" he whispered. And then he kissed me. In that instant I forgot *everything.* The whole world could have perished and starved, the whole city could have been in flames outside, but as long as I was in his arms it didn't matter.

We fell onto the bed, kissing hungrily, tugging at each other's clothes. Soon they were scattered carelessly upon the dirty floor and we were all naked need and greed, giggling and wiggling like eels, bucking and thrusting on that squeaky, shaky little bed. I was half-afraid either we were going to bang the headboard through the wall or else the whole bed was going to collapse under us and maybe even fall through the floor.

The second time was softer, slower, exquisite in every way. Passionate, yet so very peaceful. In his arms I felt safe, fulfilled in a way I hadn't been in a very long time. I had taken the precaution of inserting a sponge before I left Flatman's, so I wasn't worried about conceiving and could surrender myself entirely to pleasure. His touches were so tender, *so beautiful,* they made me ache and cry.

This was everything I had been longing for all my life, but because I was married to Jim it was accounted a sin and would be quite the scandal if it was ever discovered. Just like Hester Prynne, I would be ruined in society's eyes, judged by a bunch of hypocrites who were, in reality, just as guilty as me. In the Currant Jelly Set, while the children played innocently at musical chairs their parents played musical beds. Everyone knew but pretended not to, and as long as there was no scandal, no courtrooms or damning articles in the penny press, feigned ignorance was a veil for bliss. The *real* sin was ripping the veil away.

When at last Alfred and I had to leave, I turned to him impulsively as he was standing behind me, fastening my dress, and took both his hands in mine. "Will it always be like this?" I asked.

"Always," he promised, and kissed me again.

"Promise me"—I clung to him—"that we shall never lose the wonder of it! That every time shall be as perfect as this!"

"I promise," he said.

I took his hand and laid his palm on my chest. "Here is my heart, beloved. Feel it beating, just for you, the one it belongs to now."

He moved his hand to cup my breast, then pulled down the dress he had only half-finished fastening. He knelt and began to suckle like a starveling baby, while I grasped his hair, wrapping my fingers in those curly coppery gilt strands. I threw back my head, sighed, and shut my eyes, lost again in ecstasy.

Why did I not remember, when I looked so deep into his eyes, that blue can be such a cold color? Why did I not notice that while I was saying so much, he was saying so little? I was a fool; I saw only the charmer and missed the snake entirely.

When we returned to Flatman's Hotel, daring to linger, touching hands, for one last discreet kiss in the corridor, before going, alone, to our respective rooms, I discovered that Jim hadn't returned yet. I had been so worried that he would be there, lying on the sofa, waiting for me. I wasn't ready to face him. *He'll never know,* I kept reassuring myself. And what if he did? Did I really even care anymore? It was just a case of the goose paying the gander back in kind! But no, it was *more* than that. I had found someone kind to love me, someone who truly was the man I had taken Jim for only to discover, after our marriage, that I had been mistaken. Alfred truly was a gentle man. I could not, for the life of me, imagine him raising his voice or his hand to me.

I went and stood before the mirror; I wanted to see if my sin showed. Would I forevermore divine scarlet *A*s spelled out in the capillaries of my blushing cheeks? I had gone from being Daisy Miller to Madame Bovary in one afternoon, and there was no turning back, and the truth is, I didn't want to.

I kept watching the clock and waiting for Jim. Restlessly I walked the floor, butterflies in my belly, too nervous to sit still or even try to eat. Finally, I decided to call for a maid to help me get dressed. The tickets were already bought, they were right there, lying on the mantel, and I had a magnificent new dress of port-wine red velvet trimmed with tufts of dyed-red ostrich feathers, rolled velvet roses, and crystal beads that I'd bought especially for this occasion. The moment I saw it, it made me think of the theater, all that gold leaf and crimson plush velvet, and the roses tossed up onstage to the actors and actresses when they took their final bow. And Jim had given me a necklace and earrings of heart-shaped garnets shimmering dark as red wine in golden cups and a pair of matching clips for my hair to wear with them.

It would be a shame to waste such a spectacular gown and those tickets and Jim had carried on so about this being a special treat for me, so why should I miss it just because he wasn't here to escort me? Unless he was lying dead in a gutter somewhere there really was no reason why Jim couldn't have sent a message if he was unavoidably detained. The tickets were just lying there, so why shouldn't I go, with or without him? After all, there was another man who would be only too glad to squire me anywhere I wanted to go, and I rather relished the thought of holding tight to Mr. Brierley's hand when the man on the stage became a monster.

I waited as long as I dared. But Jim never came. So I draped my long train over my arm, picked up my fan of dyed-red ostrich feathers, and went to the Lyceum with Alfred Brierley. We had a *grand* time; the play was every bit as exciting and terrifying as everyone said it was. I loved that the frights upon the stage provided a respectable excuse for me to hold my lover's hand. After all, there were women down in the seats below clinging to strangers or fainting into their laps, so a little hand grasping with an old family friend was nothing at all in comparison. Afterward, in the cab, Alfred and I kissed and held each other tight all the way back to the hotel. He suckled my breast and guided my hand to ease inside his trousers. We smiled and giggled like naughty children making mischief behind the teacher's back, but I daresay the savvy old coachman up on his box was well accustomed to such shenanigans.

The moment I walked through the door Jim was on his feet, moving toward me. The look on his face paralyzed and absolutely terrified me. He pointed at my dress, calling it "the color of whores." He grasped the bodice and tore it down the front, then ripped the rest off me, beads, feathers, and roses flying everywhere. The long train tripped and tangled me and I fell hard at his feet. His face was almost as red as the velvet and I was sorely afraid he would at any moment be struck down by a stroke. The beads bit painfully into my palms as I tried to free myself from the tangle of velvet and wriggle away from him. Jim looked at me as though he didn't really see *me* and just kept on ranting and raving about whores, blood, and the color red and ripping that dress, as though he were determined to reduce it to a pile of velvet scraps the size of postage stamps. I'd never seen him like this. *Good God, he's gone mad!* I thought as I began inching slowly away on my hands and heels, backward, toward the door, not daring to turn my back on him for even an instant.

I was almost at the door. I was just twisting around to reach for the knob when Jim grabbed my ankle and jerked me back across the floor. He dug his fingers into my hair, pulling it so hard I was afraid he would snatch me bald. He dragged me into the bedroom and threw me onto the bed and tore my petticoats and drawers off, his nails raking long bloody scratches down my thighs.

I screamed as he pulled my breasts out of my candy-striped corset, giving each nipple a savage, twisting pinch. He clamped a hand over my mouth and warned, "Do that again, you bitch, and I'll *ram* my fist down your throat! I'll grab your heart in my hand and *tear* it out through your lying whore's mouth! I'll hold it in front of your eyes so you can see its last beat as you die!"

Somehow I managed to fight my way free of him again and made for the door, but I was clumsy in my fright and French heels. I twisted my ankle and stumbled long enough for Jim to catch hold of me again.

"*Whore!*" he roared, hurling me back onto the bed, wrestling my thighs open wide, and staring with a mixture of fury and lust at the secret pink center of me. "You would have run out just as you are! Downstairs, knowing that this hotel is full of men—men I do business with! Confess—it would give you such a thrill to show all London your cunt!"

He forced my thighs so far apart I thought I was surely going to snap like a wishbone. He drove his fist hard between my legs, punching me, as though he were trying to *ram* the whole of his fist, and his arm, up inside me to reach my heart that way.

I screamed and screamed again and begged him *please,* for the love of God and for any love he had ever borne me, to stop, it hurt *so much!* But he just kept hitting me, anywhere he could, I lost count how many times. I just wanted him to stop, I *begged* him to stop, but it was as though he couldn't hear me. There was a peculiar mad gleam in his eyes, and he just kept ranting about whores, blood, and the color red. I just couldn't understand what madness had possessed him. He'd been perfectly fine when I last saw him.

Kneeling on the bed, he tore open his trousers, threads bursting and black buttons flying, and fell on top of me. I *screamed* as he thrust inside, it hurt *so much*. I felt sure he would tear me apart before he was done with me.

I kept trying to twist free, but I couldn't; his rage seemed to only make him stronger. I wanted to shut my eyes, but I didn't dare. I couldn't look away from that mad red face, panting and grunting above me.

Just as suddenly as it had started, it all stopped. He pulled out of me, thankfully without spending; I had taken the sponge out and douched for good measure when I returned from Whitechapel. I thought he was finished with me. Then his hand was in my hair again, yanking my head back, as far as it would go, so hard I feared my neck was about to snap, and I felt a warm, sticky jet as he spent violently onto my face. His fingers dug even tighter into my hair. *"All women are whores! Damn all whores!"* he cried.

That was the last thing I heard. He flung me off the bed, into the corner, to spend the rest of the night lying there crumpled and unconscious like a broken doll. He might have cut my throat and I wouldn't have even known it.

❧ 11 ❧

THE DIARY

*Love makes sane men mad
and can turn a gentle man into a fiend.*

*C*apricious cunt! *Flighty American bitch!* I should have known! Women like her *cannot* be trusted! You give them *everything* and they *still* want *more!* I've seen the way she looks at other men, my hot little Bunny! Bright shining eyes, heaving breasts, I swear I can *feel* the heat from her cunt even under all those sumptuous layers of satin and velvet *I* paid for! She laughs, flutters her lashes, and rests her little hand on their sleeve and leans in close. Even Edwin—*my own brother!* I dropped my spoon and saw their ankles entwined beneath the table, black patent leather and pink satin. The Judas-whore! I half-expected to see her hand dip down to pet his prick through his trousers or take it out and fondle it right there at the table. I'm certain she's done it! Of course, I cannot blame Edwin; he's always been so susceptible to seduction.

I didn't want to believe it; I didn't want it to be true. I didn't want Michael to be right. But Michael is *always* right, damn his eyes, damn those silver vocal cords that have lined his pockets with gold! Command performances for the Queen, a mansion in Regent's Park! Michael is God's own gift to the world! Our parents always loved him best because he could sing; Mother always wept with pride because God had given him a voice. He didn't have to do chores like I did; he didn't have to lift a finger, only his voice to the glory of God while I wore mine to the bone taking up the slack. I was the family workhorse, the dogsbody, the slave! A poor, mediocre Liverpool lad with no special God-given talent, I spent my whole childhood dreaming of the day when I would best Michael at *something*.

I made myself rich; through sheer dint of will, I worked myself up to the top of the cotton trade. I swept floors in the brokers' offices when I was nine. Now other poor little lads come in to sweep mine, but Michael is *still* the star. God's chosen one, *always* the best and the brightest, always right, *Saint* Michael is, and he was right about Bunny too, damn him! I should have listened to him when he said I couldn't possibly be in love with someone I had known only one week, that these whirlwind shipboard romances were the stuff of novels and musical comedies and not to be trusted in real life. She was no more an "American Dollar Princess" than I was! She's heiress to two and a half million acres of fetid swamps as rank, rotten, and foul as her black whore's heart is! She learned at the knee of the best, her own mother, Caroline the Cuckolder, Baroness von *Bawd,* who uses men like handkerchiefs so she can wear diamonds and wipe her arse on pound notes! In ten years' time Bunny will be just like her. Money and whores—they're the bane of mankind's existence, they break hearts and destroy souls, but we *cannot* live with or without them! Lack, like, loathing, or loving, they'll drive you *MAD!*

I could have pretended, I could have denied it, if only I had not seen it. It would have been *so* easy to dismiss it as more nastiness and spite from the Currant Jelly Set directed at my American-born wife, "the Dollarless Dollar Princess." But I *saw,* I *saw;* with my *own* eyes I saw it!

We were in London, for some entertainment and for me to see a doctor about this vexing numbness in my cold, cold hands—cold as her heart and her cunt when I come to her bed and try to touch it! "Do let me, dear!" I implore the icy wall of her back, but silence is the only answer I ever get. There's a distressing tremor and a feeling of needles and pins—like the lies that stab my heart! Pain gnaws like starving rats at my stomach. My bowels are like rice water, and my skin sloughs off like a snake's. It itches abominably, burns, yet is so cold; I can *never* get warm enough.

Whenever I visit this great City of Whores, crawling with them like vermin, rich whores and poor whores, slim whores and stout whores, shy whores and bold whores, plain whores and pretty whores, I *always* return to Whitechapel, to visit my Mrs. Sarah and have my wedding present, the gold watch she gave me from her uncle's shop, cleaned and polished bright as new.

Of course the bitch wanted money for our five brats. I suppose they are mine; there was a time when I lay with her every chance I got. I was hot and lusty, right out of school and from under my parents' pious roof, and still believed all the preacher's prattle about hellfire and damnation and sins of the flesh, and the words of the beautiful, uplifting hymns Michael sang every Sunday. When I rented a room above the watchmaker's shop, Sarah set my loins on fire at the first sight of her. I saw her ankles on the stairs. I blushed and stammered and cast down my eyes until she left me alone so I could tend to the sticky mess in my trousers. A red-haired Magdalene with a bosom and bum like a juicy apple I longed to bite into. I was hard as a poker every time her skirts brushed against me in passing. And she *knew* it! She didn't even have to touch me! I fell asleep with my prick in my hand every night. I played with it so much I had to see a doctor. He advised me to leave it alone, that the soreness would abate with the slackening of my attentions, but I couldn't stop myself. Not even a regimen of cold baths could douse the fire Sarah lit inside me. Nor did the barbed ring the doctor recommended I wear to bed fitted snugly around the root of my cock deter me. There was no help for it—I *had* to possess her!

I thought the fires of Hell were burning me, that there was something supernatural, otherworldly, about my lust, that it was surely Hell instead of Heaven sent and the only way I could avert damnation was by marrying her. But I was *never* a fool. I knew better than to trust my prick. This was *not* a woman I would be proud to introduce to the world as Mrs. Maybrick, but she was jolly fun for an apprentice boy with a prick like fireworks always going off and having her would restore my peace of mind.

To stop her wheedling and whining, I had one of Michael's theatrical friends dress up as a preacher and bless the brass ring I slipped on her finger. I lifted her veil—made from a lace tablecloth bought cheap off one of the stalls in Petticoat Lane because of a bad coffee stain—and kissed "my own dear wife," "my Mrs. Sarah." There's a parchment with *Certificate of Marriage* in big fancy script and both our signatures—mine scrawled so illegibly not even Satan himself could read it—that she keeps framed above her bed. Proof the whore can point to that she isn't a whore even when she's lying underneath it letting the rat catcher from down the street diddle her cunt.

But *all* women are whores, in one way or another; they *all* have their price. They'll sell themselves for pennies, a kind word, a crust of bread, a tot of gin, or a bright silk handkerchief, and the most costly of all demand diamonds; it's only a matter of naming the right price. I've had whores I couldn't afford to, or didn't want to, pay for the silk handkerchief out of my pocket, and they were happy to have it. Sometimes when Edwin is out, I help myself to some of his bright, gaudy silks; the whores *love* those! You should see the way their eyes light up and their skirts flip up! That's how I get my three-penny knee tremblers for free, *ha ha!*

I had promised my darling Bunny a treat—*Dr. Jekyll and Mr. Hyde* at the Lyceum. She was supposed to be spending the day shopping while I saw the doctor and took care of some business. Of *all* the people I might have seen by chance, slumming gents and lady-whores with their veils down in the cesspool of Whitechapel, I *had* to see *my own wife,* with Alfred Brierley, a man I considered one of my best friends; I sponsored him at the Liverpool Cricket Club, God damn and blight him!

Her veil was down and she was wearing what I suppose was *her* idea of a discreet dress and hat—black with scarlet poppies blooming from head to hem—but I *knew* it was her. I saw the familiar, intimate way she leaned into him as they walked into the hotel, one of those low places where rooms are let by the hour. They stayed for two.

Pain burning like a fireball in my belly, I sat by the window at the pub across the street drinking rotgut gin and sprinkling arsenic on my palm, licking it up in long, languorous strokes, the way I used to lick her cunt when I thought she was all mine, God damn her, and watched until they came out again.

The sun went down, and it started to rain. *Even the heavens weep for me!* I thought. The hour came and went when Bunny would have been dressing for the theater. Was she alarmed by my absence? Did she make inquiries? Did she try to find me? Or did she shrug and say I must have been delayed and go with *him* taking *my* ticket, taking *my* place? And still I sat there, drinking gin and taking arsenic—I even sprinkled some in the rotgut.

I'd never felt such a rage. I wanted to *MURDER* her with my bare hands! But the children's faces kept floating before my eyes, like large, stubborn cinders obscuring my vision. I would see my hands closing around her throat, her big violet-blue eyes bulging out, protruding like a frog's until they popped, like bursting blueberries, and then I would see Bobo and Gladys staring out at me from the silver-framed picture on the mantel and I just couldn't do it. I thrust the wife-whore from me and let her fall. I stood over her, listening to her pant like a dog, *a bitch,* lying in a whimpering, quivering heap at my feet. I kicked her, and it felt *so good,* I kicked her again. Half of me hated her. The other half still loved, worshiped, and adored her. I wanted to kill her . . . I wanted to kiss her . . . I think I knew then that I was losing my mind.

I couldn't stop thinking about the children! My black-haired boy, with the rare double row of eyelashes all the ladies envy so, and my frail little girl who succumbs to every cough and fever. There is a line in Dickens's *A Christmas Carol* that always makes me think of Gladys—"always a delicate creature, whom a breath might have withered." My little angels! *Oh God, how I love them!* But oh, how they make me worry! Bobo's beauty provokes the other boys' teasing, even after his curls have been shorn. He always feels he has to prove himself the little man and sometimes takes risks he shouldn't, like the time he broke his finger playing ball in the park with the bigger boys whose company he was forbidden on account of their roughness. He tried to hide it and the bone began to knit crookedly and Dr. Hopper had to break it again and reset it. My brave little man, he tried so hard not to cry! And poor little Gladys sees Dr. Hopper almost as often as I do (last month I saw him eleven times). I sit her on my knee and put the pills into her rosebud mouth. Sometimes I give her a sip—just a *tiny* sip for a tiny girl—of my Fowler's Solution, that lovely lavender-tinted tincture of arsenic and potassium. I pray it will make her stronger!

If I killed their mother, the children's lives would be destroyed. So many people think evil is inherent in the blood. They would scrutinize the children's every word and deed, measuring them always against what I did. I couldn't do that to them. But I *had* to do *something!* The *rage,* the *furious pain,* it was like being in a room lined with iron spikes and the walls were closing in on me. I *had* to find some sort of release, some purge for my angry soul, or it would *kill* me. I couldn't keep it bottled up, letting it fester, always living with the fear that it would burst out and injure those I love best. But I couldn't trust myself alone with the bitch, the harlot with the scarlet poppies on her hat, unless I did *something* to rid myself of this rage.

I thought a walk in the rain might cool my head. I was so distraught, I didn't even care if I caught my death in the downpour. It was then that *she* scurried out of a dark alley and touched my sleeve. She peered up at me through the falling rain and I realized that beneath the brim of that battered old black straw hat I was staring into Bunny's face. The rain was washing the dirt from her hair, like mud from gold nuggets, revealing waves of molten gold just like Bunny's. Her eyes were big and blue as violets. Her lips were pink and parted, wet, and lusting to be kissed. Even in the cold, cold rain, I could *feel* the heat coming off her!

The rain hadn't cooled my rage at all. My head ached abominably, the rats still gnawed, and the fireball burned. I grabbed her arm and pulled her back into the alley. I slammed her against the wall, hard enough to jar the breath from her lungs and bring tears to her eyes. I pulled up her skirts. As I *rammed* into her, I grabbed her hair, pulling it hard, forcing her head back.

"*You hot-cunt slut!*" I hissed. "*You like this, don't you?*" I covered her mouth with mine before she could answer, biting her lips, tasting her blood, sucking at it like a leech.

I imagined her cunt *crawling* with fleas beneath the squashed cabbage leaves of her filthy green skirt, and the dingy gray petticoats that had once been pure white, the dirty pink skin crusted with the seed of all the men who had come before me, and I thought of Bunny's clean, perfumed pink-ivory skin and the neat little nest of golden curls, ticklish tendrils of gilt I loved to run my fingers through and bury my face in, teasing the little pink pearl they hid with my tongue. God and Devil *both* damn the whoring bitch! How I wished she could have seen me at that moment!

The whore whimpered and I slapped her.

"Please, guv'nor, don't spend 'pon me clothes!" she cried, hoity-toity as a duchess in velvet instead of a cockney slut in wretched rags. But it was enough. The illusion was shattered. I wanted to cut her head off! If only I had a knife! I put my hands on either side of it and twisted, wishing I could *tear* it off with my bare hands; I wanted to hear her flesh rip and see her hot red blood fall down to mingle with the cold rain. I rammed even harder; I wanted to make her bleed, the way my wife-whore had made my heart bleed. I imagined her in bed with Alfred Brierley, him on top of her on that dirty doss-house mattress, *thrusting* into her, the two of them coupling like a pair of naked savages in the worst slum in London. For a moment, all I could see was red. *BLOOD! RAGE! RED!* All I could feel was lust, excitement, fury, love, and hate all tangled up together in an impossible knot. I imagined myself standing there, at the foot of the bed, watching them, my prick fast in my fist. I'd never been so excited—or so angry—in my life!

"Particular, aren't you?" I sneered as I pulled out and slapped her dirty skirt down and spurted all over it. It gave me far greater pleasure than spewing into her filthy hole ever could!

Her lips trembled and tears rolled down her bland, boring, round as the moon face. Her eyes, I saw now, weren't blue at all but dung brown. She was a barley blonde barely sixteen by the look of her, probably fresh up from the country; she still had too much flesh on her to have been in Whitechapel for long. I pinched the big pink udders spilling from her bodice just for spite. She was *nothing* like my wife, God damn her! I threw her to the ground and pissed all over her and then I kicked her and left her whimpering on the wet cobbles.

I couldn't kill my wife-whore, but the world is *full* of whores, worthless little whores I could kill and make suffer. All the little whores of London no one gives a damn about will pay for the sins of the Great Whore!

Tomorrow I will go shopping . . . for a sharp and shiny knife.

❧ 12 ❧

I returned to Liverpool under a heavy veil, the train jolting my bruised and battered body for four brutal hours. I had to fight every moment to hold back the tears and bite my already burst and bloodied lips to keep from crying out. I had never been more surprised than when I awakened that morning, crumpled and bloody in the corner of our hotel room, to find myself still alive; I had thought surely Jim had killed me. I had never seen him in such a savage rage, the eyes of a madman staring out of his head, just like a real-life Jekyll and Hyde.

Jim sat beside me, absorbed in a medicine company's catalog, using a pencil to circle the items he wanted to order. Through the whole miserable four hours he never said one word to me. He hardly even looked at me. That was fine with me. As the wheels of the train kept turning, so was my mind, making plans, important plans to change my life. I'd stood as much as I could, more than a body should have to; I just couldn't go on like this. I'd found a new love, and now I wanted a new life.

I would go to Alfred Brierley and take off my veil and disrobe and show him what Jim had done to me. Alfred would kiss every bruise and curse Jim for the brute he was. I would tell Alfred *every-*

thing, sparing him not one single detail of the violent ravishment I had suffered at my husband's hands.

As soon as I could safely manage it, I would see a solicitor. My mind was made up. I would take my children and leave Jim, divorce him, and never set eyes on him again. I would best all the Currant Jelly belles and marry Alfred Brierley myself. We could live in Paris, where people were much more open-minded about divorce. *Hang the Currant Jelly Set! We don't need them!* We could have a perfectly *wonderful* life without them!

❧ 13 ❧

THE DIARY

I can hardly write, my hands are shaking so, just like this infernal train! I watch them move, I stretch and curl my fingers—hands of ice, heart of ice!—and grip the pen, but I hardly *feel* them; it's like they belong to a stranger! Sometimes I feel the stab of pins and needles and think the feeling is about to come back, but it never quite does. If only they weren't so very cold! I have to wear gloves, and that makes it harder to write. My stomach aches as though it were being gnawed from within by rats. I can hardly bear the pain or stand upright. The agony! I've had to take more of my medicine than ever.

I was in Manchester on business. But after the business of the day was done, I could not rest. I kept thinking about my wife-whore alone back in Liverpool. I kept seeing her lying naked on *my* bed, opening her legs wide to Alfred Brierley, crooking her finger and saying sultry soft in her syrupy Southern drawl, *Come here,* and pointing down to her golden thatch, inviting him to play with that pink pearl of flesh. *Oh, Bunny, I wish I didn't love you so!* It's tor-ture—but what *exquisite* torture!—both loving *and* hating you!

I sat alone in my hotel room, drinking red wine mixed with my medicine, sitting there entranced, watching the white powder swirl in the heart of its ruby depths. I couldn't stand it—the lust and the rage, the longing, the loathing, they were all tied up in a *tight*, *Tight*, *TIGHT* knot! I took a strychnine tablet and then another, washed down with bloodred wine. I couldn't get the pictures out of my mind. I kept hearing their lust grunts, seeing their bare limbs entwined and her golden hair spread out across the pillows as she thrashed in the throes of passion. The knot kept getting tighter and tighter. I *longed* for release. But more, *much more,* than my hand on my prick could give me. I *had* to do *something!* Destroy or be destroyed! So I went out, looking for a whore, one hopeless, God–damned and forsaken slut to stand proxy for my wife-whore.

She was selling violets, *supposedly,* though what fool buys wilted flowers fit only for the rubbish heap at three o'clock in the morning God only knows. A gaunt, glaze-eyed skeleton with a hacking cough and long lank hanks of stringy black hair. She said her name was Camille, like the brown-edged withering white flower she wore on the lapel of her tattered black coat. I almost laughed in her face. The only thing this blighted blossom had in common with La Dame aux Camélias was the lung rot that was *slowly* killing her. She was smiling at me, showing me the black empty spaces where her teeth used to be. Perhaps she thought I had come to save her, to liberate her with my love? *Ha ha!* I smiled and told her my name was Armand Duval. My little literary joke flew right over her head. As I bowed over her hand I reached for my knife.

That was the moment it *all* went wrong. Like that hot and eager apprentice boy I used to be who spent in his trousers at the mere sight of Sarah, I was too excited for my own good. I lunged. She screamed. I dropped my knife and grabbed her throat. I squeezed and pressed until she lost consciousness. I left her lying there, dead for all I know, amidst her fallen flowers, as I fled into the night, cas-tigating myself as a careless bungler.

My heart was racing. I imagined it leaping like a crimson frog from my burning throat and leaving the empty husk of my body to fall down dead in the street as it bounded along without me. Then they would find this diary and know what I had done or *tried* to do. They would shake their heads and say, *Poor fellow, he* must *have been mad!* I think that's why I keep this chronicle, so if that ever happens they will know why. *Poor fellow!* they will say, and point the finger of blame squarely at Love. *You,* they will accuse, you *did this;* you *made him mad!*

My fist curled tight around the hilt; I could not let go of my knife. My poor, poor children! How would they ever bear the disgrace? I kept imagining I heard the heavy boots of policemen pounding after me, the shrill wail of their whistles, and saw lights, like the bouncing orbs of their bull's-eye lanterns glowing in the distance behind me, coming closer every time I dared to look back.

I *had* to take my medicine! It was the *only* thing that could save me! I felt weak; it would make me strong! I was shaking too badly to attempt my arsenic; I knew my fumbling fingers would drop the precious box and spill it, and having to crouch down and lick it up from the filthy cobblestones was too nauseating a thought. I felt in my pockets and found two strychnine tablets and swallowed them quickly.

Safely back in my hotel room, I groped desperately for my silver box and sprinkled the precious white powder onto my trembling palm, lamenting each little grain that fell onto the carpet. I sat on the bed and, with shaking, icy hands, drank straight from my bottle of Fowler's Solution. The gaslights shone so beautifully through the lavender-arsenic tincture as I raised it to my lips. What a lovely color and flavor it has! I began to feel better and took another strychnine tablet for good measure. But I was overzealous. I took too much. I had to resort to bone black, and that brought it all back up. I wasted my precious store and had to take more.

Next time I will not let eagerness get the better of me. I will wait, and plan, and strike *only* when the time is right. *There will be no more mistakes!* The whores will pay, *NOT* me! I will show them all how clever I can be! When they hear of the whores ripped up like pigs in the market, gutted like fish . . . I can see them now: Michael sits at his breakfast table and frowns at the headlines over the gilt rim of his teacup. Edwin devours each deliciously dreadful word in the latest edition of the *Illustrated Police News* while his fingers distractedly shred the red carnation in his lapel. Bunny shudders, causing the frills on her breakfast cap to quiver like her quim in ecstasy and laments that such evil exists in the world as she lays aside the *Liverpool Daily Post,* all her pleasure in her morning perusal of the paper gone.

None of them will *ever* suspect that a man as gentle as their Jim could ever do such a thing. They will all be wondering what manner of fiend is stalking London and picturing some murderous, uncouth brute with wild, staring eyes and hands as big as hams. All of them will agree that no Englishman—and certainly no gentleman—could *ever* do such a thing. Inside I will be laughing all the time. The joke's on them! *Now* who's the clever one, Michael?

❧ 14 ❧

I can see myself now, sitting on my bedroom floor, hugging my knees, sobs shaking my blue velvet shoulders, tears dripping down onto my blue and cream tartan skirt, surrounded by boxes, tissue paper, and ribbons amidst the candy box clutter of my latest visit to Woollright's.

None of them meant a thing to me, but I couldn't stop myself from buying them. It was like a compulsion. But whenever I tried to persuade myself to take it all back, suddenly the most trivial trifle felt as necessary as air to me, as though the world would fall to pieces if I relinquished that lovely jade-green velvet jacket or deprived Bobo of the toy frog I had bought him. And the beautiful wax doll imported from Paris with real golden curls and blue glass eyes that opened and closed was the *perfect* gift for Gladys; one of those sweet salesgirls had even found a pretty rose-colored frock with a blue sash for Gladys to match the one the doll was wearing. What a pretty photograph that would make!

I liked the way the salespeople smiled at me, the way they picked out things that might please me, even going so far as to secrete certain items behind the counter to await my next visit, things I bought even if I didn't like them because I just couldn't *bear* to disappoint such kind, thoughtful people. They liked me; they *really*

liked me! At that time in my life, when I felt so alone and friendless, that really meant something, and I clung to it *desperately*. A
part of me seemed to feed like a vampire upon their kindness and I
couldn't live without it. I didn't want coldness to replace the kindness. And they would be *so* disappointed if I started bringing
things back.

Nothing had gone as I had expected since that stony, silent train
ride back from London with Jekyll and Hyde sitting beside me.

I'd stripped myself naked for Alfred. My bruise-mottled body
had thrilled to each one of his carefully tendered kisses and caresses.
But, as he nuzzled my breasts, his silken voice asked a question I'd
never expected: "But, my darling, doesn't this"—his fingers delved
down between my thighs, like a virtuoso harpist knowing *exactly*
which string to pluck, making me shudder and gasp as pleasure re-
verberated all through me—"these pleasures we share, make this
cross so much easier to bear?"

Where was the indignant lover leaping up, ready to grab his pistol or horsewhip and rush out to avenge me, the one I'd pictured
having to plead with and restrain from rushing right out and giving
Jim a heaping dishful of what he'd served me? Nowhere in sight!
My *gallant lover* was lying lazily atop me, my bosom his soft, cushy
pillow, languorously stroking me with his fingers, yawning, as
though it were all a colossal bore. We might as well have been talking about the weather!

"Don't rock the boat, Florie," he said. "You have a good life
with Jim, *everything* a woman could wish for, even if you must endure an occasional beating from time to time. It's not so bad as all
that. Just come to me, Florie, and I'll kiss all the hurts better." To
prove it, he pressed a row of slow kisses onto my thigh where a long
red scratch like a haphazardly embroidered seam was healing against
an ugly, mottled yellow-brown bruise.

I think that was the first time I really noticed the crystal coldness of his blue eyes. The first time I truly felt their chill as something more than invigorating and refreshing, welcoming as a
swimming hole on a hot summer's day. For the first time, in Alfred's
arms, I felt cold and comfortless. Lord, how it frightened me! I
couldn't face it then. Instead I shoved the ugly truth away as hard
as I could, but I knew then that I had made yet *another* mistake.

I'd trusted Love to save me, but Love wasn't *really* Love, just another mask donned in the Masquerade of Life. It's one of the harshest and hardest lessons a woman has to learn: Men are not kind unless it suits them. The peacock only shakes and shows his pretty feathers to coax the peahen into coupling with him; human males use kind words and sympathy, kisses, caresses, compliments, and gifts the same way. It's all a cold, cruel sham, a masquerade that goes on as long as life endures.

Indignant, I leapt up, ignoring Alfred's urgings that I stay awhile. But I couldn't do that—every time I looked at the bed I saw a snake lying amidst the rumpled sheets instead of the handsome copper-haired Apollo who had gulled and charmed me. I threw on my clothes and rushed out, yanking my veil down to hide my tears and bruises, swearing to myself that I would never go back again as I leapt into a cab and rashly rushed to the nearest law office.

I brashly brushed past the clerk and into Mr. Yardley's inner sanctum. I couldn't have cared less about a little thing like the fact that I had no appointment. But that stern old graybeard was not the *least* bit impressed when I stopped before his desk, bosom heaving, and dramatically flung back my veil, baring my face to his cool legal scrutiny, and breathlessly blurted out my story. He barely looked up from the papers he was perusing and said he dealt mostly with maritime insurance cases.

When I asked if he would be so kind as to recommend another lawyer, one better suited to my needs, he said he would not and the only advice he had to give me was to "go home to your husband, young woman, and stop making mischief!" He was an old-fashioned man, he said, who believed a husband had the right to chastise his wife. Mr. Yardley fixed me with a shrewd monocled eye and said I was clearly a conniving little minx and my husband had only been acting for my own good and if I were *his* wife he'd take a broom-stick to me for the way I was behaving right now, rushing into law offices unannounced like an actress onto the stage in some silly melodrama; he had half a mind to write to my husband and tell him all about my unbecoming and unladylike behavior and encourage him to get the broomstick ready to give me a walloping I would *really* profit from.

I stamped my foot and called him "a mean and hateful old billy goat!" I could barely restrain myself from reaching right across that desk and giving his long gray beard a good hard yank before I fled his office in tears just as I had come.

I didn't know what else to do. There was nowhere else I could go except home—though it felt like a sacrilege to call it so. Battle-crease House, its occupants and frequent guests, had made a mockery of all my dreams of love and domestic bliss. So I told the driver to take me to Woollright's Department Store.

I told the smiling, solicitous salespeople that I had been in a carriage accident in London, and they were very kind and gentle with me, bringing me a cup of chocolate, a chair, and a cushion for my back, escorting me gently from department to department, and parading their goods before me so I had only to point and say, "I'll take that, and that, and that. ..." I was so *grateful* I bought more than I should, but it was not enough, and it could never be enough, to ease the pain.

❧ 15 ❧

THE DIARY

I've done it! She's dead! I ripped her flesh like rotten old cloth! I heard it tear and give way beneath my knife! I stabbed and jabbed and then I fled, a phantom fiend, vanishing back into the night. No one saw me. I was invincible, invisible!

She was a *revolting* creature! Mouth full of missing and rotten teeth, her tits hung down like a pair of empty purses, flaccid and leathery; it *disgusted* me to touch them. She stank like the brandy warehouse that was blazing on the docks, setting the sky above Whitechapel alight with hellfire.

The whores were out en masse, drumming up trade, and the pickpockets were at their nimble best. No one noticed me. They were all too busy watching the fire. I was just another gentleman slummer.

I was *so bloody clever, so brilliantly clever,* this time! *Everything* went *exactly* as planned! How often can one say that in life? *Everything* went *exactly* as planned!

Her name was Polly. I met her in the Frying Pan Tavern. A short, stinking little strumpet dressed in shit-brown linsey with brass buttons the size of saucers on her raggedy old coat. She was going gray at the temples, streaks as wide as though someone had slapped her on each side of her greasy brown head with a paint-brush. *The old gray mare, she ain't what she used to be, many long years ago!—Ha ha!*

She was an old whore, and whores don't live to be old in Whitechapel if they aren't canny. I couldn't risk her screaming, some instinct of the gut tugging at her, shouting *DANGER!* I bought her gin though she was already the worse for it. To breed trust, I gave her a bonnet.

"Wot a jolly bonnet! I'll never lack for me doss money now, not when I'm wearin' this!" The dowdy drab preened like a peacock as she tied the bow beneath her chin and peered blearily into the bit of broken mirror she kept in her pocket.

Black straw with a band of beaded black velvet trimmed with a red velvet rose. I nipped it off a sleeping tart when I was changing trains. It was one of those sweet, opportune moments. It reminded me of the black hat blooming with red poppies my wife-whore had worn when I saw her in Whitechapel with that bastard Brierley. I thrust the bonnet under my overcoat as I passed. I was gone, boarding another train, before she even noticed her hat was. I was *so bloody clever!* A woman like that would never report the theft; her ilk usually dread the police like the pox. No one will ever know how Polly got her jolly bonnet.

I arranged a rendezvous with Polly. I didn't want to be seen leaving the pub with her. Someone *might* notice a toff in a shiny black silk topper with a diamond horseshoe in his cravat, and a long black overcoat trimmed with astrakhan, toting a black Glad-stone bag, talking to this slum-vermin bawd. Later, before our tryst, I would doff my topper and don a deerstalker. My hunting clothes. I would be dressed to kill.

"Don't you forget now," I warned, waggling a finger at her. She was so drunk her eyes couldn't even focus on it.

"Right you are, Old Cock," she slurred, and slapped my chest, nearly felling me with gin fumes. "Don'tcha worry, sir; your Polly will be there," she promised, and staggered off, weaving and reel-ing, waving her arms like a windmill.

I worried that I had given her too much gin and that she would fall down senseless in the street somewhere and sleep right through our tryst. But mistakes are meant to be learned from, and a stolen bonnet and a few pennies' worth of gin are not as grave mistakes as a scream that leads to capture, a whore's spilt blood that stains my children forever, and myself swinging from the gallows. If this whore failed to show, there would *always* be another, I assured myself. London was *full* of easy pickings and they were *all* mine for the taking.

I took more of my medicine. I lapped the white powder from my palm. I felt its power coursing through my blood, flooding me with power. People take less than I do and die, yet I've *never* felt more alive!

When I have my medicine, I can do *anything;* no one can stop me! I'm not afraid of the police, those bumbling bobbies bungling around in their big, noisy boots. I can hear them coming a mile away, *ha ha!*

She met me in Buck's Row by the stable-yard gates. It was a quiet, dark street with only one lamp at the far end. I heard a horse neigh. Was it a mare? Was she old and gray too, just like Polly?

I watched poor jolly Polly slowly weaving her way toward me, waving her arms, and singing:

> " *'Wot cheer!' all the neighbors cried,*
> *'Who're yer goin' to meet, Bill?*
> *Have yer bought the street, Bill?'*
> *Laugh! I thought I should 'ave died,*
> *Knock'd 'em in the Old Kent Road!"*

I smiled and took her hand. "The one time you are true, it will cost you dearly, my dear."

"Eh, wot's that, Bill?" she croaked as she grabbed hold of my coat to keep from falling flat on her nose. Some stitches on my shoulder popped. *Clumsy, stupid slut! I should drown her in a barrel of rum,* I thought, *only that would be a truly heavenly exit for the likes of her!*

I seized her throat and beneath her "jolly new bonnet" her eyes bulged with fright. I ached with desire as I laid her down and flung her skirts up to her nose. I like to think she died smelling the horse manure staining her hems. I stood staring down at her as I took off my overcoat and gloves. My knife slashed. My hands were cold; then they were warm, warmer than they had ever been before.

Eyes open wide, she was staring at me over her stinking, frayed hems. The scream she would have uttered came out in a weak, whistling gurgle—a new kind of music I almost wished I could share with Michael. Did I only imagine she tried to say, "God help me?" As if He would!

I blooded my knife like a knight does his sword in his first battle. I bloodied my hands, in a baptism of blood, but there were no sacred words to say, only profane ones and lust grunts. I felt the blade graze bone. The scrape sent a shiver down my spine. I spent in my trousers. Oh, the indescribable *thrill!* Ragged, jagged cuts and wet, red heat! When I bathed my hands in her blood I felt purified, exorcised, purged of my rage. I could go home to my darling Bunny and the children without fear that I would hurt them. I stabbed her flaccid, worn-out old whore's cunt and let my knife stand proxy for my prick. Her dead eyes stared up at me as I pulled on my gloves, to cover my bloody hands, and resumed my overcoat's warm embrace. I waved a hand before those blind dead eyes. Not a flicker of life. How could there be? I could see the guts like a teeming mass of snakes inside her. Not such a hot little whore now; the dead so soon grow cold. I bent and, with the tip of my bloody knife, cut one of the big vulgar brass buttons from her coat. A souvenir to take home with me. I laughed, tossed it in the air like a lucky coin, caught it, and tucked it safely inside my pocket. My new lucky charm; I shall carry it with me next time I go to the races! *Ha ha!*

Back in my bolt-hole, a quiet rented room in Petticoat Lane, I saw the button was embossed with a naked lady with long flowing hair riding a horse—Lady Godiva, *ha ha!* I wished I could show Bunny. Maybe she'd appreciate the noble sacrifice? The first honorable thing this whore had ever done in her whole miserable life, *ha ha!*

The next morning it was all anybody could talk about. " *'Horrible Murder in the East End!,'* " " *'The Work of a Maniac!,'* " " *'Ghastly*

Crimes of a Madman!,'" the newsboys were out shouting on every corner, brandishing the horrors in the face of every passerby. In the pubs those who had known the deceased were drowned in free drinks by journalists in exchange for their reminiscences.

I returned to Buck's Row. I stood, being jostled by the curious, and saw her blood still staining the cobbles. I gleefully paid my penny to go up to Mrs. Emma Green's bedroom for a bird's-eye view of those dumb, bumbling bobbies down on their knees trying to scrub away the bloodstains; they couldn't even do *that* right and ignored the shouted advice of housewives. One of the bobbies, a young officer, glanced up; our eyes met; I gave him a polite nod, which he returned. Had he but known . . . *the fools!* They can't even catch me when I stand right in front of them! The button from her coat was in my pocket all the time and her blood still caked beneath my nails under my gloves.

I've met someone. I'm bored with my Mrs. Sarah. Her looks are gone: she's bloated as a leech and whines all the time. It takes all the joy out of fucking. She's a fat sow who has suckled too many piglets! "My darling piggy," I sometimes call her. Stupid bitch, she never hears the sarcasm in my voice, only the *darling.* I'm done with her for good! It must have been Fate putting this tempting morsel in my path at exactly the right moment. Let that diddling rat catcher spend his hard-earned wages on those miserable brats from now on and see how *he* likes it! Let *him* decide if Sarah's cunt is worth the price!

Her name is Mary Jane Kelly. She's *so* deliciously low! A bawdy bawd, a ribald rut! A stout little wench, shapely as an hourglass, bosom and bum lovely and fat like well-stuffed cushions fit for a man's favorite fireside chair, but she carries it well. I *love* the way she swings and swishes her hips when she walks! A hearty young Irish whore by way of Wales with a wealth of ginger-gold hair, a ready smile—no missing teeth yet, at least none that show—and eyes as green as the Emerald Isles. They were wide with horror the first time I saw them when they looked up and met mine over the newspaper she was reading with an artist's full-paged rendering on the front page of a bull's-eye-lantern-toting bobby discovering Polly's corpse.

"What kind o' monster could have done this evil thing?" Mary Jane Kelly asked in a fascinating musical blend of Irish brogue, Welsh lilt, and cockney crudity.

What kind indeed? *Ha ha!* Sometimes monsters or angels can be standing right in front of you, staring you in the face or even speaking to you, and you don't even know it until it's too late. Some monsters even masquerade as gentle men—gentlemen—by day, but when the night falls out comes the knife and out goes the light of life.

She intrigues me like no other woman ever has, this Mary Jane Kelly. She's still young and beautiful, though probably not for much longer. She has rum every morning for breakfast. Her teeth are already starting to go; she uses the wax drippings from her candle to fill in the cavities. Oh, what a clever little whore she is!

There's something about her that reminds me of my wife-whore. I see them as two sides of the same coin. Sometimes it's spinning so fast they blur into one. Sometimes I like to imagine they're twin sisters, separated at birth, neither knowing of the other's existence, one raised in luxury, the other piss-poor. They're both twenty-six. The long, thick hair is ginger-gold, not rich molten like a melted fortune; the eyes are emerald green, not violet-blue; the hands are rough, red, and sturdy, well accustomed to gripping men's pricks, not delicate, dove white, and dedicated to the feminine art of embroidery; the voice is lilting with the musical strains of Wales and Ireland, not a molasses-thick, syrupy sweet Southern drawl.

She walks the streets in her only pair of boots, the black leather cracked and worn, to earn a living, instead of riding in a carriage to browse and buy trifles and gewgaws; she wouldn't be allowed to set one foot through the door of Woollright's Department Store. She only has one set of clothes to cover her back, not a whole wardrobe spilling over with more than a hundred dresses. She doesn't spend her afternoons sitting in the parlor with a novel or a cat on her lap. She fucks for pay, not pleasure. And yet... there's a perplexing hint of refinement about this little guttersnipe, barely a wisp, as though it were hanging on for dear life, a certain something that suggests that she used to be better than this.

I asked her if she was willing. She knew what I meant. The answer was "yes." It's *always* "yes." I gave her my arm. She laughed, saying, "Aren't you a gallant gent!" She said we could go to her room—13 Miller's Court in Dorset Street. Joe, the fishmonger she lived with, would be at work, "if he's not lost that job too!" She rolled her eyes. "I know as some would think it unlucky to live in a room numbered thirteen," she said as we walked along, "but not me—'tis one o' McCarthy's Rents, it is, an' me uncle is John Mc-Carthy himself, so I don't have to worry about him givin' me the boot! 'Twould break me da's heart if his own brother did me dirty like that! An' I've too pretty an arse for any man to be kickin' it; they'd much rather poke it instead! An' when the rent collector comes callin' I always make sure an' give him a bit o' jolly to keep him smilin' so he don't feel half so bad about leavin' empty-handed!" She winked. "I've a way with me mouth, I have, and I don't just mean the gift o' the gab. . . ."

She leaned close and her tongue darted out to tease my ear. "I know how to please a man; I can lick his cock like a little girl does a peppermint stick. *My* gents *always* go away smilin' an' they *always* come back for more!"

We walked on, newsboys darting in and out of our path, brandishing their papers and shouting, " 'Murder—'Orrible Murder!' "

"Poor Polly, God rest her!" Mary Jane sighed and crossed herself—A Catholic whore, well, well!

"Did you know her?" I asked idly.

"Aye, 'tis a sad, sad story, it is! Polly met her Bill in the Old Kent Road. That was why she was always a-singin' that song; it was *their* song." Mary Jane sang the familiar chorus:

> " 'Wot cheer!' all the neighbors cried,
> 'Who're yer goin' to meet, Bill?
> Have yer bought the street, Bill?'
> Laugh? I thought I should 'ave died!
> Knocked 'em in the Old Kent Road!"

The whore had called me Bill last night; was he on her mind even at the last?

"He had his printin' shop there, an' in the room upstairs all five of their bairns was born. It was a *good* life! But then Bill went an' ruined it all; he fell in love with the midwife that delivered their last—Little Liza. Polly took to tryin' to drown her sorrows. She couldn't bear to stay, she was just too proud to sit there an' watch another woman take her place, an' she left him, an' their brood. That was the hardest part. She used to cry for them when the horrors o' the drink were upon her, an', when she was far gone enough, for her Bill an' to sing their song. But she was in a *terrible* way, she was, not fit to take care o' herself, much less a passel o' bairns. She went to London an' fell into the life. Can't keep body an' soul together sellin' matchsticks, don'tcha know.

"One day she woke up an' took a long hard look at herself an' what she had become. Made her right sick, it did. She tried to get herself right. Some missionaries, a right pair o' teetotalers they was, butter wouldn't melt in their mouths, a preacher an' his missus, gave her a job in their house as a skivvy. She tried *real* hard, she did, but she just couldn't stand it, all that preachin', all that talk of repentance, hellfire, an' damnation, an' her with the shakes wantin' a drink *so bad* she felt like she was goin' to scream the house down, an' she fell back into her old ways, stole all the missus's clothes while she was in the bath, left her stark naked, she did, an' pawned the lot o' them an' spent every penny on gin.

"Some time after that, she met a nice bloke, a blacksmith name o' Drew. He got her off the streets for a time, he did. She tried hard to make a go of it doin' needlework an' hawkin' matches an' flowers, but it didn't last; she just couldn't give up the drink, an' in the end Drew left her too. Said he couldn't fight a ghost, an' when the horrors o' the drink was upon her all she talked about was her Bill an' how much she missed him, an' sang that song until you wanted to bang your head against the wall or hers, God love her! Her son, Will, gave her a few pence whenever he could, but he died a few years back, burned to death, he did, when a paraffin lamp exploded in his face, poor lad." She crossed herself again.

"Poor Polly, God rest her!" Mary Jane wiped away a tear. " 'An'

God shall wipe away all the tears; an' there shall be no more death; or pain, or sorrow, or cryin'; these former things have passed away.' No one can hurt her now!"

I stopped and stood and stared deep into those green eyes. It *almost* ended there. I wanted to *strangle* her; my hands shook with the urge to reach out, right there on the street, and *squeeze* the life out of her in broad daylight.

That bedraggled, gin-soaked drab I had ripped open wide and left lying like horse apples on the cobblestones was *nothing,* a worthless nobody, yet this trumped-up Irish strumpet made me see her as someone *real,* someone who *had* mattered to someone once and *still* did, even if it were only her own downtrodden ilk.

It was as though Mary Jane Kelly sat me down on the sofa next to her and opened an album of photographs. I saw the story of a life, a woman who had once been a happy wife. She'd had a husband named Bill—she had called me Bill last night!—little children had loved her and called her "Mother." She'd had a son who sympathized and gave her money, a son who had died horribly. She'd loved and lost and been betrayed, she'd had her pride, cried, and fought a powerful weakness, and she had a song she still sang because it reminded her of the happiest time in her life, before everything went wrong. She had even tried to catch herself and stop herself from falling further, and deeper, down into the cesspool. Through the window of Mary Jane Kelly's words, I saw *why* Polly had become that dirty, stinking, gin-belching hag, and I *hated* Mary Jane for it!

My trembling hands reached out for Mary Jane's throat. At the last moment they changed course. I don't know why. I cupped her face. I kissed her hard. I bruised her lips with mine. I tasted rum, sugar, and orange juice, not blood but Shrub, a drink the harlots fancied, a cheap, sweet indulgence they persuaded men to buy them by claiming "it makes a body right randy." I wanted her as I had never wanted any woman before. I wanted to hike up her skirts and fuck her right there in front of the newsboys. Lust, *not* rage or bloodlust, just plain, ordinary, pulsing, powerful lust, was hot upon me. Mary Jane knew it and she knew what to do.

She held my hand tight, stepped afore me, as the passage was too narrow for us to walk side by side, and smiled back at me as she guided me through the cramped archway. She unlocked the door to a single filthy room and took me to her bed. We fucked madly. The pine headboard banged against the wall. *Hours* must have passed. It was worth *every* penny! There was just something about Mary Jane Kelly. . . . Every time I wanted to kill her, I kissed her; every time I wanted to cut her, I caressed her. I don't pretend to know why. Maybe it really was the fabled Luck o' the Irish? Mary Jane believed in it. "Don'tcha know, I'm like a cat, I am; I always land on me feet," she always said. "Never despair, me dear. 'Tis always darkest before the dawn, but tomorrow the sun will come out." She seemed untouched by the poverty and pain that surrounded her. She was of it, as dirty and ragged as the rest of them, with the teeth slowly rotting in her pretty head, but she was still, somehow, above it; her feet never seemed to touch the ground.

In her pathetic little room, half a stub of a candle burned in a ginger beer bottle on the table by the bed next to a stale crust of bread and a half-eaten apple turning brown. A filthy, ragged muslin skirt masquerading as a curtain veiled the window. The only furnishings besides the bed were two small, mismatched tables and chairs and a lopsided washstand. The pitcher and basin were cracked and the pisspot half-shoved beneath the bed stank and was perilously close to overflowing, and empty gin and ginger beer bottles rattled against it on the bare, gritty floorboards. A dented kettle sat on the hob, and for a pathetic spot of color there was a cheap, faded print of *The Fisherman's Widow,* a desolate woman keeping vigil in a graveyard, eyes fixed upon a wooden cross. It hung over the mantel where battered tin boxes and twists of brown paper containing her meager rations of sugar and tea sat alongside a cracked shard of mirror and a broken-toothed comb.

We whiled away the afternoon with our bodies lying entwined in sheets stained with the spunk and sweat of other men, including Fishmonger Joe's. After she'd risen and had a "hard piss"—like all harlots, she believed it would keep her from conceiving—she settled herself back in my arms, as comfortable as you please, and told me the story of her life. And what a tale it was! A picaresque saga of daring debauchery and tragic travails, decadence and depravity, that would have put Moll Flanders and Fanny Hill to shame, in which our heroine went from grime to glamour, then back to grime again so rapidly it left me wondering just how much or how little of it was fact or gin-sodden fantasy; she was, after all, born of a race renowned for breeding the best storytellers.

She was born in Limerick, the only girl in a family of seven brothers, "and they'd mash any man to a pulp who trifled with me, they would," she said proudly. She'd had one sister, but she died, "poor bairn," when she was but three, "fell into the fireplace, she did, when Mam's back was turned an' bent over the ironin'.

"Mam lost her wits an' had to be sent away, to the dear nuns who knew how to deal with such things, an' Da decided to up an' move us to Wales, where he had some kin, to make a new start. 'Twas what we all needed, he said."

Her da and the boys took work in the coal mines in Carnarvonshire while Mary Jane kept house, cooked meals, and made sure they all had a clean shirt to wear to Mass on Sunday.

When she was sixteen, Mary Jane fell in love with Jonathan Davies, the boy next door. "He used to come in an' read me poetry, newspapers, an' stories, he did, while I was busy cookin' an' cleanin'. It was he who learned me what readin' an' writin' I know. The first full sentence I e'er read rightly was *I love you,* an' the second was *Will you marry me?* The answer was *Aye.*" She smiled and hugged herself. "The memory still warms me, it does, makes me knees weak an' me insides all toasty!"

But the sun set all too soon for Mary Jane and her "Jon." He was killed in a mine explosion three years later and left her with a babe new planted in her belly. The grief nearly killed her. They feared her mind would give way like her mam's. Her da and brothers, hoping the change would do her good, sent her to Cardiff to stay with a cousin, as her husband left "no near livin' kin an' a woman needs another woman at a time like that."

Ruby Ellen—that was the name of the cousin—"was a bad sort." Jealous and greedy, she resented that Mary Jane, two years younger than herself, was a great beauty and had already been a much-loved wife and had a baby in her belly before she was widowed while Ruby Ellen languished at home as yet unmarried, with no worthy prospects, "her bein' the kind men flirt with but don't marry." She introduced Mary Jane to the drink as a route to restore good cheer and to the "gay, fast company" she ran with.

Mary Jane took to the drink "as a fish does to water, I did"—"I could stop anytime I want, sure I could, but I don't want to"—and it was so very nice to feel a pair of strong, manly arms around her again. But she'd lost her luck as well as her love. She caught "somethin' heinous" from one of those fine, tall sailor boys she and Ruby Ellen picked up at the pier and landed in the infirmary. Mary Jane was there for months—"tossin' an' burnin' with fever, I was, until I feared me own brains would be fried like an egg"—and the babe, a boy, "God bless him, the poor mite," was born daft and had to be sent to a special home for the nuns to take care of.

Remembering that change is always good after heartbreak, Mary Jane decided to move on, to make a new life for herself in London. "I had to leave all that sorrow behind me or perish of it. 'Twas like an anchor, it was, weighin' me heart down, an' I thought I was too young to drown. I wanted gaiety an' excitement, an' to live while I was young an' alive, not to be tied down an' dying o' woe. The only thing for it was to start new."

When she first set foot in London—"green as a shamrock, that's how ignorant I was!"—a velvet-and-lace-gowned lady in a fine carriage driven by a Negro coachman in tight white breeches, a red tail coat, and a tall silk hat, engaged Mary Jane on the spot to be a maid in her house.

But her house was no ordinary house. It was "a gay sportin' house in the West End, it was, one o' the grandest where all the gents an' swells an' even His Highness the Prince o' Wales went.

"All pink satin an' red velvet, lace sewn with little beads that twinkled like stars, real crystal chandeliers, an' mirrors an' gilt everywhere they could think to put one an' paint t'other. There was even globes o' rose-colored glass on the gaslights. Aye, I used to lie naked as a baby in me big bed o' pink satin an' stare at meself in that gold-framed mirror an' think I looked just like one o' the ladies in those French paintin's Madame had hangin' everywhere."

Though she was hired to be a servant, Mary Jane soon made up her mind to be the gayest and most popular girl in the house. "Fuckin' beats skivvyin' any day o' the week, me boyo, an' I'd sooner be paid for lyin' flat on me back on satin than down on me knees scrubbin' floors!" At that time the reigning favorite was a novelty, a Negress known as "The Black Venus" who did a series of increasingly lewd *poses plastiques* draped—"for the first few o' 'em anyway"—in cloth-of-gold. In the grand ballroom, with the floor cleared and lit by torches held by nearly naked Negro footmen in red loincloths, she performed a wild voodoo dance with a turban on her head, gold bangles on her wrists and ankles, and a real-live snake wrapped around her shoulders and a "skimpy little scrap" of gold cloth covering her cunt, which she ripped off at the end of her dance. "All the toffs were *wild* for it . . . an' her," Mary Jane added, a tad ungraciously.

On the night of the favorite's birthday, Mary Jane, simmering with resentment, drank more than she should have of the champagne she was supposed to be serving to the guests and decided that enough was enough. She dropped her tray, full of crystal glasses, right on the floor and in her smart uniform of black dress and ruffled white apron and cap flounced into the rose-lit dining room, flipped up her skirts, and sat her bare bum right down on "that big lovely pink an' white birthday cake with a great lovely splat, frosting flyin' everywhere. After that, they all fell in love with me. Lined up to lick me clean, they did!"

I could tell she was quite proud of that memory. Soon she was being carried into the dining room every night stretched out on a big silver platter with her naked body decorated with icing roses, bows, and garlands, just like a fancy cake for the gents to devour. One night, she swore "on me mother's grave it's true!," they served her up to "good ol' Bertie, the Prince o' Pleasure, our future king, himself, Lord love an' save him!" decorated with his royal crest in icing and a regal lion and unicorn paw to hoof in icing over her clean-shaven cunt.

Another night, upon a dare for a diamond bracelet, she took a bath in a tub filled with a crate of champagne new come from Paris, "but *ne'er again!* I nearly burned me insides out, I did. Luckily there was a doctor in the house; he stuffed me snatch full o' cold sweet cream from the kitchen to cool the burn, an' all me gents were eager to comfort an' pet me, an' give me presents, an' tell me what a brave little girl I was."

True to her word, she became the gayest and most popular girl.

And, more than that, she became the Madame's favorite. "Her little pet, I slept in her bed most ev'ry night" and even traveled with her "a time or two" across the Channel to Paris, where Mary Jane worked for a time as an artists' model and posed for a few naughty photographs. But pride got the better of her, and she began putting on airs and calling herself "Marie Jeanette." "All the girls *hated* me," she said, and I could well imagine her giving orders and strutting about all high-and-mighty as though she owned the place.

But drink was her bête noire: "Me black beastie what sunk his claws in me good, it was." Gin, rum, wine, whiskey, champagne, what have you, Mary Jane couldn't do without it and didn't want to. And when the horrors of drink were upon her, she was herself a horror and "a right misery an' terror to deal with," she admitted. "Worse than the Magdalene possessed by her seven demons, I was!"

A rich man became enamored of Mary Jane and begged her to quit the brothel and be his own. He promised that as his mistress she would "lead the life of a lady" and "want for nothing."

He also promised to use his influence to help her fulfill her ambition of going on the stage. Though, having a brother who is a star in the music halls, I think I speak with some authority when I say that this was just a pipe dream. Mary Jane was only a fair warbler at best and would *never* have made even a modest success of it. And as she did not have a modest bone in her body, a "modest success" would never have satisfied Mary Jane. She was too temperamental to get on with the stage managers and other performers, drink made her unreliable, and her brogue was too thick and herself too lazy to dedicate herself to the hard work necessary to completely transform herself in order to have even a fighting chance upon the stage.

By then a new girl, Clara, a sweet little Swedish girl, a *genuine* virgin, with blond hair almost fair as snow, newly ripening breasts like little pears, and not a hair on her cunt, was poised to replace Mary Jane as the reigning favorite and in Madame's bed. It didn't help when Mary Jane, drunk and sulking upstairs, dozed off and left the water in Madame's pink marble tub running. A cascade of water suddenly crashed down through the lewdly lolling nudes painted on the ceiling and drenched the gents downstairs having a party celebrating Clara's first blood. The cake was ruined, and

Clara, who had never had a fancy cake in her life, cried for hours. Madame was *furious* and Mary Jane wisely decided it was time to move on.

She accepted the gentleman's offer. In a high drunken temper, she vowed she wanted, and would take nothing, from this house, and clad only in a pair of black silk stockings, red satin garters, and black leather high-heeled boots, she set a black velvet hat "à la Empress Eugenie" with a curling white ostrich plume flowing back over the brim held in place by a cameo jauntily atop her ginger-gold curls, pulled on a pair of long black lace gloves and her diamond bracelet—"I couldn't think o' leaving *that* behind!"—and walked down the grand staircase "regal as a queen." Out the front door she went, held open for her by a pair of astonished, gape-mouthed, white-wigged Negro footmen who thought that, after years of employment in this establishment, they had seen everything, and straight into the delighted, but mortified, gentleman's carriage and arms.

But it didn't last long. Her drunken antics and the loud, quarrelsome nature she exhibited when she was deep in her cups, coupled with her startling habit of walking around "starkers" even in the public rooms of the house in full view of the servants and any guests, and the women she sometimes brought home "for a little frolic" in her big bed, explaining that she sometimes needed "a holiday from the men pokin' their pickles inta me," soon exhausted her genteel lover's patience, and Mary Jane found herself out on the streets.

A mannish spinster lady who preached zealously against the evils of "the demon rum" took Mary Jane in, wanting to save her, but that ended after a fortnight when she staggered in starkers to have tea with the Temperance Society, singing her favorite song, "Only a Violet I Pluck'd from My Mother's Grave," and brandishing a near-empty gin bottle, and plopped herself down on the reverend's lap.

"So much for *Christian Charity*," Mary Jane sneered. "She cast me out onto the streets, to fend for meself any way I could, said she didn't care what happened to me, she did. An' her servants did me out o' a lot o' me finery; they was supposed to pack it all up, but when I opened me bags I found they'd raided the rag bin to fill 'em, an' the rest I had to pawn until there was nothin' left. I remember I stood out there, weepin' in the pourin' rain, arms stretched out, *beggin'* her to take me back. When she opened the window, I thought she was goin' to have pity, but she only tossed down a penny—a *penny* for all the joy I gave her, the sour old cunt!—then she cut me dead, she did, closed the curtains an' turned her back on me. I remember, for a long time I stood there starin' down at that penny, dirty money bein' washed clean by the rain. I wanted *so bad* to be too proud to pick it up, I did, I wanted to make the grand gesture, but in the end . . . money is money, so I picked it up, though I've regretted it ever since."

It was all downhill after that. How hard it must have been for her when every poor, deluded fool in the East End dreamed of the West End as a place where the streets were paved with gold and the people stuffed themselves on cream-filled pastries and Christmas goose every day of the week and didn't know what *want* and *need* meant. In their eyes, Mary Jane Kelly had had it *all*—the West End dream—and lost it through her own bad habits and caprice. She lived with a quick succession of lovers, each one a rung lower down upon the social ladder and occupying an even worse address, until she ended up in Whitechapel, a common whore pounding the pavements looking for trade and living, on her uncle's sufferance, in a rented room in Miller's Court with Fishmonger Joe, and them quarreling all the time because he wanted a wife, not a whore, to warm his bed at night but couldn't earn enough at his stinky labors to support either.

I'm thoroughly delighted with my spicy ginger tart! What a treat she is! So succulent, so bawdy! I've never enjoyed a whore more! I will visit her again when I am next in London. Next time I will bring her some candy sticks, to thank her for the pleasurable sensations she provoked in my prick when she went down on her knees and pretended it was one. It will be nice to have someone bawdy and fun, someone who knows how to forget herself in bed, not like those two *outwardly respectable* Mrs. Maybricks I've had the misfortune to acquire. Maybe I'll make Mary Jane the *third* Mrs. Maybrick, *ha ha!*

I left Mary Jane lying back in bed, cradling the gin bottle against her bare breasts and singing "Only a Violet I Pluck'd from My Mother's Grave." I wonder if she knows any of Michael's songs? If only he could see this bold as brass little hussy hugging the gin bottle and diddling her cunny while singing one of his sweet ballads, like "True Blue" or "Your Dear Brown Eyes"—yes, that's the *very* one!—oh, what I would give to see his face.

❧ 16 ❧

The papers were full of the most *ghastly* murder in London, in Whitechapel no less. It made me *shudder* to think of it occurring in the same spot where Alfred and I had had our first tryst. Some poor woman of the streets had been ripped open and gutted like a fish. I read every word, even though I knew I was courting bad dreams and a queasy stomach. I could not stop thinking about that poor soul. Who was she and why had she fallen so low down in life that she could never claw her way back up again?

What manner of man had done this awful thing? Did he know her and bear her some personal grievance or did she merely have the misfortune to cross paths with a madman with a lust for blood coursing through his soul? Were the horrors he inflicted upon her body truly meant for her, or was he merely acting out his anger on the first unfortunate woman who crossed his path at an opportune moment?

"I don't suppose we'll ever know unless the monster is caught," I said to Jim on one of those rare mornings when we found ourselves facing each other across the breakfast table, me with dark-circled eyes after another restless night and the toast turning to ashes in my mouth as I put the latest edition of the *Liverpool Daily Post* aside.

"I don't suppose so." Jim looked up at me and smiled as he spooned white arsenic into his tea. He raised his teacup to me as though it were a champagne toast. "Longevity and fair complexion, my dear!" he said, and drained it to the dregs. He stood up, readying to leave for his office, and bent down and kissed me. The moment he was gone I bolted from my chair and vomited into the nearest flowerpot. I just could not *bear* for him to touch me!

❧ 17 ❧

THE DIARY

It felt *so good,* I did it again! Another drab in black and brown. The only thing scarlet about these women is their morals . . . and their blood.

The charcoal-colored morning was cold and wet—I hope I did not catch a chill! I feared I had left it too long—the hour was perilously close to daybreak—but I have always been a gambler. . . .

"Will you?" I asked.

The slurred-tongued slut said, "Yes," and took my arm.

I let her lead *me* to *her* death. *She* chose the spot; the sacrificial slut led me to the altar where she would die. A quiet backyard of a house on Hanbury Street. The residents worked all hours, so they left the doors unlocked, she said. A long passage led from the front door to the back and out into a fenced yard, if you could call that pitted patchwork of earth and cracked and crumbled paving stones a yard.

There's a cat's meat shop on the ground floor that sells cubed horsemeat; a cat's a necessity for every house in these rat-infested parts. I wanted to cut this whore into bloody cubes and leave her with a note written in blood on the table for the old woman who runs the shop to sell for her customer's cats. But my knife wasn't sharp and fast enough for that, and I must be on my way before sunrise. But wouldn't I have *loved* to spend the hours! Dicing Dark Annie into cubes, cubes for cats, harlot's flesh instead of horse-flesh; wouldn't that be a *rare* treat for the pussies? *Ha ha!*

This woman was ill, I could tell. Befuddled by drink and dying of consumption, but she was no Camille. A pudding-faced hag, her features like bits of fruit floating in its cushy custardy blandness, this weary whore was short and stout, with a wobbly, waddly chin, her curly dark hair cut short as a lad's and her front teeth knocked out. How can a whore be both fat and starving? I still haven't figured that out; I only know I saw hunger and yearning in her big moon-blue eyes.

"Dark Annie," she said they called her on account of her dark, brooding moods. She wanted pity. A dollop of kindness for a dying trollop. She went on about the cruelty and unkindness of men, displaying two highly polished farthings another gent had passed off on her as sovereigns. *Money is money to a whore like you, so why are you complaining?* I bit my tongue to keep from saying. She was the worse from a fight with another whore a few days past, over a sliver of soap no less, that had left Annie with a black eye. She opened her bodice and showed me the bruises on her chest where the other whore had kicked her, and her just only out of the infirmary, she said; it was most unkind.

She had two pills; she gripped them like treasures, wadded in a scrap of paper. Afterward, I took them and left her two of my own, piled with the rest of her meager possessions at her feet. Whatever will the police make of it? Shall they waste *hours* wondering why and if this gesture is one of particular, or peculiar, significance? Don't the fools know it was only for jolly? I don't know what the pills were, but since they have done me no ill, they must have done me good; *she* certainly did. I left the scrap of paper; there was, of all the splendid ironies, an elegant *M* written on one side. I was giving them a clue if the fools could but see it; I felt as though I were leaving behind my calling card.

"Poor thing," I said. I peeled off my gloves and let my overcoat fall. The poor, weak bitch didn't have the time or strength to squeal. I twisted the scarf—her own, knotted tight, to keep out the chill of the night—savagely around her neck, like a noose, and silently laughed as her eyes and tongue bulged out. She bit it in her dying throes.

Death came silently and swiftly. It was a mercy considering what I did next.

She lay dead at my feet, tongue lolling out by my boots as though she wanted to lick them. I stood over her and licked the white powder from my palm and felt such *power,* like lightning coursing through me; I felt the strength swimming in my veins; I almost fancied I could hear it humming. I cut her throat. Her hot harlot's blood warmed my ice-cold hands. The numbness vanished; I could *feel* again! *Hallelujah!* I wanted to raise my bloody hands to Heaven and shout like one of those American fools at their tent revivals. But I *knew* better; already I was playing the ultimate game of chance—*Murder!*—risking my own life by taking another's. If I were caught now—red-handed, *ha ha!*—*nothing* could save me from the gallows!

My knife grated against bone. I worked and worried at it, sawing back and forth for longer than I should have as the sky lightened. I wanted to take her head away with me. I wanted to boil the flesh from it and make it into a vase, a memento mori, filled with bloodred roses for my study, or maybe to adorn my wife-whore's boudoir. At last I gave up. I just could not get through the bone, and there was so much more I wanted to do to Dark Annie; I mustn't squander precious time.

I flung up her filthy skirts, exposing candy-striped stockings that made me smile, recalling my wife-whore's favorite corset. I pushed up her knees and spread them wide, parting them in an obscene parody of passion or childbirth. I felt the Devil in my knife, guiding me. I slashed and ripped and tore and still I wanted *more, More, MORE!* I gutted her. I flung her innards out onto her shoulder, a fleshy—not a feather—boa for milady's shoulders. My wife-whore tells me that particular shade of pink—"intestinal pink" I shall call it from now on in memoriam of Dark Annie, *ha ha!*—is all the rage this season! Perhaps I shall visit one of the fashionable shops tomorrow and buy her a feather boa that color—and if it has accents of bloodred and shit brown so much the better, *ha ha!*—so I can look at her, laugh, and remember the little whore who died for the sins of the Great Whore.

I took her womb away with me along with some blood in a ginger beer bottle, locked in my Gladstone bag lined with newspapers about Polly's murder. I've a fancy to fry it. It's the *only* way I can bring myself to taste her! And last, from her dead finger I snatched a pair of brass rings, a wedding and a keeper, like the cheap set I had given my Mrs. Sarah, a souvenir, something to remember Dark Annie by, though I was *quite* sure I would *never* forget her.

As I walked away, I was preoccupied with pulling on my gloves, to hide my bloody hands until I could wash them, and forgot the unevenly paved ground. I stumbled and fell and barked the heel of my palm upon the broken stones—jagged and ragged like the cuts I had made. My blood mingled with hers. *We are one—one forever,* I thought as I swiftly made my way back up the passage and out onto the street. I lost myself in the early-morning market traffic, people hurrying to set up stalls, to sell their wares, or on their way to work. No one noticed me. Why should they suspect a gentleman—a gentle man—like me? The whores, they say, are wary of a Jew boot finisher who has been harassing them, a man they call "Leather Apron." I was just another slumming gent on his way back to his wholesome, respectable home after a night of wanton carousing, tomcatting in wicked Whitechapel. No one looked twice at me.

The womb was *awful, just AWFUL!* So spongy and springy I exhausted my jaw trying to eat it. Tough as an old whore! I spit it out—*damn the rotten and repulsive cunt!*

I lay back on my bed, smoked a cigar, sipped some brandy, licked my medicine from my palm, *slowly, savoring* each dainty white grain, and stroked my prick and thought of Mary Jane Kelly and my wife-whore, watching them blur together in my mind, face merging with face, two sides of a spinning coin, until I could no longer tell one from the other; they were one, sister sluts, wife, whore, wife-whore. Tomorrow, I promised myself, tomorrow I shall see Mary Jane. . . .

I found I could not sleep. Whenever I closed my eyes I saw that pathetic drab before me, begging for pity, so I rose and did what I had been *longing* to do—I wrote a letter. At first I thought to address it to the police. Then I thought better of that; it would make a far greater impression on the gentlemen of the press. The police would only file it away in annoyance, but the newspapers would be sure to publish it. But I would not mail it just yet. First, I wanted to have the pleasure of walking around with it in my pocket, knowing it was there, savoring the thrill, the thrill of the kill, and the risk of having such a damning document upon me. What if I should forget and leave it in when I gave my coat to be laundered? Oh, what a *thrill* it is, being both hunter *and* hunted!

The blood I had taken away with me was no use; it had gone dark and thick, caked inside the ginger beer bottle. Even when I tried diluting it with water, still it was no use. Fortunately, I had had the foresight to purchase a bottle of red ink. *I am so bloody clever!*

I began to write in a hand elegant enough to grace the finest wedding invitation, but scattered with a smattering of misspellings and grammatical errors no educated gentleman would ever make to further confound the fools:

> *Dear Boss,*
>
> *I keep on hearing the police have caught me but they wont fix me just yet. I have laughed when they look so clever and talk about being on the right track. That joke about Leather Apron gave me real fits. I am down on whores and I shant quit ripping them till I do get buckled. Grand work the last job was. I gave the lady no time to squeal. How can they catch me now. I love my work and want to start again. You will soon hear of me with my funny little games. I saved some of the proper red stuff in a ginger beer bottle over the last job to write with but it went thick like glue and I cant use it. Red ink is fit enough I hope Ha Ha. The next job I do I shall clip the lady's ears off and send to the police officers just for jolly wouldnt you. Keep this letter back till I do a bit more work then give it out straight. My knife's so nice and sharp I want to get to work right away if I get a chance. Good luck.*
>
> *Yours truly,*

But what to sign myself? Something catchy for the man they cannot catch. A name that will live forever. A name that will still inspire fear long after my bones have turned to ashes. I am a gentle, almost saintly, man when the rage is not upon me. . . . Saint James the Whore Slayer? Sir Jim, as Nanny Yapp calls me when I play knights with Bobo and my little princess Gladys? Something less formal? Something with a common touch for common people? I have it—*Jack!* Like Spring-Heeled Jack, with his long, icy claws and eyes glowing like fireballs, the demon who terrorized London half a century ago and still springs out to terrify audiences in stage melodramas and the penny-dreadful novels Edwin adores so. Or . . . *OH YES! YES!* Like *Michael's* Jack, the lady-loving jolly jack-tar from one of his most popular songs—"They All Love Jack." *That's it!* Jack the Whore Killer . . . Jack the Slut Slayer . . . No, something sharper like my knife. A name that will make every woman's quim quiver with fear of what I would do if only I could get my hands, and my knife, upon her. What wouldn't I do to her? Ah, I have it now; thank you, my Muse, for visiting *me* instead of *Michael.* . . .

Yours truly,

Jack the Ripper

Now they'll *never* forget me!

I stroked myself with my red-ink-and-bloodstained fingers and spent before I put down my pen.

I'll put it away now, folded carefully, for this document, the first I've signed with my new name, is *so very precious* and I might want to add a postscript later, after I've seen the papers. *Leather Apron indeed!* He's not fit to finish my boots, much less wear them.

I returned to my bed, red ink still upon my hands and Dark Annie's blood caked beneath my nails, and touched myself again, harder and faster, jerking, as though I were furious with my own flesh. This time I thought only of my wife-whore and her lover, how much they must be enjoying themselves in my absence. Does she bring him into the house, beneath the same roof where our children sleep, and fuck him in her own bed, or do they compound the insult and betrayal and soil mine?

I imagined myself standing outside, peeping in through a window, watching them naked, bucking and fucking hard upon *my* bed, the wife-whore with her golden hair unbound, straddling him, his hands gripping her hips so hard each fingertip will leave a bruise, marking her as *his* whore and himself as her master.

When I return to Battlecrease House I shall rip her skirt off and place my own fingers there. I shall show the whore who is *really* her master! I can see myself standing there in the darkness, bush at my back, thorns stabbing through my clothes, glass at my nose, my hard prick in my angry hand, jerking—*furious* pleasure, *furious* pain! *OH GOD, HOW IT EXCITES ME SO!* It shouldn't, but *it does!* Oh, God help me, *IT DOES!*

I think I shall let her continue seeing him a while longer . . . just so I can have this pleasure, so I can lie here alone afterward and imagine . . . London is full of little whores who can pay for the Great Whore's sins and keep my children safe from the rage I would, without their sacrifice, most assuredly turn upon their whore-mother, my wife-whore, and, God help me, in my madness, maybe even them. I cannot bear the thought! That fear is enough to keep my knife sharp! I would kill every whore in the world to save Bobo and Gladys!

In Mary Jane's room, I savored her fear as well as her sex. I lapped it up like arsenic. But damn her green eyes, when she talks about those drabs she makes them come back to life; she resurrects the human flotsam from the cesspool where they would have drowned had it not been for me and my merciful knife and brings them back to haunt me.

I now know Annie Chapman was a guardsman's daughter who, despite spending her life surrounded by men in military barracks, thought she was destined to die an old maid until, most unexpectedly, at the forlorn age of almost thirty, she fell in love with a coachman—John Chapman. The happy couple made their home in Windsor. They posed for a photographer once, Mr. Chapman in checkered trousers and watered-silk vest, and Annie in a lilac calico crinoline with a pattern of white stripes and little flowers, her late mother's Bible on her lap and her long brown hair gathered back, the curls smoothed and subdued and coiled in a fat bun at the nape of her neck with a tortoiseshell comb. She'd shown Mary Jane that picture once, though the frame had long since been pawned, still so proud of that long-vanished dress and its skirt, made from yards and yards of material billowing over the then fashionable hoop. She'd sat there and pointed and told her what color everything was, painting the colors back in on what was now only a faded sepia memory.

Those were the days before it all went wrong. John Chapman was a man, fickle like any other. Time and familiarity bred boredom, and another, younger and prettier, soon caught his fancy. Annie found that the children he had given her were scant consolation and turned to the bottle. She had a son who had to be sent away to a home for cripples and a daughter who married up, moved to France, and forgot all about the folks she left behind her.

Forced to fend for herself in London, Annie had tried to earn her keep by doing crochet work and selling flowers. In desperation, she had even sold her hair to a wig maker.

When suicide seemed the only alternative—" 'twas either that or the river"—she became a whore, "an' hated herself every moment for it." Annie sought oblivion in gin. She could no longer bear to face her own Bible and, not having the heart to pawn it, left it abandoned on a bench in Hyde Park, hoping someone would find it and give it a good, and more deserving, home. "She didn't half seem to care when the doctor told her she was dyin'. 'Sometimes I feel like I'm already dead,' she'd say to us who knew her; her sisters in sorrow, she called us."

The papers are full of my naughty deeds, but, curse them, they keep crediting them to this *Leather Apron!* How *dare* he try to fill *my* shoes! I shall have to send my letter soon and set the fools straight! I bought them all and read them aloud to Mary Jane, taking fiendish delight in her fear. I'd never seen a woman not facing my knife so afraid. I wanted to whip it out and show her, let her *feel it* cold against her throat, or maybe her cunt, but her terror excited me so much I gave her my cock instead, to comfort her, the *dear* little whore. She wanted more, and I wanted more, and we gave it to each other. We suit each other *so* well!

Some think I'm a doctor driven by some unholy madness onto the streets, to use my skill to kill, to take instead of save human lives—if you can even call a whore human. And then there's this "Leather Apron," a whore-hating Jew boot finisher. Already the whores cower and creep about cautioning each other to "beware of The Knife!" and "watch out for Leather Apron!" I didn't see it, but apparently there *was* a leather apron folded under a water tap—I also missed that, or I could have washed my hands!—not two feet from where I slew Dark Annie. The street lamps in Whitechapel are so scant, it's a wonder anyone who goes about at night can see their hand before their face, or Jack's knife, when it comes out of the dark.

I shall have to send my letter soon and set the fools right or else this poor fellow might end up a gallows dancer.

I've fooled them *ALL*—police, press, and populace, and all the witless whores who live in terror of my knife. I've made the City of London the City of Fear, the City of Frightened Whores! I've baptized it in blood—*whores'* blood.

The gentlemen of Scotland Yard are running around like chickens with their heads cut off. The blind leading the blind! Catch me if you can! I *howled* with laughter over *Punch*. There was a cartoon of a blindfolded bobby playing blindman's buff with a group of ruffians and beneath it the caption "Turn round three times and catch whom you may!" *May*—the first three letters of my surname, right there in the paper for all to see, a clue hiding in plain sight—*May, clever, clever, so bloody clever!* They'll *NEVER* catch me! It's so *frightfully* funny!

Across the breakfast table the wife-whore shudders and swoons over the headlines and wonders, "*Why* don't the police *do something?*" I comfort her as best I can. I, the most hated and hunted criminal since the world began, play the loving husband and pat her shoulder or hand, kiss her cheek, and tell her that our police force here in Liverpool is one of the finest in the world and such things could *never* happen here—I'm not such a fool as to soil my own backyard!—or to women of *her* class; the whores of Whitechapel die as they live, on the knife's edge of danger. Every time they toddle drunkenly up to a man and say, "How's about a poke, Old Cock?" they're taking their lives into their own drink-trembling hands. They're asking for it every time!

How my dear little wifey frowns and worries over those damned dead whores! Bedraggled hags who are better off dead! If she only knew that it is *her own sins* I am punishing, every little no-account whore I kill is dying in *her* stead! They die so *she* can go on living, so our children's names will never be sullied by her sins and my crimes of punishment by proxy, so I will never make the mistake of bringing my hate home with me. What would she do if she knew? Would she give me, and herself, away? Would she think of the children like I do? She's such a selfish bitch, my wife-whore, she would act impulsively; she doesn't have the sense to stop and think about tomorrow. She would only think of the moment, the lives lost, and the blood spilled, not that it might stain our children. The bitch is lucky to have me; *I* think of *everything.*

I've mailed my letter. I'm tired of reading about Leather Apron and speculation that I'm a doctor or a mad butcher and that no Englishman could ever do such a thing. Others trying to snatch the gory glory away from me! It's time for me to take it *ALL* back!

Before I sent it, I couldn't resist adding a postscript:

> *Dont mind me giving the trade name Ha Ha.*
>
> *wasnt good enough to post this before I got all the*
> *red ink off my hands curse it.*
> *No luck yet.*
> *They say I'm a doctor now Ha Ha!*

Soon I will be more famous than the Queen herself. Now there will be no more talk about "The Knife" and "Leather Apron," only Jack—the Ripper!

I'll no longer be an unknown killer, a knife plunging out of the pea soup fog and darkness, slashing at whores' throats, sagging udders and hungry bellies, and filthy flea-crawling cunts; *now* I have a name. Mothers will caution their kiddies: *Jack the Ripper's going to get you if you don't watch out; Jack the Ripper's going to get you if you don't come inside right now; Jack the Ripper's going to get you if you don't eat all your vegetables, mind your manners, and say your prayers.* They'll *never* forget me; they'll forget Michael's jolly jack-tar, but they'll *never* forget me! You can take all your sea chanteys, sentimental ballads, and humble hymns, Michael, and shove them up your arse along with Fred Weatherly's prick. This name, taken with my medicine, will make me *invincible. NOTHING* can stop me now! I'm Jack, Jack the Ripper, my knife is my scepter, and *I* reign as the Red King over this Autumn of Terror. Long live King Jack; long may he hack!

Soon I shall get to work again, soon. . . . I stroke the sharp edge of my knife and my cock, sometimes the one with the other, but *gently, oh so gently,* and dream of what I shall do to the next. Ribbons of blood, rivers of blood. I want to take their heads, boil the skulls down to bare bones, and use them as vases. I want to fill them with bloodred roses or candles and arrange them on the altar at St. James's Church in Piccadilly where we were married and *BURN* that cathedral of lies to the ground.

Michael—*damn, Damn, DAMN HIM!*—is worried about me; the wife-whore has persuaded him that I'm taking "too much strong medicine" for my own good and am "always the worse for it after." Well, I gave *her* worse for it after! When I found out she had betrayed me, I *beat, Beat, BEAT* her! I made the bitch *BEG* for mercy and then I didn't give it to her. Oh, how the bitch *cried, Cried, CRIED.* She *begged, Begged, BEGGED* me not to hurt her. Like an angel of love, I caressed her bruised and bleeding face. I promised never again. But I *lied, Lied, LIED.*

I've seen two more doctors, one of them Michael's *personal physician*—Dr. Fuller. He's a *FOOL!* He said I was a hypochondriac—*ME!*—how can I be a hypochondriac when I'm sick all the time? He cannot crawl into my skin and feel what *I* feel, the agonizing ache in my belly that sometimes bends me double and makes me cry out as though rats with fangs of fire were gnawing me, the pains in my head, sharp as spikes being hammered, the *blazing* burn in my bladder, stools like rice water, the *maddening* twitching of my eyelids, and the *awful,* terrifying icy numbness in my hands. Sometimes they tingle as though they are fighting, trying with all their might, to feel again, but always, *always* failing. I watch them move, but it is as though they belong to a stranger. I'm going to see another doctor tomorrow, and then, then . . . *Oh, I cannot wait!*

❧ 18 ❧

I should have known better than to trust Michael. Desperate as I was, I should not have looked for even an ounce of chivalry in his cold, arrogant soul. Michael told Jim all that I had confided about the drugs I believed were transforming him into a real-life Jekyll and Hyde.

Jim came home from London and flung the front door open with such force it cracked one of the stained-glass panels and charged upstairs and beat me with his umbrella until it broke and then he threatened to put my eyes out with the finial. When I tried to crawl under the bed to escape him, he wrenched me out by my ankles, flipped me over, beat me with his fists and kicked me with his boots on, and raped me. I could not show myself in public for over a week even with paint on.

That awful autumn, while the madman that was my husband consumed my waking hours, that unknown madman, Jack the Ripper, stalked my dreams; he seemed to dog my fitfully slumbering soul's every step. I'd see myself as a fallen woman, pathetic, dirty, haggard, and raggedy. It was *so real* I could even smell my filthy flesh and taste my fetid breath and rotting teeth and feel the itch of fleabites beneath the rancid rags I was wearing. I'd catch my reflection in a window and see all my beauty gone, worn away by worry and want, and feel so very tired, as though I hadn't slept in a thousand nights or more but had spent them walking aimlessly, lost in the fog, fear stabbing my heart every time I heard a sound or turned a corner, never knowing if it would bring me face-to-face with the faceless fiend none could recognize.

That, I think, was the most frightening part. He might appear benign and grandfatherly, like a genial old doctor, a priest with the most blessedly comforting countenance, or a favorite uncle. Surely he did not go about with the mark of evil clearly upon him like a tattoo on his brow or else none would ever steal into the shadows with him beside them.

Those wretched women surely were not fools or they wouldn't have survived on those hellish streets as long as they had. I thought so much about those women, I felt that we were, in some strange way, sisters beneath the skin, that though our lives had been very different, I would have understood them and they would have understood me. Maybe they could have told me how to break free? How to burst the shackles and chains of the comfort, luxury, and respectability that held me fast, to just let go of it all, of myself and the velvet cushion life I had always known and didn't believe I could survive without. Perhaps they could have told me how to *really* not care anymore, not just to pretend not to. Every time I told myself I no longer loved or wanted Jim, that I was done with him, my conscience shouted, *Liar!* in a whisper that was also a scream.

I thought about the Ripper too. What manner of monster was he? Are such men born evil, or do they become so? What could turn a man into a flesh-ripping monster? I sat and pondered in the parlor and speculated as I tossed sleeplessly in my bed at night or after being rousted out of yet another foggy nightmare in which I walked the streets of Whitechapel, knowing to the very depths of my soul *exactly* what it felt like to have lost everything that mattered, along with all one's hopes and dreams, always awaiting the inevitable, the knife that flashed so fast it left me no time to scream. Would I know him when I saw him, or would I only recognize him when it was too late? Would anyone hear my dying screams? Would anyone come to save me or could only I save myself? I now wonder, decades too late, was that what these dreams were truly trying to tell me?

Though I had sworn that I would never go back, I went back to Alfred Brierley's bed. I can't even offer a justifiable reason; even when my life hung in the balance I couldn't explain it. It was just something I did. Maybe I was hoping it would be different this time? Maybe I was hoping that, in time, he would truly come to love me? Maybe I couldn't let go of the dream that someday we would be together, living and loving in Paris or some other sophisticated city that took divorce in stride? Maybe I was just one more woman seeking some kind of comfort in a pair of arms that were willing to hold her while a cock nested inside her? Maybe it's a fair price to pay for just being held? We all want some kind of love. Sometimes it's not enough, and sometimes it is.

All I know is that one day I was there at his door, in his arms, then naked in his bed once more. He was a kind, generous, and skillful lover; it was only when he talked that he showed himself insensitive. I still ask myself, *Why wasn't that enough?* Why couldn't I be content with his sensual finesse? Why couldn't I be happy with what we had? Why did I let it make me so very sad? Why did I run to him when I knew all too well that icy cold sadness lay beneath the burning heat of passion? There really is a unique sort of sadness that goes hand in glove with the act so often called "making love," though love often has little or nothing to do with it. *Strange how being filled can leave you so empty,* I'd think every time as I wandered through Woollright's after leaving his bed, frittering the rest of the afternoon away making frivolous purchases before I had to go "home" again.

❦ 19 ❦

THE DIARY

Double event this time! The first bitch squealed a bit. The pony and cart were almost upon us. The driver reached out his whip and poked the dead whore with it. But he didn't see me. I had to flee before I was done with her. I knew I was invincible—the name, the powder, the power—I knew they couldn't stop me, but for a moment... How I trembled and my heart raced! I could not keep up with it! It was like a drum in my ears as I fled, beating faster and faster. The scent of blood was in my nostrils, on my hands, on my lips where I had lapped it up along with my medicine. The lust was hot upon me. I was not sated; like a man interrupted in the midst of fucking, I *had* to seek another, for the *full* satisfaction. I would know no peace until I did! It had been three weeks since my last kill. I could endure no more, stifling, bottling up the rage, holding it back, while my wife-whore fucked Alfred Brierley behind my back! I *had* to kill, to *purge* myself; I could not go home until I was free of it!

But first... the first... The tall, "fair" Swedish liar.

"You would say anything but your prayers," I said, and kissed her.

I have her prayer book in my pocket now. It's in Swedish so I cannot read it, but there's a crude woodcut of the Devil stained with the whore's own blood. Long Liz! Tall and lank. I wanted to yank her head back and *rip* that lying tongue out by its roots!

Nothing but a tired old whore now, but she must have been a blond beauty in her youth, the signs were still there, but you had to squint and look hard to see them. Haunting gray eyes—like tarnished silver left out in the rain. She claimed to have the second sight, but the bitch *never* saw what was coming or else she would have run from me and not *clung* to me. I couldn't wait to *cut, Cut, CUT* her! Dark yellow hair, like burned butter, hanging down in stringy, greasy hanks, hair fit for a hag, framing a face haggard and gaunt. But what fine cheekbones! A sculptor would have loved them! Good bones tell. I traced them with my fingertip. I couldn't wait to bare them down to the bone; I wanted to see it shining white as a pearl in the moonlight. *Who's the poetic one now, Michael?* She had no upper teeth; she'd lost them, she said, in the *Princess Alice* steamship disaster. Her husband and nine children had been amongst the seven hundred who died when a collier rammed it. As she clambered up a ladder, always just a step above the rising water that threatened to suck her back down to a watery death, the man above her slipped and his heavy work boot kicked her in the mouth and knocked her teeth out, caved the roof of her mouth in, and cleaved her upper palate clean in two.

She seemed to mourn the loss of her teeth more than her family. It would be a *pleasure* to send this selfish whore to Hell! I would take my time and *savor* each moment! I couldn't wait to start cutting, to plunge my knife in and *twist* it around, stirring her innards like some foul witch's brew! I would show the bitch that there are worse things than losing one's teeth.

Second sight, my arse, you silly bitch! While I smiled and charmed her, inside I was taunting the vain fool: *Why ever did you let your family go aboard the* Princess Alice? *Why didn't you save them and your precious teeth? Why don't you now? You still could, you know! And now you're promenading like a lady in the park with the man who's about to take your sorry whore's life—second sight indeed!*

I saved her life. She thought that meant she could trust me, that I would *protect* her. What *fools* women are! They have no sense of danger; they never see it until it's right in front of their faces and too late to run! The knife's already at their throat before they even think to scream and then they're paralyzed with fright! Women are born to be the victims of men like me.

It was a rain-sodden Saturday, a cold, dark night. I first saw her through a curtain of rain. She was standing in the doorway of the Bricklayers' Arms pub, taking shelter from the rain, trying to keep warm, huddled and crammed in with several other men and women in the same plight. There was a man with her, dark haired with a droopy mustache.

"That's Leather Apron you've got cozyin' up nexta you," one of the men nudged and teased her, jerking his head at her companion, but she just laughed and clung tighter to his arm. She seemed to know him well . . . well enough not to be afraid.

That remark about "Leather Apron" got my attention. I followed them. In Berner Street, they rested against a wall. He leaned over and whispered something in her ear. She put her palm against his chest, shook her head, and gave him a playful little push.

"Not tonight, some other time perhaps," she said. A whore who said no; how intriguing!

To his mind, that was clearly the wrong answer. He tried to pull her through the gate. She kicked and fought him. He shoved her down. She screamed. He grabbed her head with one hand while the other fumbled past his heavy overcoat to unbutton his trousers. She screamed again.

"Lipski! Lipski!" some fool, paused to light his pipe upon the opposite pavement, shouted, pointing at the man, who did have a distinctly Jewish appearance. It's an insult they use in these parts; it was the name of a Jew who killed a girl a few years back. That stopped the man cold with his cock wilting and his trousers sagging.

The man with the pipe trembled and took off with the whore's assailant in hot pursuit, running toward the railway station. I wonder what he did to him when he caught him? That would teach the fool to go around shouting, *"Lipski!"*

Like the Good Samaritan, I helped the fallen woman up. I straightened her bonnet, tweaking the limp black crepe ruffles as though I were the finest milliner in Paris proud of my latest creation, and retrieved the brass thimble and wad of black thread that had fallen from her pocket. She stroked the diamond horseshoe on my black tie with a covetous gleam in her gray eyes—the bitch would nip it if I did not watch her!—and told me I had brought her luck. I was her hero, her savior; she could not thank me enough!

I gave her one of Edwin's gay silk handkerchiefs—a green-and-yellow-checkered one. I knotted it playfully about her neck, wanting to *twist* it tight, but not yet, not yet. . . . With my own handkerchief I wiped the grime from her cheek where she had grazed it against the wet pavement. I gave her a pack of pretty pink cachous from my pocket; her breath stank of gin and rot and I hoped she would take the hint and make immediate use of them, but she merely held them in her hand, awkwardly, admiring them—"such a pretty pink!"—as though she didn't know what to do with them and was afraid to ask. I bought her a red rose, backed with maidenhair fern, and pinned it on her shabby black jacket.

I lulled her with kind words; I soothed her with sweet deeds. I wanted her to trust me; I *needed* it. It would make the horror when it came so much the sweeter! I wanted to see the hurt and betrayal in her eyes as she died! I wanted this to be sublime, an experience I would *never* forget! I wanted this whore to close her eyes in rapture, to submit to me like the most willing lover, the one she had dreamed of all her life but never found. I wanted her to expect delights, to dream of them, only to awaken to a nightmare in my arms that was all *too* real as I plunged my knife in and *twisted* it around.

I strolled her down the street; I told her even though it was raining—a light and inconstant drizzle—the sun shone for me every time I looked at her. A fruiterer's shop was still open though it was nearing midnight, with a tempting array of white and black grapes arranged in his window. He was yawning and about to close his shutters. I bought half a pound of black grapes and shared them with her, but the ungrateful bitch merely chewed them, then spit them out into the street. She said she didn't like how they felt going down her throat. At least she had the decency to use her own handkerchief to wipe the juice from her chin and not the fine silk one I had just given her. The cheap and vulgar tart, she had no refinement at all!

The International Working Men's Educational Club was having a meeting, a bunch of socialist Jews and armchair anarchists who used politics as an excuse to get a night away from their wives once a week, and music was coming from the open windows of their clubhouse, so we strolled up and down Berner Street listening to it, Long Liz sometimes singing along when she knew the words. Then I drew her close and whispered, "Will you?"

Coyly twirling a grape stem, she said, "Yes."

They *always* say yes to a toff like me!

Stupid bitches, they think clothes make the man, that coarse clothes and manners means a brute and that they can trust a suit and spats, a fine black overcoat trimmed with astrakhan, a mammoth gold watch chain gleaming on a man's vest, a diamond horseshoe twinkling in his tie, and a tall silk topper or deerstalker hat. Because a man is dressed as a gentleman they think he is a *gentle* man. They don't realize it, but I'm dressed to kill! I don a deerstalker *only* when I go hunting.

I followed her through the gate, the same one that surly chap had tried to drag her through. This time she went willingly, leading me by the hand, looking back at me with bold eyes. Oh yes, she must have been beautiful when she was young! Eyes like a gray dove's plumage; what a pity she was so soiled.

The night was cold; so were my hands, and even colder my heart. I am a man of ice, *angry* ice, through and through! My hands were numb, but they would soon be warm. She turned away, fussing with the fastenings on her jacket. I drew my knife out. Just then she happened to glance back. She opened her mouth to scream. I grabbed the knot of the checkered silk handkerchief and *twisted* it viciously tight. I silenced the bitch with scarcely a whimper. A little worn-down stub of a knife, the blade barely a nub, fell from her lifeless fingers. How *dare* the bitch even think of trying to fight for her life; didn't she know it wasn't worth it? I stuffed the knife in my pocket—another souvenir. I took her prayer book too. She had shown it to me earlier, to prove that she knew what the Devil looked like.

I lowered her to the ground. I drew my knife across her throat. I felt my fingers tingle as I bathed them in her hot blood. A horse neighed nearby—*too* nearby! I started and glanced back over my shoulder. Hooves flailed the air. A man shouted; a whip cracked; the pony kicked the air and shied, refusing to pass through the gate. They call horses "dumb animals," but they are so much more sensitive than we humans are. The horse knew what his driver didn't. I scrambled back into the shadows, tensely awaiting my moment as he leaned forward and poked at her hip with his whip. I could not be trapped here in this courtyard. I groped for my silver box. I licked my medicine from my bloody palm, I tasted her blood along with its power. I felt strength surge through me. I *knew* everything would be all right!

The driver got down and struck a match. It was a windy night and the match immediately went out. He tried again. It must have been enough for him to see the blood. He ran into the club, jabbering in his Jew tongue. I saw my chance and seized it. I drew my overcoat tight about me and stepped swiftly past the cart, out into the street, and walked calmly but quickly away.

The bloodlust was still upon me. It drove me relentlessly onward. I couldn't stop! As I walked, I sprinkled more of my medicine onto my palm and licked it. I moved deeper into the city, losing myself in the dark labyrinth of tangled and decaying, stinking, rubbish-strewn streets.

My hands were numb again and cold, so *very* cold, like my heart. I was shivering. The blood cools so quickly; I *needed* its warmth, that feeling of release, to be reborn in a bloody baptism. I *had* to kill again, I needed to *rip*, to hear the flesh tear, the grotesque musical gurgle of burbling blood and air escaping from a severed windpipe. They'd never sing again; I always took their voices away, and then their lives. But a slashed throat was *never* enough. I *had* to plunge my hands inside and grope and plunder. I had to feel the life go out and the hot blood turn cold. I *had* to know that thrill again!

I'd romanced a young whore called Rosey in Heneage Court earlier that evening. We spooned, sitting on a dustbin, but we had been interrupted, by a bumbling fool of a bobby no less. I pointed to my black bag and said I was a doctor, and the girl backed me up—bless her sweet, trusting soul!—so I spared her. I kissed her brow and called her "a sweet young thing" as I gently took my leave of her. Now I almost wished I hadn't. . . . The next bitch I would make pay for my thwarted kill; I would do *everything* I intended for Long Liz and more, *much more!* Her own mother wouldn't recognize the whore when I was done with her.

*   *   *

Katie. She was the liveliest of the lot. A trampled red cabbage rose with an untrammeled spirit, that's how I shall always think of her. However had she kept her hopes alive in Whitechapel all these years when it seemed to suck the life out of everyone else?

She was a dainty bit o' fun. The top of her head scarcely reached my shoulder, with bright hazel eyes and a mop of deep auburn curls, clean for a whore in this dirty city, apple cheeks, a pointed chin, and a cheery smile beaming from beneath the brim of a black straw bonnet with amber and green glass beads.

When I happened upon her, she was leaning beneath one of the sparse street lamps, having a smoke from a clay pipe, to steady her stomach, she explained. She'd been drinking all night and was just out of jail. She'd been having "a bit o' fun" marching up and down Aldgate High Street pretending to be a fire engine, "bringin' a bit o' cheer" to the crowd that had gathered to watch her, when a constable came along and took her off to jail, to sleep it off.

"My man'll give me a damn fine 'idin' when I get 'ome," she groused.

I just smiled. I knew what she didn't know—she would never go home again.

She was fresh up from the country, "been 'op pickin' with my man down in Kent I 'ave."

Apparently the "lady" lacked luggage; she was wearing every bit of clothing she possessed. I teased her about being plump as a Christmas goose, but she said, "No, 't'ain't really so, gov; I'm really turrible skinny. See!"

She juggled the fulsome folds of her paisley silk shawl to better free up her arms, hiked up her grimy gray apron, and proceeded to reveal herself to me layer by layer. I was instantly reminded of the set of Russian nesting dolls I had given Gladys last Christmas. With increasing amusement, I watched as Katie lifted a dark green alpaca skirt, with an ornate pattern of golden lilies and Michaelmas daisies, a rich castoff from a stall in Petticoat Lane no doubt, another of brown linsey trimmed with black silk braid, followed by a much-soiled sky blue with three red rickrack flounces—she was so proud of those flounces!—then the petticoat her man had just given her to mark their anniversary ("been together eight years we 'ave!"), a triple-flounced pale pink chintz with a pattern of tiny bright flowers.

But she didn't stop there. With a playful smile, she lifted a rank, ragged yellowed chemise stained with spots of reddish brown that must have been blood shed in months past, and showed me a pair of stick-skinny legs in brown ribbed stockings rising out of a pair of mismatched mud-caked men's work boots.

She giggled and lifted her fat armful of skirts even higher and showed me her hairy cunt. The hair was deep red like that on her head, the color of freshly drying blood. I couldn't wait to stab it!

I'll leave this one her heart, since she's already given it to "her man," I charitably decided. Her liver or perhaps a kidney will do nice enough for me! "You must let me add something to your layers," I said, caressing the bare skin above her bodice where ruffles galore framed her plump little breasts. "I'm afraid you will catch cold if I don't." She giggled as I tied another of Edwin's gaudy silks around her neck. "There! It brings out the red in your hair and cheeks."

She led me to Mitre Square. "It's dark an' quiet this time o' night an' we can take our time an' be alone there." The poor little whore was *so eager* to please me!

"Are you *sure?*" I blew playfully on the back of her neck and whispered, "It's haunted, you know. Are you not afraid of ghosts?"

I told her the story of the mad monk, Brother Martin. Driven insane by lust, he had murdered a nun upon the altar of the church that used to overlook the square during the reign of Henry VIII.

Katie laughed. "Lord love ya, no! I 'aven't a cowardly bone in me 'ole body! There's not a ghostie or a beastie o' the two- or four-legged sort that frightens me! An' if me word's not good enough to prove it, I'll tell ya somethin' more. . . ." She glanced swiftly from side to side to make sure no one was near enough to hear us, but we were quite alone; I had already made certain of that. "I've come back to London early, to earn the reward for capturin' Jack the Ripper. I think I know 'im!"

"*You do?*" I arched my brows and leaned forward eagerly. "Truly, I am agog with curiosity! Won't you tell me who he is?"

But she laughed and playfully jabbed me in the ribs. "Get on witcha now; I ain't tellin'! Lose me reward, I should think not!"

"Oh my dear." I drew her close and kissed her brow. "As if I could *ever* deprive *you* . . ."

Oh, Katie . . . if you only knew what I had in store for you. . . .

I smiled and followed this ragged coquette into the darkened square.

I swiftly scanned the dark, empty windows of the warehouses that surrounded it as I maneuvered her into a corner and turned her to face the wall. I nuzzled her from behind, but she was wearing so many layers I doubted she could even feel my cock.

"*Oooh . . .*" she purred. "Fancy it from behind, d'ya?" With a gay little laugh she leaned forward and flipped up her flounces like a French dancer and swished her bare bottom at me.

I reached for the handkerchief around her neck and gave it a jerk and a savage twist. I pulled her back and watched her eyes bulge out as her nails clawed frantically at the red silk, trying to loosen it. "Breath and voice gone forever," I whispered in her ear. "Who did you think he was? Surely not *me*? Well, it doesn't matter now; you were wrong, and you won't live to tell!"

She went limp and I lowered her to the ground. I eased off my overcoat and stood staring down at her as I stripped off my gloves. The life had gone out of her eyes. I closed them. Her arms lay limp and loose at her sides, palms up, like a desperate woman begging for mercy or alms. I searched the blind eyes of the windows again and then took a deep breath. . . . I had much to do and so little time. . . .

I fell upon her in a frenzy. I flung her skirts up, over her head, and slashed and jabbed like mad. There were so many layers that sometimes they fell down and got in my way. I didn't stop; I cut them too. I ripped her from breast to cunt. I cut so deep I feared I would lose myself in her. I tore and flung her innards out. My hand closed around a kidney. I severed it. Maybe it would make a nice supper? Surely it couldn't be worse than that womb.

Breathless, I sat back on my heels and spent in my trousers. Her face bothered me. It seemed so peaceful, as though she had gone to a better place, a safer place, and was now mocking me with the tranquility of the shattered husk she had left behind her. My fist tightened around my knife and I slashed off her nose, then each of her earlobes. I meant to take them away with me, to send to the police, but I forgot. I remembered Long Liz's fine cheekbones and laid Katie's open to the bone. Beneath each eye I carved an inverted V. If you ignored the space between, where her nose had been, and put them together ^^ it formed the letter *M*—*M* for *Maybrick*. But the police are such fools they'll *never* see it for what it is—a clue!

I cut a corner from her apron to wipe the blood from my knife. Before I put it away, my trusty friend, my steel prick, I kissed it.

With silent mirth I swiftly pulled on my gloves as I stood and stared down at her. There was a brooch at her breast, nearly lost amidst all the ruffles, a little pink flower under glass now stained with blood. Was this cheap trinket another gift from her precious man? I pocketed it—another souvenir for my collection.

Shaking with silent laughter, I tipped my hat to Katie, lying dead at my feet with her bent legs splayed wide so that the bobbies when they came bumbling onto the scene would see another cheap pink flower, only this one sprinkled with drops of blood instead of dew.

As I was leaving the square, I passed a young bobby on the street and nodded politely to him and wished him good night. "Same to you, sir," he said. I *do* hope he was the one who discovered what I had done to Katie! Would he remember me afterward and always wonder if he had said good night to Jack the Ripper? I hope the thought will haunt him *all the rest of his life.*

I knew they were looking for me, the hunter had once again become the hunted, but I also knew they wouldn't catch me. I strode confidently, swift and sure, through the dark, mean streets, every twist and turn leaving them farther behind me, lost like blind rats in a maze.

In Goulston Street I paused to catch my breath. I leaned against a wall, tore off a glove, and shakily sprinkled arsenic onto my bloody palm. As I lapped up its power, I remembered the chalk. I had put a piece in my pocket, in case a clever little rhyme and the opportunity to write it came to me. I had hoped inspiration would strike while I was standing over a whore with a convenient wall behind, but you never know when the Muse will call; she's fickle like any other bitch.

Upon the black dado wall of a darkened tenement, I scrawled in stark, startling white against the dead black:

THE JUWES ARE
THE MEN THAT
WILL NOT
BE BLAMED
FOR NOTHING

Take it and make of it what you will, you damned, bloody fools with all your speculation about doctors, butchers, Jews, and Yids! You'll stop and scratch your confounded heads and beat them bloody against the wall trying to figure it out, and I'll be on to the next whore and then the next while you're *still* trying to make sense of it.

If the fools have wits enough to realize it really is a message from me, I hope it will free the Jews from suspicion. They're hated enough as it is and I've nothing against them.

When I was an apprentice lad, so hot for Sarah but unable to have her, I used to notice the Jewesses walking through Whitechapel in their black wigs. Their religion decrees that they must shave their heads after marriage and let no man but their husbands see them uncovered.

There was one young, shapely wench I always admired. A young bride with a face as pretty as a cameo beneath her black wig. One day, when I was burning with pulsing, mad lust for Sarah and sure I would go mad if I did not soon possess her, the beautiful young Jewess crossed my path. Acting on a sweet, mad impulse, I snatched the wig from her head and ran up an alley. Of course, she followed me.

Weeping with shame and trying to shield her naked head with her shawl, poor thing, she begged me to give back her wig. I backed her against the wall and hoisted her skirts. Tears ran down her face and she wouldn't even look at me as I filled her. When I tried to caress her face, she jerked her trembling little chin away, still refusing to look at me. That only excited me more! I pushed her to her knees and spent all over her sacred bald scalp.

She never let me catch her alone after that; I never saw her again except in a gaggle of Jewesses. I've *always* remembered her fondly.

"For the fair Jewess," I saluted my scrawl. I wouldn't want one of her relatives to be molested or hanged for my naughty deeds. My soul is *still* kind, after all! It's only whores I'm down upon.

I flung the scrap of bloody-shitty apron I'd used to wipe my knife down beneath it, another calling card from Jack the Ripper.

I heard the church clock strike three. Maybe they had blood-hounds after me? I'd read some such speculation in the newspapers. But I was like a bloodhound myself, relentlessly drawn to the scent of sex. Mary Jane was near. I was *so close,* I fancied I could almost smell her cunt. I thought of my succulent ginger tart—my spicy, ribald Mary Jane lying in her bed with her gin bottle, a song on her lips, her stained and sweaty shift hiked up to her hips, and her fingers fiddling away like mad. It was a most amusing habit she had; some women fidget with a lock of hair, a piece of jewelry, or the trimmings on their gown, but Mary Jane plays with herself. There was a little fountain set just a few feet off the road, for the denizens of Dorset Street to wash in, and I quickly peeled off my gloves and washed my hands and made myself presentable. I remembered to take the prayer book and brooch from my pocket and lock them in my black bag where Katie's kidney was biding its time, waiting to become my dinner.

What a rare treat it would be for me, juicy with blood and red, red wine. I couldn't wait to taste it! Maybe I would share it with Mary Jane or take it home to dine with my wife-whore? Or maybe the press or police would care to partake? Wouldn't that be jolly? Let's all make a feast of Katie's kidney! So many men have had her in life, why not a few more in death? My bag was equipped with a good, sturdy lock. As an added precaution, I had left the key back in my bolt-hole. You can *never* trust a whore, and if I fell asleep Mary Jane might riffle my pockets. I smoothed down my clothes. The best thing about black is that it doesn't show blood, especially in the dead of night. If there was any spot of blood on my white shirt, cuffs, face, or hands I would claim a nosebleed, mention it even before the bitch had the chance to notice it.

I plunged boldly into the darkness of the narrow archway leading to her room. Number 13, lucky for some, unlucky for others. I
peeked through the window, around the makeshift muslin curtain,
worn thin as a bridal veil. I was in luck. I caressed the diamond
horseshoe on my tie and smiled like the Devil. She was alone. Fishmonger Joe was nowhere in sight. I'd been half-afraid that he would
spoil everything. I'd thought about watching them fuck through the
window, the way I fantasized about my wife-whore and Alfred Brierley. The candle in the ginger beer bottle was burning bright and
Mary Jane was lying there on the rumpled bed just as I had pictured her. I could hear her singing softly and slurrily about that
damned, infernal violet on her mother's grave.

Let the police go on playing hunt the Ripper, let them have their
fun, while I had mine.

With the dawn I rose and left Mary Jane sprawled in sweet
drunken slumber. On my way back to my cozy little bolt-hole in
Petticoat Lane, I passed a policeman. He handed me a handbill.
On it was my letter, printed in facsimile, in red ink no less, above an
urgently worded request for any who recognized the writing to
come forward. As I walked along I saw that they were also pasting
posters on the walls. I wanted to laugh right in their stupid faces.
Safely back in my bolt-hole, I took a postcard and my bottle of red
ink from my travel desk and sat down to write:

> *I wasn't codding dear old Boss when I gave
> you the tip. Youll hear about Saucy Jackys
> work tomorrow double event this time
> number one squealed a bit couldnt finish
> straight off. Had not time to get ears for
> police thanks for keeping last letter back till
> I got to work again.*
>
> *Jack the Ripper*

That "tomorrow" would really confound them and make them
wonder if I had really stopped in the midst of my bloody labors to
write and mail the postcard or if instead it was the act of a prankster.

Once again I addressed myself to the gentlemen of the press, at the Central News Agency; I knew they wouldn't disappoint me.

I changed my clothes and went out to pop my postcard in the post, enjoying my walk and the cries of the newsboys, shrilling out the latest horrors to befall the harlots of Whitechapel. I watched the women cluster together, cowering close to one another and their menfolk for comfort. I *savored* the terror in their eyes. *Which one of you,* I wondered, *which one of you will be the next for Jack?*

I bought every edition, every paper I could find. I stopped at a bakery for an assortment of pastries, drizzled with icing, caramel, and rich chocolate sauce and filled with spicy cinnamon, jam, or sweet cream. I am *always* good to my whores. I knew these sweets would please Mary Jane, as would the present in my pocket and inside the gay striped satin hatbox I was carrying.

She knelt naked upon the bed as I placed the emerald taffeta bonnet on her sleep-tousled ginger-gold head and tied the ribbons in a big beautiful bow beneath her pretty chin. I watched her ravenously tear into the buns, tearing into them like I tore into whores. And guzzle from the bottle of rum I'd brought her, knowing this was her favorite breakfast. White cream, tawny caramel, red jam, and dark chocolate staining her face, she sat there, shamelessly naked, legs wantonly sprawled; ravenously licking her sticky fingers when all the sweets were gone. She was an adorable greedy glutton begging for more and I would give it to her.

I watched as she leisurely rolled the green silk stockings—"as green as the Emerald Isles and as beautiful as your eyes," I said gallantly—up her fine, shapely legs. She remarked that it had been such a "terrible long time" since she had felt silk against her skin and lifted a leg and twisted one green-clad ankle this way and that to admire it. "I've hooked many a man by showin' me ankles on a rainy day!" she said as I smiled over the newspapers and read to her all about Jack the Ripper's double event.

I watched her shudder and cross herself and reach for the rosary lying on the table beside her bed and begin idly fingering the beads instead of herself.

"Sometimes I dream," she confided with wide, frightened eyes, "that he's comin' for me! Sure as the Mark o' Cain, I'm marked as one o' his, an' there's no help for it; even if I run, he'll find me!"

Her terror fed my need and my greed, and soon I must let the papers fall to the floor and take her again, plunging my knife of hot flesh, not cold steel, into her until she *screamed* with pleasure and begged for more and for me to stop all in the same breath. Women—two-faced, two-minded, duplicitous, deceitful whores all of them!

Do all the whores in Whitechapel know one another? There are so many whores here, *thousands* of them, it seems impossible. Yet Mary Jane knew Long Liz and Katie. Like the miserable ghost of Marley rattling his chains at Ebenezer Scrooge, Mary Jane brought them back to haunt me, accusing eyes, angry mouths, and, underneath, throats gaping open like second mouths, hungry for life but filled only with death—raw, bloody death! Filthy whores, they degrade everything they touch, even their own sorry lives! I did them all a favor by killing them. I relieved them of their misery; it was the nicest thing anyone could ever have done for them. I let them sacrifice their lives for a good and noble cause—to keep two sweet, innocent children and their undeserving mother-whore safe. Why can't they be grateful? They should go down on their knees and thank me, not haunt me and rattle those damn phantom chains!

The tall, gangly, flaxen-haired farmer's daughter Elisabeth Gustafsdotter—Gustav's Daughter—was born in "Torslunda or somethin' like it." She loved to read *anything* she could get her hands on. She dreamed of becoming a schoolteacher, but all her hopes were shattered when she was sixteen. She was working at her first job, as a maidservant in a fine house in Gothenburg, "servin' the gentry," when she let the charming young master, Lars Fredrik, the adored only son of the house, seduce her. She thought he loved her. In those days Liz still believed all the fairy tales about peasant girls who became princesses.

He left her pregnant and with a dose of "somethin' heinous" that landed her in the infirmary, with the blame *all* upon her.

The young man claimed that *she* had seduced *him,* wept when he knelt down before his gray-haired old mother, and confessed that Elisabeth, the housemaid, had stolen his innocence and infected him with some shameful ailment that had left a canker on his doodle and made it burn and weep a foul discharge.

Liz's daughter was stillborn. She was heartbroken when the

doctor told her that she could never have another. Her good name and all her hopes gone, she took to drink and walking the streets.

Eventually she emigrated, hoping for a new and better life in England. She threw herself on the charity of the Swedish Church in Trinity Street. She loved to visit the reading room and pore over the papers from the old country. Sometimes she let the Swedish sailors who brought them buy her favors and drinks, *always* drinks.

Then along came John Thomas Stride, a good man believing in redemption, that everyone deserves a second chance. They married and opened a coffeehouse in Crispin Street. Liz was always kind to the poor, sick, downhearted, and downtrodden, especially the whores. "There but for the grace of God go I," she always said as she filled the coffee cups and served thick, generous slices of the cinnamon-spice cake or another kind filled with creamy cheese and luscious tarty-sweet red raspberry jam, and special cookies rolled in white sugar, all baked from her own mother's recipes.

Though Elisabeth was certainly a tall girl, I learned from Mary Jane that her height had nothing to do with her being called "Long Liz." It was her habit of telling tall tales and her vast knowledge of Swedish folk and fairy tales, with which she regaled the coffee-house customers for hours.

But of course it didn't last. Disease raddled Mr. Stride's fine, generous mind; he raved and turned violent. It was a *dreadful* sight to see a man so horribly transformed. "Truly, had you known him before, you would not have known him after," Mary Jane said. "He was altogether a different man when he'd been the soul o' sweetness before." He had to go to the asylum, where he soon afterward died. "Liz said they sawed his skull open an' found his brain full o' holes like moths had been at it."

His brother did Liz wrong, cheating her out of the coffeehouse, and, sunk deep in despair, she sought solace in drink and the arms of strangers again. "She just couldn't resist those sailor boys from Sweden." She had to earn her keep. She'd already seen what happened when body and soul parted ways—"when that happened to you, you were like to end up in the asylum like Mr. Stride." She whored and begged charity and drinks, always drinks.

As I had suspected, the *Princess Alice* tale was just a figment of her imagination, bait for sympathy, originally concocted to take advantage of the charity fund established for victims of the disaster. "The closest Long Liz ever got to a ship after she docked in England was the sailors she fucked." Mary Jane laughed. The boot of some surly drunk or a pimp Long Liz wouldn't pay—depending on which story you chose to believe—had kicked most of her teeth out; the rest she had lost to decay.

She'd lived off and on the last few years with a dockside laborer called Michael Kidney—Kidney! I perked up, remembering the treasure sealed up tight, floating like a mysterious blob-shaped creature at the bottom of the sea, in a jar of red wine locked in darkness inside the black Gladstone bag I'd left beneath my bed in Petticoat Lane. But "she couldn't quite stick to it. For long spells she'd be fine; then off she'd go, carousin' with sailors, livin' an' fuckin' an' drinkin' like there wasn't goin' to be a tomorrow."

Mike was a good fellow, but he found Liz hard to handle. He grew weary of all the arguments and gave up trying to make her stay, contenting himself with knowing that she would always come back. *Until Jack's knife flashed,* I added silently as I snuggled against Mary Jane's bare back and gave her earlobe a dainty nibble when what I really wanted to do was *bite it off!*

Would the police find Katie's earlobes that I had sliced off? What would they do with them? Would they sew them back on in the mortuary? What did they do with dead whores? Did they bury them in pieces or try to sew them back together again like rag dolls, to give decency in death to those who had lived so long without it?

In my mind's eye, I saw the ghost of Long Liz standing at the foot of the bed, blame blazing in her eyes, severed throat gaping, pointing an adamantly accusing finger. The fireball in my belly churned and burned. The rats gnawed. I gasped and gripped Mary Jane's breasts so hard with my cold, numb hands that she cried out, "Play gentle now, Jim!" I heard the rattle of phantom chains and swallowed hard. My throat burned as though I had drunk acid, and pain drove spikes into my head. *Damn you, Mary Jane! You should be hosting séances instead of peddling your cunt! Through you the dead live again, damn, Damn, DAMN you!*

But she was done talking of the fair lying Swede. Now Mary Jane was on about Katie. Catherine Eddowes, the name she had been given at birth, or Kate Kelly as she liked to call herself, proudly taking her man's name.

Mary Jane *would* know her too! Would I *ever* kill a whore who would elicit a shrug and a blank stare from Mary Jane instead of "oh yes, poor harlot, I knew her well!"?

Katie and her many siblings had been left to run wild after her mother died in childbed, while their father worked hard to earn their keep making tin plates. At sixteen she'd fallen hard for a smooth-talking pensioner, Thomas Conway. He'd persuaded her to have his initials tattooed in blue ink upon her arm and given her three bastard babies, "but no weddin' ring, though their life together was like a circle unendin'. First he'd beat her, then Katie'd run out an' try an' soothe her hurts with gin, then he'd come after her, pick her up out o' the gutter or some other bloke's bed, say some sweet words that'd make the poor fool fall in love all over again, an' home they'd go, until it all happened again, an' there was no reckonin' when that might be, two hours, two weeks, or two months, but it *always* happened again. Like livin' on a floor covered in broken glass, it was, knowin' that no matter how carefully you set your feet down you were bound to get cut sometime." But then Tom Conway up and disappeared, and no more was ever heard from him.

Katie mourned, then moved on. She was lucky. She found her *true* love with an Irish market porter, John Kelly, who was *determined* to give her a good home and wean her off the gin. Though she suffered an occasional slip, it wasn't often, and he'd made it plain to her that she was *his* woman and he wasn't a man to suffer her being with another.

"She wasn't a reg'lar whore, not like me an' the rest," Mary Jane said. "She was just a poor soul tryin' to get by, one day at a time. But when the thirst was upon her, an' the bottle had gone dry, an' the money had run out, an' her still cravin' more, she'd do whatever she had to to get another nip, an' if that meant lettin' some gent hoist her skirts, so be it. What Johnny didn't know wouldn't hurt him."

Katie and her Johnny lived one day at a time, renting a double bed most nights in a doss-house in Flower & Dean Street, him working as a porter in the market and her hiring out as a char and taking in washing and needlework or hawking flowers or what have you in the streets. She was a bit of a magpie, with a fine, quick eye and a knack for picking up little treasures to pawn, things the finer folk threw away or lost, like quality buttons of metal or ivory, sometimes ones set with stones, or pillboxes and cigarette or card cases. Once she even found a pair of silver spectacles set with little diamonds and flashy black stones so fine she thought "they must've belonged to the Queen" and was half-tempted to go to the palace to return them. Every autumn Katie and Johnny would join the mass of migrant workers heading for the country to pick hops and enjoy the sunshine and clean air and all the fresh milk and wholesome country fare they could eat. It was something they looked forward to all year; it was such a welcome change from the miserable muck and murk of foul and foggy London.

Now *two* ghostly whores were rattling their chains at me. I wanted to *strangle* Mary Jane Kelly with those phantom chains, but when I looked in her green eyes all I could say was, "Back down on your back you go," and roll on top of her and thrust deep inside her. *Why* was it *so hard* to kill this one? She was *only* a whore like all the rest of them!

Back in my bolt-hole, I cut Katie's kidney in half and fried and ate it with onions and carrots. I sprinkled my medicine in my glass of fine red wine and watched the white powder swirl and melt into its ruby-red depths. Warmth flooded my icy fingers, filling them to the very tips. It was *very* nice! *Almost* as nice as bathing them in a whore's hot blood. The other half, bloody and raw, sopping and wine sodden, I put into a little brown cardboard box and tied it up tight with string, then sat down with my red ink to write a new letter, this one addressed to Mr. George Lusk, the Chairman of the newly formed Whitechapel Vigilance Committee, who had vowed not to rest until I was brought to justice and was offering a substantial reward for my capture. I had met the man before; he specialized in decorating music halls and was a fellow Freemason in Michael's lodge. Lusk thought Michael was "a gem of a man" and always wanted the halls he designed to be the perfect setting for him, so it gave me *great* pleasure to address him in the guise of Jack the Ripper.

> *Mr. Lusk*
>
> *Sor*
>
> *I send you half the Kidne I took from one women prasarved it for you tother piece I fried and ate it was very nise I may send you the bloody knif that took it out if you only wate a whil longer*
>
> *signed*
>
> *Catch me when you can Mishter Lusk*

I wrote it in strong, bold red letters, delighting in my crude misspellings, so contradictory and bizarre that it would make them wonder if I was *really* that ignorant or just playing games. What illiterate cockney knows that *knife* starts with *k* and writes such an elegant copperplate? But *this* time, as much as I wanted to, I did not sign my name, just to toy with them. They would *know* who it was from; Katie's kidney would leave them in no doubt about that! I could think of no better calling card, except one with my *real* name engraved upon it, and *that* the fools will *never* have, *ha ha!*

I lay back on my bed and licked white strength from my palm. I furiously fondled my cock and thought of my wife-whore sucking Alfred Brierley's while I stood at the foot of the bed and watched. I glanced at my watch. Tomorrow, after I mailed my parcel to Mr. Lusk, I must catch the train back to Liverpool. How I wished I could catch my wife-whore and Brierley in the act, burst in on them naked in bed. I wanted to whip out my cock and scream at them to keep fucking until I spent all over them!

I held my watch up over my head, swinging it by its heavy chain, like a pendulum. My Muse blessed me then with a *wonderful* idea. I found a pin and, after carefully prying off the back of the casing, slowly, painstakingly, inscribed dead in the center of it *I am Jack the Ripper!* and, below it, my signature, *James Maybrick;* then, like planets orbiting the sun, I surrounded it with four sets of initials: *PN, AC, ES,* and *CE.*

It served the last whore right to deny her her man's name at the end. *E* for *Eddowes,* her maiden name, though her days of maidenhood were long past. Now the whores are *always* with me! As long as I have my watch, I will carry them with me wherever I go. The victims I know them *so well!* Let them rattle their phantom chains, God damn them!

❧ 20 ❧

I couldn't bear it anymore, this endless back-and-forth between loving husband and the mad, rampant monster. I would have to resort to drastic measures. If I could not divorce Jim, I would have to make him divorce me. I'd managed to make a few discreet inquiries amongst solicitors, and they all advised me, for the sake of the children, to aim for reconciliation. Even Dr. Hopper, who had pretended all along with me that my injuries were the result of tumbles down stairs and other careless accidents, agreed that it was all for the best when I turned to him, hoping he would testify for me. I'd tried to write Jim a letter, asking him to set me free, a long, rambling, bumbling, surely bungled thing that I ended up shoving into the depths of my desk in frustration. It was no use! Since no one would take my side and help me, Jim would just have to divorce me; I'd have to force his hand.

I decided to do the most brazen thing I could think of. I reserved the bridal suite at Flatman's Hotel in our own names, Mr. and Mrs. James Maybrick. I told Jim an old aunt of mine was ailing and in London to see a surgeon and was begging me to visit her, fearing it might be the last time she would ever see me on earth. Of course, Jim said I must go. He even gave me a lovely speckled fur cape lined in orchid satin as a substitute for his "warm embrace during these dreary and lonesome days we must spend apart," explaining that his business prevented him from joining me, as I knew perfectly well it would; that was why I had chosen that week in particular.

But it wasn't Mr. and Mrs. James Maybrick who checked in at Flatman's but Alfred Brierley and Mrs. Maybrick. Several of the cotton brokers who frequented Flatman's recognized us. They knew at once that the man registered as James Maybrick and sleeping in bed with Mrs. Maybrick was not Jim, and that was just what I had intended.

But I didn't count on Alfred walking out on me after the first night. He'd seemed so delighted when we'd made the arrangements, congratulating me on being so clever and saying how perfect it all was. But the fantasy didn't quite match the reality. He was sullen and peevish instead of passionate. He accused me of trying to drag his name through the mud, of using him and wanting to see him named co-respondent in a divorce scandal. He said he didn't love me, we'd had our fun, and he was done, he had no intention of marrying me.

"You mean nothing to me," he said bluntly as he was putting his clothes back on and packing up his trunk, ignoring the lovely dinner I'd ordered brought upstairs for us, "no more than any other woman, just pleasure for pleasure's sake, nothing more, and I cannot fathom how you ever thought otherwise; I certainly never said anything to give you that impression. If I like her, and the lady is willing, I'm willing to oblige her until I get tired of her. Afterward, if she doesn't cling and cry too much and try to hold on to me, sometimes we can resume as friends, after a suitable interval, of course. That's how I live my life, and I see no reason to change it; I'm having a thoroughly marvelous time being a bachelor, I couldn't be happier."

At first I couldn't believe what I was hearing.

"No! You don't . . . you *can't* mean that!" I cried.

"Oh, but I do," he was quick to assure me, eyes and words cold as ice, *freezing* me.

In that moment I felt my heart break like a trifling little crimson glass Valentine's Day bauble. It was only when I was losing him that I realized how much I loved him. I just couldn't bear to let him go.

I was so upset I snatched up the crystal bowl of jewel-lovely fruit medley and poured it over his copper head and slapped his face, sending fat, glistening drops of sugary-sweet syrup and chunks of pineapple, diced peaches, grapes, and cherries flying everywhere. *"You cad!"* I shouted. "You haven't a chivalrous bone in your body!"

I wept up a storm and went back to Liverpool on the very next train. I told the people who saw me crying that there'd been an unexpected death in my family.

Aching with loss and longing, I returned to Battlecrease House, with leaden feet, to await the inevitable; the storm was bound to break soon. No one was expecting me, and when I walked heartsore, travel weary, and tearstained into my bedroom I was astonished to find none other than Nanny Yapp, blind as a bat with her spectacles off, dancing and twirling before my mirror wearing my candy-striped satin corset and a flurry of pink and white ruffled petticoats trimmed with red satin bows and ribbon-threaded lace that also belonged to me. She lifted and shook them like a French dancer, displaying a pair of my frilly drawers and pink silk stockings. She even had her big flat feet crammed into a pair of my little red satin French heels, her toes bulging out at the sides in a way I supposed must be quite painful, and had my bracelets, a veritable fortune in icy-glistening diamonds, stacked up to her elbows over a pair of my pink satin opera gloves. She was singing in such an awful off-key manner I was suddenly immensely grateful that Jim and Mrs. Briggs had never seen fit to entrust her with the children's musical education.

> *"While strolling through the park one day,*
> *In the merry, merry month of May,*
> *I was taken by surprise by a pair of roguish eyes,*
> *In a moment my poor heart was stole away,*
> *Da da da da da da*
> *Da da da da da da. . . ."*

This was simply *too much;* I just *had* to walk away. Luckily she was singing so loudly and without her spectacles she was so blind that she never noticed me standing in the doorway. I went back downstairs and told May I was feeling right poorly and would she please be so good as to draw me a hot bath; that would surely give Nanny Yapp time to get back into *her* clothes and out of *my* room.

While I was soaking in my bath, luxuriating in the rose-perfumed steam, I asked May to bring me any letters that had come for me during my absence.

Much to my surprise, amongst the many bills I found a letter from Alfred Brierley. He said he feared he'd been "far too precipitate" and "egregiously mistaken." He'd been feeling foolish and out of sorts and worried after several men he habitually did business with had recognized him in the lobby, and one must expect a certain amount of fear and trepidation when a man sees the end of his bachelor days upon the horizon. That fear had made him unkind and he fully deserved being called a "cad" as well as having the fruit medley dumped over his head. I was "the most exciting, intoxicating woman" he'd ever known, and he couldn't bear to go on without me. We *must* reconcile at the first possible opportunity or else he would find himself sitting with a pistol in his hand one night contemplating self-destruction, and did I *really* want a man's blood, his heart's blood that pulsed *only* for *me,* staining my lovely lily-white hands?

"Oh, Alfred, Alfred, Alfred," I sighed. "Your love is just like a noose, always keeping me dangling!"

I tried to tell myself to buck up and show some pride and not go running back the moment he beckoned. But I knew myself too well to lie to me; I knew I would soon be back in his arms and in his bed again.

The warm, fragrant water lulled me into a doze, and I awakened with a start to a sudden splash. I was no longer alone. Edwin had crept in and disrobed, in such haste to join me in my perfumed bath that he had forgotten to remove his socks. I laughed until I cried, and then I laughed some more. Edwin laughed with me, pointing and braying at his sodden green socks. It was almost like old times except we were naked in the bathtub.

When my laughter subsided, I tried to shove Edwin out, but he only laughed all the harder and pulled me onto his lap. He assured me that we were quite safe; Jim had gone up to London. My absence had put him in a fond and forgiving mood, and he had decided to surprise me by settling all my debts as the first step on the road to the new life we would be starting down together the moment he returned tomorrow evening. We were only a scant few months away from a new year, 1889, and he truly wanted this New Year to be a new start for us, devoid of all deception and lies.

"He told me to tell you," Edwin said, "when he takes you in his arms and kisses you at the stroke of midnight, he wants to kiss you that way every day for the rest of his life. I think he means like this. . . ." Edwin proceeded to illustrate until I succeeded in stopping him by shoving a cake of pink rose soap into his mouth.

I jumped out of the tub and threw on a robe. Foolish creature that I am, the words were scarcely out of Edwin's mouth before my heart went leaping after Jim, leaving Alfred Brierley in the dust. Then, just as suddenly, it stopped and sank like a stone. By now Jim would have already inquired for me at Flatman's and discovered that Mrs. *and Mr.* Maybrick had already checked out. The catastrophe I'd set the stage for could not be averted. The only hope I had was to pray for a miracle and, barring God's intervention, to somehow brazen it out. If only I could persuade Jim to hold on to that spirit of forgiveness, then maybe, just maybe, there was some hope left for us after all. I suddenly wanted that new start more desperately than I had ever wanted anything in my life. I knew then, no matter how I might try to pretend, I *still* loved Jim. I wanted to be a wife, *his* wife, not any other man's mistress.

I dressed in green, the color of spring, and waited for Jim to come home. Someone had once told me that butterflies were a symbol of rebirth, so I put the lavender and mint jade butterfly comb in my hair and sank down on my knees and prayed with all my might that if God would help me disentangle myself from this foolish fix that was entirely of my own devising I would never look at another man again, that henceforth there would be no one but Jim. That's the way it should have always been, but I'd made mistakes, out of anger and hurt pride, a spirit of revenge, and a longing for what was lacking, and now I wanted desperately to atone.

I'd kept Mrs. Humphreys slaving in the kitchen all day. I ordered her to prepare, with especial care, a replica of our first meal as man and wife. Everything must be *exactly* right—the rosemary chicken, tender green asparagus, new potatoes seasoned with herbs and butter. I'd ordered the lemon custard cake from the bakery this time, Mrs. Humphreys not being so adept at fancywork as I would like, and asked that a dove with an olive branch in its beak be drawn in icing atop the dark chocolate frosting.

I jumped up and ran downstairs the instant I heard Jim at the door. My foot hadn't even left the final step before his fist felled me. As stars danced before my eyes blood streamed from my nose and my consciousness wavered like a dying candle. I fully expected to feel his hand in my hair dragging me upstairs, followed by the crushing power of his fingers around my throat, but he left me lying right where I fell. It was his way of telling me that he was done with me. I wanted to roll over on my stomach and *drag* myself up the stairs after him and find a way, *some way,* to win his love back, but I didn't have the strength. I never wanted anything more until after I knew I had lost it. *Tomorrow,* I promised myself as the stars stopped dancing and everything went dark, *tomorrow* . . .

❧ 21 ❧

THE DIARY

My life is a house of cards. It's threatening to fall apart. I'm afraid that soon *all* will come a-tumbling down. Blinding headaches, bad dreams, and bellyaches, I do believe I'm done for; I'm afraid I am damned in this world as well as the next. Even my medicine's strength seems to be flagging. I need *so much* now that every time I take it I know I am taking my life into my own hands . . . one grain too many and Death's scythe will strike me down. I feel awed and *enslaved* by its power, yet I would not give up *one* precious grain of my white powder.

The icy numbness that afflicts my hands is creeping down into my legs and feet. My fingers and toes are like nubs of ice. Sometimes I sit on the side of my bed and hold up my unfeeling hands and stare down at my bare feet. I wiggle my fingers and toes. Sometimes they tantalize me by tingling, but that's all. It's a queer sensation. I walk but cannot feel the floor beneath my feet. I stepped on one of Bobo's lead soldiers; his little sword broke through the skin and drew blood. Had I not stumbled and looked down, I never would have known it.

Dead whores stalk my sleep, rattling their chains and pointing fingers of blame, alongside images of my wife-whore writhing naked on my bed with Alfred Brierley while I stand at the foot and watch, furiously jerking my cock, and our children's woebegone faces float before my eyes, and something else—I'm haunted by the gentle man I used to be. Sweet and solicitous to my wife, kissing and caressing her, I liked to pretend she was my little girl with golden curls and no one could spoil her even half so well as me. "Kiss Papa," I would whisper when I hung jewels around her slender white throat and pressed a kiss to the gently throbbing pulse.

"The *best* father in the world!" Bobo and Gladys used to call me. I always took such pride in that!

Suddenly my grand scheme, to make all the little whores pay for the Great Whore's sins, seems so futile, so pointless! I don't want to be Jack the Ripper anymore! My God, what was I thinking? *I MUST have been mad!* Why did I ever stray from the path of right-eousness? I want to be the man I used to be, the one who won Bunny's heart; I want to forget the crimes I committed when I was consumed and transfigured by rage, lust, and madness. I want ab-solution and to make amends.

I went to visit my parents' graves today. It was my fiftieth birth-day. I can scarcely believe I've lived half a century. I didn't sleep at all last night. I dreamed I cut my darling Bunny up instead of a birthday cake and, with a devilish smile and a mad gleam in my eyes, served pieces of her—heart, cunt, kidneys, liver—to the chil-dren and guests. I woke up screaming. I flung off the covers and ran and woke Bunny up, hugging and kissing her a thousand times. I was so very glad that she was still alive and all in one piece, that I hadn't risen from my bed in a trance and hacked her to bits. We made love, *really made love,* for the first time since this horrid busi-ness began. She gave freely and willingly; I didn't just take. Warm and welcoming, she took me into her body, into her sweet arms, comforted me, and told me that she still loved me and always had. *I want so much to believe her!* "I never stopped loving you, Jim!" she cried as she clung to me. "It was just that I was so hurt and mad!" Hurt and mad, we both had been hurt and mad, but in my pain and madness I had become the Devil's tool. *God help me! I was a mad FOOL!*

I stood for a long time gazing down at my parents' graves, slumbering serenely in perpetual peace in the shadow of a stone cross. I prayed for tranquility and guidance, for God to shine a beacon on the path to absolution to help me find my way back. How I wished that they had loved me! Sometimes I think that's why I love my own children so much, because I know what it is like to grow up lonely and unloved. When Mother died, her hand in *mine, not Michael's*—*mine, Mine, MINE!*—her last words to me were a plea that I endeavor to be more like Michael. When I remembered that, I kicked the cross and trampled the violets I had brought my parents, *CRUSHING* them, *PULVERIZING* them with my heel, *GRINDING* them, leaving a pulpy purple, green, and brown dent in the sacred ground.

I get no rest. I toss and thrash and talk in my sleep. Fever burns my brain. Pain gnaws my belly. There are hours when my limbs are locked and useless as iron bars. Sometimes I rise and walk without waking. Damn Edwin for telling Michael! I am writing this from his house in Regent's Park. Michael insists I see another specialist. He's taken to locking me in at night so I don't fall down the stairs and break my neck.

The doctors are *useless, Useless, USELESS;* I see that now. Were they not necessary to procure prescriptions I would be done with the lot of them altogether. I'm more down on doctors now than I am on whores, but I lack the energy to start a new regime of ripping. They use words like *hypochondria, melancholia, gross indulgence,* and *dyspepsia* and dose me with harmless tonics that might as well be sugar-water for all the good that they do me. *Liver pills! Digestive lozenges!* That fool Hopper actually had the gall to caution me against trebling the doses of his prescriptions, as though one spoonful of anything ever did anyone any good, and mixing them with other drugs. He said if I continued to do so I might do myself a *grave* injury! That's his polite and careful physician's way of saying I might kill myself. If I didn't take matters into my own hands and dose myself with arsenic and strychnine I would be dead already!

None of them understands how sick I am! They call me a hypochondriac, ignoring the obvious fact that I am sick *all* the time! Dr. Humphreys even gently alluded to the tale of the boy who cried wolf as though I were a child in the nursery! Of all the impertinences and absurdities! Drysdale actually had the gall to roll his eyes when I told him our neighbor had just been diagnosed with diabetes and I was afraid to have him over for dinner and cards lest I catch it. The doctors think I just want attention, to be coddled, that I *like* being sick! That *IDIOT* Drysdale thinks my condition is due to "suicidal self-indulgence at the dinner table," nothing more! Haven't I just reason to be afraid? The coldness and numbness continues creeping over my limbs. I fear I will wake up one morning and find myself paralyzed and not able to move at all, not even an eyelash; it almost makes me afraid to go to sleep. The pains in my belly bend me double; the doctors think I'm just being dramatic when I say it's like rats gnawing or a blazing fireball burning me from gullet to bladder. One quack suggested I try cold cream enemas and pills of powdered rhubarb and a healthful and replenishing tonic of celery! *COLD CREAM ENEMAS! RHUBARB! CELERY!*

I'm so afraid of dying! I'm afraid of going to Hell and of who will be waiting for me at the portal. I'm afraid of phantom whores rattling chains, waiting for me on the other side of Heaven to drag me down to Hell, where even I know I belong. *God help me; no one else can!*

I've been *beastly* to the children! I *DESERVE* death for scaring them! What has become of the father I used to be? So loving, so kind! When they prattle on about Christmas—more than a month away! Will I even live to see it?—and try to coax me into revealing what presents I will give them, I lose my temper and snap, *"A nice sharp knife like Jack the Ripper's!"* and watch their little eyes fill with tears and terror before they run away from me, the man who used to play for hours with them on the nursery floor and buy them licorice and toffee apples. *My God, how I have changed!* I don't know myself anymore! God help me, even *I* am afraid of *me!*

I keep telling myself I will be better in the spring—the season of rebirth will replenish, renew, and restore me. I will be born again in the spring. It has always been my favorite season. I will feel better when the flowers bloom and the robins sing outside my window. By the time spring comes, I will have made all the wrongs right. We will be a happy family again and lead a happy life.

The wife-whore has sent me a letter, a long and lovely letter that brought tears to my eyes. She begs my forgiveness for all her mistakes, the debts and Alfred Brierley; *more than anything* she wants us to make a new start. We've said the same things so many times before, dare we make one more attempt? That's what I want too— a *new* start! *New Life, New Love, Love Renewed! Oh, Bunny, my dear, precious Bunny, you've awakened springtime in my heart!*

I will give up Mary Jane, fond of my ginger tart though I am. I hate to leave her in the lurch, but we *must* part. Fishmonger Joe has already walked out on her and the rent is nearly thirty shillings in arrears, and Uncle John is losing his patience.

Fishmonger Joe caught her in bed with another whore, her friend Julia, "havin' a harmless little frolic, not hurtin' a soul," Mary Jane protested. They'd even offered to let him join in, moving over to make room between their naked bodies, stroking their nipples and spreading their thighs wide to entice him, but he demurred. "He's such a prude, Joe is!" Mary Jane snorted with contempt as she related the details of their parting. He'd been so angry he'd punched his fist through one of the windowpanes to keep himself from striking her and wouldn't even linger long enough for her to bind his wounds.

I want to do something for my spicy ginger tart. I have destroyed four whores; let me now save one. I think I shall see if I can find the money to pay her passage back to Ireland, to give her a fresh start too in a land of green that reminds me of spring. I've heard her more than once before warning young girls, "Whatever you do, don't you do wrong, an' end up like me." She's only twenty-six; it's not *too late* for her to change her life. She's clever enough to crawl out of the gutter and *stay out!*

I'M GOING TO MAKE EVERYTHING ALL RIGHT!!!

I WILL ATONE FOR ALL MY SINS!!!

I'm tired of being Jack the Ripper. I want to throw my knife in the Thames and vanish into the fog as *suddenly* as I appeared.

I'm tired of being James Maybrick too. I'm just tired. *TIRED, TIRED, TIRED!* I can't *STAND* the strain or the pain anymore! *God help me! IT'S KILLING ME!* Lightning bolts stab my brain, the rats gnaw, and my bowels and belly churn and burn like Hell is already inside me! I feel the demons' pitchforks stabbing; they spin my innards around like noodles upon a fork! *GOD HELP ME!*

I JUST WANT IT TO STOP!!!

MY GOD, WHAT HAVE I DONE?
WHAT HAVE I DONE?
OH GOD, WHAT HAVE I DONE?

When I opened my eyes, I thought I had lost my mind. I thought I was lying naked in a slaughterhouse, embracing a hunk of dead meat, a freshly slaughtered cow, but, God help me, it was Mary Jane. Blood gummed my lashes and flies buzzed in my ears. Sticky redness blinded me; I could hardly see. Blood was in my nose, in my mouth, in my hair, covering my whole body as though I had bathed in it. All was red in Mary's Jane room. The walls ran red with gore.

I wanted to believe it was all a bad dream. A nightmare from which I would soon awaken. I wanted to forget, but it was all coming back to me . . .

Walking in the rain, wishing it would cool my fever . . .

"Come along, my dear; you will be comfortable. . . ." My spicy ginger tart leading me back to her room, undressing me, and, for me, lying down, opening her legs, all juicy and pink. . . .

She was drunk and sleeping. She never had a chance to scream. When I plunged the knife in I saw her green eyes open wide with fright and surprise, over the edge of the sheet, just like I had first seen them staring at me over a newspaper. *"Oh . . . murder . . ."* she gasped, that and nothing more, as her head lolled back and the blood gushed out. She lay back unabashedly for her new lover—

Death—limp with limbs a-sprawl. My ginger tart . . . she surrendered *so easily* to the knife . . . no fight at all.

All the Devil in me must have come out to play. . . .

Her lovely face was gone. I—it *had* to be me—had cut it away in strips. Only her death-glazed green eyes, staring up blindly at the blood-spattered ceiling, and her long ginger-gold hair, sopping up the blood like a sponge, remained to show that she had once been human, not just a butchered beast. Her breasts, nose, and ears were on the table, beside the bloody heap of her intestines, and other piles, blobs, mounds, and strips of flesh I couldn't and didn't even try to identify. What did it matter? Even if I could put it all back together, like a jigsaw puzzle of flesh, it would not bring her back. Her liver lay between her feet, knees bent, thighs agape, as though she had just given birth to it and her cunt had spit it out in a bloody mass onto the sheets. Her thigh was bared to the bone, nicked by my knife, like someone carving a notch for every lover. Her left hand reached into her empty abdomen, like a greedy child groping for some hidden prize, but there was nothing left. . . . Blood dripped like red rain to pool on the floor beside and beneath the bed. The thin mattress was soaked through, dyed red, the harlot's color, saturated, still wet, with it. I had even—it must have been me, though I cannot remember actually doing it—scrawled my wife's initials, a crude *FM,* written in blood on the wall amidst the spatter. Will anyone even notice it amongst so much blood and carnage?

> *And all the Queen's horses,*
> *And all the Queen's men,*
> *Can never put this harlot together again!*

I *had* to kill her. I know that now. It could never end any other way. She was the mirror and I had to break her. She was the medium who resurrected the whores I killed and brought them back to haunt me, to rattle their phantom chains and stand at the foot of my bed to rob me of peace and rest. I couldn't close my eyes without seeing them. I couldn't stand to look at myself anymore in the green mirror of her eyes. The women I killed I thought were worthless, human dross no one gave a damn about, penny fuckers who would even spread their legs for a stale loaf of bread if you offered it to them, but *she* made them *real;* through her own peculiar Irish-Welsh witchcraft, her storyteller's tongue, she made them live again. She made me see them as something more, women more worthy of pity than scorn. Some of them had fought to redeem themselves. Even if they ultimately failed, *they had tried!* The earnest attempt counted for far more than the failure! She showed me how life's misfortunes had made them what they were when I, Jack the Ripper, mighty, invincible, with my arsenic and my nice sharp knife, made them pay for another woman's crimes, crimes she might never have committed had I been a better husband.

She was the mirror and I had to break her. I couldn't stand to look at myself anymore, mirrored in uncanny green. Jack the Ripper masquerading as a gentle man—a gentleman—reflected in the emerald mirror of her Irish eyes! I saw a condemned man every time I looked in them. I saw my jury of four, my jury of whores— Polly, Annie, Liz, and Katie—declaring me guilty, damning me to Hell, every time. Some people believe that when someone dies violently the last thing they see is imprinted upon the retinas of their eyes and a photograph will reveal it. I shudder to think what the police will see if they bring their lights and cameras to photograph Mary Jane's magical green eyes. The coward in me wanted to gouge them out, to grind them like grapes beneath my boot heels, so that could never happen, but I hadn't the heart; I hadn't the right. Let her eyes condemn and damn me; they already have. Even if they don't lead the police to my door, I'm damned. Saucy Jacky is no more!

It was better this way, I tried to console myself as I sat on the edge of that bloody bed weeping and holding her dead hand, feeling her flesh as cold as my own. Drink would have destroyed her beauty all too soon; men are brutal creatures by nature and would not spare her the boot or the fist or their syphilitic cucumbers. She would have lost her teeth and roamed about Whitechapel miserable, drunken, riddled with lice, fleas, and disease, fucking for pennies to drown her sorrows in gin until despair drove her to the river, to suicide, another haggard, ugly whore, sick and old before her time. If not my knife, some other's knife might have killed her, a scorned lover, a pimp who thought she owed him a share of her meager earnings, an abortionist on a bloodstained table in some dark back alley, Fishmonger Joe, or another man like him, who couldn't tolerate her "jolly frolics" with other females. My knife was really the kindest cut of all. In my own way, I loved her.

In the fireplace I burned the green stockings and the fancy bonnet I had given her. I took some old clothes her laundress-whore friend had left behind and added them to the blaze. I couldn't risk these pretty bits of greenery being traced back to me. I still had to think of my children.

I took Mary Jane's heart away with me. I held it in my icy, trembling hands and imagined it still beating, pulsing faintly with life, just for me. And some souvenirs: a lock of her hair, the key she was forever misplacing, and a naughty French postcard, superbly hand tinted, the only one she had left to remember her decadent days in Paris by—Mary Jane striking a risqué pose, looking every bit the elegant lady in a mint-green and turquoise satin gown, with her long ladylike white gloves, lace fan, and high-piled mound of gleaming curls garnished with red roses. A saucy, mischievous glow lit up her face as she impishly lifted her skirt high to show she hadn't a stitch on above her red-gartered stockings.

I stood over her and stroked her hair and kissed the bare, bloody bone of her brow. She just stared at me with eyes like cold green glass. I saw accusation, understanding, and tenderness in their glassy, dead emerald depths and *knew* I was forgiven . . . by her . . . but not by me, nor God, I fear; the Devil shall yet claim me as his own. I've a feeling a flaming throne is reserved for me at the left hand of Satan.

I left with the dawn. I left her more naked than naked. More naked than she had ever been in life.

The rage is suddenly all burned out of me. A cold and quivering husk, I stood for a long time gazing down into the black waters of the Thames. I wanted to jump, but I didn't have the courage. There's a poem about despairing whores taking their lives, jumping from the "Bridge of Sighs." They had more courage than I did. My hands were cold and shaking so, I couldn't bring myself to raise the knife and slit my throat. I emptied the contents of my silver box onto my palm, a little mountain of white snow, and swallowed it all, but I've become accustomed; it would take more than that to finish me. It only made the rats in my belly bite harder, sinking their teeth in deep to *gnaw, Gnaw, GNAW.* My eyelids *twitch, Twitch, TWITCH!* If I weren't already mad, I think it would drive me so. My brain and bladder *burn, Burn, BURN! The pains of Hell have got hold of me!* Tears rolled down my face. All I could do was throw my knife in. I watched it flash silver as it fell. The dark waters were the last thing it would ever stab.

Back in my bolt-hole, I mournfully etched her initials—*MJK*—onto the back of my watch. I will never forget her. I will always regret her. In my dreams, she holds me in her arms, my head cradled lovingly against her breast, as she rocks me gently, like a child, strokes my hair, and croons her favorite song:

> *"Scenes of my childhood arise before my gaze,*
> *Bringing recollections of bygone happy days,*
> *When down in the meadow in childhood I would roam;*
> *No one's left to cheer me now within that good old home.*
> *Father and mother they have passed away.*
> *Sister and brother now lay beneath the clay;*
> *But while life does remain, to cheer me I'll retain*
> *This small violet I pluck'd from Mother's grave.*
>
> *"Only a violet I pluck'd when but a boy,*
> *And oft times when I'm sad at heart, this flow'r has*
>   *given me joy,*
> *But while life does remain, in memoriam I'll retain*
> *This small violet I pluck'd from Mother's grave.*
>
> *"Well I remember my dear old mother's smile,*
> *As she used to greet me when I returned from toil;*
> *Always knitting in the old armchair,*
> *Father used to sit and read for all us children there.*
> *But now all is silent around the good old home,*
> *They all have left me in sorrow here to roam;*
> *While life does remain, in memoriam I'll retain*
> *This small violet I pluck'd from Mother's grave.*

THE RIPPER'S WIFE   207

> *"Only a violet I pluck'd when but a boy,*
> *And ofttimes when I'm sad at heart, this flow'r has*
> *   given me joy,*
> *But while life does remain, in memoriam I'll retain*
> *This small violet I pluck'd from Mother's grave."*

But she was the mirror and I had to break her. I couldn't stand to look at myself anymore! Wherever she is, Mary Jane will know the truth by now, and I *know* she will understand. Who was it—some author, though I cannot recall the name or the book—who said that God sometimes sends us the strangest angels; we never know they have been to visit us until after they're gone. Mary Jane Kelly was undoubtedly one of the *strangest* angels the Lord ever sent, an angel masquerading as a whore for a murderer masquerading as a gentle man. She ended Jack the Ripper's bloody reign. The Autumn of Terror is over; winter is about to fall.... I killed the messenger, *God's messenger* . . . **GOD HELP ME!** Shall I live to see springtime? I buried her heart by moonlight at the base of the flowering may, the hawthorn tree, in our garden. Sometimes I look out and fancy I see her standing there . . . watching, waiting for me . . . keeping vigil . . . my saucy ginger tart angel . . . *Why didn't you tell me God, not the Devil, sent you?*

❧ 22 ❧

In November he killed again—Jack the Ripper, the faceless fiend who slashed his knife and chased me through my dreams. She was young and fair, an Irish girl, twenty-six, the same age as me. Mary Jane Kelly, that was her name. The papers said her lover could only identify her by her hair and eyes after he was done with her. Before he cut off her face, I wonder, did she in any way resemble me? He butchered her on the very bed she took him to, thinking only of his lust and money, not blood and butchery. What risks we women take! What savage carnage wrought on one only seeking coinage! He left her lying there naked, stripped of her very skin. How he must have *hated* her, or someone, very much.

I could not keep my breakfast down after reading the papers. I vomited everything back up and ran upstairs, dots dancing before my eyes, like fireworks doing the polka, and flung myself onto the bed May had only just finished making with only seconds to spare before I swooned. I lay there for *hours,* not daring to move, the flat of my palm resting on my queasy, fluttering belly, my heart galloping as though it were determined to win the Grand National.

God had seen fit to punish me, by sending me that which I most feared. I was pregnant again and I had no idea who the father was—Jim, Edwin, or Alfred. I'd been so distracted these last few months, maybe I forgot to insert the little sponge or a womb veil, or maybe it failed me? Maybe it happened one of those times when I was taken by surprise and the seed was already planted before I could even try to uproot it with a caustic douche? If I even remembered to do that? There were days when I felt as though my head would float away like a hot-air balloon if it weren't tethered by skin and bone to my neck! Just trying to sort it all out made my head feel like it was swimming in syrup!

I tried to undo the pregnancy, with the most powerful, stinging douche I dared. I pilfered a tiny, tiny pinch of Jim's arsenic even though it scared me so and added that to the mixture. In the privacy of my pink and ivory bathroom, I lay huddled on my side, next to the tub, with my knees drawn up tight, holding on to them as though for dear life, the bathroom tiles cold as ice beneath my burning body, and stuffed a towel into my mouth so no one would hear my screams and cried and cried. I nearly burned my insides out. It felt as though Satan himself had struck a Lucifer Match inside my womb!

When the blood began to trickle I thought I had done it, that everything would be all right. I lay flat on my back, gasping with relief and the last lingering vestiges of the unmerciful pain that had mercifully rid my womb of its unwanted burden, softly sobbing as I shakily applied great daubs of cold cream to my stinging, raw lady parts.

But the blood was only the result of irritation; I'd simply scalded that most delicate skin bloody raw. My womb was not void of its terrible, unwanted burden after all. I had heard horrible stories about desperate women who resorted to the knitting needle when all else failed, but I didn't have the courage to chance it. Bobo and Gladys needed me, and I *had* to go on living for their sake. I could only pray that after God's punishment would come a small mercy and He would see me through the horrors of childbed one more time.

I knew I would have to tell Jim soon, before my face and belly began to exhibit the telltale roundness. I would keep my secret as long as I could, but all I could really do was hope and pray that my baby would not be born a miniature mirror image of Alfred Brier-ley. Thank heaven for small mercies and I didn't have to worry about any resemblance to Edwin. That would be entirely under-standable and wouldn't cause even one single eyelash to flicker, as all the Maybrick men had brown-black hair and similar features.

❧ 23 ❧

THE DIARY

I've tried three times to kill myself. But I am still alive. Suicide seems the only honorable thing to do. Bunny and the children will think it was an accident. I take so many dangerous medicines, it should be quite simple. There would be no shame to blacken their names, and perhaps, someday, they will look back and remember their "poor Jim," "poor father," with kindness. But each time I quaked with cowardice and reached for the charcoal, the bone black, and saved myself at the last instant. I've journeyed to the threshold of death, only to falter and turn back.

There are moments when all I want to do is die and others when I want, with all my heart, to live. A little voice in my head says that if Jack the Ripper were brought to trial he would be executed, so my taking my life is only Justice donning a different cap; it wouldn't *truly* be suicide and a sin but an *execution*. I think that little voice is right. I want to heed to it. It will not be quieted and needles at me so, sharper than the delicious pinch of the hypodermic. I know, in my heart, ignoring it is wrong; it is the Voice of Righteousness, the Voice of God. But I haven't the courage to be my own executioner, so I just lie here, my guilty heart swollen sore with remorse so that each sluggish beat is a torment to me, and pray that soon it will stop.

Every night and day I pray that God will give me the courage to die. But I just *can't* do it! It seems so simple; arsenic and strychnine have slain so many, through mishap and malice, but it's not; *it's not!* Oh God, it's so damned difficult! I took their lives, callously, without regard, but I *cannot* take my own!

It fills me with horror to contemplate the knife-wielding monster, the maniac, I let myself become. Everyone believed me the kindest, the gentlest, and the most loving of men. Edwin always used to joke that I would not even suffer them to use flypapers in the kitchen to kill innocent flies. What would he say if he knew I had murdered five harlots? I fooled them all, but I can no longer laugh about it. It *sickens* me to look back on what I have written and know that monster was me and that he still lives because I lack the courage to kill—to execute—him.

Christmas was *dreadful!* The beast is still alive in the black heart of me. At our Christmas Ball, I saw Alfred Brierley lay his hand on Bunny's bare shoulder and lean and whisper something in her ear as she lit the candles on the Christmas tree.

When Bunny and I had bid good night to the last of our guests, I swooped her up in my arms, carried her upstairs, tore off her gown, ripped the jewels from her neck and the pearls from her hair, and *beat, Beat, BEAT* her! I didn't stop there; I raced into my study, flung open the safe. I marvel now that my *cold, Cold, COLD, numb, Numb, NUMB* hands and my *hot, Hot, HOT* head had the wits to unlock it. I brandished my will in her face.

"Do you know what this is?" I taunted.

I tore it up, scattering the pieces like snowflakes in her hair. I left the bitch penniless, and then I flung her to the floor and *fucked, Fucked, FUCKED* her harder than I have *ever* fucked a whore before.

As I crouched over her, mercilessly pounding her bleeding cunt, pulling her hair, *relishing* every plea and whimper, feeling blood trickle through her hair to warm my cold, numb fingers, suddenly I chanced to look up. I saw four little white feet innocent as doves. Bobo and Gladys were standing hand in hand in the doorway in their white nightgowns.

With a cry like a dying animal I wrenched myself—*my monstrous self!*—off their mother and fled into my study. I locked myself in. I gulped brandy straight from the decanter and swallowed every potion, powder, and pill I could find. I tried to end my life again, but, at the last crucial instant, the bone black beckoned and the coward in me reached out like a drowning man to grasp it and let it pull me back to life—Sweet, Horrible, Wonderful, Wicked Life!

❧ 24 ❧

Was there ever a more *wretched* Christmas and *unhappy* New Year? Alfred was at our Christmas Ball, vying with Edwin to see who could be the most attentive, both of them clinging to me like ivy vines. I couldn't turn my head without my garnet earbobs flying out to slap one or the other of them in the face as my hand was itching to do. Jim, thank goodness, had always been stone blind to Edwin's ardor, but he might as well have been looking at Alfred Brierley through a telescope.

Acting as though we were still the most intimate of lovers, Mr. Brierley sidled right up to me and said I had never looked more "breathtakingly beautiful" and he wished he was an artist so he could paint a portrait of me standing there by the candlelit Christmas tree dressed in my sumptuous, artfully draped layers of port-wine red and wintergreen velvet trimmed with deep flounces of creamy lace, with pearls woven through the burnished gold pompadour of my hair and a white dove of peace perched on top and long ringlets cascading down over my shoulders. Once he even reached past me to seemingly admire one of the ornaments and in doing so brushed his hand against my breast. When my nipple instantly perked up, he smiled, so gloating and triumphant that I wanted to slap him.

"You can't deceive me, Florie," he whispered. "I *know* you still love me! See, your own body betrays you!"

Looking across the room at Jim's angry red face, I could see him, sweating and shaking, clenching his fists and quaking, like a pot about to boil over. I don't know how he got through the evening without striking either or both of us. I had *terrible* visions of him hurling himself at Alfred and the two of them falling, knocking over the Christmas tree, and the candles setting the curtains and the whole house afire.

How I dreaded the moment when the last good-bye was said and I was left alone with Jim. I prayed to God that the morning sun would find me still alive.

Jim gave me his worst, as I knew he would. After beating me bloody he ran and got his will from the safe, rolled the parchment into a tube, and beat me about the head and shoulders with it, then tore it into confetti and flung it in my face and said I'd seen and spent the last penny I would ever have from him. Then he hurled me flat, onto the floor, so hard I lost my breath along with my senses and awoke moments later to the most excruciating pounding, piercing pain and to the even more painful sight of my poor, innocent children standing in the doorway seeing for the first time in their innocent little lives that the act of love can also be an act of violence.

I felt so shamed before their wide-open eyes that I had to shut mine and turn my face to the wall. I was so ashamed to have them see me, see us, their father and mother, that way that I just wanted to die.

It was that exact same sight, and realization no doubt, that tore Jim from me as violently as though God Himself had reached down from Heaven and yanked him off me. Bawling like a baby, he ran and locked himself in his study, and it was up to me to drag my bloody, battered body off the floor, tug together the tatters of my gown, and force myself to smile and reassure the children as I led them back to bed.

The next morning I awoke to a bloody discharge trickling from between my thighs. When it persisted and grew heavier and I began to feel pains quite unlike those that often accompany the onset of a lady's monthly, I had to summon Dr. Hopper. I just couldn't lie there and let myself bleed to death; my children needed me! Before I let him examine me, I made him promise not to tell Jim. I said he didn't know and it would be just too great a blow if he were to discover that in chastising me he had also murdered our unborn child. There was no telling what he might do, and I wanted to spare him.

As I lay there, knees open and bent, my nightgown turned up over my bruise-mottled stomach, silently submitting to Dr. Hopper's ministrations, I never thought a day would come when I would find myself actually grateful for a beating.

❧ 25 ❧

THE DIARY

I am still he; he is still me. *GOD HELP ME!* I thought myself freed of this demon!

"For I know that in me (that is, in my flesh) dwelleth no good thing: for to will is present with me; but how to perform that which is good I find not. For the good that I would I do not: but the evil which I would not do, that I do. Now if I do that I would not, it is no more I that do it, but sin that dwelleth in me."

I was dreaming, of a red waterfall, a waterfall of blood, and Mary Jane, waiting, on the other side of that red river for me. The other whores were there too, pointing the finger of blame, rattling their chains.

I awoke. It was as though my soul floated above the bed where my numb body lay, paralysis slowly overtaking my limbs, limbs I saw and commanded to move but no longer felt. I rose. I dressed. I went out. Because I was so weak, Michael didn't think he needed to lock me in. I am visiting him again, to see a new doctor. I wanted to shout, *NO!* I wanted to shake and slap myself awake. But I was *powerless,* and I was awake yet not, I think, awake. On and on my body moved, no longer mine to command, wholly in the demon's power.

She was a short little woman, a widow in black, as round as a barrel. "Victoria, like Our Gracious Queen," she said her name was. Another whore with a tale of woe: driven onto the streets in dire need with seven kiddies at home to feed. Her black hair was striped with broad bands of gray. I wanted to laugh. It reminded me of my gray-and-black-striped cravat. She leaned forward and flipped her skirts up, revealing a fat, rosy pink, dimpled bum.

The phantom shade of Mary Jane must have slapped me awake. I awoke from my trance and stood there dumb and blinking with a knife, taken from Michael's kitchen, glinting in my hand, not knowing where I was. The questioning glance, from over her shoulder, turned to one of sheer fright. She screamed. My skeleton nearly leapt out of my skin. I do believe I was as scared as she was. I dropped the knife and fled into the night.

I am still he; he is still me. *Oh God, what can I do?* I thought it was in my power to stop him! But the fiend I have made incarnate, the demon I have summoned up from the bowels of Hell and given a name, is still alive. . . .

I awakened in my bed, in Michael's house, the next morning. Mud and manure tracked across the carpet told me I did not just dream it . . . it was all most terrifyingly *real!*

❧ 26 ❧

When my body had healed and I could safely show myself in public again, I defiantly rekindled my romance with Alfred Brierley. Our passion for each other must have been the most stubborn, tenacious flame that ever burned. It just would *not* die out; try and douse it though we might, it persisted, flickering, sputtering, and flaring. One or the other of us just kept fanning the flame, keeping it alive; we might as well have been throwing kerosene on it for all the good it did us.

We were seen together at the races in a pose some might call at best unwise and at worst compromising.

We'd all gone down to Aintree for the fiftieth anniversary of the running of the Grand National. Everyone who was anyone would be there, including the Prince of Wales. Jim and I were making a party of it with Edwin, Alfred Brierley, the Samuelsons, and Mrs. Briggs and her unfortunate husband, Horace.

Some mischief-maker with a camera took a photograph of Alfred and me, by intent or by chance, I'm still not entirely certain. They captured us standing close together, much *too* close apparently for it to be quite socially seemly. My kid-gloved hand was resting intimately on his arm, and we were staring into each other's faces with raw and naked yearning. His hand, in elegant dove-gray kid, was resting lightly on the waist of my periwinkle-blue linen suit, fingers fanning down to lightly graze my hip.

The photographer printed out a copy and sent it to Jim suggesting he might like to have the negative, for a mere pittance of course, as though any sum with three zeros following a comma and a two-digit number could be accounted a pittance by anyone whose last name wasn't Vanderbilt.

"Damn it, but I will *not!*" Jim declared, and balled the letter up and flung it into the fire.

I was proud of him for refusing to pay it.

I suggested he brazen it out and paste the picture in our album to show the world how much it truly did *not* matter, that some greedy fool was just trying to stir up a tempest in a teapot where none existed and Mr. Brierley and I had just been sharing a joke about the Prince of Wale's latest amour. I'd said I would not sit so close to a man with such a notoriously gargantuan appetite if I were wearing a whole stuffed pheasant on my hat lest his stomach feel a grumble and he be tempted to reach up and tear off a wing. We were, after all, friends, we'd been sitting together in the same box, so really what was the harm of our strolling out together?

Jim was still smarting about it when we sat down to play cards with the Samuelsons that evening. I wondered idly if Christina was still bedding down with him, but I was long past caring if she was. I had Alfred, after all. Jim could do what he liked, with Mad Sarah, Christina, or any other willing party. I knew now that peace would never reign within our marriage. Fidelity, like honesty, was an unattainable dream.

The truth was we were both just *too* weak. Neither of us could make a promise and stick to it. We'd tried and tried and failed and failed each and every time. Jim couldn't stop striking me, beating me bloody black-and-blue, anytime he was of half a mind to; his promises of "never again" had long ago lost all meaning. He wasn't willing to renounce the medicines that brought out the beast in him, and I couldn't stop shopping or keep out of Alfred Brierley's bed, at least not for long. We were just treading water, and we all knew it. We'd just have to own up to our failure and figure out the right way to end it. I'd written to Mama about that last beating and the destruction of Jim's will and told her that as long as the children were provided for nothing else mattered; I didn't care.

Jim sat gloomy and glowering over his cards, displaying none of his usual charm. His eyes were dull and dead, and he never once smiled or even lifted a finger to stroke his diamond horseshoe. Mr. Samuelson either was too big of a fool to realize anything was awry or gave such a fine impression of being one that the stage was surely much poorer without his presence. He was clearly far more interested in a crystal dish filled with pretty fruit-shaped marzipan candies than he was in the flirty eyes his wife was flashing at my husband. Alfred and I kept quiet and mechanically played our cards. Only Christina was her usual giddy, giggling, simpering self, full of gossipy prattle, so annoying at times I wondered how all of us had the restraint not to shout at her to just *SHUT UP!* When the game was *finally* over and she had lost, Christina, with her typical redhead temper, burst into tears and threw her cards in her husband's face and cried, *"I HATE YOU!"* and fled the room in a flurry of tears and teal taffeta.

Poor Mr. Samuelson sat there blinking in astonishment, cheeks puffed out with marzipan and a lot of bewildered hurt in his big innocent blue eyes. I felt so sorry for him that I just *had* to reach out and say kindly, "You mustn't think anything of it; I say 'I hate you' to Jim all the time." Words I would later come to regret; sometimes a kindness given freely ends up costing us dearly.

In April we were invited to a masquerade ball at the Wellington Rooms; it was to be the event of the season. Every dressmaker and tailor in town was worn to a shadow trying to meet the demand for costumes, each more elaborate and fanciful than the last, with every member of the Currant Jelly Set vying to outdo the rest.

Jim had taken to his bed again, moaning that this was surely the end and he would never rise again. I don't mean to sound dispassionate, but it was the same old talk of cold hands and feet, numbness, paralysis, migraines, and bellyaches, and more than I wished to know about the state of any person's stools, including my own. Our parlor had become like a waiting room for doctors; one would be going out while the maid was going in to announce to Dr. So-

and-So that Mr. Maybrick would see him now. Even when Jim had their prescriptions in hand, he did nothing but criticize and disparage them and triple every dosage as though he knew better.

When he heard about the ball, Jim determined to rouse himself and summoned his tailor to make him a matador's gilt-encrusted *Traje de Luces,* Suit of Lights.

I bit my tongue, to keep from saying, *Darling, do you* really *think that's the right costume for you?* Though he was ailing, Jim's paunch was still as prominent as a watermelon. In fact, he complained more than ever of "bloating pains" in his belly, so I just couldn't quite picture him striding boldly into a bullring in a pair of skin-tight trousers that betrayed every bulge. But he was so like a little boy in his newfound enthusiasm, smiling and sitting up and taking an interest for once in something besides his health, that I just couldn't bear to spoil it. So I just smiled and said I thought that was a "grand idea." And for a few—*too few!*—heavenly days he was once again the man I had fallen in love with aboard the *Baltic,* the same charming overgrown boy whose smile lit up a room. My heart and arms reached out to hug him, and I just couldn't help but love him.

"You know, Bunny," he said to me, "this costume has filled my mind with thoughts of sunny Spain. I'm sure if there's *any* place in the world where I could recover my health it's there. Just think of it, Bunny. We could rent a place by the sea, with a garden filled with orange trees, and I could sit and soak up the sun like a lizard and glut myself on oranges! What say you?" He reached for my hand and squeezed it. "Shall we take a trip? We've not had one since our honeymoon."

"Oh yes, Jim, yes!" I cried, and let myself be caught up in the fantasy of "one more chance" one more time.

My emotions were such an excited bundle, it was no wonder my face broke out in blemishes. I looked everywhere I could think of, but I simply could not find the prescription Dr. Greggs had given me ages ago in New York. Despite my initial fear of it, that facial wash had worked better than anything I had tried before or since to eradicate those unsightly pimples.

I have always had a good memory and I thought I remembered

the ingredients well enough to attempt to replicate it, so I sent to the druggist for the necessary ingredients—elderflower water and tincture of benzoin. Of course there was arsenic aplenty in Jim's medicine cabinet, but the very thought of it made my skin crawl. Even though I had pilfered a pinch for my attempt at abortion, I was still scared of the stuff. I was afraid that what seemed a small pinch to me might in reality be *too much* and I might end by ruining my skin. I had *horrible* visions of the stuff burning like acid, gnawing my face away down to the pearly white bones. And I didn't like to ask the druggist, fearing his smirk and knowing eyes or a flip comment that Mr. Maybrick should know better than anyone. So I decided to improvise. I remembered a trick I had seen young girls in Germany and Switzerland employ to create similar concoctions. So I ordered some flypapers and soaked them in a basin of water to release a mild and much-diluted dose of arsenic that I could then add the benzoin and elderflower to.

I thought I had done the right thing until I walked in one day after a fitting with Mrs. Osborne for my costume, a lovely re-creation of the billowing peach gown and shepherdess straw hat worn by the lady on the swing in the famous Fragonard painting, and caught Nanny Yapp in my room peeping under the towel that I had draped over the basin to prevent the solution from evaporating. I was in no mood to be trifled with. I stamped my foot and ordered her out. The next thing I knew she was downstairs in the kitchen, gossiping with the maids, their heads together like criminals plotting over their teacups.

By the evening of the ball, Jim was too ill to accompany me after all. When I said I would stay home and nurse him he wouldn't hear of it and insisted that Edwin go in his stead and the tailor was hastily summoned to take in the green and gold Suit of Lights to fit the still slender Edwin. I must say it suited him splendidly! But the way he looked at me with that devilish grin and matching gleam in his eyes and that unmistakable velvet-covered bulge in his breeches pointing at me, I *knew* what was coming.

But I was *so angry* at Jim for disappointing me, and even though he was lying there with a grayish-green tinge to his face, moaning like a cat in heat, I stamped my foot and pouted and cried and then

I grabbed Edwin by the arm and yanked him out the door, shouting back at Jim, "All right, I'm going to the ball. I'm going to drink champagne, dance, and enjoy myself, and not spare a single thought for you, just like you told me to. I'm going to have such a good time that I wouldn't mind dancing with Jack the Ripper himself, much less Edwin!"

"Why, Florie, I'm flattered!" Edwin smiled and sidled closer.

"Don't be!" I snapped. "I didn't intend it as a compliment!"

On the way to the Wellington Ballroom, the fool actually tried to make love to me in the carriage. He flung my full, billowy skirts up over my head and wrested off my frilly pink-beribboned drawers and tossed them out the window. I slapped his face and shoved him off me, stuffed my breasts back into my bodice—it was cut so low that they had popped out during our tussle—and snatched off one of my peach satin slippers and brandished it at him like a weapon, threatening to knock a hole right in the center of his forehead with the heel if he dared touch me again. Edwin just sat and stared at me, then flung himself back against the seat cushions laughing to such a degree I feared—and almost hoped, as then we really would have to turn back—that he would burst the back seam of his skintight breeches.

In spite of my boastful words, I did *not* have a good time at the ball. It was *dreadful!* The whole time I was there all I wanted to do was go home. Alfred was cooling toward me again and doling out his attention freely, like a king dispensing alms, amongst the Currant Jelly belles. He seemed not to have one smile to spare for me and, try as I might, I just could not get him alone, nor could I shake off Edwin. The fool should have come dressed as an octopus instead of a matador—he really was all arms that night, and back in the carriage it was more of the same thing. Finally I just gave up struggling and let him have me. It really wasn't worth fighting about. I knew that just as soon as he had spent his lust he would stop pestering me. "Have your way and be done with it!" I cried. And he did, rutting and grunting like a wild animal as the wheels of the coach rolled on, bearing us back to unbearable Battlecrease House.

When I crept in to check on Jim I was greatly alarmed. His breathing seemed so labored and, in the gentle golden glow of the lamplight, there was a distinctly cadaverous appearance about his face. His head against the pillows looked like it had been carved out of wax, like something straight out of Madame Tussaud's Chamber of Horrors.

Icy fingers of fear gripped my heart and I burst into tears and flung myself against my husband's body, clinging to him desperately and taking comfort in feeling the rise and fall of his chest and hearing his heart, still beating.

"*Please,* Jim, *please* get well! I *need* you! I *love* you!" I cried. "Think of Spain, sunshine and oranges! Our new start! *Please,* don't leave me; don't ever leave me! I'm sorry for *everything!*"

Despite his pain, Jim smiled at me.

"There, there, Bunny," he whispered. "You mustn't worry. I've *never,* no matter what I've said and done, stopped loving you for an instant. I sometimes think this pain I'm suffering now is God's punishment for the pain I've caused you. But I shall soon be well, God is merciful, and I've been praying for His forgiveness. It's spring you know, my favorite season. And you know what spring means—rebirth and renewal—and I hope, I pray, it may be so with us. . . ."

"It will, *it will!*" I cried fervently. "It *will! Everything's* going to be all right; I just *know* it!"

And in that moment I believed it. I wanted it so bad I could almost taste the morsel of our future happiness melting like fine chocolate upon my tongue even as Fate hovered nearby threatening to snatch it away. I curled myself up into a little ball at Jim's side, laid my head on his shoulder, and held him tight, trying to will him well, to send some of my strength into his body. I didn't leave him again until morning's first light.

❧ 27 ❧

THE DIARY

I've taken to my bed. I shall never rise again. Doctors come; doctors go. They dose and poke, prod, and purge me. Syringes—for veins and anus. I am pumped full of drugs, except the *one* I crave *most*—they stint so on the arsenic, and I am too weak to reach my private store!

Morphine suppositories, hydrate of potash, bromides and bicarbonates, Fowler's Solution, nux vomica, potassium salts, soda water and milk, mustard in steaming-hot water to soak my ice-cold feet and purge my stomach, double doses of bismuth and brandy, Tincture of Jaborandi, Extract of Aloes and Chamomile Flowers, sulphur lozenges, laudanum, Du Barry's Revalenta, chlorodyne, Valentine's Meat Juice, Neave's Invalid Food, prussic acid, lemonade gargles, celery nerve tonic, liver pills, antipyrine, enemas, and even leeches.

Dear Edwin sneaks me sips of champagne on the sly and assures me I will soon be better.

Why can't I have my arsenic and strychnine tablets? I grow weaker and weaker without them, but the fools won't give me any no matter how much I beg and plead. Michael says it is very ill becoming of me to behave in such a whining, petulant manner, like a tot throwing a tantrum because he is denied a toffee apple. I'm *dying, Dying, DYING* for want of arsenic! But all they will let me have is just a little sip, a very tiny, tiny, tiny, minuscule, occasional sip, of Fowler's Solution that only tantalizes me.

They hover together like a flock of blackbirds in their black coats for their consultations; they argue and contradict one another, blabbering about inferior sherry and chronic dyspepsia, indiscreet dining, a chill from when I was caught out in the rain last time I went to the races, or too vigorous a toweling at the Turkish baths. Have you *ever* in your entire life heard *anything* more absurd? Death by toweling in a Turkish bath! Each one thinks *he* knows better than the rest. Bunny weeps, Edwin frowns and rages, "I tell you it's those damn strychnine pills; he's been taking them like candy!," and Michael glowers and summons more doctors.

My legs are as stiff and useless as dead things. They lie there stretched out before me, rigid as steel bars.

It's May outside, but my windows are shut tight. "Nature," John Calvin so rightly said, "is a shining garment in which God is revealed and concealed." But not revealed to me . . . only concealed. . . . The velvet curtains are drawn tight against the fresh, sweet air, blue skies, and sunlight. My children will never again grab me one by each hand and pull me out to walk in the park, to fly kites, chase hoops, and sail toy boats, feed the birds and squirrels, and buy them toffee apples and ices—lemon for Bobo, raspberry for Gladys. The next time my little girl brings me a bouquet of bright flowers it will be to lay upon my grave.

Outside my window, Gladys and her little chums are skipping rope. I hear God's voice in the nonsense rhyme they are chanting and it brings me a peculiar kind of peace:

> "Jack the Ripper's dead,
> He's lying on his bed.
> He cut his throat
> With Sunlight Soap,
> Jack the Ripper's dead!"

I pray God she will never know, that a day will never come when she looks back with those heart-melting violet eyes and remembers herself as a six-year-old child, in bouncing black ringlets, big satin hair bow, button boots, and purple plaid frock, and realizes just how *close* she came to the truth:

> Jack the Ripper's dead,
> He's lying on his bed,
> He hasn't the courage to
>   cut his throat,
> But Jack the Ripper's dead.

Today will be the last time I confide my thoughts to this loyal diary. I've made up my mind, I am going to give it to Bunny to read and reveal to her in all his blood-crazed jealous madness the Jekyll and Hyde monster she married. Afterward, I will most humbly implore her forgiveness and *beg* her to find the courage and strength to do what I cannot and kill me.

A public trial and execution would destroy our children; they would be forever tainted, tarred and feathered, as the accursed spawn of Jack the Ripper. But Justice *must* be done. I *cannot* suffer the beast inside me to go on living, and he *will* as long as I draw breath. Bunny must be brave and kill the husband she once loved; it's the *only* way.

This diary I will ask her to hide away, somewhere secret and safe, and hope someday, long after Bunny and my dear children have departed this earth, when the truth can no longer touch or hurt anyone I once loved, someone will find it and those who read it will understand that love can make sane men mad and turn a gentle man into a fiend and they will find it in their hearts to forgive me.

God have mercy upon my sorry, tormented soul, grant my guilty heart peace and my unquiet spirit eternal rest, forsake me not, instead *forgive,* and remember the gentle man I was before love's madness made me into a monster.

Signed, for the **LAST** time, in red, for my heart's blood and in memoriam of that I have spilled, from the depths of my guilty heart . . .

Yours Truly,

Jack the Ripper

❧ 28 ❧

Bicker, bicker, bicker, that's all the doctors did, and all the time Jim just kept on getting sicker and sicker. He was sinking so fast, and no one seemed able to pull him back up. And I was caught right smack in the middle of it. I just didn't know what to do or who to believe. They kept saying words like *gastritis* and *nervous dyspepsia* and *melancholia* and talking about bad sherry and gross indulgences while dining, and pumping more drugs into his poor body through every orifice. He moaned and groaned and tossed in terrible pain, and every time they gave him anything in the way of medicine or food he was sick at one end or the other, sometimes both at the same time. Finally they would let him have nothing to eat but a kind of bottled invalid food, a weak beef broth, called Valentine's Meat Juice, since everything else seemed to disagree with him.

But Jim kept crying for champagne, lemonade, and, most of all, arsenic and strychnine, insisting that he would soon be right as rain if he could only have his "pick-me-up" tonic. But everyone acted like they were deaf and dumb, as though my poor husband were a man deranged by delirium crying out some vile obscenity that it was best to ignore for propriety's sake.

In desperation, I sought advice in Jim's own medical books.

When I found a passage suggesting that sudden and complete deprivation could be deadly to a man accustomed to arsenic eating and brought it to the physicians' attention they just smiled at me, patted my hand, and said I must put my trust in them and advised me to try to calm my nerves with needlework and prayer.

Michael came up from London, *furious* that I hadn't called in more doctors and nurses; it was obvious Jim was in need of more specialized care than Liverpool could provide. When Edwin interjected that it was "those damn strychnine pills; he's been killing himself with them!" Michael snapped at him to be quiet: "When you attain a medical degree I will be pleased to consider your opinion, but until then I will thank you to keep your mouth shut!" Poor Edwin just stood there blinking and baffled; he'd only been trying to help, and what he'd said made a lot more sense than any of the doctors' prattle about inferior sherry and too vigorous a toweling at the Turkish baths.

Mrs. Briggs agreed with Michael that I was quite incompetent and flooded his ear with tales about the "slipshod fashion" in which this household was run, then proceeded to take full charge. Then I looked out a window and saw Nanny Yapp in the garden gesticulating wildly, talking urgently to Edwin. Later I came across the two of them, with Mrs. Briggs and Michael, huddled in the hallway outside Jim's room thick as thieves. They broke apart at my approach and the looks on their faces almost froze my blood. Suddenly I found myself forbidden access to the sickroom without supervision. There would be times when I would hear Jim calling for me and I would try to go to him and find the door barred against me by a nurse whose features were as hard as her marble heart. "Can't you hear he's calling for me?" I would cry as the door was closed firmly in my face.

I didn't know then, but I had made another mistake. Alfred Brierley had informed me by letter that he had made up his mind once and for all to end everything between us forever and go away to South America. Jim being so ill and me feeling so friendless, alone against Michael, Mrs. Briggs, Nanny Yapp, and the dizzying array of doctors and nurses marching in and out of the house, I just couldn't bear the thought of parting. All I could think about was Alfred lazing away the days amidst coffee beans and brown-skinned beauties wearing little more than beads fanning him with palm leaves. The cold tone of his letter made me long suddenly for the warmth of his body and the comfort of his arms. I know better than any just how horrible that sounds, with my husband lying there sick, maybe even dying, and me weeping and wailing and walking the floors and hardly sleeping, hoping and begging and praying that he would get well, wanting, yet again, to make yet another fresh start. Heavens, but I do look a contrary, contradictory, deceptive, duplicitous female! Even I can see it. Yet the purpose of this memoir is truth, and I cannot deny what I felt, even if that truth shows me in the poorest and most unflattering light.

I had dashed off an impulsive letter to Alfred, to try to stop him from leaving, the words flying from my pen so fast I hardly knew what they said, thrust it into an envelope without giving it a second glance, and told the maid to mail it. She left it lying on the hall table, and it happened that as Nanny Yapp was passing, to take the children out for "their afternoon constitutional," she saw it. She would later say that she gave it to Gladys to carry and that my little girl, skipping along on the way to the post office, excited about doing this favor for Mama, had dropped it in a mud puddle.

Being the kind, considerate woman that she was, that viper who had nursed at Satan's own teat, Nanny Yapp decided to open my letter and put it in a fresh envelope and in so doing discovered my shameful adultery and decided that it was her "Christian duty" to alert Edwin and Michael, choosing that time to also tell them about the flypapers I had been soaking in my bedroom before the ball.

There had been a dreadful murder case a few years back in which a pair of sinister spinster sisters who ran a rooming house had sent some of their lodgers to the grave with arsenic they obtained by soaking flypapers, and Nanny Yapp leapt to the conclusion that I was no doubt up to the same thing, endeavoring to "hasten the poor master's end," and my "sinful passion for Mr. Brierley" was the reason.

Melodrama had leapt right off the stage and become real life! No wonder they regarded me with suspicion! But I was too overwrought; I couldn't see it through their eyes then, so I missed the chance to take precautions to protect myself. Murder had never even tiptoed to the threshold of my mind at any time! And Jim took so much arsenic himself and was even then lying there in his sickbed bleating for it like a baby for its mother's milk. . . . I thought everyone who knew him, even casually, knew about his habit; he was always whipping out that silver box, dropping a pinch into his wine, and raising his glass to wish everyone "a fine complexion, good health, and longevity!" I was too blind and weary to see it then, but I was playing right into their hands. Michael would see to it that Jim's reputation would be safeguarded at all costs, while my own already-tarnished honor would be sacrificed, even if it meant my life must also be lost. But I didn't know until after . . . and by then it was already too late. . . .

Jim sent for me to sit with him. This time they allowed it. Outside in the hall, where I was left waiting, I heard him arguing with them, demanding would they deny a dying man his final wish, the consolation of what just might be his last meeting with his beloved wife. Michael and Mrs. Briggs tried to speak against me, but Jim, to his credit, would not hear them.

"She's my wife," he said, "and I love her, and I *will* see her *alone—without* busybodies and chaperones!"

And in the end, they let me in.

"Oh, Jim, I'm so afraid!" I cried, clutching at his hands. The skin was gray, cold, and clammy and looked waxy and dead. It was an *awful* thing to hold and part of me wished I didn't have to, but another part of me never wanted to let go.

I bent forward, meaning to kiss him, and nearly vomited right onto his chest. It took *all* my strength to persevere and deliver the intended kiss. His breath was absolutely *fetid*. I'd never smelled anything so foul coming out of a human mouth.

"Oh, Jim!" I sobbed, wishing I had strength and power enough to pull him back to health and life.

"Hush, now," he said, his voice weak and raspy, and squeezed my hand. "It's all for the best." He smiled gently at me, a *real* smile this time that was in his eyes as well as upon his mouth.

"But, Jim," I protested, "when we married we swore for better or worse, in sickness and in health. . . ." And now, when I could see the very life ebbing out of him, I knew I had failed to keep the most important promise of my life, the one I had intended *never* to *ever* break. Yet I had broken it again and again, so many times, and now it was too late to make amends. I had done the unforgivable, and even if Jim could find it in his heart to forgive me I could never forgive myself. In that moment I *hated* Alfred Brierley and Edwin too, but even more than them, those Devil-sent temptations I had succumbed to, I hated myself.

"Hush," Jim said gently, raising, with a mightily trembling hand, my own to his lips and letting his cracked, fever-hot lips linger there. "It doesn't matter now. I forgive you for everything, and I hope you can forgive me—"

"Oh, I do, I do!" I cried. *"Anything! Everything!"*

"Not yet . . ." he said with an adamant shake of his head, "not yet, not until you know . . . all."

It was then that he pushed from beneath the covers a black book. After a moment I recognized it as the diary I had bought for him all those years ago as a happy young bride skipping spontaneously into a stationer's shop to buy a gift for her husband. I'd wanted to give him something for his study, to lie on his desk and to say for me, whenever he touched or looked at it, *I love you* and *I'm thinking of you.* I hadn't seen it since; in my silly, frivolous way, I'd forgotten all about the gift after the pleasurable moment of giving it had passed; I'd had no idea that he had even kept it.

"Before I give you this," he said in a raspy, rough, whisper-soft voice, "you must promise me first that after you've read it, no matter what you think of me, you *must* come back and sit, talk with me again, one last time."

"Of course I will!" I assured him, a trifle baffled as to why he would even ask such a thing. Of course I would come back; I would be with him every moment if only they would let me! How could he think anything written in that silly old book could change that, and at a time like this, when his very life was in peril? It all seemed so absurdly trivial!

Jim shook his head. "This is a promise you *cannot* make lightly, Bunny. If you give your word, you must be fully prepared to keep it, no matter what you find in these pages." He tapped the book's black cover.

"I promise," I said, thinking no doubt that he had chronicled his adulteries, or gambling debts I had no inkling of. But given my own sins, I could surely face his. Knowing the details might hurt, I couldn't deny that, but I could bear the punishment; maybe I even deserved it after the way I had carried on with Alfred Brierley. "I promise faithfully, no matter what you've written, I will come back to you after I've read it."

"Even if you find a monster inside?" he persisted, his eyes boring like nails into mine.

"Even if I meet a monster inside," I promised, "you are *still* my husband, and *I love you,* and I will *always* come back to you, as God is my witness. I mean it, Jim; this is *one* promise I *will* keep!"

Jim nodded, satisfied, and pushed the book across the bed to me.

"Leave me now," he said, "go and read it, and then, come back to me, and, if you can, forgive everything."

"I'll come just as soon as I can." I rose and pressed a kiss onto his brow.

As I reached the door, just as my hand was on the knob, he called out to me, forcing his weary, worn voice to carry—how it must have hurt his poor throat to make that effort! "It was all for love, Bunny; you *must* believe that!"

"I do!" I assured him. "I do! We've both hurt each other *so much,* my darling, but it really was all for love! People do bad things in Love's name all the time; we're not unique in that. I think we've just made a worse muddle of it than most do." I forced myself to smile through my tears.

"Indeed we have!" With a wry, weak little chuckle, Jim nodded and lay back and shut his eyes. I had a sense, in that moment, that I had, with my words, given him a sense of peace, and I was glad that that at least was something I could give him.

The time I spent alone in my bedroom with that book changed my life forever.

It took me *hours* to read it because I kept stopping, sick with horror, dumbstruck and disbelieving, going back and reading the same lines over and over again, hoping I had misread it, that I was tired and overwrought and imagining things and that *this time* the barbaric mutilation of a woman of the streets would become a mundane business luncheon where the talk was as dry as the cotton the men were discussing.

I sat and stared and ran my hands, like someone blind groping gently to discern a person's features, over that mad, erratic, furious scrawl, so different from my Jim's genteel, gentlemanly hand. *This can't be him,* I kept telling myself. *It just* can't *be. This is not the man I love, the man I married. . . . It* must *be the drugs; it* had *to be the drugs!* Combined with the ghastly and lurid stories filling all the newspapers and the anger he was feeling toward me, the jealousy and betrayal, it had all combined, melded into one mad arsenic fever dream and given birth to this medley of horrors. It was no more than a ferocious, furious fiction! Oh God, *please,* let it be so! It just couldn't be anything else! Because if it was the truth . . . that was just *too horrible* to contemplate.

The more I read, the more incredible it seemed. My blood turned to ice and the horror cut through me just like Jack the Ripper's knife. I shivered so hard there were times I could scarcely read the words; whether I held it in my hands or laid it on my lap, the book shook so badly, and there were moments when my face went green and I had to thrust it from me and grope blindly, through my tears, for the chamber pot.

I just couldn't believe it! I didn't want to believe it! If this was true . . . Oh God, it *couldn't* be true! I wanted to believe that my husband was mad, better a madman who sat and wrote out his crazed, drug-fueled fantasies than a murderer, because with madness there was always hope, hope of a cure, of a return to normalcy, but with murder it meant a life for a life, prison until the last breath was drawn or he perished on the gallows!

But it all seemed so terribly *real!* I could *feel* the hate burning off every page, and the *rage* that wielded the pen, and the knife, it was all so vividly real to me. This was *not* Charles Dickens drawing the reader into a story, spinning and binding a spell with words; this was too terribly, nauseatingly, horribly *REAL!* And the pain . . .

Oh God, those poor women! I could *see* their faces, I could *feel* their fetid breath upon my flesh, along with their heart-pounding fear the moment when they realized . . . It was as though I were standing right there, looking over his shoulder, helpless, deaf and dumb, unable to warn them, unable to shout, *RUN! SAVE YOUR-SELF!* I had no choice but to stand there and watch them die, watch him—*my Jim!—kill* them!

If these wild, wicked words were true . . . Jack the Ripper was no longer a faceless fiend stalking the streets of Whitechapel and my own bad dreams, he had another name, an ordinary mundane man's name, James Maybrick, and he was my very own husband, the father of my children. If this sick fantasy was indeed fact . . . my husband was a killer and *I* was the cause! I was the blind White Queen who had reigned, unwittingly, beside the mad Red King over that Autumn of Terror! He had projected my sins onto those poor, unfortunate women, so, in a way, *I* killed them too; they had died because of me. No matter how horrified and sickened I was by what he had done, I could *never* forget *that*—that *I* was the cause of it all. Our damaged, distorted, and perverted love had brought death, in the most violent, frenzied form, to five innocent women.

With his words he took me back, back to where I never wanted to be again, back onto the wretched streets of Whitechapel, the site of my first illicit tryst with Alfred Brierley, and even further, Jim took me to *Hell* and showed me such horrors there that I *knew* I would be forever scarred by them. He introduced me, one by one, to his victims, so that they could never again be just names in a newspaper. Polly Nichols, Annie Chapman, Elisabeth Stride, Catherine Eddowes, and Mary Jane Kelly—now they were all real women to me! I had seen them through his eyes, and through his hands I *felt* them; I felt their blood surge and their hearts race with terror and then grow cold, still, and die. I wanted to fall on my knees and beg their forgiveness. I now knew just how true it was that one small pebble cast into a pond creates great ripples that spread far and wide and can indeed touch and change, horribly and incredibly and indelibly, many lives. My sins were no longer my own; others had suffered and died because I was vain, hurt, lonely, foolish and weak. God help me, I was in my own way, a murderer too!

Love makes sane men mad and can turn a gentle man into a fiend, my husband had written. I now knew what he had meant when he had called after me as I was leaving his room, "It was all for love, Bunny; you *must* believe that!" The horrible thing was that I did, I *did* believe it, I *knew* it was true. Love, like Justice, is blind, but only Love is mad and impetuous and shouldn't ever be trusted to wield a sword; it causes only more harm, leaving hearts and lives lying broken and bleeding in Love's debris. Do the dead and wounded, I wonder, weep for the ones left behind to pick up the pieces? Or is it a penance they are destined to pay? God alone knows the answers.

As I lifted the diary from my lap a brass key fell from its binding. I was catapulted at once back through time to the morning I had sat as a young, naïve bride at my husband's desk and rattled the locked drawers. My life had indeed turned out to be a fairy tale after all, only not one of the pretty, happily ever after stories but the most sinister one of all—I was indeed Bluebeard's bride, Jack the Ripper's wife. And amongst the many secrets my husband was harboring was a cachet of murdered, butchered women, like the dead wives in Bluebeard's secret chamber. When I had opened the covers of that diary I had peeked into that secret room, and now, now I held in my hand the key. . . . *God help me!* I prayed as I walked into my husband's study.

Seated behind his desk, I shuddered and stared at the snake-haired Medusa heads that stood guardian over each keyhole. *My blood is already turned to ice; if she turns my body to stone that just might be a mercy,* I thought as I forced myself to try the key in each one until the third lock yielded. I was as afraid as though I knew it contained a live serpent that would rear up and strike me. I sat there for quite some time, the little brass handle at first cold growing hot in my hand, rattling gently as I trembled, trying to find the courage to open that drawer.

Finally, I could bear it no more. I took a deep breath, gave the drawer a tug, and found myself staring down at a candy box beauty with big, innocent blue eyes set in a porcelain and roses face, framed by a pompadour of golden curls and a big pink picture hat trimmed with tulle and roses. She might have been me at my best. With trembling hands, I lifted the box out and set it on the desk.

Whoever would have thought such a beautiful box that had once contained the most heavenly, exquisite chocolates—cream centers, caramels, liqueurs, jellies, nuts, nougats, pralines, and juicy red cherries floating in sweet pink cordial—could now be the repository of such horrors? Grisly trophies, souvenirs of the foulest murder, not tenderhearted tokens of love, sweet love, letters and valentines. One by one, I laid them all out in a row, knowing that I would never look at a chocolate box in quite the same way ever again.

A big brass button embossed with the figure of a naked lady with long flowing hair on horseback, it had to be Lady Godiva; two brass rings; a little prayer book in a language I now knew was Swedish, its cracked binding flopped open to reveal a crude woodcut depicting the Devil, stained reddish brown at the edges with the life's blood of the woman who had owned it; a stubby little knife; a cheap glass brooch with a pink flower inside, like a sad valentine, the fluted ruffle of gilt metal that framed the poor, pathetic little thing turning green and black in spots like moldy, mildewed lace; a well-worn key with a long lock of braided ginger-gold hair threaded through the top and tied with a fraying green ribbon; a bottle of red ink; a cache of newspaper clippings about the Whitechapel murders; and several slim volumes bound in innocuous, unadorned cardboard covers with some rather suggestive, titillating, and thought-provoking titles: *Freaks of Youthful Passion; Lady Lilywhite & the Lumberjack; A Case of Early Morning Stiffness; Three in a Coach: The Clergyman, the Countess, & the Cowpoke; The Schoolmaster & the Waif; The Schoolmarm's Birch Rod; The Amorous Adventures of a Kentucky Farmboy in New York; The Minister & the Milliner;* and *The Vicar of Make-Love.* Last, there was a postcard, delicately tinted, to put roses back in a now dead woman's cheeks and recall the vibrant green of her eyes and the ginger-gold of her hair, the only parts of her left for her lover to recognize her by after the carnage.

Despite the vulgar, indecent pose the elegantly clad model was striking, brazenly lifting her skirts high to reveal her naughty, naked, lasciviously rosy-tinted lady parts, it was her face I sat and stared at. It was the face that had been carved away in the Ripper's mad frenzy, and I knew, sitting there at my husband's desk, that I was the very last person to look upon the now effaced and forgotten features of Mary Jane Kelly.

Was it my imagination? I reached across the desk for the silver-framed photograph my husband always kept of me and held the postcard up alongside it, trying to will my hand to stop shaking and the tears to stop pooling long enough for me to compare them. Her hair was gingery while mine was pure spun gold, my eyes were limpid violet-blue and hers a saucy, insouciant emerald, and hers was definitely the more voluptuous figure, but we might have been sisters raised in two different worlds. The same lively hint of mischief tweaked at both our smiling mouths, mine more refined, gentle, and sedate, while hers was entirely unrestrained, but it *was* there just the same.

"He might have left you be had it not been for me! God forgive me!" I laid the postcard facedown in the bottom of the candy box and piled my husband's other souvenirs back on top of it. Last, I added the diary. It fit perfectly, as though it belonged, like a big, deep, dark chocolate heart at the center of it.

There was no turning back and retreating to blissful ignorance. I could no longer doubt and deny it, make up excuses, grasp at straws, and pretend. These grotesque souvenirs were the last nail in the coffin; all hope was dead. I now knew, beyond all doubt, that my husband was Jack the Ripper. This night he had taken me to Hell and shown me his very soul with my own, damned alongside it, shackled perpetually to it by guilt.

I caressed the band of gold on my left hand, which now seemed to me suddenly to have become a golden shackle. "Bound forever," I whispered, "till death *and* ever after!"

I started to lock the candy box away, back in its drawer, but at the last moment I hesitated and took it with me instead, back to my room. I had some peculiar notion, an urgent, unexplainable compulsion to keep it safe, protect and preserve it; I had become the sole guardian of a terrible secret. I knew if Michael got his hands on it, it would be in the fire before I could even blink an eye. He wouldn't hesitate to destroy the truth to maintain the fiction of the Maybricks' outward respectability.

In my dressing room I kept a lovely little tapestried chest that I'd had since I was a girl in Germany; I called it "my treasure chest." Inside were my postcard album and some odds and ends, postcards I had not yet pasted in, photographs, pretty or amusing pictures, advertisements, stories, poems, articles, recipes, and anecdotes and such that I'd clipped from various periodicals with the idea of someday creating a scrapbook, and stray buttons, ribbons, and trinkets. It had a deep tray that lifted out, made in such a way that one didn't immediately realize it, so it had the effect of having a false, or secret, shallow bottom compartment. Into this I put the candy box, burying it under all the scraps of pretty fabric I'd been saving for years, intending to make a quilt someday.

Satisfied that the candy box was now safe, I took a few moments to compose myself, and then I went back to Jim, just as I had promised.

The night nurse didn't argue and let me in; she was so wrapped up in the romance she was reading I think she would have let Satan himself in with scarcely a nod over those enthralling pages. She resumed her cozy seat by the fire and just let me and Jim be. At times I heard her murmuring what sounded like "kiss her, kiss her!" as though urging the hero on to loving action.

When I sat down on the bed beside him, Jim opened his eyes and looked at me, searching, hopeful, and wary.

I just sat and looked at him with tears welling in my eyes.

He hesitated a moment, then took my hand. I think we were both surprised that I didn't pull it away. There was a part of my mind and my heart that just couldn't reconcile it. Jim was still Jim, yet he wasn't. . . . But how could I reproach him? I had made him what he was. I was the potion that had brought evil Mr. Hyde out of gentle Dr. Jekyll. If I had been a better wife, a faithful wife . . . those five women would still be alive.

"You've come back to me," Jim said, his voice so coarse and faint I had to lean down to hear it.

I nodded. "And forgive everything," I added as the tears overflowed my eyes.

"I always knew you were as kind and gracious as you are beautiful," Jim said with the ghost of his old gallantry. "I was the *luckiest* man in the world to have you. I'm sorry I didn't value you as highly as I should. My own bloody temper, and my wretched stupidity, my secrets, and lies, my dalliances, led to your own—"

"I was weak and foolish too!" I sobbed.

"You were a sweet, beautiful child. I spoiled and neglected and abused you in my fashion," Jim said, "and you had every cause to rebel. You deserved better, Bunny, much better—"

"You were everything I ever wanted; you *still* are!" I cried, and laid my head down on his chest until his nightshirt was soaked clean through with my tears.

"Bunny." Jim plucked gently at my gown, trying to pull me back upright so I would sit up and look at him. "Bunny, all is forgiven that can be between man and wife, but there is one thing more I must ask of you. . . . Compose yourself, my love, and be brave, and listen. . . ."

I sat up, mopping at my eyes, though the tears welled right back up, seemingly unending.

"You know now, having read the book, what a frightful coward you married. I need you now to do what I cannot."

I started back in shock. "Jim, you *can't* mean . . . !"

He nodded with the gentlest, most understanding little smile and reached out for my hand again. "It will be *so easy,* my dear, and you will have *nothing* to reproach yourself for. Remember, you do not do murder, but *Justice!* You are sparing our children the shame that would forever tar them if I were to stand trial. I'm so sick already, and the doctors don't know what to do for me. Instead of making me better, they keep making me ill, so this, what you are about to do for me—and I *know* you will be brave and do it, Bunny! It will be so simple; the meat juice is right here." He indicated the nightstand. "And my coat is in the dressing room, and my silver box within the pocket. They've weaned me, against my will, and my body can no longer withstand the doses it once could. Just add a pinch or . . . make it two for good measure, since, as I've always said"—his face lit up once again with the same boyish smile that stole my heart on the decks of the *Baltic*—"one spoonful, or pinch, of anything never did anyone any good, and I will slip quietly away and face my Maker, and His justice, and take my guilty secret to the grave, and with it, my undying love for you—"

"Oh, Jim!" I dissolved in tears again. *"I can't!"*

"You *can.*" Jim hugged me close as I imagined my tears soaking clean through his chest to drip on his heart. "You *can* and you *will,* because you *know* this is the *right* thing to do. If I were to go on living, *he* would go on living too. You've read . . . you know . . . I'm slipping, Bunny. I can no longer chain the beast inside me. It was just the Devil protecting his own that kept me from being caught that last time, but luck doesn't last forever. . . . It's only a matter of

time, and the *only* way to kill *him* is to kill me. You *must* do it;
there's no one else I can trust. Think of the children, the scandal, if
I should be caught, the trial, the gallows, the infamy that would live
forever. I would be taking their lives too, just like I did . . . the others' . . . Be brave, for *both* our sakes, Bunny, and the children's, and
be my Lady Justice! My life is in your hands, and I want, *I need,*
you to take it!"

Slowly, I stood up, half-blinded by my tears. I knew he was
right. If he lived and was captured and tried it would mean the gallows for him and perpetual disgrace for all those he left behind.
But he was asking me to act as judge, jury, and executioner and
take another human life, and I . . . I just couldn't believe that could
be right. But my children, their future . . . Like one in a trance, I
began walking slowly around the bed toward the dressing-room
door.

"That's my brave girl." Jim smiled.

"*I love you!*" I sobbed as I picked up the bottle of Valentine's
Meat Juice. "I never realized how much until now, but I do. . . . I always have. . . . I always will!"

"And it's because of that great love you bear me that you will be
brave enough to do this for me now," he said, "because you know
in your heart that it *is* right. My love"—he stretched out his hand
again for mine—"you are only being the instrument of Justice and
you must *never* think otherwise or waste one single moment re-
proaching yourself. Come now, just two little pinches of my white
powder, and the truth will die with me; no one will ever know."

I didn't know what to say, so I said nothing. I cradled the brown
glass bottle against my breast and walked into the dressing room,
hoping and praying that God would guide my hand.

I found Jim's coat and slipped my hand into the pocket. The silver box felt like ice in my hand. I sat there holding it for quite some
time, staring down at Lady Hamilton as a near-nude nymph of
health.

Could I *really* do this for him? I looked at myself in the mirror,
trying to see the noble Lady Justice blindfolded and sword wield-
ing in her robes of flowing white, embodied in the weak and
wretched, teary-eyed, disheveled blond woman in the black lace dress
staring back at me, her reflection blurring and wavering through

my hot tears. Instead of the scales of Justice I held Jim's silver box
in one hand and the onion-shaped brown bottle of Valentine's
Meat Juice in the other.

"Courage, Bunny!" Somehow Jim's weak, raspy voice reached
me through the half-open door. *Do it quickly; don't think about it!* I
told myself. I sat the silver box down and uncorked the bottle. My
hands shook so badly some of the brown juice splashed out as the
cork came out with a *POP!* and an untidy snowfall of white powder
billowed down around the neck as I quickly added two tiny
pinches of arsenic. I took out my handkerchief and quickly mopped
up the mess I'd made, praying every second that God would give
me a sign that I was doing the right thing.

But a moment came when I could delay no more. It was now or
never. I knew my courage would fail me completely if I dallied any
longer. As I headed for the door I realized I'd forgotten the cork. In
turning back, I stumbled over my skirts and fell to my knees.
Through my bleary, tear-blind eyes I saw that about half the bottle
of meat juice was now lying pooled on the floor with little messy
clumps of white powder, like sodden sugar lumps melting in the
brown heart of it.

I gazed heavenward. Was *this* the sign I had been asking for? I
hurriedly grabbed my handkerchief and wiped the whole mess up.
Then I stood, took a deep breath, trying so hard to steady myself,
and replenished the bottle with water until it was full again, hoping
I was diluting whatever, if any, of the poison remained inside it. In
that moment a certain sense of peace came over me, like a comforting mantle of downy angel's wings, and I *knew* that God had sent
one of His angels to reach out a heavenly foot and trip me. It wasn't
meant for me to take justice into my own hands and end Jim's life;
I didn't have that right and it was wrong for me to even contemplate usurping it.

When I walked out of the dressing room I saw that Jim, thank
heaven, was sleeping peacefully, so I didn't have to look him in the
eye and confess that I had failed him. I just couldn't bear to see the
hurt and disappointment in his eyes.

The dreadful Nurse Gore was just then coming in with the
dawn to relieve the night nurse, whose name escapes me, watching
me with eagle eyes as I crossed the room and set the bottle on the

mantel, well out of Jim's reach. *Out of sight, out of mind,* I prayed, hoping slumber would bring forgetfulness and he would never ask me again. I smiled and nodded pleasantly to the two nurses in passing as I left the room and returned to my own.

In my room I fell onto the sofa in an exhausted swoon. I hadn't the strength to take off my clothes, wash, and put on a nightgown. I knew that if I tried to take one more step I'd fall. I promised myself I would just lie down for an hour or two. The gray sky was streaked with orange when I closed my eyes.

I awakened some hours later to a loud bang, like a gunshot—my door had just been kicked open!—and Edwin was leaning over me, grasping my shoulders, and shaking me *hard,* demanding my household keys. *"Your keys!"* he kept shouting right into my face. *"I want your keys!"* Out in the hallway Michael's voice, as commanding as a general's on a battlefield, was telling someone that Mrs. Maybrick was no longer mistress of this house.

Suddenly my doorway was filled with faces—doctors, servants, neighbors, nurses—all of them staring in at me as though I were some rare, exotic animal in a zoo.

"JIM!" I sprang up screaming. *"JIM!"* I hurled myself through them like a cannonball, before any of the hands they reached out could stop me, and ran to his room. I knew in my heart that he was already gone. He'd slipped away while I was sleeping; their faces told me so. But I didn't want to believe them. I *had* to see him one last time.

I flung open the door and thought I'd just stumbled across the threshold of Hell. The bed was stripped down to the bottom sheet, every gaslight in the room was blazing, and Jim lay there naked, blind dead eyes staring up at the crimson velvet canopy. His poor, wasted body, sagging skin white as a fish's belly, had been cut open from breast to groin, and three men, doctors I presume, stood over him. One was busy writing; another was scooping out Jim's innards in a big bloody heap and depositing them into the big stone jar yet another man was holding out for him. An image of Jim in a much more dark and squalid setting, alone, enacting a similar scene, standing over Mary Jane Kelly flashed before my eyes, and I fell with a scream.

When I opened my eyes I was back in my room prostrate on the sofa again. A dull ache filled my heart as I realized it had not all been just a terrible dream. Jim was dead and he'd taken Jack the Ripper with him to the grave and everyone was treating me, his widow, abominably, and I couldn't understand why.

Nurse Gore was sitting by the door, speaking words I couldn't quite comprehend and had to ask her to repeat again and again—the words just wouldn't sink in—until I finally understood that I was forbidden, on "Mr. Michael's orders," to leave this room. I was now a prisoner in my own home. I saw then that my desk had been ransacked. It stood there with every drawer open, and those papers deemed meaningless and unimportant strewn carelessly across the carpet, but all my personal letters, my ledger, and my household keys were missing. Anything that might have vindicated me or reflected badly upon Jim had been destroyed. I knew even before I found the fragile fragments amongst the ashes in the fireplace that the love letters Edwin had written me had been burned, just as surely as Alfred Brierley's had been taken into Michael's safekeeping.

"My children!" I bolted up with a sudden cry, racing for the door. How could I have been so thoughtless, lying here in a swoon like this, instead of rushing straight to them? Their father was dead, and they needed me. I had to explain what had happened and give them what comfort I could. I needed to reassure them that everything would be all right.

But Nurse Gore was there, barring my way, her hands closing with an iron grip around my tender wrists, pushing me back, away from the door.

"Sit down and be quiet!" she ordered. "It does no good to make a fuss! Your children have been taken away, on Mr. Michael's orders, where *you* can't get your hands on them!"

"My children . . . *gone? . . . Taken away? . . . Why? . . . Where?*" I stared up at her uncomprehendingly. "I must go to them. I must—"

The door opened and one of the doctors came in. There was something in his hand as he came toward me, and I shrank back into the sofa cushions, wishing there were some safe haven I could run to. The syringe glistened menacingly in the gaslight, the needle pierced my arm through the black lace of my sleeve, and my mind turned into a sopping-wet cotton ball, my limbs felt weighted with lead, and all I could do was sleep. In those days, whenever my brain bobbed blearily back to the surface, before the sharp bite of the needle sent it sinking back down, I discovered that I was more in love with Sleep than I had ever been with any man. The comfort and oblivion I found in darling Sleep's arms kept all the terrible pain, the cruel world, and the wolves howling, clawing, and clamoring at my door at bay.

The next I knew it was daylight again and Nurse Gore was shaking me roughly awake. "If you want to see the last of the husband you murdered you had better stand up." She pointed to the window.

I struggled unsteadily to my feet and stumbled and tottered my way to the window, my head swimming with every step, and clutched desperately at the windowsill to keep from falling. It was then I saw the coffin, covered with white carnations, being carried out to a glass-sided hearse drawn by four black horses with puffs of ebony ostrich plumes on their heads. I swung round, my skirts tangling in my feet, the heel of my shoe catching in the black lace and tearing it with a loud *RIP!* as I lurched toward the door.

"Stand back!" I screamed in Norse Gore's cruel gorgon face. "Stand back, I say! I must go to him! I must! Jim!"

Nurse Gore, who looked like a wrestler dressed in nurse's garb, shoved me back hard, sending me tottering and flailing over the sofa arm with my feet flying up in the air. "You are not to leave this room," she said, positioning herself before the door, arms folded across her breast, with an expression on her face just *daring* me to try to get past her.

I had no choice. I was trapped. I rushed back to the window and watched as Jim's carnation-covered coffin was loaded into the hearse and the glass doors closed upon him. Hysterically I began to hammer on the glass with my fists, shouting his name, "Jim! Jim!" as though I expected the din I was making to rouse him from his coffin and for him to push off the lid and sit up and look back to see what I was making such a god-awful ruckus about. In my desperation, I picked up a little footstool and was swinging it toward the window, meaning to shatter it, when Nurse Gore grabbed me and wrested it from my hands. "No! No!" I fought her as hard as I

could. "Leave me be! I must go to him! Jim! Jim! Don't leave me!"
I fell sobbing to the floor, irrationally crying out for him not to
leave me, even though I knew he already had and, what was even
worse, he'd left me alone against the world in a house filled with
enemies.

Then the doctor was there again with the needle and sweet
oblivion opened its arms to catch me as I fell. I was dimly conscious
of Nurse Gore picking me up by my shoulders and the doctor taking hold of my ankles and the two of them swinging me like a sack
of potatoes onto the sofa. That's the last thing I remember.

I kept dreaming I was a bride again in my blue linen suit waltzing through Versailles with my happy, smiling husband, so handsome, so charming, in his black Savile Row suit with the lucky
diamond horseshoe sparkling in his black-and-gray-striped silk cravat. We were so in love, laughing, and smiling into each other's
eyes. We danced through every room, the vast grand ballroom, the
presence chamber, and the Hall of Mirrors, and down every corridor, up every staircase, even through the kitchens. Jim even lifted
me up onto a long banqueting table and we danced across its
smooth, polished surface before he swung me back down onto the
marble floor again. Then we were out in the garden, dancing down
the pebbled paths and even on the rims of fountains.

We must have waltzed for *hours!* Every time I started to float
back to the surface, to glimpse reality through the glassy waters, I
felt even more exhausted, as though I really had been dancing all
that time without ever stopping to catch my breath. I'd feel dizzy
and my stays pinching, even my feet aching, and before I broke the
surface I sank like a stone gratefully back down into the thick,
warm mud of sleep. But in no time at all I would be back in Jim's
arms, waltzing through Versailles again.

During the days that followed—I never was sure just how
many—someone must have carried me to my bed, but they didn't
care enough to undress me and put me properly to bed, so when I
awakened I found myself still wearing the same black dress, now
grown quite rank and smelly, and my petticoats stained by urine
and a light, bloody discharge, too faint to be the onset of my
monthly courses but similar to the "sanguineous discharge" I'd

suffered before. They hadn't even cared enough for my comfort to take off my shoes or to pull the pins from my hair, which now had the appearance of an oily, frizzed, and matted yellow rat's nest.

I sat up, blinking and rubbing the sleep from my eyes, to find a policeman standing at the foot of my bed. That horrible nurse, Michael, Edwin, Mrs. Briggs, and Nanny Yapp all crowded behind him, staring at me. Then the doctor was feeling my pulse, nodding, and declaring me fit.

"Mrs. Maybrick," the officer began, "Mrs. Maybrick, you are in custody on suspicion of causing the death of your late husband, Mr. James Maybrick. If you choose to reply, be *very* careful, because whatever you say may be used as evidence against you."

"Please!" I managed to blurt out before I lost consciousness again. "Somebody send for my mother!"

Apparently Edwin, who would never forgive me for Alfred Brierley, found it in his heart to do me one last kindness. He sent a cable to Mama in Paris that I was in trouble and needed her desperately.

She came at once as I knew she would. "The indomitable Caroline," Baroness von Roques, barging right in, as fearless as an angel entering a burning building, coming to my rescue, not a knight in shining armor but a voluptuous white-blond matron clad head to toe in lavender chiffon trimmed with silk periwinkles and the most enormous hat I'd ever seen. Pearls and diamonds clacking, she shoved past Mrs. Briggs and Nanny Yapp, sending the maids scattering and Edwin running for cover, swinging her handbag and parasol left and right, like a medieval warrior's mace, warning them to get out of her way or she would knock them all down like bowling pins.

When a policeman caught up with her on the stairs, telling her I was under arrest on suspicion of murdering my husband by administering an irritant poison, she poked him aside with her parasol and said, "Don't be absurd. If anyone poisoned James Maybrick it was James Maybrick; that man was a drugstore walkin' on two legs. I'm surprised he lasted this long! Now unhand me, sir. I'll have you know that my second husband was the grandson of Benjamin Franklin an' the illegitimate son of Napoleon III! An' another of our illustrious ancestors stood right beside Christopher Columbus on the deck o' the *Mayflower* holdin' the map that he steered by!"

Then she was there, in my room, gathering me in her arms, and I, just like a terrified little girl, was clinging to her and crying, begging my mama to help me, saying that I didn't understand what was happening and why they were treating me like this.

Apparently they'd searched the house and found packets of arsenic I'd never seen before marked *"POISON!"* hidden amidst my underlinens or rather *planted* there; it certainly wasn't mine. And they'd collected a vast array of medicines; I believe the tally ran to 147 different pills, potions, and powders. But those were *all* Jim's. I had *nothing* to do with them! And Nanny Yapp wouldn't shut up about those damned infernal flypapers, which I'd only used to replicate Dr. Greggs's prescription to get rid of my blemishes in time for the ball. Then there were those two sacks labeled *Industrial Arsenic* that Jim had been bragging about his "stupendous luck" in acquiring from a business associate. On the whole, the policemen said, there was enough arsenic in Battlecrease House to do away with the entire British Army and take a good bite out of the Navy too.

I told Mama the truth, except the bit about my husband being Jack the Ripper, of course, and that all I'd done was sprinkle a little white powder into the Valentine's Meat Juice bottle at Jim's bidding, because he was suffering so and swearing he needed it. But, before I could give it to him, and I was already thinking twice about it, I tripped and spilled it. I had refilled the bottle with water. Most of the white powder had been left on the floor in undissolved clumps. I had mopped it up myself. And what, if any, was left in the bottle was surely not enough to have killed him. Yet apparently Michael had sent the bottle out for testing and found a trace amount of arsenic in it. My handkerchiefs had also been examined and one of them was found to have arsenic on it. But that must have been either from wiping my face, after using the facial wash, or from when I mopped up the mess I made when I spilled the bottle of meat juice; it had to be one or the other.

"Surely I am guilty of no crime?" I looked up at Mama uncertainly. "Jim has been taking that arsenic for *years,* and there was only a teeny-tiny amount found in the meat juice bottle, not enough to kill anybody. I heard the doctors saying so! They said the attempt was clearly 'inept' and 'the work of a bungler'!"

"Listen to me, Florie." Mama braced her hands on my shoulders. "You are *not* to blame for this. This was bound to happen sooner or later. Jim had been poisonin' himself for years, an' there's no telling what all those doctors have been givin' him. In tryin' to cure him they may actually have killed him. But he wouldn't have been in this state anyway if he'd treated his body like a temple an' kept it pure o' all that poison! Arsenic an' strychnine!" She rolled her eyes. "An' now he's died and left you in a devil of a fix! I shall have a lawyer for you by this afternoon," she promised, "an' we'll clean this mess up so you can bury the past with Jim an' come back to Paris with me and put all this behind you!"

That was my mama, "the indomitable Caroline."

While she was in the guest room changing her dress, someone locked her in. That was when they took me away to jail. I was so weak I couldn't walk. They had to carry me out in a chair. Mrs. Briggs yanked a silk cord from the window curtains and tied me to it to keep me from falling out as I slumped there, swooning. Two constables carried me out the door, with Mrs. Briggs and Nanny Yapp following, *graciously* thanking them for taking the trash out.

❧ 29 ❧

My trial began on August 1, 1889, in the worst heat of summer; it was one full week of unrelenting torment. I sweltered in my black crepe widow's weeds, shrouded in thick veils, in the crowded courtroom at St. George's Hall in Liverpool and shivered in my tiny jail cell that was like a living tomb carved out of Arctic ice.

You'll forgive my indignation I hope, but I simply *cannot* think back to that time without getting my temper up.

They tell me as many as seven thousand people observed my trial. That includes those who just stuck their head in for a peek at the accused murderess, "hiding her guilty face from the world behind her impenetrable black veils."

Many of them were people I knew, members of the Currant Jelly Set I had danced and dined with. Ladies came, dressed in the height of fashion, in huge hats to the dismay of those seated behind them. They came to my trial as though it were a matinée, a fun, festive occasion, not my very life and death, my freedom, at stake. Many brought a boxed lunch so they need never relinquish their seat and risk losing it to another, and opera glasses through which to gawk at me, and chatted gaily with the journalists who obliged them by describing their hats and dresses in detail in the newspapers in return for their opinions and reminiscences about me.

Women I knew who were avid players of the game of musical beds, couples who indulged in discreet wife swapping during weekends at genteel country houses, all sat there frowning, shaking their heads, and mouthing, *SHAME!* and calling me a "brazen American hussy" just like the Puritans who had surrounded the marketplace scaffold where Hester Prynne had stood, staring at the scarlet *A* embroidered with flamboyant defiance upon her breast. Their eyes bored into me and they put their heads together and whispered about me and Alfred Brierley, who had, upon his physician's advice, conveniently set sail for South America. The papers reported that Alfred "appeared reserved and to feel the delicacy of his position most acutely." Before he went, he issued a terse statement to the press: "I have figured more prominently in this case than my real connection with it warranted. Besides this I have nothing to say regarding anything."

As I stood there in the dock gazing out at them through the hazy black of my veil it was all I could do not to shout, *You're all a bunch of hypocrites!* These people who were so fickle and free with their affections, not a one of them would have recognized *true* sincerity, instead of the feigned variety they donned and doffed just like carnival masks, if it had come up and slapped them in the face or kicked them in the pants!

They even put up a waxwork figure of me in Madame Tussaud's Chamber of Horrors, "most carefully modeled after actual photographs," gowned in "an authentic replication" of my widow's weeds. A packet labeled "ARSENIC!" peeked from my pocket and a red taffeta petticoat peeped from beneath my black skirt as I, with my hand also clutching a black-bordered mourning handkerchief and a bottle of Valentine's Meat Juice, coyly raised it to give the people a glimpse. For weeks, they tell me, people were lined up around the block from morning till night, over fifty thousand of them, waiting to get in to see it, and souvenir postcards of it sold so briskly the printing presses were taxed to keep up with the demand. Edwin even dared flash one at me, when I was being led out of the courtroom, smiling and saying, "I'll save one for you, Florie, in case they don't hang you." I didn't know whether to spit at him or slap him. I felt like doing both, but, of course, I did neither.

With all the eyes of the world upon me, just waiting to catch a glimpse of the evil they were convinced was lurking inside me, it wouldn't have been wise. All I could do was "accidentally" tread upon his toes, then falter and gasp out an apology, and we both knew just how sincere *that* was!

From the start Judge Stephen displayed a shocking prejudice against me, describing my late husband as a man "unhappy enough to have an unfaithful wife" and using words like *adulterous intrigue* every chance he got. Every single time he addressed the jury he seemed more concerned with my infidelity than whether the evidence presented was truly sufficient to convict me of murder. In truth, he seemed quite bored with that, though given the dry, ponderous nature of the medical testimony I could hardly blame him. There were moments when those doctors and scientists were on the stand when I could hardly keep my eyes open and was grateful to my heavy black veil for hiding my yawns. Time and again Justice Stephen would swat the medical arguments aside like a bothersome fly, commenting on their complexity and declaring them too difficult for his mind to grasp, and draw the jury's attention back to my adultery. He seemed to particularly relish the reading aloud of my love letters and the testimony of those witnesses brought in to provide proof of my illicit trysts. Like a Bible-banging zealot he saw in me the reincarnation of all the evil women of history—Eve, Delilah, Jezebel, Salome, Agrippina, Cleopatra, Messalina, Catherine de Medici, and Lucrezia Borgia, to name just a few he cited in his apparent passion for the subject.

There was a lengthy parade of scientific witnesses largely consisting of bickering doctors. I wondered even if you could get them all to agree to the sky being blue if they would fight one another like tigers over the precise hue; I could picture them coming to verbal blows over *celestial* versus *cerulean*. The tide seemed to be turning unexpectedly in my favor when a Mr. Davies who was an analytical chemist, brought in by the prosecution no less, admitted that the traces of arsenic found in Jim's organs were too slight to be measured and insufficient to cause the death of a normal person, let alone a habitual arsenic eater like James Maybrick was said to have been. But then a Dr. Stevenson, an esteemed toxicologist, took the stand and spoke with such a resounding air of authority when he declared, "I have no doubts that this man died from the effects of arsenic," that the jury could not fail to be impressed.

Michael was there every day, staring at me, smiling like the cat that got the canary, and stroking his gold Mason's ring. When he was called to the stand he emphatically declared that Jim was not a person given to dosing himself with medicines. Michael recounted Nurse Gore's tale of my tampering with the bottle of Valentine's Meat Juice, claiming "my brother grew gradually worse from that time on." When queried about Jim's habitual use of arsenic, Michael briefly lost his composure, sitting forward with his fists clenched. "Whoever told you that is a damned liar!" he said, his eyes daring anyone to disagree. "They should think of my brother's children before uttering such rubbish!"

Then it was Edwin's turn. He admitted that he was "very fond of Florence, and I would never have believed anything wrong about her . . . until a letter to a man was found. . . ." Judge Stephen *loved* that! He was actually leaning over, nodding encouragingly at Edwin, almost *begging* for more, and Edwin, his pride still smarting, eagerly acquiesced. Following in Michael's footsteps, Edwin feigned ignorance about Jim's use of drugs, which he *knew* to be habitual; standing over what turned out to be Jim's deathbed he had blamed his brother's sad and sorry state on those "damn strychnine pills; he's been taking them like candy!" Edwin sat there, after laying his hand on the Holy Bible and swearing to tell the truth, insisting that "on the whole my brother enjoyed very good health and only occasionally took digestive remedies as prescribed by his physician." There was a moment of comedy when Edwin sought to mop his sweat-beaded brow in the sweltering courtroom and drew out a whole string of rainbow silk handkerchiefs and couldn't quite manage to cram them all back into his pocket, so that when he exited the stand they were trailing behind him like the tail of a kite. I would have laughed if I hadn't been crying.

Then the servants had their moment to bask in the sun of fame or infamy, call it what you will. They got to see their names and pictures in the newspapers, souvenirs to save for their grandchildren. Everything I had ever done suddenly seemed sinister and suspect to them in hindsight and they tattled and prattled on endlessly about my ineptly run household and the occasionally violent quarrels between the master and mistress, the cause of which was, no doubt, some grievous fault of mine, since it was quite obvious by this point that James Maybrick had been a saint. I was expecting Judge Stephen to usurp the Pope's authority and canonize Jim at any moment. Jim and I got along like a house on fire in our passion and our fury. There was no denying that; even I would have admitted it if anyone had ever asked. Mr. Maybrick, each and every one of our servants avowed, had been the best and kindest master and gentleman it had been their pleasure to serve; he was one of the finest men who ever lived. And it hurt all their hearts to see how Mrs. Maybrick, to save her own skin, was trying to paint a picture of this goodly and godly Christian gentleman as some kind of drug fiend. They were simply appalled when my counsel *dared* to bring up the fact that Jim had a mistress and *five* bastard children to try to balance the scales when everyone knew it was different for men and what was good for the gander wasn't necessarily appropriate behavior for the goose. *Oh, what hypocrites!*

Next Nanny Yapp came flouncing up the center aisle, for all the world like a Floradora girl—a *blind* Floradora girl, since she had forsaken her spectacles for this performance. She was wearing one of *my* dresses, custard-yellow satin trimmed with rows of black velvet bows and black lace flounces, with stuffed canary birds perched amongst frills of black lace on her—*my!*—hat, twirling her—*my!*—parasol like a flirtatious belle promenading in the park trying to catch a gentleman's eye. I could just hear her in my mind again singing, *While strolling through the park one day, in the merry, merry month of May . . .*

She took the stand and regaled the crowd with a melodramatic rendering of how she—the heroine of the hour!—had alerted the household to my murderous intentions, rousing the alarm by crying out in turn to Edwin, Michael, and Mrs. Briggs that *"the mistress intends to poison the master!"* With stage-worthy gestures, Nanny Yapp vividly recounted her discovery of the flypapers soaking in my bedroom, in a washbasin covered with a towel in the hope of concealing my "nefarious intentions," and how in innocently intending to do a good deed by putting the letter my little girl had soiled by dropping it in a mud puddle into a clean envelope she had inadvertently discovered my adultery—the obvious motive for my crime! She went on to tell how she had been the one to discover the packets of arsenic nesting amidst my underclothes and yet more hidden in the linen closet. "I always *knew* she was up to no good!" she cried, staring daggers at me before bursting into tears. "Oh, the poor master! The poor, poor master!" she blubbered into her, or rather *my,* handkerchief; I spied my initials embroidered upon it in sky-blue silk.

Judge Stephen looked like a stage-door johnny wanting to shower Alice Yapp with gems and roses after that performance! He actually told the jury that she was "an exceedingly nice young woman" and that "her courageous act in retaining the letter and handing it to Mr. Edwin Maybrick must be commended."

When she was asked about any medicine she might have seen Jim taking she was simply aghast. Mr. Maybrick had been "the most godly and temperate man" she ever knew, and she knew for a fact that he was loath to take even a simple cough remedy, preferring to trust Jesus Christ, Our Savior, to save him from any earthly infirmity. *BALDERDASH!* Not one year ago, my husband had stood right in the middle of the nursery, in *full* sight of Nanny Yapp's adoring eyes, and drunk straight from a bottle of cough syrup to prove to the children, who were both sick, that it didn't taste bad. He ended up drinking the whole bottle right then and there and having to send out for more—for himself *and* the children!

Mrs. Briggs took the stand in full mourning, replete with a complaisant air that seemed to confirm without actually saying a single word that she always knew something like this would happen from the moment she discovered that Jim had jilted her for me. She behaved as though Jim had been her husband, weeping as she recounted how Nanny Yapp, in a state of wild, weeping despair and frenzy, had met her at the door, crying out, "Thank God you have come, Mrs. Briggs! The mistress is poisoning the master! For God's sake, go up and see him for yourself!" Wings must have sprouted from her heels, she flew so fast to his side, and found him a mere faint and fading shadow of his former self. She pooh-poohed the "absurd and ridiculous notion" that Mr. Maybrick had been an arsenic eater, then went on to enumerate all my grievous and many faults, harping, for the benefit of the housewives in the audience and all those who judged a woman by her house, on my inept and ill-managed household, my extravagance, shopping sprees, racking up debts that led me into dealings with moneylenders, and then, of course, there was "that business with Mr. Brierley. . . ."

Nurse Gore and the two other nurses who had been in attendance at Battlecrease House also had their little tale to tell, namely how Michael had forbidden me the sickroom and cautioned them to be very vigilant whenever I was near and to report any suspicious behavior on my part promptly to him.

And Mr. Samuelson, whose wife had betrayed him with my husband, took the stand against me to testify to my admission that I often said I hated Jim, taking it totally out of context and turning what I had intended to be an act of genuine kindness against me.

Mr. Schweisso, the headwaiter at Flatman's Hotel, was the sensation of the sixth day when he was called to give evidence about how I had stayed there with Alfred Brierley, registering the two of us as man and wife—Mr. and Mrs. James Maybrick—and confirming that the two of us had slept in the same room, in the same bed, together.

I had for my defending counsel the flamboyant Irishman Sir Charles Russell, an inveterate gambler with the air of exhaustion clinging to him like a wet cloak despite all his bluff and bluster after mounting a grueling defense of Parnell, the Irish Nationalist fighting a charge of sedition. Russell came at great cost, a retainer of five hundred pounds and an additional one hundred pounds a day, but Mama said he was worth it. He was a most gallant gentleman who from the start viewed me as innocent and the case against me as a house of cards he was determined to topple. "Don't worry, Mrs. Maybrick; the English have ever loved an underdog," he said. "The tide may seem against you now, but it *will* turn in your favor." He always referred to me as "that friendless lady" and told the jury that it was all very simple; there were just *two* key points they must consider: (1) Was James Maybrick's death due to arsenic poisoning? and (2) If so, was that poison administered by his wife?

The gallant Sir Charles did his best to demolish the prosecution's case and produced several solid, unshakable witnesses who testified in detail to my husband's hypochondriacal tendencies and long-standing habit of casually taking dangerous medicines, namely strychnine and arsenic. Some witnesses even came all the way from America in the interest of seeing justice done. Sir Charles summoned the black valet who had attended Jim in Virginia and a madam, Mrs. Hogwood, whose brothel Jim had frequented, both of whom testified that they'd been scared to death he would suddenly drop dead on account of the white powder he was always taking and that they might in some way be held accountable. He also had the druggist, Mr. Eaton, whose shop Jim was accustomed to frequenting several times a day for his "pick-me-up" tonic, take the stand and give a detailed account of Jim's steadily increasing dosages and visits. The druggist even told how once when Jim had gone away on a business trip he had *insisted* that Mr. Eaton prepare *sixteen* vials of this tonic for him to take with him just in case he couldn't find an obliging druggist to cater to his special needs. Sir Charles brought in other doctors to counter the prosecution's parade of learned medicos, all stating firmly that Jim had most likely died of gastroenteritis, insisting that in reviewing the case as well as the postmortem findings they had found no solid proof of arsenical poisoning, though years of abuse had most certainly taken a toll on his constitution.

Gradually what Sir Charles had promised began to happen; public opinion began to swing round to my side. I was becoming a cause célèbre on both sides of the Atlantic and the "friendless lady" was not so friendless anymore. People were actually getting into fistfights over the subject of my innocence or guilt and just how Jim had died. The papers were full of us; there was even a daily column in one of the local papers called "Maybrick Mania."

But Judge Stephen simply could not let the matter of my adultery rest. He kept harping on it incessantly, worrying it like a bad tooth his tongue couldn't keep away from, and it was the jury's opinion and not the public's that mattered. He dismissed the contradictory twaddle of complex medical opinions and repeatedly stressed that my "adulterous intrigue with Mr. Brierley" was a "very strong motive why Mrs. Maybrick should wish to get rid of her husband. It is easy enough to conceive how a horrible woman, in so terrible a position, might be assailed by some terrible temptation."

It took the jury only thirty-eight minutes to convict me.

When they came back and the judge asked me to rise, I knew I was going to die. Not one man sitting in that jury box could look at me; they all turned their faces away.

"*Guilty!*" the foreman pronounced, and I tottered back as though I had been struck a physical blow.

Judge Stephen asked me if I had anything to say. This would be my first and most likely last chance to speak, since the law at that time denied accused murderers the right to take the stand in their own defense, so I forced myself to stand up straight and look him square in the eye.

"My lord," I said, "everything has been against me. Although evidence has been given as to a great many circumstances in connection to Mr. Brierley, *much* has been withheld which might have influenced the jury in my favor had it been told. I am *not* guilty of this crime!"

Judge Stephen's eyes were smiling as he put the black silk cap on over his white wig and sternly spoke the following words to me: "Prisoner at the bar, I am no longer able to treat you as being innocent of the dreadful crime laid to your charge. The jury has convicted you, and the Law leaves me no discretion, and I must pass this sentence upon you: The court doth order you to be taken from hence to the place from whence you came, and from thence to the place of execution, and that you be hanged by the neck until you are dead. May the Lord have mercy upon your soul!"

According to the law, since three Sundays must pass before a condemned person could mount the gallows, I had eighteen days left to live. There being no Court of Appeal in England at that time, my only hope was a royal pardon.

A great crowd had assembled outside and there was much outrage expressed about the verdict, so much so that Judge Stephen, being hissed as "Mr. *In*justice," required a police escort home and had rocks thrown through his windows.

Surrounded by a quartet of constables and a prison matron, I was taken out a side door to the prison van, the infamous Black Maria. But, of course, the crowd found me. Though many hissed, spit, shook their fists, and hurled insults at me, there were a great many who shouted, "God go with you, Mrs. Maybrick!" and in the crush and press of the crowd someone snatched my veil away, as a souvenir I suppose.

The Black Maria was like a coffin on wheels, stultifying and terrifying. The taps and knocks the populace gave to the vehicle's sides meant, no doubt, by most, I'm sure, as a show of support, to let me know I wasn't really alone, were like clods of earth crashing down upon my coffin's lid, only I wasn't dead yet. I was still alive, trapped and sealed inside, waiting tensely to draw my last breath.

As the van drew away, I saw, through the barred window, a gentleman I recognized as one of my countrymen, come from America to show his support—Mama said he had been most assiduous raising funds to aid my defense—lift his hat to me. Then, holding it over his heart, he began to sing in a fine baritone voice that brought the crowd to a sudden awed silence:

> *"In a cavern, in a canyon,*
> *Excavating for a mine*
> *Dwelt a miner forty-niner,*
> *And his daughter Clementine.*
>
> *"Oh my darling, oh my darling,*
> *Oh my darling, Clementine!*
> *You are lost and gone forever,*
> *Dreadful sorry, Clementine!*
>
> *"Light she was and like a fairy,*
> *And her shoes were number nines,*
> *Herring boxes, without topses*
> *Sandals were for Clementine.*
>
> *"Oh my darling, oh my darling,*
> *Oh my darling, Clementine!*

You are lost and gone forever,
Dreadful sorry, Clementine!

"Drove she ducklings to the water,
Every morning just at nine,
Hit her foot against a splinter,
Fell into the foaming brine.

"Oh my darling, oh my darling,
Oh my darling, Clementine!
You are lost and gone forever,
Dreadful sorry, Clementine!

"Ruby lips above the water,
Blowing bubbles, soft and fine,
But, alas, I was no swimmer,
So I lost my Clementine.

"Oh my darling, oh my darling,
Oh my darling, Clementine!
You are lost and gone forever,
Dreadful sorry, Clementine!

"In a churchyard on a hillside,
There grow roses well entwined,
And some posies amongst the roses,
Flowers for my Clementine.

"Oh my darling, oh my darling,
Oh my darling, Clementine!
You are lost and gone forever,
Dreadful sorry, Clementine!

"In my dreams she still doth haunt me,
Robed in garments soaked in brine.
Though in life I used to hug her,
Now she's dead, my Clementine.

"Oh my darling, oh my darling,
Oh my darling, Clementine!
You are lost and gone forever,
Dreadful sorry, Clementine!

"Then the miner forty-niner
He began to weep and pine,
For his darling little daughter,
Now he's with his Clementine.

"Oh my darling, oh my darling,
Oh my darling, Clementine!
You are lost and gone forever,
Dreadful sorry, Clementine!"

As the last notes of his song died away, the world through that little window seemed to shrink to the size of a postage stamp; then everything went black. The last thing I remember thinking, as the prison van swayed and shook over the cobbles, was that Death was rocking me to sleep.

❧ 30 ❧

Holed up in that dank, dark, icy-walled little cell, sitting huddled, shivering on the floor, with only the clothes on my back—the same black mourning gown I had worn to my trial—I felt like I had already been buried, walled up alive, behind stones so thick no one could hear me scream. Even Sleep had forsaken me. Whenever I lay down, longing for him to come and take me in his comforting arms, I imagined, so vividly I thought my sanity had deserted me too, a sword hanging by a fraying rope dangling over my head. I could not close my eyes and lay there all night tense and alert, every part of my body stiff and aching.

But I was *not* dead, though I lived every moment in the shadow of death, marking the ever-dwindling eighteen days that stood between me and the gallows. Even for the half hour each afternoon when I was let out to walk in the high-walled prison courtyard, though the sky above me was light and sometimes the sun even shone down on me, I walked in darkness and I walked alone. "My God, why have you forsaken me?" I used to whisper, straining my ears, listening, and hoping for an answer that never came.

My counsel, Sir Charles Russell, the only one who was allowed in to visit me during those dark days, assured me that the world had not forgotten me. He took my hand and said most gallantly,

"The friendless lady has more friends than she knows." There were petitions circulating on both sides of the Atlantic—why, one in London alone had already garnered half a million signatures—beseeching Queen Victoria to spare my life. Every edition of every newspaper was full of vigorous arguments in my favor from doctors and lawyers and just ordinary people who thought my conviction a travesty and grave miscarriage of justice. Pictures appeared depicting me as a frightened and penitent Magdalene, cowering against a wall, with Jesus Christ standing between me and an angry mob led by Judge Stephen, who were ready to stone me, with a caption reading: "He who is without sin amongst you, let him cast the first stone."

But the days dwindled and passed. I laid out little bits of stone I chipped from the wall to mark their passage—18, 17, 16, 15, 14, 13, 12, 11, 10, 9, 8, 7, 6, 5, 4, 3 . . .

And every day I kept thinking about that diary, hidden away behind the smiling face of a candy box beauty, tucked safely inside my tapestried trunk. It was now safe with Mama. She'd managed to save it, as I knew she would, even when Michael ordered Battlecrease House stripped and everything—all the furnishings, books, and bric-a-brac, my personal possessions, and even the children's toys and clothes, so that nothing need ever again touch them that would remind them of me—be sold at public auction.

It had been the unhappy task of Sir Charles to inform me while I was awaiting trial that everything—*almost* everything—was already gone. Sensation seekers had even gone into a bidding frenzy over my frilly, ribbon-trimmed drawers. But Mama had not failed me; she was the one person I could always count on, and she had managed to save the one thing that mattered—the tapestried trunk. She had even succeeded in saving my Bible, the one I'd had all my life, by sending her own clever maidservant to view the goods prior to auction. She'd substituted another Bible of the same size and color in its stead while another of Mama's servants created a diversion by falling down in a fit. "I hope the ghoul who would bid upon a falsely condemned woman's Bible pays two hundred pounds for it!" Mama told me afterward. It actually sold for £225. I wonder what Michael spent the money on. Did any of it go to my poor children? Did he spend one penny to provide them with new toys?

Sir Charles told me by the terms of Jim's will, the one he had written in a fit of anger after tearing his old one up, I was completely cut off and, although I technically remained the beneficiary of Jim's insurance policies, he had defaulted on the premiums. Now all the power was in Michael's hands. He could do anything he liked with money or goods and my children's bodies and souls; he could turn Bobo out to work as a chimney sweep and send Gladys out to skivvy if he wished and no one could stop him. I had no power except . . . if I dared . . . the diary. . . . It was my trump card if I only dared play it. Murder would become execution. The truth would set me free; I had only to tell it.

But would it make any difference to my children's lives or would it only be packing and piling on the sins, crushing their dear little shoulders beneath the weight of shame? They would grow up with Michael poisoning their minds against me—no doubt he'd already begun, believing that I had killed their father—but if they knew their father was Jack the Ripper . . . But the world would also know, and once the truth was told it could never be untold. It would *never* be forgotten; they would live out their lives as Jack the Ripper's children, endlessly pursued by journalists and curiosity seekers, pointed and stared at everywhere they went, never knowing a moment's peace. The father they had loved, the man who used to read them stories and get down on the floor and play with them, would be lost forever; horror would steal all those sweet memories away.

Every time I got so frightened of the hangman's noose that I was tempted to hammer on my cell door and beg them to send for Sir Charles I imagined my son and daughter grown to beautiful man- and womanhood, falling in love with someone wonderful they wanted to spend the rest of their lives with, only to be denied, cheated of that love, maybe even having it turned to hate and disgust, because their father was Jack the Ripper and, if that were not bad enough, their shameful, wanton adulteress mother had been convicted of murdering him. Such evil, people were sure to believe, must run in the blood, and they would stare at my children, scrutinizing their every move, suspiciously citing their every human foible and mistake as proof that bad blood tells. They would *never* be free! I couldn't take the chance, I just *couldn't* do that to them!

Sometimes the greatest love of all demands a sacrifice, and mine would be my silence, and my life.

To further guard against weakness and temptation, I made Mama promise to lock that trunk away in a very safe bank vault in London and bring me the key. I would hide it away, drop it in a crack or crevice somewhere so that it would never be found until they tore this prison down and maybe not even then, and if it was . . . would anyone *really* care about an old key? I would do that, I promised myself, before they led me out to die. I would leave it to Chance, the Fool's name for Fate, and the eternal curiosity of mankind to find that key and where it fit and reveal the truth long after anyone it could hurt was dead. *Tempus Omnia Revelat,* Time Reveals All— my husband had indeed chosen a most fitting motto. God, Who knows all, past, present, and future, must have been guiding his hand that day.

Until then I kept that key close to me, hidden in a seam in my dress, feeling it burn like temptation through the black cloth every time the fear threatened to overwhelm me. But each time I would fight it back down, like a mother lion defending her cubs, by think-ing of Bobo and Gladys and the *one* thing it was still in my power to give them. I couldn't save them from being my children, but I could save them from being Jack the Ripper's. The world would only pity them for being mine—a weak and foolish woman who had thought a pinch of white powder was the path to passion's ful-fillment. It was better this way.

The morning I laid the seventeenth stone down, Mama was al-lowed to see me. They led me into a little room where she was al-ready waiting, with two sharp-eyed, stiff-backed matrons standing sentry to make sure she didn't slip me any poison or a razor to help me cheat the hangman. Wordlessly I fell to my knees before her, burying my face in her black taffeta skirts. Both of us were so over-come by emotion the words stuck in our throats. We clung to each other and cried the whole half hour allotted to us to say good-bye.

When the matron said it was time to go back to my cell, I clung to Mama like a frightened child, even as the matron reached to pull me away. Mama clasped my face between her two hands and smiled through her tears and kissed me; then she gently put me from her.

"You must be very brave," she said. "Because you are innocent, you must be strong and carry yourself without reproach, with all the confidence, grace, an' pride of a queen. I will be there, right beside you, darlin', walkin' with you every step o' the way, an' God will be on the other side o' you, bearin' you up, givin' you strength. Whenever you feel yourself about to falter, you can lean on us, lean on Him. We'll see you through to the end."

"Yes, Mama." I nodded through my tears, gazing back at her longingly as they led me away. The rest of the day I spent weeping with the silver-haired and spectacled prison chaplain, clinging to him, groveling, and swearing my innocence upon my very soul, until he began to cry too because, though he was fully convinced of my innocence, it was not within his power to grant me earthly salvation.

The next morning, as I sat and watched the sky of my last morning lighten to buttery gray between the bars of my tiny window, I laid down the eighteenth stone. I knew it was only a matter of hours that stood between me and the great mystery of death.

I steeled myself, pacing the floor, praying God to help me be brave. I thought of Marie Antoinette on her last morning in the Conciergerie, golden hair bleached white by sorrow, her once beautiful face haggard and careworn, still regal and proud even when stripped of all her grandeur, preparing to face the guillotine, making her peace with God and man. She had mounted the scaffold with her head held high, every inch the queen she had been in life. No matter how much they degraded and insulted her, they could not take away her dignity and grace. That was the woman I wanted to be during the last precious moments of my life. "It takes courage to live, not to die," she said as they led her out to the tumbril. I repeated those words like a prayer until they were engraved upon my heart.

I stood in the center of my little cell, hugging myself tight with my own arms, since there was no one else to hold me. I shut my eyes and hummed a waltz. And in that moment I was in Jim's arms again, in my blue linen suit, whirling through the vanished splendor of Versailles. He was smiling down into my face, and I was gazing up at him, a young bride, her heart in her eyes, and it was so good to be alive! Soon, I knew, we would be dancing together again, in Heaven where we would never hurt, dishonor, or disappoint each other ever again.

"I didn't lie," I whispered to his shade. He felt so near me now, like he was waiting for me just on the other side of a veil. I could almost reach out and touch him. "All really is forgiven."

When the door of my cell opened and the prison governor and the chaplain came toward me, all my courage disappeared. I cried out in terror and fell fainting to the floor.

When I next opened my eyes I was lying on a cot in the infirmary, a matron holding a vial of vinegary smelling salts under my nose. I saw the governor and the chaplain hovering over me, and only their hands, raised in a staying motion, and the smiles lighting up their faces stopped me from fainting again.

No, no!" they cried. "It is *good* news!"

It wasn't a pardon; Queen Victoria was of the same mind as Judge Stephen and firmly convinced that I was a wicked woman who truly deserved death. But Sir Henry Matthews, the Home Secretary, had become convinced that the medical evidence was insufficient to condemn me without lingering doubt. The end result was that I was reprieved from the gallows and my sentence commuted to life imprisonment. Even as I was sitting up groggily, gingerly touching my bandaged temple, the Black Maria was waiting to take me to the train station, to begin the journey to Aylesbury Prison, where I was to spend the rest of my life.

"God help me," I whispered as they assisted me, weak kneed and shivering, into the black van. "I am only twenty-seven!"

As I sat on the hard, swaying seat, my handcuffed hands folded primly in my lap, I saw myself growing old and gray, wrinkled, stooping with a dowager's hump, my sight dimming, my steps slowing, and my hands gnarled with rheumatism, as the weeks became months, and the months became years, and the years stretched into decades. My children would grow up without me, and I would never know love, maternal or carnal, ever again. I was alive and I knew I should be grateful and fall on my knees and thank God that I had been spared, but a life devoid of warmth, comfort, and love was scarcely a life at all.

I felt the key burning me through my gown. I felt so weak and frightened then I wanted to scream out the truth, but I thought of Bobo and Gladys and bit my lips until they bled. At Aylesbury Prison they would take my clothes away and that temptation, the key that could set me free, would go with them to be locked in a storage box until the day I died. If it was found then . . . Chance is the Fool's name for Fate and I've been a gambler all my life.

❧ 31 ❧

At Aylesbury Prison the first thing I lost was my name. Henceforth, no one would call me "Florie" or "Mrs. Maybrick." I was now L.P. 29, the twenty-ninth woman in the year of 1889 to be condemned to penal servitude for life.

The second thing I lost was my clothes and with them the last tattered shreds of my dignity. They made me stand stark naked in the center of a cold little room as a hard-faced matron with rough hands scrutinized every inch of me while three others and the prison doctor stood by and watched with bored, unfeeling eyes. Somehow the brusque, businesslike way her hands moved over me, the way they had rudely, intrusively brushed over hundreds of women before me, seemed worse than all the beatings I had endured at my husband's hands. At least he had loved me. Now I would never be touched in love again. Afterward I was ordered to lie upon a table, deprived of even the modest veiling of a sheet, with my knees up and my thighs parted wide, while the doctor poked his impatient fingers into my most intimate parts. I yelped as his fingers twisted within me like a corkscrew and he snapped, "Hush! I can't possibly be hurting you!" I could tell by his tone that he would not have cared if he was.

When I got up, shaking on unsteady feet, I was ushered out into a long room where I was ordered to fall into line behind the other women who had gone before me. Petty thieves, prostitutes, pickpockets, failed suicides, abortionists, and condemned murderers like me. *We're all criminals now,* I thought. Some were very young—one girl looked no more than fifteen—some were very old, gray and bent backed with gnarled fingers, and there were all ages in between, slim and stout, fair and dark, all stripped naked of their name, clothes, and anything else they had ever called their own. Some stood blatantly, brazenly naked, as though the cool air felt deliciously refreshing upon their bare skin, occasionally scratching a crotch or hairy armpit, while others, faces aflame with shame, hunched and huddled and tried to hide themselves like me. A matron grabbed my arm and yanked me back, barking my vulnerable bare heels on the cold, stone floor, and said sharply into my ear that I must *always* remain three full steps behind the woman in front of me whenever we were in a line or else I would be punished and a notation made in my permanent record. I was also informed that *any* attempt at conversation between inmates, or even murmuring, singing, or humming to oneself, was strictly forbidden.

I who had once enjoyed hot rose-scented baths in my own private tub was forced to wade quickly through a long vat of cold, dingy gray water. When I emerged, the soles of my feet feeling like they were coated in slime, a blast of white powder hit my crotch in a billowing puff to kill any lingering vermin and a matron barked at me to put my hands behind my head so she could fumigate my armpits in the same manner. The powder and my pride stung and brought tears to my eyes.

I followed the line to a long table where I was given one rough petticoat stenciled "AYLESBURY" in bold black letters, the mud-brown linsey prison uniform, a baggy long-sleeved sack of a dress, a pair of thick, ribbed beige woolen stockings, and big brown heavy-soled boots, stout enough to last a lifetime. No drawers or stays were permitted. Nor were nightgowns allowed; we must sleep in our uniforms.

The third thing I lost was my hair. That weighty golden glory I had once worn piled high in a gilded pompadour or cascading in curls was chopped off high at the nape of my neck. The matron in charge of my shearing gathered my hair tight in her big meaty fist, pulling so hard my scalp burned and tears pricked my eyes, and determinedly hacked away with her scissors. Every rasp of the blades broke my heart. She briskly wound a length of twine around my hair, forming what looked like a long gold horse's tail, and handed it aside, to be put in storage with my clothes. Then, not content with leaving me shorn short as a man, she went to work with her shears again, cutting what was left of my hair as close as she could to my scalp. When she was done, she tossed a white linen cap into my lap and shouted, "Next!"

I was led down a long, dark corridor of thick, double-bricked walls. The matron paused to unlock a door, set with an abysmal little postage-stamp window, barred as though a grown woman could ever hope to shimmy and crawl through it when that would be hard for even a baby. And even if she got her hand through somehow what could she hope to grasp except air? The matron motioned me inside and locked the door behind me.

That was when I stopped counting what I had lost and started counting what I had. Seven normal-sized steps took me across the width of my cell, and another seven measured the length of it. One barred window, my only light, set with thick glazed glass, set up high, so that even when I strained and stood on my tiptoes I seemed to view the world through tears. A wooden plank bed covered with a thin mattress stuffed with coconut fibers, and a gray serge blanket. A bucket for one's bodily needs sat beneath it. There was also a second bucket filled with cold water, for washing body and cell and eating utensils. A stool and a small table that I might use at my labor and my little leisure. On a shelf, set recessed into the wall, not nailed there lest some clever or deranged convict pry it loose and wield it as a weapon, sat a tin plate, bowl, cup, and spoon, a small dish of salt, and an ounce of soap, a whole week's allotment, a comb, a slim volume to instruct me in prison etiquette, a hymnal, and a Bible.

I would be permitted a bath, a fresh uniform, and barbering once a month as needed, essentially a repetition of the deplorable process I had just endured. After the initial to-the-scalp shearing, my hair would be allowed to grow no longer than my earlobes, but if any vermin were detected I would be shorn down to the scalp again.

This would be my life from now on, a living death entombed by bricks piled and mortared double thick, suffered in silence, *always* silence. There were moments when I *longed* to scream just so I could remind myself what my own voice sounded like, to lose myself completely and be like the madwomen whose tormented banshee shrieks sometimes shattered the silent nights. Sometimes when one of the matrons, the warden, or the chaplain spoke to me, allowing me to speak in return, I'd stumble over the simplest words, they had grown so unfamiliar to my tongue. I must have sounded like a simpleton, dumbly groping for words that once rolled off my tongue smooth as silk. I never thought I'd live to see the hour when a sneeze, a cough, or even a fart would be welcome because it broke the omnipresent silence without inviting dire punishment.

I had thought the days in which I stood in the dock, on trial for my life, then those, after I was condemned, when I sat in my cell waiting to die were the darkest days of my life, but I was mistaken. I think now, no matter how bad things may seem, there is *always* something worse.

Every morning I must rise at six o'clock. I must be waiting, standing at the door, with my bowl and cup, for weak tea and lumpy gruel with a few morsels of gristly mutton and a hunk of brown bread so hard and gritty it was murder on the teeth and jaw. By the time the bell rang for chapel I must have thoroughly scrubbed my cell, down on my knees, with cold water that caused my hands to crack and left my knuckles rough and raw, carefully portioning out my meager supply of soap. At seven o'clock we were led out, leaving our scrub buckets and brushes outside our cell doors as we went, walking a full three paces one behind the other, to the prison chapel for a thirty-minute service. Then it was back to our cells for work duty.

Sewing shirts for soldiers, that was mine. I was required to produce at least five completed shirts each week, with no faults or sloppy stitches, as each would be minutely inspected. If I failed or disappointed in any way my rations would be cut, my weekly library book and letter and visitation privileges revoked, and a notation made in my record. Every evening when I heard the matron making her rounds to collect our sewing implements I stitched all the faster, praying for time. There were nights when I went to bed and couldn't sleep for worrying over an unfinished shirt, fearing that I would fail to meet the requisite quota by the week's end.

At noon we paused in our labors for another meager meal of tough mutton, weak tea, and brick-hard bread. For the following hour, we were let out into the prison yard, walking, three paces between each body, round and round in circles, never stopping, staring straight ahead, mouths sealed lest the vigilant matron suspect us of talking. What else was there to look at except the backs of one another's heads? Only the high stone walls, the flat gray flagstones beneath our boots, and the sky above, mocking us each moment with its expansive blue freedom and clouds that could drift wherever in the world they wished. By two o'clock we were back at our labors.

For supper at six, we stood at our cell doors, cups and bowls humbly outstretched for the greasy meat stew, tepid tea, and hard bread. After our meal, a prisoner, who had earned the ultimate privilege of working in the library, would roll a cart down the cell-lined corridors taking back the books we had finished and letting us select new ones.

We were allotted one hour of "leisure" before bed in which we might read, pray, or sit in quiet contemplation over a loved one's letter or photograph. We were each allowed one small box in which to keep these precious paper treasures, subject to inspection, of course, to make sure we never came into possession of anything forbidden. All our letters were read before we ever laid eyes on them. *Privacy* was another one of those words my tongue could no longer form or fathom; it had lost all meaning to me.

ᴥ 32 ᴥ

I counted the stitches, stitches in time, sewn throughout the years, every instant feeling like a taffy-stretched eternity. I thought about my children growing up without me, and, in my woman's heart, I dreamed of Alfred Brierley.

Those numerous sleepless nights were passed in foolish fantasies in which I was magically set free and he was waiting at the prison gate for me, to sweep me up in his arms and carry me away in a hot-air balloon. I imagined us swooping down and scooping my children up. Then away we'd all go to a new and happy life together. I hoped and prayed that he was thinking of me too, that he would wait for me. But a day came when Mama, during the precious half hour we got to spend together every three months, talking through a grille, with a matron standing by me, told me that he'd married.

I'm so glad it wasn't me, a little part of my heart took me by surprise by saying. It took me a *long* time to realize that little voice was the voice of truth. We could never have *really* made each other happy. He was just a fantasy, a dream I tried to will into reality, and even when he was flesh and blood and throbbing manhood in my arms he was still just a dream. I was just too hurt and blind to see it at the time. But even when I knew that dream was also lost to me, I never did stop thinking of him lustfully; we all need someone to dream about. Why must loss, lust, and love be tangled up so?

I thought of the diary, and I thought about Jim and that whole impossibly tangled mess we'd both made of love and lust, resentment and revenge, passion and pain. So many, many times I felt Jack the Ripper's knife twist in my heart. Jim's confession could set me free . . . but at what cost! This sacrifice, this penance, this silence, this imprisonment for a crime I had briefly contemplated but never, thank God, committed! Would the reality for my children truly be as bad as I feared? Why was it *so* hard to know if I had done the right thing? Why did I keep torturing myself by traveling up and down that road? Why couldn't I make peace with the decision I had made? Why couldn't I be stalwart like a saint and stoically endure my fate, knowing that I had made a noble sacrifice? I was so weary of wrestling with my conscience, day after day, night after night, always wondering what was wrong and what was right. All I truly knew was that once black and white paint are mixed together they can never be pure and separate ever again, only some shade of gray.

Other books tormented me too. One day I impulsively took Mr. James's *Daisy Miller* from the library cart. But that was a mistake. In its pages I found the ghost of the girl I used to be, the fun, foolish, flighty, and frivolous young madcap, and she came back to haunt me, bobbing bustle and ringlets, saucy manner, and vibrant, flirty smile, dancing through life with her head in the clouds and stars in her eyes. I also found shades of me in the prison's illicit copy of *Madame Bovary,* that scandalous book stitched inside the cover of a book of sermons to be secretly savored by all of us who could read; there I was the discontented wife, racking up debts and recklessly running off to rendezvous with her lover. That story ends with poison too, only it's the wanton wife who dies, not her ditchwater-dull doctor husband. Hawthorne's *Scarlet Letter* I found peculiarly comforting now that I wore an ineradicable invisible *A* upon my breast that could never be put off, not even in death—*A* for *Arsenic, A* for *Adulteress.* And *Lady Audley's Secret* I could not suffer to have near me. Never would I take it into my cell, not even when it remained alone in the library cart the only volume I had not read. It reminded me that I also had a secret. *East Lynne* I likewise shunned. It made the unrelenting ache for my children even more unbearable; Lady Isabel was my sister in sorrow.

I became slothful and indifferent. It's hard not to when all you have to wear is one baggy brown dress and you're all but bald beneath your cap. I also became dispassionate and, in a sense, numb. When before the sight of a mouse or some ugly creepy-crawly insect would send me shrieking up onto the nearest stool, now I sat, in the stony gloom of my living tomb, and stared at the mice and black beetles scuttling across my cell, amazed that any life would come willingly here.

The ever-present chill crept into my bones, lodged there, and would never leave, bringing with it, uninvited, the most unwelcome and tenacious houseguests—fevers, chilblains, bronchitis, catarrh, rheumatism, burning throats, and hacking coughs.

And so the years crept past. Slowly, slowly, slowly. The old year dragging into the new one like the deadweight of a corpse being dragged from a river. Every New Year's Eve I would stand on my toes, gazing out the window, seeing nothing but the dream of what might have been. Christmases spent with my children. Being spoiled and petted, kissed and lavished with gifts. Champagne and waltzes, a new gown, sparkling jewels, diamonds and pearls, and a man who loved and desired me taking me in his arms and kissing me at the midnight hour. Some years I imagined it was Jim; others I dreamed of Alfred Brierley. What did it really matter? They were both lost to me. My bare shoulders bundled in costly furs, a ride home through snow and moonlight, then falling into a bed of love, my body opening like a flower beneath my beloved's kiss. Sometimes, in those dark hours, when the world I used to be a part of was embracing and celebrating, bidding the old year good-bye and welcoming the new one with champagne, and my fellow prisoners slumbered, dreaming their equally hopeless dreams, I dared lift my mud-hued skirt and in my stocking feet, humming just as softly as I could, waltzed across my cell in the arms of a phantom lover.

My children grew up without me. Michael arranged for them to be adopted by one of Jim's doctors who had testified against me at my trial, Dr. Charles Fuller, and his wife. For one hundred pounds per annum they would raise Bobo and Gladys as their own and send them to spend every summer with their chilly, arrogant, and otherwise indifferent uncle Michael at his house on the Isle of Wight. The Fullers even changed the children's names. Bobo was now James Fuller—he'd even dropped my family name of Chandler, which he'd been given as a middle name—and my daughter became Gladys Evelyn Fuller.

Michael was *determined* that they should despise me. But Mrs. Fuller at least had a heart. No matter what else she might have thought of me, she knew the pain of a mother's heart, perhaps because a string of miscarriages had dashed her hopes of having children of her own. Every Christmas without fail, she sent me a photograph of Bobo and Gladys, so I could, from this sad, disgraced distance, see the changes each year wrought.

How my heart lived for those pictures! I was as greedy for them as any child for toys and treats on Christmas morning. No present, not even the jewels and dresses I used to take for granted, could ever have meant as much to me as those precious pictures.

Through still images, frozen moments captured in sepia tone, I got to see my beautiful black-haired boy, dressed like a man in miniature now, in suit and tie, growing up, tall and slender, so handsome he should have been posing for artists and preparing for a career on the stage. When he posed in profile, I saw his lashes were as long and luxuriant as ever. Only he was never smiling in these photographs. It worried me so to think of that laughing, happy little boy I had known becoming such a dour, frowning sourpuss, so grave and serious, cold and arrogant. I remembered how he loved to cuddle, kiss, and hug and could not reconcile those memories with the strange cold-fish little character staring morosely back at me with blank, bored eyes. I wished I had magical powers so I could reach into those photographs and shake him and shout, *No, Bobo, no, this is not who you were meant to be!* He was becoming Michael in miniature, and there was nothing I could do to stop it. I was forbidden to write to my own children. I was like a beggar every year waiting with hands outstretched and yearning for those pictures. Michael, I knew, was determined that the children be brought up strictly. "A flawed tree grows from a flawed root," he had told the Fullers, making that an ironclad condition of the adoption. The summer visits were his means of ensuring it was being enforced.

Gladys showed every sign of blossoming into a great beauty. A violet-eyed, black-haired, porcelain-skinned belle, she had a flat, boyish figure that was gradually rounding into the tantalizing promise of beautiful, bountiful womanhood. Mrs. Fuller sent me a lovely hand-tinted picture of Gladys wearing a lilac chiffon dress. I could see so much of myself in her, the longing almost killed me. She was at an age when a girl really needs her mother, and I could not be there for her, not even by letter. Her little bosoms were just appearing when the pictures abruptly stopped coming.

After I had been in prison six years Christmas came, but the pictures didn't. I was so upset I couldn't stop crying or keep down my food and had to go to the infirmary for a fortnight. When Mama came to visit me I *begged* her to go and see Mrs. Fuller and find out what had happened. I was *terrified* some awful fate had befallen my children. Or maybe Mrs. Fuller had died and no one else knew of the yearly charity she had unfailingly dispensed to me? Perhaps Dr. Fuller or Michael had found out and forbidden her to continue? Mama wept herself to see me so distraught and frantic, gnawing my nails bloody, and my eyes bloodshot and dark circled from crying through so many sleepless nights. She promised she would find out and an explanation would be in her very next letter.

Trapped behind iron bars, I had no choice but to wait . . . and hope. Maybe the pictures had been lost in the mail or misdirected, which had caused a delay in their delivery? Or maybe an illness, not a serious one, from which the children, or Mrs. Fuller herself, had quickly recovered had merely postponed the pictures' being taken and mailed in time for Christmas?

I thought there was nothing left of my heart to break, but the truth is the human heart endlessly regenerates itself and there's no counting the number of times it can break over the course of a lifetime. No one was dead or dying and England's postal service was as prompt and efficient as ever. Nor had Dr. Fuller or Michael forbidden Mrs. Fuller this act of charity; it was my son.

With no one to pet and feed him lumps of sugar my little Bobo had, as the pictures had made me fear, grown hard and sour. Bobo—it was impossible for me to think of him by any other name, though I knew he now answered only to the strictly formal James— had been thoroughly persuaded of my guilt. He believed that I had deprived him and his little sister of a loving father. And the fact that I was permitted the pleasure of gazing upon Bobo's and Gladys's features once a year made him sick. Maybe that was why he was never smiling in those pictures? Had he been sending me a silent message all along and I had failed to see it? Now that he had attained the age of fourteen and was standing on the cusp of manhood, he had adamantly expressed the wish that no further photographs be sent to me. And everyone felt, given his age and the maturity with which he had expressed himself, that this was no childish whim and that his wishes should be respected. And Gladys . . . Gladys felt the same; she also hated me. Michael had patted them both upon the shoulder and promised, "She will forget your faces, just like you have forgotten hers."

How could anyone be so cruel? To deny me even the one tiny consolation of seeing my children's faces, printed on paper, once a year at Christmastime? My heart all but died that day. My chest hurt so bad, assailed by the most awful pressures and pains, like a giant's fist was gripping my heart and *squeezing* it, trying to wring every last drop of blood out, while bearing down with all his might upon my shoulder with the other hand, that I had to be taken to the infirmary again.

Every year thereafter, as the years crept *slowly* by—1896, 1897, 1898, 1899, 1900—a whole brand-new century, just think of it!—1901—the end of an era, Queen Victoria died—1902, 1903—I sat at my table every Christmas and lined up the pictures I had in a row and tried to imagine what my children looked like now. Where they were, what they were doing, how they were spending this Christmas? And did they ever spare a thought for me?

Bobo's voice would have changed; he would have found the first whisker on his chin and started shaving. Did he sport a fine mustache like his father or agonize over the cultivation of a straggling, puny little one or prefer to remain clean shaven? He would have finished school and gone to work. Where? At what? What were his interests? Was his work just work or was it a passion? Did he share his beauty with the world or hide it away in a dull, dreary office?

Gladys would be a woman now; she would surely have beaus. I bet the boys just flocked to her and her dance card was never empty. A little beauty like her, she might even be engaged or actually *be* married for all I knew. And what of Bobo? Was there some sweet girl who set his heart afire and made his soul sing?

My mother's heart ached to know. I would sit and stare at those photographs until tears blurred my eyes and I could no longer bear it; then I would fall weeping onto my cot.

I wondered if Queen Victoria had any idea when she commuted my sentence that sparing my life would be so much crueler than putting a quick end to it on the gallows?

❧ 33 ❧

Near the end of January 1904, a miracle happened. The king, Edward VII, Victoria's fun- and lady-loving son, Bertie, the one everyone used to call "the Prince of Pleasure," decided this wicked woman was indeed worthy of redemption.

My cell door swung open wide and I walked out a free woman, a lady again, with my head held high.

I was taken to a little room where a dusty cardboard box containing my belongings had been set out on a table, with a hand mirror facedown beside it, lying there just like a snake waiting to bite me, between a beautifully wrapped pink dress box tied with shimmering ribbon and a big pink-and-white-striped hatbox that Mama had sent me from Paris.

A bath—with *hot* water, the first hot bath I'd had in fifteen years!—and an entire cake of soap just for me, awaited me in an adjoining room. A tiny, strictly utilitarian bathroom, no frills and nothing fancy, but in that moment it seemed the most beautiful sight my eyes had ever seen. A toothbrush—another luxury that had long ago vanished from my life—was lying on the sink. Part of me wanted to sit and luxuriate in the hot soapy water and steam for hours, but now that I was free . . . I didn't want to tempt fate. I was half-afraid that if I lingered a matron would come barging in and inform me that a mistake had been made and bundle me back to my cell again.

Sheer white silk stockings, pink satin slippers with French heels and big silvery buckles on the toes, drawers and chemise of the purest angel-soft white batiste trimmed with pink silk ribbons and lace, a corset, candy pink, the first that had embraced my waist in fifteen years, a shirtwaist of white eyelet trimmed at the collar and cuffs with pink ribbons, and, to fasten at the throat, a brooch, a big, round opal, with a whole flashing pastel rainbow captured in its milky depths, set into a bouquet of carved coral roses, a beautifully tailored suit made of candy-pink linen with a long, straight, narrow skirt—bustles were *long* gone!—and a jacket that flared out around my hips. I was dressed like a lady again, and for the first time in fifteen years I actually *felt* like a lady! And the hat! Oh, what a hat! An extravaganza of pink satin roses and ribbons covering what looked like an upside-down washtub woven out of golden straw, with a long hatpin topped by a green and white enameled ruby-throated hummingbird hovering above the roses. There was an exquisite white lace mobcap to wear beneath it, with a cascade of pretty lace to frame my face. Mama had thought of *everything*. She knew I would be embarrassed about showing myself to the world with my head shorn.

It was only then that I thought about my hair and opened that musty old cardboard box. It was still there, a shimmering gold horse's tail tied at one end with twine. I sat down and, with my lips puckered in concentration, tried to braid and roll it into a bun I could wear until my own hair grew out, but I was too nervous, I just couldn't manage it, the silky strands kept slipping through my fingers. With a defeated sigh, I stuffed it into the pink satin hand-bag Mama had sent. I would deal with it later.

It was only then, with the lace cap covering my cropped hair and that wonderful hat on top, that I had the courage to finally face the mirror. I almost wished I had remained a coward. I shrieked and dropped it. It shattered upon the slate floor, and staring up at me I saw my face reflected a dozen times, thin and marble white with hard, harsh lines chiseled deep about the eyes, nose, and mouth. My eyes were sunken and dark circled and the skin around my lips had with age achieved a faint permanent pucker, like the finest tiny pleats. My shorn hair, now shot with silver, had darkened to a deep muddy yellow, rendering that shimmering fall of radiant hair in my handbag utterly useless. If I wore it, no one would believe for a moment that it was my own. And my body—for a moment the new suit had made me forget—my curves had long since melted away, my bosom now hung pendulous and slack, and my body was practically a broom handle with arms and legs like toothpicks. And my hands . . . I quickly pulled on the white kid gloves to cover them. I had grown up believing you could always tell a lady by her hands. I now had the hands of a charwoman who spent her spare time picking cotton.

"I'm just not that girl anymore," I whispered to my multitude of miniature reflections staring mournfully up at me from the gray slate floor. "Good-bye, Florie!"

That girl, that Florie, was gone; nothing but memories were left of her now. She'd slipped quietly away while I was in prison. I'd been expecting to see her, waiting excitedly to greet me, for this candy-pink suit and rose-festooned confection of a hat to make her come running. But no, it was not to be. She was lost and gone forever, dreadful sorry, Clementine. Now this grim-faced, skinny forty-two-year-old shadow that long gone golden girl had left behind her had no choice but to go forth bravely into the world and forge a new life for herself and find out who she was now that she couldn't be *that* Florie anymore.

I reached back into the box and drew out my black mourning gown, old and stale, fifteen years out of fashion, and grown rusty with age. For a moment it looked so much like bloodstains upon the black fabric that I felt nausea rising. I shuddered and dropped it; it made my skin crawl. I shut my eyes, took a deep breath, willed myself to be strong, and reached in again. I quickly removed the key from its hidden seam and let the dress fall forever. I dropped the key, badly tarnished and no longer golden, just like me, into my new pink purse. "Burn the rest!" I said imperiously to the matron on my way out.

To my surprise, a sweet little Swiss nun was waiting for me. A Sister Patia, she had come all the way from the Convent of the Epiphany in Cornwall, where she was to take me now, it being their way of gently reintroducing those who had spent so many years in solitude behind bars back into the world.

"It grows busier and nosier every year, my dear. You will find it very much changed from the way you remember," she said.

Mama had been notified and would meet me there and take me back to Paris with her after I'd had a few weeks to readjust and recover from the shock.

"*Shock?* What shock? I'm ready to go *now!*" I cried, chomping at the bit until a horn blared loudly, nearly startling me out of my skin, and I leapt back, clinging to Sister Patia, as a motorcar drew up outside the prison gates when I'd been expecting a horse-drawn cab to take us to Paddington Station.

Sister Patia just smiled and gave a knowing little nod. "This way, my child," she said, gently ushering me into the back of the shiny black automobile.

The way that "taxi" zipped and darted through the traffic of the London streets, where only a few horse-drawn equipages stubbornly remained, I felt certain we would be killed at any moment. I clung to my hat with one hand and Sister Patia with the other while she just sat there smiling, sometimes giving me an encouraging pat or a reassuring word. "We're going to die!" I kept crying out, though the chipper cockney driver just smiled back at me—how could he take his eyes off the street for even an instant?—and assured me, " 'Aven't lost one yet, missus; just you sit back an' relax now!" I was so afraid of imminent death, of being impaled by the crush and grind of metal, I could hardly take in the sights outside my window. Every time a horn blared—and good Lord there were a great many of them!—I jumped. I was sorely afraid I would end by losing control of my bladder and ruining my pretty pink suit.

But apparently this was the way people got about nowadays and there really was no cause for alarm. Sure enough, we arrived at Paddington Station safe and sound. Sister Patia led me to a chair in the waiting room and, when she was sure I was sufficiently calm, left me for a few minutes and returned with a stack of magazines for me.

Casually flipping through them, I saw few faces I recognized and but a few tried-and-true products still going strong in this new century, like Cadburys; suddenly I wanted a taste of chocolate *so* badly I was salivating like a mad dog. The names of all the songs and dances and popular books and stage plays, actors and actresses, seemed bewilderingly new and I feared I had fallen too far behind to ever catch up. It was *too much* to take in, and I left the magazines sitting in my lap and just sat and watched the people pass by.

I already knew the fashions had changed, but the march of progress had trod over everything. Harsh electricity had replaced the romantic kindness of gaslight. Life seemed to move at a faster pace; people seemed to walk and talk faster, though perhaps it only seemed so because of the silence and isolation I had endured in prison. Sister Patia told me pictures even moved now. "The flickers" or "movies," "motion pictures," she explained were a popular form of entertainment and growing more so every year. People paid to go and sit in a theater and stare at these pictures in motion projected onto a big white screen. I wasn't at all certain I would like such a thing—I was half-afraid it would make me dizzy and faint or hurt my eyes—but Sister Patia smiled and said she thought not, they only lasted a few minutes, hardly time to do such damage, and most people liked them, though, of course, they weren't on a par with the legitimate stage and would never replace the music halls, but they were good fun all the same. "Though perhaps I am biased." She smiled. "I confess, they are my guilty pleasure."

When we stepped off the train in Cornwall, Mama was right there waiting for me, just as Sister Patia had promised. I was so happy to see Mama, without iron bars between us, I ran and hurled myself into her arms like a cannonball and nearly knocked her off her feet. All the way to the convent, we clung to each other and cried.

I ended up staying at the Convent of the Epiphany for six weeks, going out into the world a little each day, visiting shops, walking about town, and sitting in parks listening to band concerts or watching children play, learning to speak up and use my voice again. It was harder than I ever realized it would be not to shy away from people, to stand my ground and look them in the eye and speak to them just like I always did before my troubles began. It was a battle royal I fought with myself now not to hang my head and hurry away whenever the salesclerks approached and not to spend half an hour walking round in circles before getting up the nerve to go into a little café and order a pastry and a cup of coffee or tea. I felt like everybody was staring and whispering about me. There were times when it seemed like I was afraid of everyone and everything, including my own shadow.

Mama had miraculously saved my pearls—her pearls—the ones she had given me on my wedding day. She fastened them around my neck my first night in the convent, when I sat up in bed, in my new white nightgown, hugging my knees and glorying in being able to even temporarily call that starkly simple whitewashed room my own and to actually be able to brush my teeth, undress properly for bed, and have hot water and wash myself whenever I wished. She told me the pearls would help restore my confidence. "Nothing makes a lady feel more like a lady, darlin', than pearls!" She also cut a lock from my hair and sent it on to London. She'd made inquiries and discovered that the best wig and hairpiece maker was a Frenchman named Armand, and she let it be known she expected to find a selection of fine falls and hairpieces that perfectly matched my hair waiting for us when we arrived.

I went out with Mama at first, clinging to her at every step like a toddling child terrified of falling, despite the pearls hanging like an anchor around my throat vainly trying to steady me. And then, at Sister Patia's gentle insistence, after the first week, I ventured out on my own. Walking boldly into a drugstore and asking if they stocked the pink rose-scented cold cream I had always liked without turning and running away like a scared rabbit felt like one of the greatest triumphs of my life. The clerk was a very kind young man and apologetically informed me that brand was no longer being manufactured, but, if I would allow him he would be pleased to recommend a substitute many ladies found agreeable. "If you would be so kind . . ." I nodded and soon I left the shop smiling with the pretty pink tub of cold cream in my handbag. Back in my little white room in the convent, I spent *hours* sitting on the bed in my camisole and drawers slathering it on my parched and hungry skin, soaking it in, basking in its cool, silky pink sweetness. After fifteen years in prison, I doubted I would take *any* luxury, not even a little thing like cold cream, for granted ever again.

Strolling by the tempestuous gray sea, I had many long, private talks with Sister Patia. We talked about the children and Jim, Michael, and Edwin, and though it shamed me to say his name to a nun, knowing that she knew what we had done, we spoke of Alfred Brierley, and the anger and guilt she could sense, without my even saying it, that I was carrying like a cancer inside me.

"You cannot forget until you forgive." She spoke these simple words so matter-of-factly I knew that she was right, but I couldn't stand still and face it; all I wanted to do was run. I had been through *so much* . . . I just *couldn't* let go! "And when I speak of forgiveness," she continued, "I do not just mean others; I also mean yourself. God has forgiven you, my child, and given you the gift of a new beginning; if He has forgiven you, why should you not forgive yourself as well as those who have judged and trespassed against you? Until you are ready to do that, I am afraid you will never truly know peace."

"I know, Sister, I know!" I sighed. "I just don't know if I can do it . . . not yet! Have I not just cause for bitterness? And anger?" I demanded. "Look at all they took from me! They stole *fifteen years* of my life! *My freedom!* My children lost to me, their love turned to hate, my reputation. They *lied,* stood up in court, swore on the Bible, and *lied,* not even caring if I died for their lies!"

"You are not alone." Sister Patia reached for my hand. "He died for the sins of others, and yet He rose again, and forgave, as *you* must do. 'Remember ye not the former things, neither consider the things of old. Behold, I will do a new thing; now it shall spring forth; shall ye not know it? I will even make a way in the wilderness, and rivers in the desert,' " she quoted with the most beautiful, tranquil serenity, it brought tears to my eyes.

"I hear what you say . . ." I started, and stopped, tears streaming from my eyes. I felt torn and tugged in every direction; I knew and yet I didn't know. My ears heard her, but my heart, I was afraid, was deaf to her wisdom. "I know . . ." I started, to try to explain, if only I could. . . .

Sister Patia smiled gently and patted my hand. *"You will,"* she said confidently.

* * *

When the time came to leave the convent, I found I didn't want to go. "I don't know if I can do this," I said suddenly, turning on the steps and reaching back for Sister Patia's hand. "Maybe I should stay . . . just for a little while longer—"

"You'll be fine." She took both my hands in hers and gave them a squeeze that was both comforting and confident. "Sometimes, my child, the only way a person can grow stronger is after they have been knocked down as you have been. Now it's time for you to get up and go back out into the world again."

I nodded uncertainly, but I didn't like to disappoint a nun, especially one who had been so kind to me. "I hope so, Sister Patia; I most sincerely hope so!" I said, and squared my shoulders and started down the steps again to where Mama was already waiting in the cab.

"But what if I fail?" I turned back suddenly and caught desperately at Sister Patia's hands. "I'm so afraid of failing!"

"You mustn't be," she said with the most serene, beatific smile I had ever seen. "Sometimes, my child, failure is a gift from God, though it may not seem so at first glance. Failure is the chance to start again; it is not an end, but a new beginning."

I nodded and swallowed down the last vestiges of my fear. "A new beginning!" My eyes lit up with longing. "I'd like that more than anything, Sister Patia!"

"And God has given it to you." She smiled. "Ask and you shall receive, seek and you shall find, and that is what you must do now. Godspeed, and good luck to you, Mrs. Maybrick!"

With renewed confidence, I went out boldly into the world in my candy-pink suit, rose-heaped hat, and pearls, *determined* to have that new beginning. Mama said some people pray all their lives for a second chance and it is never given to them and I was one of the lucky ones. I was alive, and with life there is *always* hope! I was on my way to Paris, but first I was going to London to see my children.

It took every ounce of courage I could dredge up to knock upon the Fullers' front door. Not even all the pearls or finest French fashions and hairpieces in the world could give me confidence enough, but I *had* to do this. When the maid opened the door, I turned pale as her little white ruffled cap and swayed so that she had to reach out and steady me.

"Merciful God, missus!" she exclaimed. "You're not goin' to faint here on the doorstep, are you?"

"I'm all right, thank you." I gulped my fear down and took a deep cleansing breath. "I've come to see Mrs. Fuller; is she in?"

The Irish skivvy gave me a queer look. "In, mum? The Fullers haven't lived here in *years!* This is Dr. Pearson's house now. They up and moved to America, to New York, years and years ago!"

"And the children?" I asked anxiously. "Did the children go with them?"

"Mr. James and Miss Gladys?" There was that queer look again. "Why, yes'um! Them being such a close family, I could hardly imagine any of 'em willingly putting an ocean between 'em!"

"America!" I gasped, tottering on my French heels. "Thank you!" I nodded and, pressing a coin into her hand, hurried briskly back down the steps onto the street again.

I kept walking. I didn't dare turn around lest I see the maid still standing there staring after me. I wanted to stop and catch my breath, but I kept walking. I don't know how many blocks I went before I just had to stop. When I looked around I found myself in an unfamiliar part of town, a crestfallen, dreary part where all the buildings seemed in want of painting and the people in need of new clothes. A pretty blind girl with a tattered green shawl draped over her red hair was leaning against a wall, a tin cup in her hand, singing a song that Fate seemed to have intended just for my ears:

> *"Oh, no! We never mention her, her name is never*
> *   heard;*
> *My lips are now forbid to speak that once familiar word.*
> *From sport to sport they hurry me, to banish my regret.*
> *And when they win a smile from me, they think that I*
> *   forget.*
>
> *"They bid me seek in change of scene the charms that*
> *   others see,*

But were I in a foreign land, they'd find no change
  in me.
'Tis true that I behold no more the valley where we met,
I do not see the hawthorn tree, but how could I forget?

"For oh! there are so many things recall the past to me,
The breeze upon the sunny hills, the billows of the sea,
The rosy tint that decks the sky before the sun is set;
Ay, every leaf I look upon forbids me to forget.

"They tell me she is happy now, the gayest of the gay;
They hint that she forgets me too—but I heed not what
  they say.
Perhaps like me she struggles with each feeling of regret:
But if she loves as I have loved, she never can forget."

Tears in my eyes, I emptied the coins from my purse into her cup and quickly hailed a cab. I had to get back to the hotel and tell Mama I was not going with her to Paris, I was going to America to find my children and, God willing, to make amends and a place for myself in their hearts again.

❧ 34 ❧

I returned to America on the same ship that brought me to England, Jim, and my destiny, twenty-four years ago, the *SS Baltic,* only it was a brand, spanking new *Baltic;* they'd retired the old one years ago but kept the name. It seemed somehow strangely fitting that I'd been with both *Baltics* when they were maidens, only I wasn't a young girl anymore, a hopeful bride-to-be of eighteen, though there were moments when I stood at the rail that I sensed her ghost standing beside me. My reflection reminded me every chance it got that I was a worn and weary middle-aged woman whose future remained uncertain. But I was still hoping for a new and better life; that hadn't changed. I was alive, and life and hope are bound together like Siamese twins; you can't have one without the other.

When our ship glided gracefully into New York Harbor and I saw the Statue of Liberty I fell on my knees, the most grateful tears I had ever shed streaming down my face. Let the others stare; I didn't care. I more than any one of them understood what *liberty* truly meant. I'd lost it, I thought forever, and now it was mine again, and I would *never* be such a fool as to take my freedom for granted.

The moment my foot, shod in a dainty new boot of black patent leather and gray suede, to match my new striped traveling dress and silver fox stole and muff, touched the gangplank a band began to play "Home, Sweet Home." I was so overcome that Mama had to hold me up. The press of the crowd, though they were a kindly bunch, all calling out good wishes and God bless, frightened me, as did the numerous journalists, crying out questions and aiming cameras at me, making me feel petrified with terror, like I was facing a firing squad, and I clung to Mama all the more and tried, with trembling hands, to pull my veil down.

"*Please!* I am too overwhelmed to speak!" I kept crying as I slumped against Mama.

The next thing I knew I was seated in the opulent velvet-cushioned softness of a sleek silver motorcar and a broadly smiling man and woman, Mama's friends, my ardent supporters the Densmores, were pressing enormous bouquets of pink and white flowers into my arms and I was being whisked away to the quiet and splendid seclusion of their country estate, Cragsmore House. I was so stunned I couldn't take in a single word. I merely sat there, dumb as a mute, trying to just breathe and staring at the back of the chauffeur's head while Mama and Mrs. Densmore sat on each side of me, patting my hands, and Mr. Densmore kept smiling so much I'm sure his mouth must have ached long before we reached Newport.

It was a world I thought lost to me forever, only a dream I vaguely remembered—manicured lawns, sweeping marble staircases, antique statuary imported from digs in Roman ruins, crystal chandeliers, forest-green, plum, and deep blood-crimson plush velvet portieres, gilt accents, like golden lace to trim this lavish life, stucco embellishments, rich-veined woods, polished until they shone like brown eyes lit by love, brocade, damask, velvet, and leather upholstered sofas, chairs, stools, and benches, ancestral portraits and Old Masters in rich golden frames on every wall, photographs framed in silver, Wedgwood, Sevres, Dresden, Chippendale, Sheraton, Brussels tapestries, Aubusson carpets, graceful rococo splendor evocative of the vanished opulence of Versailles vying with discreet intrusions of the new, exciting and frightening, fast modern world tap-dancing to the tune of progress. I felt like a child, walking through a museum, afraid to touch anything. This world I had once taken for granted was now alien and frightening to me; I was a fish out of water terrified I'd never get back in it or, if I did, it would be only to discover that I had forgotten how to swim. That golden-ringleted girl who had flopped with careless, casual grace into Chippendale chairs didn't exist anymore. That girl was dead, but I, the shell, the weary old husk, she left behind her, was still alive, desperate and frantic to find *something* to fill up that emptiness.

I was shown into a lovely rose-colored room, filled with light and vases of roses. I smiled and nodded politely whenever my hostess spoke to me, saying she hoped I would be comfortable and happy here, but all I could do was inwardly pray that my closely entwined feelings of unease and awkwardness would soon abate. I had to learn to swim again, and quick! This pretty room felt too good for me, as though by just being here, touching it, sleeping in that beautiful rose-pink bed, sitting in the fireside chairs, reading by the light of the rose silk–shaded lamps, I would pollute or damage it, as though black stains would spontaneously appear wherever I touched.

There was a balcony with a fine view overlooking a vast rose garden, with fountains and statues. A little lacy white wrought-iron table and chairs had been set out with one of the chairs drawn back as though in readiness for me.

"I thought you might like to work out here in the sunshine and fresh air sometimes," Mrs. Densmore said.

"Work?" I asked, recalling instantly the hundreds and hundreds of shirts I had sewn in prison. I thought all that was over! I had, perhaps foolishly, thought that I would never have to work again. I had just assumed I would always be taken care of from now on. I'd never had to fend for myself or earn my own living before, and I feared I was rather old to start now.

Mama and Mrs. Densmore exchanged a lengthy look. Then Mrs. Densmore made her excuses and left me alone with Mama, to settle in and rest after my long and tiring journey.

"Work?" I repeated.

"Your book, o' course," Mama said as she pulled me back into the bedroom and, just like I was a little girl again, began to divest me of my hat, muff, wrap, handbag, and gloves. "You'll want a hot bath; I remember that was always the *first* thing you wanted whenever we arrived in those happy days of our travels—"

"What book, Mama?" I persisted.

"Florie, dear." Mama went to sit on the bed and patted the rosy coverlet beside her. "I don't like to say it, but you *must* be practical. It is an unpleasant but unavoidable fact that you will surely want for money, an' soon. You *cannot* live off the generosity of your supporters and admirers forever. People are fickle, an' their interest *will* fade. In this day an' age when every edition of the newspaper proclaims a new sensation it is only a matter o' time before they forget you entirely now that you have won your freedom an' procuring that freedom has ceased to be a cause for them to champion. In short, your days o' fame *are* numbered, darlin'. You have to make the most o' them while you *still* can; you simply *cannot* afford to let an opportunity pass you by; you're no spring chicken anymore an' you've your future to think of. Your story *must* be told, an' *now* is the time to tell it, an' who better than *you* to tell it? An' in a way that will provide you with an income until such time as we can find you a new husband. So, you're goin' to write a book. Isn't that excitin'? Your agent, Mr. Charles Wagner, has already arranged *everything,* includin' a generous advance for you, an' then you're goin' on the lecture circuit. He's already started bookin' a tour for you, a hundred appearances at fifty dollars per, an' that's just for starters. If you look pretty an' tell your story in an engagin' fashion, so that all the women weep for you an' all the men want to protect you, you might be able to stretch this out for a few years, maybe more!"

"Mama . . ." I sat there stunned and staring. I didn't know what to say. This scheme of hers went against *everything* I wanted. I didn't want any more notoriety. "Mama . . . I don't want to do this! *Please,* don't make me! I want to be forgotten; I don't want to be remembered or reminded! I've paid the price, and now I want to live quietly, and I want my children back—"

"Florie!" Mama started back as though I'd struck her. There was a wounded look in her eyes that brought tears to mine. "I'm only thinkin' o' what's best for you, darlin', an' if you want to secure your future, an' not spend the rest o' your days a pauper, relyin' on the charity o' others, then *this* is the most logical course. I'm

sure I don't know what else you can do, darlin'. Mama's not a magician; she cain't pull wealthy bachelors out o' her hat, you know.
You no longer have your youth an' beauty to fall back on, darlin'.
You're going to have to make *some* effort, an' use what you *do*
have—your tragic story o' how the world has wronged you—to
rouse their chivalrous an' protective instincts. Men like to feel like
knights in shinin' armor ridin' to the rescue of a damsel in distress;
they want to think they can wrap her up in their arms an' keep her
safe like no other can. An' *you,* Florie dear, *are* a damsel in *most*
distressed circumstances, an' they're only goin' to get worse, darlin', if you don't do *something,* an' quickly. An' your children are all
grown-up, darlin'. Why, Bobo must be twenty if he's a day! There's
just no way you can have those years back; they've grown up an'
forgotten all about you. You've got to face facts, darlin'; that dream
is stone-cold *dead!*"

When this only made me hang my head and weep, Mama said,
"I'll tell you what you do, darlin'. You write them a nice long letter
layin' your heart bare. I'll give it to the chauffeur an' have him take
it straight to the Fullers' door. If they want to see you, they'll answer, an' if not . . . you just move on, the same as those ungrateful
brats have."

So I wrote a book, or rather a very efficient bespectacled spinster secretary whose fingers flew with alacrity over the keys of a
typewriting machine that Mr. Wagner sent round wrote a book
while I supplied the story of my woefully unfortunate life and the
Hell on earth I had endured behind prison bars and ate bonbons
and waited for a letter that never came and for my hair to grow out
and was fitted with a new wardrobe to start my new life in courtesy
of the ever-generous Densmores. A melodramatic plea for prison
reform packaged between midnight-blue covers with some choice
details about my alleged crime and the travesty of my trial thrown
in for good measure, the book appeared on bookstore shelves as
Mrs. Maybrick's Own Story: My Fifteen Lost Years, and Mama and I
packed up, bid a fond farewell to the Densmores, and went on the
lecture circuit.

I wasn't the great success everyone envisioned—I was nervous
and fraught with worry and gnawed my nails before every appearance—but Mama just whispered, "Make 'em fall in love with you,

Florie; that's all you have to do!" and shoved me out onstage, slapping my hands away when I tried to turn and cling to her in fright. The truth is I *hated* every moment of it. My life might read like a melodrama, but I was totally unsuited for the stage, and it wasn't long before everyone knew it.

It's devilish hard to be likable and engaging and stand there looking pretty as a picture while you're talking about the death of your husband, the father of your children, the man you almost went to the gallows for murdering, and recounting all the horrors and deprivations and punishments packed into fifteen years of imprisonment. It hurt me so having to endlessly relive it and answer the audience's prurient and often impertinent questions about it. And there's just something downright tasteless about standing there with your now rounded and well-fed woman's body dressed in the latest fashions and top-dollar hairpieces with a fortune in pearls draped about your throat while describing the dismal prison uniform and the humiliations of having your head shorn down to stubble and not having the use of a nightgown or toothbrush for fifteen years. Every time I'd talk about the heavy, ill-fitting prison boots I'd feel every eye in the house being drawn down to my elegant little boots or French heels and silk stockings. I felt like a fraud and just as much a hypocrite as every man and woman I'd ever met in the Currant Jelly Set.

My body might have looked well enough, but my face was haunted and haggard. I couldn't sleep. Every night I lay there with my heart galloping, racing fast enough to win the Grand National, my mind endlessly replaying scenes from my life, trying to pinpoint what I could've and should've done differently and how I might have averted this fate. Some nights I was the strong, independent woman who threw up her hands and said, *The hell with you!* and walked out of Battlecrease House with her children in tow without ever looking back. Other nights Jim and I succeeded in waking dreams where we had failed in real life and found a way that was not altogether clear to me to be the happily ever after fairy-tale couple and grow blissfully old and gray together and dance at our children's weddings and our own golden anniversary. There were nights when I, the giddy bride exploring her husband's private sanctum, found only towels and toothbrushes in the bathroom cabinets and others when Jim, reformed and repentant, poured all his drugs down the drain, then took me in his arms and told me that I was the only drug he needed and couldn't live without.

Suffice it to say, it was all bound to fizzle. The only surprising thing is that it lasted as long as it did, almost five years, thanks to Mama and Mr. Wagner working so relentlessly to prolong my popularity. The best I can really say about my stint on the lecture circuit is that I got paid fifty dollars every time I stepped in front of an audience and I wore some very fetching frocks, smart suits, stupid hats, and shirtwaists with cameo brooches, flowing lace jabots, and pouter pigeon breasts.

Ultimately Mama decided I should marry a Texas cattle baron, a big, beefy, barrel-round, pink-faced man with buck teeth and bushy white hair and surprisingly small feet crammed into ornate silver-tooled black leather boots whose silver spurs jingle-jangled everywhere he went. He was given to whooping ecstatically at the least provocation and danced a little jig whenever he was happy and sometimes, in particularly exuberant moments, discharged his pistols into the air, then casually doled out hundred-dollar bills to pay for any damage he had caused to chandeliers and ceilings. One evening when he came to my hotel room, to dine and afterward take me to the opera, he told me I was the calf he had set his heart on roping and he wasn't about to take *no* for an answer, whereupon he wrestled me onto the bed and had my drawers off so fast I wasn't at all surprised that he had won so many awards for speed in hog-tying and calf-roping contests.

I tried to be sensible and think of my future like Mama said. I was no longer young and beautiful, and marriage really was the easiest route for a woman in my predicament. I had no practical accomplishments to fall back on that could guarantee me a living. God never intended me to be a seamstress or typewriter girl. . . . So I lay back, looking forward, listening to his spurs jingle-jangle as he mounted me—he kept his boots on, to give him traction, he said, and his big ten-gallon Stetson hat too, though for that he gave no reason. But he weighed *so heavily* upon me, crushing me like a great big writhing and snorting pink hippopotamus trying to attempt coitus with me, and it had been *so long* since any man had touched me that my body had forgotten how to give and receive pleasure. I was tight as a virgin down there, and it hurt *so much,* I just wanted him to stop. I kept telling him he was hurting me, begging him to stop—*"Please!"* I kept screaming and pounding his back with my fists and when that didn't work planting my palms on his chest and trying to push him away. *"Please!"* My tear-filled eyes kept turning desperately to the vase of roses on the bedside table. I wanted to grab it and smash it over his head, but each time I saw terrifyingly vivid visions of him lying there dead and bleeding on the floor, policemen pouring in, handcuffing me, and dragging me downstairs crying and pleading every step of the way, and pushing me into the Black Maria, to await a second trial and condemnation, and I just *knew* that if that happened there would not be a second reprieve. If I went back to prison again I'd never leave it alive.

Later, when I was perfumed and presentable again in café au lait satin overlaid with black diamond-dusted Alençon lace, naked neck and wrists weighed down with diamonds and pearls, my big braided bun of a hairpiece straightened and secured again with diamond-tipped pins, and a rag stuffed in my drawers to sop up the bleeding, he sat me down to a gargantuan steak and lobster dinner, with potatoes bigger than my shoe, and opened a red velvet–lined box, flashing a diamond ring as bright as the stars at me. When I saw that it was shaped like a horseshoe, I blanched; I just *knew* it was a bad omen.

My mind flooded with pictures of Jim, remembering all the times we had both stroked the diamond horseshoe he always wore in his tie, caressing it like a pet; it had even been, at his request, buried with him when he died. I sat there like one lost in a trance, remembering all the good times, the smiles and laughter, excitement, dances, champagne, wagers, and nights of love we had shared with that horseshoe sparkling all the time, like the sparks of exploding diamond-white fireworks raining good luck down on us as we danced through life together. And I just couldn't do it. I closed the lid on that great big gaudy sparkler and got up from the table without a word and walked out of my own room and just kept walking, on and on, wearing holes in the fragile soles of my black satin French heels, with the ghost of Jim always on my mind. In the darkness before dawn I found myself standing, shivering bare shouldered and bare armed without my fur, and staring down into the black river. I didn't throw myself in; I didn't even think of it. Instead, it was the chance the cattle baron was offering me, to again live a life of luxury and ease ensconced like a queen within the respectable and secure embrasure of marriage, that I threw away.

In 1908, when attendance at my lectures was growing alarmingly sparse and the booking bureaus were starting to look upon me as the Typhoid Mary of the lecture circuit, Mama and Mr. Wagner decided motion pictures were the answer. The flickers were so popular that if a photoplay was made of my story it would surely boost attendance to standing room only, my bookings would soar, as would my price—Mama and Mr. Wagner would see to that!—and I would soon be the darling of the lecture circuit again.

They made an appointment with the top man—"*we* don't deal with underlings," Mama said scathingly, and Mr. Wagner agreed—at the American Mutoscope and Biograph Company on East 14th Street and Mama and I duly arrived decked out in big hats and feather boas, with Mama carrying Napoleon, her fat and ornery Pekingese, and wearing enough jewelry to stock the front window of Tiffany's.

"If we look like we don't need it, they're more likely to give it to us," Mama said shrewdly. "An' remember, Florie, mention our cousins the Vanderbilts ev'ry chance you get; nothing impresses these *movie* people more than knowing you are intimately related to someone rich enough to use dollar bills for matches. They will feel privileged that *you* are willing to *consider* lettin' *them* make a photoplay o' *your* life. Remember, it's *you* doin' *them* a favor, darlin', *not* the other way around, even if the idea originally came from us!" Then she looked me over good in my new lemon linen suit trimmed with bright green silk braid and fancy frogging fastening the front of the jacket and adorning the skirt and decided that I would do.

When we stepped into the studio's office, early despite Mama's insistence that we be late, Mr. Wagner, who was to meet us there, hadn't arrived. We were greeted by the *sweetest* boy, soft-spoken and somewhat shy, not chatty or cheeky like the bellboys at the hotels we stayed at whom Mama always likened to "Satan's imps in training." He had a film can and the menu from a nearby restaurant tucked under one arm and was holding a broom in his other hand, and a torn costume was draped around his neck, all of which he immediately set aside as he took the time to greet us, see us seated comfortably, and ask if he could get us anything while we waited.

Acting for all the world like Catherine the Great sitting on her throne, twiddling her pearls and stroking her Pekingese, Mama imperiously demanded sauerkraut juice, watermelon relish, sweet potato pie crowned with pink whipped cream two inches thick, a bottle of champagne, caviar, and a dish of creamed chicken hearts and livers for Napoleon. She'd already told me that whether I actually appeared in the picture or was only on the set in the capacity of a consultant I should "constantly endeavor to tax the ingenuity an' resourcefulness of the go-for boys an' keep 'em runnin'," as it would make these theatrical types respect me more. "Bein' demandin' keeps you from bein' treated like a doormat, Daughter!"

But at the startled look on the boy's dear little face I quickly intervened and assured him Mama was just teasing, at which news he seemed greatly relieved and quickly offered us coffee or tea instead, assuring us that both were freshly brewed.

I have a spot in my heart soft as a marshmallow for sweet boys with dark hair and brown eyes, especially ones at ages I missed being with my own boy, and there was *something* about this one that just tugged at my heart. This licorice-whip-skinny boy didn't have Bobo's breathtaking beauty or his vibrant vivacity, but there was *something* there. . . . I simply could *not* take my eyes off him. I wanted to cup his face in my hands and drink him in, and my arms *ached* to reach out and hug him and never let go. I reckoned he was about fourteen, the age Bobo had been when he'd taken his stance about the photographs. Looking at him, I practically had to sit on my hands not to reach out and smooth back the brown hair falling carelessly over his brow, and before I even knew what I was doing I was already reaching for my handkerchief, thinking to wet it with my mouth, to scrub away the smear of green paint staining his left cheek. Mama read my mind and yanked the hanky from my hand and barked at the boy that tea would be fine, "with milk, sugar, lemon, an' cream if you please! An' some little cakes would not be unwelcome! Bake 'em if you have to, but don't keep us waitin', boy!"

While he scurried off to see to our tea—I think he just wanted to get away from Mama, and maybe even me, the way I kept looking at him like I wanted to *devour* him—I stood up and wandered over to the window, to stand before it without actually looking out and just be alone with my thoughts. I wanted to block my ears to Mama's stinging cat-o'-nine-tails tongue castigating me about "that longing look" I got sometimes and could never hide whenever a boy possessing a certain coloring and quality came along to remind me of what I missed most of all. Restlessly I turned from the window to the desk. It was then I saw the stack of schoolbooks bound with a leather strap and the violin case lying beside them. He must have come straight from school. My fingers reached out to caress them and the gray cap lying beside them, my fingers lingering, lovingly tracing over the herringbone pattern of the tweed.

It was then that I *really* started thinking and realized that I could *not* make this movie no matter how much Mama and Mr. Wagner wanted me to. What if my son and daughter saw it? Some pretty young blond actress up there on the screen pretending to be me, reliving the whole sordid, scandalous, and sensational spectacle, not as a valentine to their dead father or validation of their mother's innocence but as an *advertisement*—that's really *all* it amounted to—for my book and lectures, both of which I *loathed!* I just *couldn't* do it! Mama and Mr. Wagner just kept stirring it all up, bringing it back to a full roiling boil, when all I wanted was for the flames to die out. I didn't want to be remembered or reminded! Why couldn't anyone understand that?

Decisively I crossed the room to stand before Mama. If at fourteen my son could decide he didn't want to pose for photographs anymore, at forty-six I could certainly put my foot down to quash every notion of this photoplay!

"I'm sorry, Mama," I said. "I know you want this, you think it's in my best interests, but I don't. I won't do this, and you can't make me!"

I was walking toward the door just as the boy came back in with a heavily laden tea tray. God bless his eager to please little heart, he had even found some cake somewhere. He politely stepped aside to make way for me. With a nervously trembling hand, I dared reach out and lightly caress his cheek, smooth and baby soft, such a sweet, endearing face, and brush back the fall of dark hair tickling his brow.

"Thank you, darling; the tea looks delicious. I wish I could stay and have some. I'm sorry we put you to all this trouble for nothing," I said, turning away quickly as the tears caught in my throat and overflowed my eyes.

What was it about *this* one? There had been boys before, briefly glimpsed, who had caught my fancy and become my adored-from-afar objects of obsession, only to be forgotten when I moved on and the next one came along, but this one was different. . . . I already knew he was going to be haunting my dreams for a *very* long time. As much as I wanted to stay and try to figure out why, I *had* to leave.

"Florie, you get back here!" Mama shouted after me. "We have an appointment; you *can't* just walk out! I didn't raise you to be so rude, inconsiderate, an' ill-bred! Remember who you are! One o' your ancestors acted as ring-bearer when Marie Antoinette married Napoleon! An' I assure you, he didn't attain to that high honor by actin' the way you are now! *Get back here!*"

"I'm sorry, Mama." I turned briefly on the threshold, just in time to see Mama, struggling with Napoleon, who had entangled himself in her feather boa and caught his claws in the lace yoke of her bodice, exasperatedly fling him aside, actually throwing the poor animal through the air, shouting, "Here, boy—hold Napoleon!" so that the poor lad had no choice but to drop the tea tray or have his head slammed into the wall by a fat, flying Pekingese.

I had said all that I had to say; I didn't want to talk about it. I was afraid I was too much of a coward to stand my ground if I actually had to stay and stand there. I hitched up my skirts and ran out into the street, with Mama hot on my heels. She turned back only long enough to tell the boy, who had managed to catch Napoleon and was holding him against his chest, stroking him soothingly, while standing with the ruins of our tea on his shoes and spattering his skinny legs, that the diamonds on Napoleon's collar were real and they'd best still be there when she got back if he knew what was good for him and she meant to count them—all 117 of them.

Poor thing! I almost went back to comfort him. The very idea that that darling boy would ever pry diamonds out of a dog collar was too absurd for words! For God's sake, there was a *rosary* dangling out of his pants pocket! I had been tempted to tuck it back in so he didn't lose it, but I knew boys that age could be a trifle skittish about being touched so familiarly by strangers and I didn't want to scare him. But if I went back . . . that would mean facing Mama and having to go through with the appointment, with both her and Mr. Wagner, when he arrived, and maybe even the motion picture man, if he liked the idea, all against me, all talking and shouting at once, badgering me until I gave up and gave in and turned my poor brain back around to their way of thinking, and, as much as I wanted to see that child again, I just *couldn't* do it. I *had* to keep moving, running as fast as I could, away from there, turning my back on yet another chance.

Without even looking, ignoring the blaring horns, screeching tires, and shouts of angry drivers, I darted out into the street and dived into the first cab I saw. *"Drive; just drive! Get me away from here!"* I shouted at the driver.

I flung myself back against the seat and wept; I never thought a day would come when I would run away from Mama. She was the only one who had never abandoned me, and *this* was how I repaid her, by leaving her standing on the sidewalk stamping her feet, snorting like a mad bull, and shouting at the top of her lungs outside a movie studio. I'd made her so mad she'd actually thrown her precious Pekingese into the air! As ornery as Napoleon was, I was glad the boy had caught him. *I'm sorry! I'm sorry!* I kept sobbing hysterically, beating my fists against the leather seat, but in my heart I knew I really wasn't, I had done the right thing, and that, peculiar as it sounds, only made me feel worse.

Of course Mama was heartily disappointed in me. First I had forsaken the cattle baron and then the chance to have a movie made of my life.

"Heaven helps those who help themselves! Maybe someday you'll learn that, Florie, my girl!" she said, her voice tart and scalding as she flung her furs around her shoulders, picked up her first-class ticket and her Pekingese, and flounced aboard the luxurious

White Star liner that would carry her back to Paris, leaving me alone, to fend for myself, in New York.

The lectures gradually dried up and the book went out of print and people just weren't that interested in me anymore. Invitations and marriage proposals stopped coming. Everything Mama predicted came true. But in my heart I was glad. That was not the life I wanted. I was tired of being a curiosity, a novelty, invited just so people could stare at me and pose impertinent questions or experience the thrill of being in the same room as a condemned murderess. All I wanted was my children and to live long enough to live my notoriety down, to just be me—whoever that was—again.

I could not stop thinking about them, even though they had never answered my letter. I knew where the Fullers lived, and several times I set out to knock upon their door again, the way I had in London. I'd done it once, I could do it again, I kept telling myself. But every time, I'd walk past posters with my picture, posed in profile, wearing a Paris gown and a big, fancy feathered hat, advertising my lectures, or I'd pass a bookstore window displaying my book, or someone on the street would rush up to me, to shake my hand or launch into a lengthy speech about how grievously I had been wronged, and every time my courage would falter and ultimately fail me.

I would think about Bobo and Gladys walking past those same posters, maybe even stopping to look, appalled, disgusted, hanging their heads, feeling sick to their stomachs at the sight of me and the vulgar way I was profiting from their father's death. They might even be moved by curiosity to read my book, but what if they did and felt only shame, not sympathy? Every time I stood on the stage I'd find myself scanning the audience, squinting at every dark-haired young man and woman and wondering if my children had come to see me. After every show I'd wait and hope they would approach, but if these young people I'd spied ever did, nearness always revealed they were not the dear ones I was longing for.

I was so ashamed of this new notoriety I had acquired that I just *couldn't* face them.

Sometimes I made it all the way to the street where they lived. I'd stand at a discreet distance and stare and curse myself for a coward for not going up and knocking on that door. Every time it opened or a car drew up before it my heart would leap into my mouth and I'd stand there frozen, rooted to the spot, hoping for a glimpse of them. And when I did see them, it was a balm that both comforted and burned my heart.

I saw Gladys first, her face exasperatingly overshadowed by a huge red-rose-laden straw hat. She was in the midst of a gaggle of gossipy girls of similar age, in the back of a big chauffeur-driven car crammed full of parcels, fresh from an afternoon of shopping in New York's finest stores. As Gladys traipsed gaily up the front steps, swinging her sables and only slightly hindered by her pea-green hobble skirt and high heels, she turned and waved and called back to her companions, confirming a date at a fashionable tearoom the following afternoon.

My heart beating like a drum, I was there the next day, seated at the table nearest theirs, devouring my daughter with my eyes. She was *so beautiful*—porcelain skin, violet eyes, and a pompadour of jet-black curls crowned by a hat piled high with purple and lavender roses, dressed in a lavender linen suit, with amethysts at her throat and a silver fox stole swaddling her slender shoulders. It reminded me of the grand birthday party I'd given her, the mammoth rose-covered cake, and the fairy princess costume she'd worn. Some things at least never change—Gladys apparently still adored purple.

But her conversation! It was *Dr.* this *and Dr.* that! Twice she even pulled a pretty porcelain-lidded pillbox out of her purse and popped a couple of pills into her mouth! She told her friends she was going visiting in Saratoga for two weeks because Dr. Glass recommended rest and Dr. Hartley recommended exercise and she didn't like to disappoint either of them on account of they were both so handsome and, with luck, one of them might be her husband someday. She could think of *nothing* more exciting than being married to a doctor, all the prescriptions he could write for his loving little wife free and gratis, and just think of his hands caressing her in passion and discovering a hitherto-undiagnosed ailment, which reminded her, she had quite made up her mind to let either Dr. Bramford or Dr. Ashe, she wasn't quite sure which, remove her appendix when she returned from Saratoga. All that horseback riding she planned on doing was surely bound to agitate it; why, she might even have to go straight to the hospital the moment she got home for an emergency appendectomy! The way her violet eyes lit up you would have thought the girl had been invited to open a royal ball by dancing with a prince! But she was bound and determined to have Dr. Tafford, and no other, take her tonsils out! Then she was on about another doctor; she was seeing him twice and sometimes thrice a week for her "poor shattered nerves," for specialized treatment involving intimate paroxysm inducing stimulation with some sort of vibratory device that didn't sound at all like proper medical treatment to me.

In the prime of her life, my daughter already had more ailments than an old granny woman! With a sad, sinking heart, I realized that even if I could, by some miracle, find a way back into Gladys's life again, I couldn't help her; she was already drowning deep in medicine's magical thrall. *Just like Jim,* I thought as I walked away, *just like Jim.*

Seeing Bobo—or "James Fuller," as he now called himself—was just as bad. He had grown into the man I had feared he was becoming. Michael must have been so proud of the walking, talking ice sculpture he had created! Even from a distance, I could see the hard, harsh set of my son's stone-serious face, often bent over a thick stack of papers he was reading as though his very life depended on their contents. He seemed almost never to look up, and when he was with anyone his conversation was terse and monosyllabic. I never saw him smile or heard him laugh. The mouth was firm and flat, and, even worse, the brown eyes, despite their warm shade, were cold and dead. Such grave austerity greatly diminished his beauty. The features were still very fine, but without that inner warmth lighting them up like the candle in a jack-o'-lantern . . . this was *not* the same little boy who used to sit on my lap and gobble sugar cubes from my fingers and wrap his arms around my neck and promise me a kiss for every one I fed him. I couldn't even see the ghost of that winsome little fellow in this cold, grave young man in his conservative gray suits and boring black ties. Black hair, white skin, gray suit—he was as devoid of color as the voiceless actors in the photoplays, only they possessed emotions and projected varying degrees of personality. He was already old and cold, even in the bloom of youth. *A lost cause; all hope is dead,* a little voice I didn't want to hear whispered inside my head.

Seeing Bobo so sadly changed made my tears fall like rain. Part of me wanted to bring a sugar bowl and race across that street, knock him down, straddle him, and shove just as many sugar cubes as I could into his mouth, in the vain hope of restoring at least some of his sweetness, though I would most likely be carted off to the nearest madhouse if I tried. Then the door of that stately tomb-gray town house would close behind him and I would find myself walking slowly back to whatever hotel was standing proxy for "home" and dreaming about that sweet boy at the Biograph studio and wishing he was mine.

Sometimes I'd meander down East 14th Street and catch a glimpse of him, always from afar, rushing in or out on various errands, coming straight to work from school or on his way home. But I never had the courage to approach him either, not even just to nod and say hello in passing like normal people would to any chance acquaintance they met on the street. Even though I had become accustomed to standing up and speaking in front of an audience, I had become increasingly shy and wary of people and what they might think of me. And I guess I always knew how strange and silly I seemed even to a child. All my easy, graceful charm had been lost in prison and I never got it back. I was always afraid that my unconcealed, unfulfilled yearning, that naked lust that wasn't carnal at all, only a mother's desperate longing for the son she had lost, would scare them, like the witch in "Hansel and Gretel" trying to lure them with candy, and send them running, screaming, for their parents or the nearest policeman.

It wasn't every child who crossed my path that did this to me, thank God, for the world is *full* of brunet boys. There were just certain ones who through some combination of demeanor, coloring, or features or some special quality I can't even name cast a spell over me without their even knowing it, and that Biograph boy cast an enchantment deep enough to drown me if I let it. All I had to do was look, and love and longing would bite like a bear trap, clamping its steel-sharp teeth deep and hard into my hungry heart. But all I could ever do was dream, and love these special ones from afar, ethereally, never in any tangible way, not even as a self-appointed eccentric auntie who loved to spoil and dote on them and buy them toys and candy. I could catch glimpses of these boys on the street or playing in the park, but I could never hold them, touch, or talk to them, or worm my way into their little hearts, and, in the end, I always had to let them go and move on, to another city, lest that unquenchable desire and that unshakable, insatiable yearning drive me mad.

The afternoon I found myself standing out on the sidewalk like a fool in the pouring rain that had already pounded my black umbrella down like a witch's pointy hat several times, hoping for just a glimpse of the Biograph boy, I gave myself a good hard shake, packed up my bags, and caught the next train to anywhere.

❧ 35 ❧

The next two years I tried to lose myself and maybe find myself at the same time. I vowed that I would never set foot on a stage again. I was done with lectures and book signings. I wanted everyone to forget me, so I tried to forget me too, hoping they would follow my example, and, for the most part, they did. It's shocking just how easy it is sometimes to fade from memory. You can be the world's darling one day and a forgotten soul the next.

I drifted with the tide of life, hitching rides and hopping trains, living off bad coffee and not much better pie at greasy, decrepit little diners, ravenously devouring candy bars and more daintily indulging myself with dishes of ice cream and strawberry sodas, sitting at drugstore counters leafing through magazines and watching the world go by without me. I told everyone who cared enough to ask that my name was Florence Graham. I got the idea from a box of crackers that was staring me in the face the day a lady asked my name in a little country grocery store.

Little by little, piece by piece, to pay for my food, hotel rooms, and train tickets, I pawned my jewelry and clothes, except for my pearls. Mama always said pearls were the emblem of a true lady, so I thought I should hold on to those; they just might be the anchor that kept me from sinking too far down in the world. But the rest were just a burden weighing me down when I wanted to be light and free as the air. I wanted my whole life to fit inside a single suitcase, to pick up and go as I pleased. I pawned my big, heavy trunks and cast all the couture confections out of my life, saying good-bye to all the easily wrinkled satins and silks, heavy, hard to clean velvets, and crinkled chiffons, opting instead for simple, serviceable clothes and sturdy shoes I could walk a mile or two or three in any day and practical hats to keep the sun from my eyes.

Of course the money eventually ran out and I had to find other ways to pay my way. I was still too proud in those days to sup in soup kitchens or ask the Salvation Army for a bed.

I pulled myself together for a time, persuaded a kindly landlady to launder and press my best black suit and white shirtwaist, polished my shoes, and pinned up my silver-streaked burned-butter hair in a neatly braided bun, put on my pearls, and got myself a job behind the gingham counter in a department store. They could tell I was a lady who had known better days and they were happy to have me. But I *hated* dealing with the customers—flighty, featherbrained, obnoxious, arrogant ladies who couldn't make up their minds about the color or length of a simple thing like gingham. *The customer is always right, even when they're wrong*, I had to constantly keep reminding myself. I couldn't sleep nights for dreading what the next day would bring—I found those women insufferable, and I *hated* gingham and all that cutting and measuring, folding and packing, and writing out sales slips, always with a smile. I'd lie awake staring at the ceiling or the gradually lightening gray square of the window *dreading* the first true light of morning. And after I slept in once too often, they let me go. They weren't paying me, after all, to waltz in whenever I pleased, at half past noon or even one fifteen, the manager said; some ladies are simply not suited to employment despite the reduced circumstances that compel them to pursue it.

Next I found a job peddling books and magazines door-to-door. That didn't last long either; the Southern sun was hot, and I'd much rather sit in the shade and read them than try to sell them. In Georgia—or was it Iowa? I'm not altogether sure—a man with a chicken farm asked me to be his housekeeper. But I was woefully inadequate at that kind of thing, and just standing in the doorway, observing the inside of his house, which looked as though a hurricane had swept through it, made me feel weary and oppressed. And when I discovered that the free room and board he was offering meant sleeping in *his* bed I simply *had* to decline. Despite my slide into increasingly shabby circumstances, I was still rather fastidious, and I wasn't sure which smelled worse—him or his chickens.

Like adding beads onto a string, there were a lot more little jobs along the way, some lasting a month or a week, maybe two if I could make myself stick, and some not even a whole day.

There was another time in another department store, during the Christmas season, I stood behind a counter in my good black suit and snow-white shirtwaist and pearls with a sprig of cheerful holly on my lapel and sold children's toys. But the desperate gleam in my eyes and the way I knelt down and gazed hungrily into their faces and held their little hands as though I never wanted to let go frightened the children and disturbed their parents and I was let go. I encountered a similar predicament the week I spent working in a candy shop. My employer said I made the children nervous and I was caught giving certain boys extra portions too many times. "We *sell* candy; we don't distribute it as charity," he kept telling me, but it did no good. When I was staring mesmerized into a certain pair of chocolate-brown eyes and my fingers were twitching, itching to reach out and smooth back a careless fall of dark hair . . . toffee, licorice, and spice drops were the only way I could safely show my affection. Mr. Hershey's were the only kisses I could give them.

Still fancying I possessed some ladylike pretensions, I wasted a few of my precious pennies and advertised myself as a companion for invalid ladies. The first one to avail herself of my services was unbearably flatulent and crotchety and cursed with an obsequious oily-haired toad of a nephew who was very eager to come into his inheritance. When he started dropping discreet hints about his auntie's medicine, that a few more drops might finish the old girl off and if we went about it just right no one would ever suspect anything, I was so frightened that I never went back. I snatched up my suitcase and hitched a ride into the next state and from there took a train into another. I was *terrified* that Fate was trying to play some cruel trick on me, and I wasn't about to relive the past if I could help it.

I next tried tutoring a little blond-haired girl in geography and history—I thought she was a safe choice since my heart only succumbed to brunet boys—but she ended up failing to make her grade. Apparently the War of the Roses had nothing to do with horticulture at all; *thank you, Mama!* The girl's parents blamed me and turned me out of their home without a cent or a letter of recommendation.

Then I fancied I could play the piano and sing well enough to sell sheet music in a music store, but I was wrong. I was even more mistaken when I thought I could operate a typewriting machine and take dictation; that was a most humiliating failure. As was the tactfully worded rejection when I applied for a job modeling ladies' ready-to-wear fashions and found myself the only applicant over twenty-one. I fared no better when I responded to an advertisement for a counter girl at a combination tobacco and confectionary shop; the proprietor told me that mostly men frequented his establishment and they liked seeing a pretty young girl behind the counter they could flirt with. He didn't have to say more. Time hadn't been very kind to me.

I eventually found myself sewing shirts again just like I had done in prison, the *one* thing I'd sworn I'd *never* do, paid by the completed garment, not by the hour. I *leapt* at the offer to leave that behind and go work in a bakery's kitchen after-hours. But I found the heat and exertion of baking bread and lifting big trays of biscuits far too wearying for words and had to resign.

I told fortunes at a county fair, read tea leaves in a tea shop, and dropped too many trays and broke too many dishes to get paid when I tried waiting tables; I ran away from that job owing more money than I earned. I sold matches and flowers, apples and peanuts. I even picked fruit; at least it left my mind free to wander and dream.

I knocked on doors again, this time hawking boxes of laundry soap instead of periodicals, until I sprained my ankle and fell into a ditch running away from a barking dog. The soapboxes that I pulled along on a little wagon tumbled into the muddy water after me and I found myself sitting there soaking with white suds up to my shoulders. My employer was not a smidgen sympathetic and insisted I pay for the damages out of my own pocket or he would have the law on me. Terrified by any mention of the police, and the prospect of jail, I emptied my purse into his palm.

My pride was slipping fast, down and down the rungs of the ladder of success. But I had to eat. I needed to bathe and wash my clothes—I just couldn't bear the thought of stinking. I needed some pillow on which to lay my weary head, somewhere safe, out of the elements. And I had to keep moving along. If I lingered in any one place too long there'd inevitably be another brunet boy who unknowingly took my heart hostage, like the Biograph boy who still haunted my dreams, waking and sleeping, merging with memories of Bobo and fantasies about what might have been and could never be. All it took was for one special boy to cross my path and I'd find myself forsaking my work and spending hours sitting in parks or casually meandering past schools, churches, or the place where he worked after school, waiting, hoping, and longing just for a glimpse to feed my love-starved heart and fuel my futile dreams.

From time to time a New York paper would find its way to me, bearing word, in the social columns, about my children—travels to Europe; summers at Newport; Gladys's beaus, all handsome young men of prominent families, squiring her to dances, opening nights of plays and operas, exhibits at art galleries, garden parties, and horseback riding in Central Park, the columnists assiduously cataloging the beautiful clothes my daughter wore—she still loved purple. And Bobo, serious as the grave about his work—my son, like a nun forsaking the world and all its pleasures, fun, and romances, had wholeheartedly embraced the boring, facts and figures world of engineering. How that made me cry! My beautiful boy should have grown up to grace the stage and screen as a matinée idol; there were plenty of ugly men in the world to do all those dreary calculations! Sometimes there were even pictures in the papers, pictures that I *treasured!* I bought a little scrapbook from a five-and-ten-cent store and some paste. These newspapers were both a balm and a blister to my heart and always left me longing for more.

The new year of 1910 found me back in Alabama where I was born. I had come full circle and found myself back where I started from. There was a man, let's call him Fred. He was the proprietor of the Moran Hotel, a big, graceful white former plantation house, with stately columns supporting a broad front porch and balconies.

He bought me a green silk dress and paid for me to visit the beauty parlor, where a clever woman banished the silver and made my hair shine like gold again. I spent my days sitting on the front porch in a rocking chair, lazily plying a palmetto fan, sipping iced tea and mint juleps, and admiring the dogwood trees, plate-sized magnolia blossoms, and blazing pink azaleas that thrived under the Southern sun.

It was there that word reached me that Mama had died in a French convent. She did it in style, in a cream lace nightgown trimmed with yellow ribbons, with her hair freshly coiffed, piled up in a mass of gleaming, lacquered white curls, sending out for enough yellow roses to cover her bed to help alleviate the stink of the sickroom and death when it came. At the end, a photographer came and took her picture and afterward hand-tinted it and sent it to me. That was my last sight of Mama, lying there oh, so peacefully framed by a fortune in yellow roses. The florist, hairdresser, and photographer sued her estate to have their bills paid, but there was nothing left, for them or for me.

Fred was kind. He held and comforted me. He bought me a black lace dress and hat, new black shoes and silk stockings, ordered masses said for Mama's soul, and introduced me to the consolation of Catholicism. But, after a decent interval had passed, he asked me about the land.

It turned out that Mama, *still* trying to help me after all, even though I thought she'd long since given up, had written to him secretly, asking him not to tell, as I had had some bad experiences with fortune hunters that had left me rather sensitive, confiding in him about the two and a half million acres of land I would inherit whenever that vexing legal knot was finally untangled. It was like a bucket of ice water in my face. I told him there was no land; that was just one of Mama's fairy tales. I was heiress to nothing except the free air.

He lost his temper. I couldn't really blame him. He'd wasted so much time and money on me, not to mention all those tender words and touches at night in his bed. I was a fraud and he was a fool, he said. I just sat there on the floor and cried, cradling my cheek, smarting and pink from where he had struck me. He told me to get out. I'd grown accustomed to the comfortable life again, regular meals and a soft bed and wearing pretty clothes, and hats and shoes more frivolous than practical, and I wept even harder at the thought of taking to the roads again.

But Fred was not entirely without a heart. He offered to see if he could get me settled in an old-age home. Fancy that! And me only forty-eight! It was downright *insulting!* The thought of being confined in an institution again with rules to govern everything I did, when I got up, when I went to bed, what I ate and wore, made me *sick* to my very soul. I told him to go to the Devil and that I would rather die in a gutter than go to a place like that. He told me to do it then and get out. I packed my bags—I had enough to fill two suitcases by then—and hitched a ride in the back of a truck carrying pigs. At that moment those fat, oinking pink creatures seemed a lot better company than Fred!

By judicious pawning, I reduced my possessions to a single suitcase again and made my way slowly back to New York, inch by inch, trying to get my courage up. I had by then discovered that gin is wonderful for drowning cowardice. Mama's death had made all my longings for my children bubble right back up to the surface again. I couldn't stop thinking about them no matter how hard I tried. I was *determined* to be brave this time and see them face-to-face. Surely enough time had passed . . . the lectures and the book, and me along with them, had faded from public memory. I was their mother; I had every right. I had *never* surrendered my rights; they had been *taken* from me by force, by Michael Maybrick and a pack of liars in his pocket. I told myself to stop dillydallying and hiding and fight for my right to hear Bobo and Gladys call me "Mother" again.

I arrived in New York in time to stand outside the cathedral and see Gladys emerge as a bride, gowned in white lace with delicate touches of lavender ribbons, tiny crystals, and seed pearls, trailing *yards* of white lace train and veil behind her, and a dozen bridesmaids wearing chiffon dresses in three different shades of purple. There was an *enormous* emerald-cut slab of a deep purple amethyst flashing on her finger. I smiled; clearly my daughter had her own ideas about engagement rings.

"No more beautiful bride ever lived!" I cried as she walked past me, without a glance, taking the compliment as simply her due if she even heard it, and climbed into the back of the big silver car decked with bunches of lavender and white ribbons, roses, and bunting.

She'd married late, at twenty-nine. I hoped it meant she had taken her time and chosen right. I found a newspaper and carefully tore out the article for my scrapbook. His name was Dr. James Frederick Corbyn, a dark-haired physician of Welsh descent and quite handsome. Dusty and shabby as I was, I went into the cathedral. I took one of the purple ribbons tied to the pews to keep as a souvenir. I found my way into the little room where the bride had waited, hoping Gladys had left a handkerchief, embroidered with her initials, so I would know for certain it was hers, and found the empty pill bottle she had left behind instead. There was that familiar frog on the label, giving advice to a baby, the same nerve pills her father had favored. Apparently they were still around; they'd outlasted even the rose-scented cold cream I was fond of. I went back into the church proper and lit a candle. I prayed that Dr. Corbyn would always love Gladys and treat her well and that God would grant him the wisdom and the strength to steer my daughter off the path to self-destruction drugs were leading her down, just like they had her father.

I didn't see Bobo amongst the wedding party, but my eyes had been glued to Gladys the whole time, I hadn't even noticed the groom. I rented a room, bathed, and made myself presentable and went to a library and pored over old newspapers until I found out that Bobo was in Canada, working as a mining engineer at the Le Roi Gold Mine. I pawned the little gold rosebud earrings and matching pendant Fred had given me. They were so sweet and dainty, I had hoped to keep them, but this was more important; they would take me to Canada and my boy.

I don't know how I did it, but I did, and without the false courage of gin. Wearing the blue-gray suit that had replaced my old trusty black, and a new violet-blue silk shirtwaist that paid the perfect compliment to my eyes, a gray hat adorned with silk violets, and my pearls—I never needed that ladylike reassurance more!—with my hair freshly gilded, I found myself standing in my son's office at the Le Roi Gold Mine. He'd apparently just been called away. His lunch—a sandwich, a piece of cherry pie, and a bottle of milk open as though he'd been about to pour it into the glass sitting beside it when the telephone rang—was laid out on the paper- and book-piled table that doubled as his desk and laboratory. There was a microscope and some glass slides and bottles of chemicals nearby, *too* near for my liking. I shuddered, seeing the skulls and crossbones and the word *POISON!* screaming from all the labels. He'd also left his watch behind.

My heart stood still. My blood froze. A knife stabbed and ripped my heart wide open. It was his father's watch. I picked it up with the same trepidation as I would have handled a live rattlesnake. I opened the back and squinted down at the secret scratches etching a terrible confession into the gleaming gold—*I am Jack the Ripper! James Maybrick*, ringed by five sets of initials: *PN, AC, ES, CE, MJK.*

"What are you doing? Who are you? What are you doing here?" a voice behind me demanded. I whirled around and found myself face-to-face with my son. I wanted to grab his face and kiss him and feel those glorious long black lashes fluttering like butterflies against my face. "That's my watch!" He snatched it from my hand. "A thief—I should call the police—"

"Please don't do that, Bobo," I said softly. "I was just looking at it, remembering. . . ."

He gasped and recoiled from me as though I were a leper. The watch fell from his hand onto the floor. "No one has called me that since I was a child!" His eyes widened and I knew he recognized me.

"Get out of here!" He pointed at the door. "I have *nothing* to say to you!"

"Bobo, *please,* I've come a long way, it's been such a long time, please . . . hear me out. . . ." I dared to cross the distance he had put between us and lay my hand, and with it my heart, on his sleeve. "Just this once . . . If I never see you again, *please,* let me tell you the truth. . . ."

He jerked away from me. "*Your* version of the truth, you mean! Well, whatever you have to say, I don't want to hear it; go tell it to your lover, the man you killed my father for!"

"Alfred Brierley was one of the great mistakes of my life," I said, and knew it was the God's honest truth. "I haven't seen him since

1889, and I didn't kill your father, for him or anyone else. You *must* believe me! I *loved* Jim!"

"A judge and jury of twelve men, my uncles, Mrs. Briggs, Nanny Yapp, the servants, the police, who are accustomed to investigating these matters—you were not the first woman to attempt to use poison to rid herself of an inconvenient husband—and all the doctors and chemists"—Bobo ticked them off on his fingers—"they were *all* wrong?"

"Yes." I nodded. "They had their reasons, and science is not equipped to answer every question yet, but, yes, they were wrong. Some of them lied outright, some of them just didn't know the truth, or knew the right answers and couldn't admit it. There are certain men who can never say 'I don't know,' and I'm sure that's quite an embarrassing admission for men who are called experts to make, especially when the eyes of the world are upon them. There was much that was not told, many lies covered truths, and my sins, my *carnal* sins, blinded and distracted many, but if all had been revealed, perhaps . . . the outcome would have been different."

Bobo snorted and shook his head. "That was all *years* ago." He shrugged. "I have my own life now, and you will never be a part of it. I'm not your son anymore. None of this has any bearing. My heart declared you dead when I learned what you did, or were accused of doing," he quickly mollified when I took another step toward him, "and I will permit no resurrection now. There's *nothing* you can say that will change that. I'm going to be married soon, and I've no desire to revisit the past, or to have my future wife and in-laws troubled by old scandals being dredged up after I've worked so hard to lay them to rest. Now please go. Leave me in peace and never trouble me again."

All the things I'd meant to say, all the questions I was longing to ask, died upon my lips. What was the use? I felt crushed, defeated; I suddenly wanted a drink more than I ever had in my life. Gin drowns more than cowardice; it also numbs sorrow.

"All right, Bobo." I nodded. It was then that I noticed the watch still lying on the floor and bent to retrieve it. Just this once, in innocently returning it, placing it in his hand, I could touch my son for what I knew, with complete and utter certainty now, would be the last time.

"Thank you," he said. I was halfway to the door when he cried out, "Wait!"

My heart lurched and leapt with renewed hope. Had some miracle occurred? Had God sent an angel to whisper in his ear and change his mind?

"What are these scratches?" Bobo demanded. "What did you do to it?"

My heart sank like a stone. "Nothing; they've been there all along."

"All right." He nodded, his back still to me. "You can go."

"Good-bye ... Bobo. ..." I lingered, one last long moment on the threshold, hoping, praying, to hear him call me "Mother," even if it had to be coupled with "Good-bye."

But he said nothing. I waited a moment longer, staring at the back of his gray coat, and the immaculately brilliantined black hair I *longed* to glide my palm over. He resumed his seat at his desk, and I knew I was still waiting for a love that was never going to come. I blew the back of my son's sleek head a kiss and softly shut the door.

I was halfway down the hall when I heard the glass break.

I ran back. Bobo lay upon the floor, his body twisted, spine arched, fingers gnarled, brown eyes staring wide, his face a frozen mask of contorted horror, the perfume of bitter almonds hovering above his gaping mouth. Broken glass lay like a halo around his dark head and the telephone, scattered papers, the chair he had been sitting in, and his lunch all fallen around him. Had he been trying to call for help? After I left him, he must have wanted a drink as badly as I did. In his distraction, he didn't look, he reached out blindly for the milk bottle, to pour into the glass, and his hand found the bottle labeled "Cyanide" instead. He'd gulped it down without a glance. Luck for the boy born with the lucky double row of eyelashes had run out.

As I knelt beside him, closing his eyes, feeling those long, long lashes caress my palm one final time, the glimmer of gold caught the corner of my eye. The watch! It was there beneath the microscope! I stood up and looked and, many times magnified, I read the words I already knew by heart. Bobo, in his last moments on earth, had learned the truth. Now I would never know for certain ... that fatal drink ... had it *really* been an accident? Or had I, in trying to plead my innocence, shown my son a truth he could not live with? *Oh, why did I pick up that watch?* He might never have noticed those scratches if I hadn't! I should have left it, and him, alone!

I couldn't stay; I couldn't explain. I couldn't let anyone know who I was or why I had come there. What if they thought once a poisoner, always a poisoner? They wouldn't understand that my whole life had been poisoned, maybe because *I* was poison. When Lady Luck turned her back on me she truly became my enemy and left me with a curse—to bring death and misfortune to everyone I loved.

I put the watch back in his pocket, kissed my son good-bye forever, and left him lying there for someone else to find. There was nothing else I could do for him but disappear; he'd made it quite clear he didn't want me there. I had embarrassed and shamed him in life; I wouldn't do it to him in death, so I left, I just left . . . another piece breaking off my heart with every step.

❧ 36 ❧

As soon as I got back to New York, before I even left the train station, a woman I hadn't seen in years bumped into me and started to commiserate about Bobo's passing. The Fullers were family friends; she'd heard the news almost as soon as they did. I cut her off, my voice like an ice pick; later, when she recounted our encounter to the press, stirring all the old scandal up, she said my eyes were blank, cold, and dead. "I have no son. The past is dead. That boy has been dead to me for more than twenty years," I said, and walked on. *The past is dead, the past is dead . . .* I kept on telling myself.

Then and there I decided to try to reinvent myself. If I couldn't lose myself, I reasoned, maybe I could change myself so much that I wouldn't even know me. Straight from the train station, suitcase still in hand, I marched into the first beauty parlor I saw.

"I want to walk out of here a whole new woman!" I said, and laid my money down.

They took me at my word and went to work on me. I left there with a bright red hennaed head, finely plucked and high-arched brows lending me a perpetual expression of surprise, a sack of cosmetics to replicate the painstaking paint job they'd given me after rubbing and slathering oils and cold cream into my skin, and perfectly manicured nails, shell pink and shimmering. I stopped and bought three new dresses. "Out with the old, in with the new!" I rebelliously cried as I stood before the fitting-room mirror, hands on hips, modeling a persimmon silk dress and a long strand of pink coral beads.

On the way to the pawnshop to sell my old clothes—money was, after all, still a loathsome necessity of living, and I never wanted to see that gray suit and hat or that violet-blue blouse ever again—I caught a glimpse of my reflection in a store window. I truly was a new woman now. "A *scarlet* woman!" I laughed. Then I thought of the blood of those long dead women and the initials etched on the back of Jim's watch—*PN, AC, ES, CE, MJK*—and I felt the immediate urge to shave my head. Instead, I got drunk and stayed drunk for a *very* long time.

I floated to the surface again weeks later and found myself staring up at a single flickering lightbulb swinging like a pendulum from the dusty water-stained ceiling above me. I was naked except for a pair of grubby pink panties reeking of urine. I had vague memories of a man telling me that this was a magic glass, it could never be emptied, and the gin would never run out no matter how much I drank, and of myself laughing too loud, a hand inching up my thigh, clumsy feet and even clumsier kisses, scuffling and staggering in the darkness, and the creak of rusty bedsprings. My battered beige suitcase was flung in a corner and my clothes scattered across the coarse crimson carpet littered with coral beads. My purse was empty and my pearls—the only thing of real value I possessed—were gone, stolen by a man whose face I didn't remember and whose name I don't think I ever knew.

"Mama always said pearls were the emblem of a true lady; now I can't even pretend anymore!" I sobbed into my pillow, suddenly feeling even more naked now that the last pretense of respectability had been stripped from me. As soon as I was able, I staggered into a store and sought a set of "imitation pearls for an imitation lady!" I laugh-cried when I tried them on. I didn't buy them; it just didn't feel right.

I was *desperate* to get a job, but once I got one I didn't want to go. I pulled the threadbare coverlet up over my head the next morning and peeped out from time to time at the moving hands of the clock, knowing, for a little while, that I could still make it if I tried, that if I went now a good excuse for my tardiness would surely suffice—the woman had been nice; she'd seemed to understand how much I needed this job—but I pulled the covers up and closed my eyes until I knew it was far too late and the chance had passed me by. Later I sat tousle headed, musing over a cup of tepid tea, wondering why. I still haven't found the answer.

I started to sell myself, the only thing I had left. Now that I knew I couldn't trust myself to hold a job, I guess I thought maybe I could hold a man's cock for five or ten minutes at least. Whenever I led another stranger into a dark alley to grunt and thrust into me I thought my gin-bleary eyes saw the ghosts of the women my husband had murdered looking at me over his shoulder, watching me with sad eyes. We truly were sisters now. Sometimes I even selfishly borrowed their names so it didn't have to be me doing this.

I began accepting charity from the Salvation Army, a cup of coffee, a bowl of soup, a bed for the night, even if it meant I had to listen to a bunch of do-gooders spouting platitudes that only made me feel worse. "A fallen woman is a sister to be saved, not a sinner to be punished"; "No one escapes this life without suffering"; "There but for the grace of God . . ." It was like being surrounded by a bunch of squawking parrots. I wished they'd all go back to converting cannibals and leave me in peace; I really only wanted the soup and sometimes a bed I could lie in alone without some man's prick poking me.

There was one particularly earnest young preacher who tried to wean me off alcohol and got me a job in a secondhand store. He saw things in me that I had forgotten I possessed. He wanted to help me save myself and have me put on the uniform and stand up in front of other poor, wretched sinners and tell my story. I got roaring drunk and turned on him like a tigress; I almost brained him with a gin bottle. "You're not Jesus Christ, and I'm not Mary Magdalene; you *can't* save me!" I remember shouting as I stormed and staggered out, back onto the streets and into the arms of the first man who was willing to buy me a drink.

Now that I was no longer too proud to take charity, I started writing begging letters to some of the rich society people who had once been my most ardent supporters. They felt sorry for me, but not enough to embrace and welcome me back into their world again, thank goodness! Small sums of money began to trickle in from time to time; the envelopes had a knack of showing up just when I needed them most. I tried to tell myself that it was God's way of looking after me.

In those years I existed, nothing more. Even reinvented, I still needed to lose myself in a world of dreams; it was the only way I could survive. First in rented halls with a white sheet tacked up onto the wall in front of a row of benches, then in opulent, gilded movie palaces with plush velvet seats, I sat enthralled, safely out of the elements, surrounded by people who were more or less just like me, trying to escape life's problems and the dreary drudgery of reality even if it was only for an hour, breathing in air perfumed by melted butter. Subsisting on popcorn, ice cream, candy, and soda pop, I let myself be mesmerized or lulled to sleep by those silent black, gray, and white flickering images. Sometimes an organ or a piano played; sometimes the only accompaniment was the audience—laughing, murmuring, coughing, belching, or shouting at the magical moving pictures up there on the screen. This was my twilight world where all that existed was a dream within a dream.

I adored the comedies—jolly Fatty and blank-faced Buster, and Charlie, the Little Tramp; life has enough tears and tragedies, so why should we spend our nickels and dimes to see those things projected on a screen? Better to laugh than to cry if you can.

I worshiped Theda Bara, the black-haired vampire with blood-red lips and dead white skin who devoured men's souls and bank accounts until she'd drained them dry. I tore pictures out of magazines of her voluptuous scantily draped body leaning over a skeleton as though she'd just delivered the fatal kiss and of her holding up her long hair like devil horns. To think that I would live to see a day when such a wicked woman was adored and celebrated! She could have played a husband-murdering adulteress and the world would have thrown roses round her feet! When the title card gave her an imperious voice that cried, "KISS ME, MY FOOL!" I laughed and applauded her power.

But I didn't care much for the virginal "virtue is its own reward" valentines—Mary Pickford, that girl with the golden curls, reminded me too much of the late, lamented Florie, and the Gish sisters with their candy box beautiful faces always called to mind another candy box and all the ugly secrets concealed inside it. I'm sure they were very nice girls, and talented, but whenever I saw them I twiddled the key I now wore on a chain around my neck, wondering if a day would ever come when I would dare go back to England and unlock my own Pandora's box filled with evil. I couldn't stand to watch them; it was just *too* painful for me. Whenever they appeared on the screen, I drifted back out into the sun or night, the sudden intense need for gin drawing me like a siren's song. Only when I felt my back hit a wall, hard flesh stabbing soft, rough fingers digging into the tender white skin beneath my thigh, and heard animal grunting and heavy breathing in my ear would I stop thinking about that key and what it would unlock.

I liked the big, sprawling historical spectacles best. Even if I fell asleep, which I often did, there was always something interesting to see when I woke up. *Intolerance* was my favorite; I think I stayed in my seat for every showing of that one. I *loved* the wild, magnificent decadence of ancient Babylon, Belshazzar's bacchanalian feast, the wanton virgins in the Temple of Love, and the pillars of palaces topped by giant white plaster elephants with their trunks turned up for luck. The massacre of the Huguenots on St. Bartholomew's Day made me weep; I kept hoping it would end different each time and that the hero would carry the girl, his beloved Brown Eyes, over the threshold as a bride instead of a ravished corpse. And when Christ intervened and saved the adulteress from stoning, proclaiming, "He that is without sin among you, let him cast the first stone," I wanted to kiss His feet in gratitude.

But it was the modern story that had me on the edge of my seat, riveted and tense, frightened enough to want to run, only I didn't want to miss a moment, and in truth I don't think I could have moved unless someone had set off dynamite beneath my seat. It was *my* story, only it was a young man playing the part. Truly innocent but accused and convicted of taking a life, he had a questionable reputation, a past, that counted against him.

Even though the film was silent—the actors had no voices then—his dark eyes truly were a window into his innocent soul, and I could "hear" his cries of "I didn't do it!" *clawing* at my heart. There was just *something* about his face; even with that dark mustache, I'd never seen one more innocent. How could the judge and jury not see that too? I kept crying, shaking my fist, and railing at the screen, even though I knew it was all a fiction, not real life. Several times the ushers had to come in and quiet me down by threatening to throw me out if I didn't sit down and shut up and stop spoiling the show for the other patrons. I kept thinking that I knew him, and maybe I had seen that actor in another film before, I saw and slept through so many, but I finally persuaded myself it was just an illusion, a trick of the mind. Seeing him bringing to life a story so uniquely like my own had worked a strange magic and created a false sense of kinship and familiarity.

"The Boy"—that was the only name the character had—was condemned to die. He passionately protested his innocence and fainted in the prison chaplain's lap, just like I had, even as his young wife raced to waylay a speeding train and beseech the governor's pardon. There was something otherworldly about his thin, pale face and the dark eyes he raised to Heaven when he took the Last Sacrament. I had to shake and pinch myself every time. I was so caught up in his magic, it was almost impossible to believe that this was just an actor playing a part, all in a day's work for him. He made it seem *so real,* like all of us sitting out there spellbound in darkness were truly witnessing an innocent young man preparing to die. He made it all the way up to the gallows; the black hood was on his head and the noose around his neck before reprieve came at the last possible instant. It sent chills down my spine every time. I was so afraid the reprieve would come too late and that I would have to sit there and watch him die.

Then it was 1917 and the world was at war. I didn't read the papers anymore, except the social columns now and then to try to catch a glimpse of Gladys, and I couldn't quite wrap my bleary, weary mind around what it was all about. All I knew was that the streets were full of brave young men in uniforms and the walls papered with posters trying to coax more to join up. If my son had been alive he would have been one of them. I didn't like to think about it, so I drank and drank. I still thought about the Biograph boy; he was rarely out of my thoughts for long. He must have been well into his twenties by then. Was he in uniform too? Was that baby face sporting a dapper mustache like so many of these boys, trying so hard to be brave and grown-up, were wearing nowadays? One evening when I woke up after sleeping all day with him still on my mind, so vivid I could almost reach out and touch him, I staggered into the nearest church and lit a candle and prayed that he would be spared, wherever he was. Even though I didn't know his name, I was sure God would.

One day I woke up with the morning and took a cold bath, put on my most plain and decent dress, did what I could with my faded hennaed hair, and went out and tried to volunteer as a nurse, but one glance told the Red Cross how utterly unsuitable I was. So I gave what comfort I could to those poor boys going off to war or coming back wounded, missing limbs, and shell-shocked, in dark doorways and alleys, where the darkness and dim, distant streetlights still knew how to be kind to an aging woman.

❧ 37 ❧

The tail end of 1920 found me in Atlantic City, recovering from jaundice and a gallbladder operation, performed at a charity hospital by a doctor who was adamant that I should give up drinking. Something he said must have struck a chord so deep within me I couldn't consciously hear it. I had, incredibly, come out of the darkness into the light. It just happened. Maybe it was one of God's tiny miracles? I just woke up one day and decided that I was tired of being drunk, tired of being pushed, punched, and pawed, and just tired of being tired all the time. I had a little money. A Mr. Alden Freeman, a philanthropist who used to attend my lectures, had died and remembered me with a small bequest in his will. So I made my way to Atlantic City. I thought the salty air might bring clarity and help me find a new and better way to live.

I hadn't felt better or more hopeful in years. I had even woken up that morning thinking I might like to take up china painting again. I'd always loved it so when I was a girl and had time for such things. Maybe I could rent a little stall and sell my handiwork? I was letting my hair go natural after years of hennaing and dyeing it a harsh, brassy blond, and letting my skin breathe freely, devoid of makeup after years of tumbling into bed drunk with more paint on my face than a Rembrandt.

After my operation, my hair had gone all stringy and started to fall out and I had reluctantly surrendered to the nurse's suggestion that I have it bobbed. After all those years of enforced prison shearings I thought that was another thing I'd *never* do again. I shut my eyes and trembled and tears seeped out from under my tightly clenched lids when I felt the cold steel of the scissors against the nape of my neck. But afterward I was glad that I did it. My head felt surprisingly light and cool, and all the ladies at the salon said the style suited me *beautifully* and took *years* off me.

As soon as I got to Atlantic City, I had bought myself a new blue-and-white-striped dress and a white straw hat with long blue ribbon streamers and was strolling idly on the boardwalk, smiling over a little sack of pink and white saltwater taffy, remembering how I used to love my candy-pink dresses and candy-striped corset until Alice Yapp put it on and spoiled it for me. I could almost laugh about it now without being too bitter. I was thinking that I might like to try for a job in one of the tiny taffy shops that dotted the boardwalk. I was older now and I was *finally* starting to make peace with the loss of my son. Maybe I would be calmer now and not frighten the shop's eager little patrons? It was worth a try, I thought, and popped another taffy into my mouth. When I bit down I felt the most *excruciating* pain.

Fortunately, I was able to procure a dentist's appointment that very afternoon on account of a last-minute cancellation and I had money enough to attend to that rotten tooth. I was sitting there waiting, flipping through a copy of *Photoplay* magazine and trying not to be too nervous, when I came to a picture that made my heart jump.

It was him—the Biograph boy! Full page, in profile, it was unmistakable! Handsome, sensitive, sweet, and vulnerable, he still had the power to pull at my heart. All grown-up, he was still that same boy. My mind raced back to 1908, where I could see him in living color not just as a flat black and white printed page, and the day I had dared brush back his dark hair and let my fingers linger caressingly over his face. At last I learned his name; it was Bobby— Bobby Harron. It suited him perfectly; no other could be more fitting. I smiled. However had I missed him becoming a movie star?

Had I *really* been that tired and drunk? I'd have to make a point of seeing his next picture; I was so excited I was of half a mind to wait until the nurse's back was turned and tear the page out for my scrapbook, I was *so* proud of him. My own son had shunned the gift of beauty God had given him and chosen math and mechanics over being worshiped and adored as a matinée idol, but, I couldn't believe it; my sweet, shy little Biograph boy—I still couldn't help but think of him as mine even though I only knew him for a few precious minutes all those years ago—had become a movie star! Then I read the small print under his picture: "The boy you knew"—Why was it in past tense? I started to feel the sneaking creep of fear, but I kept on reading—"on the screen was the real Robert Harron, 'Bobby,' as friends and fans called him—human, lovable, genuine. His passing, as a result of an accidentally inflicted bullet wound, left a place no one can fill."

I automatically turned the page, hoping for more details, as though knowing more would in any way change anything. Even if I knew everything he would still be dead, just like my son. My eyes skimmed over the words without reading them until one popped off the page like a boxer's fist—*Intolerance.* That was why he'd seemed so familiar! But I hadn't been able to see past the drama and the dark mustache he was sporting for that particular picture. Distracted by the similarity to my own story, I let myself be convinced that it was all a trick of the mind, only it wasn't; there was another, much deeper, reason he'd been able to capture my heart without saying a word. "The Boy" on the screen was *my* Biograph boy. And now he was dead, just like my son. Bobby was only twenty-seven. Bobo died at twenty-nine.

Accidental—The papers said my son's death had been accidental too. He had everything to live for, a successful career, a girl he meant to marry, a bright, bright future. But they didn't know what I knew; they hadn't seen the watch under the microscope, the evil confession signed and spelled out in scratches. Surely it really was an accident. It just *couldn't* be anything else! That would be *too* cruel! Accidents happen all the time. One young man, troubled and distracted, pours cyanide into a glass and drinks it down like milk; another one drops a gun on the floor and puts a hole in a perfectly good heart—and it *was* a good heart. I could tell that from the first glance. They were both so young and had everything to live for. But in the end only God knows for sure.

I remembered that soft, baby smooth cheek against my palm; I could *feel* his skin, just as real, living and warm, after all these years as though I had only just touched him. When I caressed him that day in the Biograph office had I also cursed that sweet, innocent boy with the death and misfortune I brought to all my loved ones?

I got up from my chair and walked out of the dentist's office without saying a word, the magazine trailing listlessly from my hand, pages flapping against my ankles like the wings of Death. I stayed more or less drunk for the next ten years. I never went back to that dentist or any other; I let that tooth rot and fester in my jaw as a penance and numbed the pain with alcohol.

I went back to Chicago and then New York and started painting my face and coloring my hair again. I returned to the vagabond vagrant's world of Salvation Army cots and soup kitchens, meaningless couplings in dark alleys against walls, just for the money, and the only place I found any small measure of happiness—the movies. My diet was every child's dream—any given day for breakfast, lunch, or dinner I might have Cracker Jacks or hot buttered popcorn, orange, grape, or strawberry soda, or even Coca-Cola, which had replaced coffee and tea in my heart, and a handful of sticky peanut butter Mary Janes or some of Mr. Hershey's blissful Kisses, with an Eskimo Pie for dessert, and in between I was constantly sucking on sassafras, horehound, or red anise drops, peppermint stars, and butterscotch buttons. I was profoundly disappointed in myself, but I just didn't care enough to do anything about it.

The world was moving even faster now. The twenties really were roaring. Faster cars, faster music, faster dances, and faster women in shorter skirts and shorter hair, who were not afraid to show their stockings and drink homemade gin brewed in somebody's bathtub even if it meant risking death or blindness. They just thumbed their noses and laughed and made jokes about it. The world just kept evolving and revolving at a faster speed, in both morals and motion. Corsets, like bustles and crinolines, were a thing of the past, and I had a terrible time getting used to these new dresses without structure that hung as loose as society's morals now blatantly and unapologetically did. I didn't know whether I had been born too late or too soon or to laugh or cry or just curl up and die.

My daughter was all I had left now, the only one to love, even if my love was unwanted and always given from afar. Though well into her thirties, Gladys didn't show it; she was still beautiful and fit right in with the bright young things of the 1920s. I'd catch a glimpse of her sometimes, in the society columns or with my own eyes, getting out of a car in a cloche hat, t-strap high heels, and a bright purple coat trimmed with monkey fur to attend a ladies luncheon or a charity event at a fashionable hotel or restaurant and in sparkling evening dresses, encrusted with crystals or covered with tinsel fringe that flowed and danced over her slender body like liquid silver or gold.

One of those rare summers when I was less drunk instead of more, I floated to the surface in Newport. I was going through one of my resurrection phases and decided to clean myself up. I left my badly faded red, yellow, and gray streaked hair alone and stopped painting my face, put on a dowdy plain dress, and went in search of respectable employment. I was hired at a fashionable country club as an urgent last-minute replacement for a ladies' washroom attendant who had just eloped with a wealthy stockbroker's nitwit son.

That night I couldn't believe it. I found myself in the same room with Gladys. So close I could have reached out and hugged her. Because I was wearing what amounted to a maid's uniform I was all but invisible to her and her glossy, gorgeous friends. In their eyes I was no better than a coatrack or an umbrella stand.

For one so beautiful, my daughter's disposition was distinctly dour. Her constant complaining made crabapples suddenly seem as sweet as sugar candy. She was wearing the loveliest black lace dress, with cascading flounces floating over her shoulders and down her back, and yards of skirt billowing over a sheath of black satin beneath, and a lavender satin sash encircling her tiny waist. Her hair hung down to just above her waist in a mass of perfect inky black ringlets, with clusters of lavender roses at each side of her head. She looked a full dozen years younger than her actual age.

But was Gladys satisfied? *No!* She was sulking and pouting and stamping her feet and complaining because her husband wouldn't let her bob her beautiful hair and she was tired of looking like Mary Pickford in mourning, with black curls instead of golden.

"If he wanted Mary Pickford, he should have married her instead of me!" She flopped down petulantly onto a velvet bench and hitched up her skirts, dug into her purse, and drew out what I thought at first was a spectacles case, popped it open, and proceeded to nonchalantly fill a silver syringe and inject it into the white thigh above her black stocking top.

"Heroin is simply heavenly!" she sighed, glancing round at her friends and extending the case as though it were a candy box.

Her friends very wisely demurred—*apparently not all young people these days are devoid of sense,* I thankfully thought—and changed the topic of conversation to that perennially popular feminine subject: the prevention of pregnancy.

Gladys, fumbling around in her purse again, shrugged it all off. "Dutch caps and watching calendars!" she snorted. "I don't have the time or the patience for all that! I'd rather just have an abortion! I've already had nine; it's a *wonderful* excuse to go to Paris and shop for Poiret gowns! I simply adore Dr. Jacquard!"

"Couldn't you see Dr. Jacquard without having to have an abortion?" one of her friends asked, to which Gladys insolently barked, "*Shut up, Mimsy!*"

Just as quickly, Gladys's angry snarl transformed into trills of the gayest laughter. "You all should have been with me the last time I was in Paris! I made Jim take me to the Café du Rat Mort—the Café of the Dead Rat. I was there the same night Olive Thomas drank the mercury poison," she boasted, mentioning the beautiful young actress who had died a few years ago under mysterious circumstances. After a late night of partying in Paris she and her husband, Jack Pickford, had returned to their hotel, where she had drunk, intentionally or accidentally, no one knew for sure, the mercury solution he used for treating his syphilis sores. ". . . and we ate the most *delicious* food," Gladys continued, glossing over this vibrant young woman's sad and untimely passing, "watched a Negro bite the head off a giant rat, and some whip dancers—I tell you the welts they raised were *real!*—and then we danced to the gypsy orchestra, and they had these girls come round to all the tables offering lovely little bouquets of fresh flowers that they sprinkled with cocaine from silver shakers. I'd said I would have one, *merci beau-coup,* and was already sniffing it when the girl held out her hand and told Jim that would be twenty francs; you should have seen his face! He complained that the cost was exorbitant, but by then it was too late; it'd already gone up my nose and wasn't coming back. And they have the most *wonderful* cocktails there—brandy and ether with a dash of liquid morphine and a spritz of essence of violets. I tell you, they're the *best* in the world!"

She finally found what she was looking for in her purse and came and shoved me aside and swatted at the rose marble counter between the two sinks with her lacy skirt, then began to carefully tap out two lines of white powder from a little golden vial. She took a dollar bill and carefully rolled it into a hollow tube and, bending over the counter, stuffed one end of it up her nostril and proceeded to suck the white powder right up her nose, while her friends just looked on shaking their heads and rolling their eyes. Apparently they were well accustomed to Gladys's antics.

When she was done, she casually flung the dollar in my direction; I suppose that was her way of tipping washroom attendants.

"I'm tired of this!" she declared, turning back to regard her reflection in the big glass mirror over the counter. She reached back behind her and untied the bow of her sash and with a playful whoop flung it high in the air. Then she reached down and began tugging at her skirt. "Devil take you, black lace valentine Mary Pickford!" she cried, balling her lace overdress up and sending it sailing over the nearest stall door, into the toilet. Standing before the mirror in her slinky black slip, she began to do a shimmy dance, pulling her slim skirt up, inch by inch, to reveal her stocking tops. She stepped out of her black satin step-ins, explaining that they "spoiled the line," and kicked them aside.

Then my daughter spoke to me. For the first time since she was six years old, Gladys Evelyn turned, looked me right in the eye, and spoke to me, her mother.

"*Scissors!*" she bellowed, thrusting out her hand. When I hesitated she got right up in my face and yelled, "Are you deaf or just dumb? I said: *SCISSORS!*"

I opened the drawer and took out the pair of silver shears we kept on hand for ladies who needed help with hanging threads or repairing a sagging hem or loose button. She didn't give me a chance to hesitate and snatched them from my hand.

With Gladys's girlfriends, I watched in horror as my daughter laughingly tugged at her corkscrew curls, pulling them down and watching them spring back up, "just like a piggy's tail!," then started to snip them off one by one. "Won't Jim be surprised?" she cackled, blindly thrusting the scissors back at me, points first, like a dagger, then skipped out the door, calling back to me, "You can keep the dollar!"

She never noticed the tears in my eyes as I stood there with the ruins of my daughter's beautiful curls scattered round my feet, remembering the day her brother had given himself a haircut in imitation of the illustration of Oscar Wilde's Happy Prince.

Shaking their heads, Gladys's friends tipped me with various coins and some generous dollars and followed her out.

Alone, I knelt, gathered up my daughter's curls, and cried and cried. I couldn't bear to stay, to see her like this. She was certain to kill herself one day and I didn't want to be there to see it. I'd had enough of death. As I stood up I caught a glimpse of my face, haggard and ashen in the mirror, and I had to stop and ask myself was I any better? I was a poor hag who drank and sold her sagging body for a few cents, while my daughter danced, wore designer gowns, injected heroin, and snorted white powder. Was Gladys another victim of my curse? Had she imbibed the seeds of death and destruction with the milk she'd sucked from my breast?

I deserted my post then and there. I wouldn't be paid, but I didn't care. I got my coat and hat and went to the bar. There was something in my face that silenced the barman's protests that I wasn't supposed to be in there. He gave me the glass of gin I demanded.

"This is the last one I'll ever have!" I said, saluting him with the glass before I downed it.

As I walked through the club's ballroom, I caught one last glimpse of Gladys through the open glass doors. She was standing, balanced precariously, on the edge of the swimming pool's diving board while her husband and friends anxiously tried to coax her back down. She attempted to dance a Charleston and fell, suffering a concussion and a broken arm. Dr. Corbyn, her husband, fished her out, gently wrapped her in a blanket, and carried her out to their car. I noticed as he passed me, with Gladys moaning and whimpering in his arms, that Dr. Corbyn didn't look at all well. Though he was still in his late thirties, his hair was already gray as a tombstone, the lines on his face were carved quite deep, and behind his spectacles his eyes looked woefully weary. Marriage—or should I say marriage to Gladys?—clearly did not agree with him, it had aged him terribly.

That last glimpse was well and truly enough. I never set eyes on Gladys again. And I can't honestly say, even though she was my daughter and I loved her very much, that I wasn't glad. There are some things a mother just shouldn't have to see.

❧ 38 ❧

I was sitting in a movie theater surrounded by sighing half-swooning females all staring up at the screen, with longing eyes and heaving breasts, caught up in the fantasy that their idol hadn't just died, dreaming that Valentino was still alive and, as The Sheik, was carrying them instead of Agnes Ayres across the desert sands to ravish inside his tent. Suddenly it occurred to me that I was just like them. I'd been a white zombie walking through life with the same glazed longing in my eyes.

I'd spent my whole life waiting for someone to save me, to just swoop me up in his big, strong arms and carry me away from whatever troubles I was facing. James Maybrick had rescued me from the aimless, roving existence I led with Mama and given me a wedding ring and a home to call my own. Countless nameless, faceless salesclerks had sold me the illusion I was more than willing to pay for that buying pretty things could cure me of my doldrums, discontent, and boredom. Before he became my undesired paramour, Edwin had been my playmate in evading adult responsibilities; it had all been one long, diverting game of follow-the-leader. And Alfred Brierley had helped me escape the painful reality of my marriage when it all went sour; he'd been my Sir Lancelot, the knight in shining armor come to carry his Guinevere away to a squalid rented room that she saw, through dewy wet-violet eyes, as Joyous Garde, and the exotic desert sheik who would turn his lily-white, golden-haired captive into his love slave, all rolled into one magic carpet of a man who in real life could never measure up to those fantasies. It was a terrific burden, I realize now, to heap upon the shoulders of a man who only wanted a lover, not love. My dreams were all I'd had to sustain me in prison, ludicrous fantasies about soaring high and making love in a hot-air balloon with my beloved, or waltzing with my husband, feeling his kiss again, welcoming his touch the way I did when I was a new bride. And, after I was miraculously set free, released into a new wall-less, bar-less prison of book signings and lectures, gin and flickers had helped me keep ducking and dodging in the perpetual game of blindman's buff I was playing with the truth about my life.

"Why have you brought me here?"—"Are you not woman enough to know?" the title cards were asking in what seemed like an omen when I got up and walked out into the misting rain. The past was *not* dead because *I* would not *let* it die. "Time heals," the sage Salvation Army angels in their midnight-blue wool uniforms said, "but time heals *slowly*." "Yes," I agreed, "but how long does it have to take?" They didn't have to tell me the answer; I already knew—*Sometimes, a lifetime.* When I reached the dilapidated sagging-roofed rooming house where I was staying I sank down onto the wet front steps and hugged my knees to keep from shivering. A voice I thought I had forgotten spoke to me, like a phantom whispering right in my ear. It was Sister Patia saying, *You cannot forget until you forgive. . . . I do not just mean others; I also mean yourself. . . .*

I'd been carrying around that anger, letting it fester, eating me up inside just like a cancer, and feeling sad and sorry for myself for more years than I liked to tally. And it didn't start with my trial or prison term, much as I liked to pretend it did, and it certainly didn't end there. If I couldn't be bothered to save myself, why should anyone else lift a finger or bother?

Sometimes, my child, failure is a gift from God, though it may not seem so at first glance. Failure is the chance to start again; it is not an end, but a new beginning, the shade of Sister Patia said to me.

Suddenly I knew I had to go back to England. I curled my fist determinedly around the key resting in the hollow between my breasts. It was time to reclaim the diary. I'd left the truth sleeping in that dark bank vault far too long.

"Remember ye not the former things, neither consider the things of old. Behold, I will do a new thing; now it shall spring forth; shall ye not know it? I will even make a way in the wilderness, and rivers in the desert."

Thank you, Sister Patia!

I got up and started walking. There wasn't time to write a letter and sit around waiting and hoping; this time I was going to go and hold my hand out for charity. I knew where the Densmores and a nice old spinster lady with a penchant for hopeless causes lived, and between them I was certain to get enough cash to carry me across the sea to England.

I went first to the house I had hoped would be my home. I could still see myself as a giddy young bride, falling in love at first sight with what I thought then was "home, sweet home," dreaming of all the *wonderful* things I expected to happen within those walls. I could see myself impetuously wishing "to live and love here forever with Jim." Thinking the Cupids smiling down on me in my bedroom would ensure that I would always be lucky and loved.

Battlecrease House had been broken up into bed-sit flats and wired for electricity. Nothing was the same anymore, except the outside structure, though a closer inspection revealed chipped paint upon the windowsills and a couple of cracked panes. The lavish gardens were gone; where once Jim and I had strolled arm-in-arm or sat kissing beneath the gracious trees and I had sat with the children feeding bread crumbs to the silver and gold fish or coaxing the peacocks to eat from my hand there now stood a parking lot.

Giving my name as Mrs. Graham and presenting myself as a widow with her veil down—I was still afraid someone might recognize me even after all these years—I went in and inquired about a room. I just *had* to see inside that house again!

Though the face had changed, the grace remained; it was and it wasn't still the same. All our furniture was long gone and cheap linoleum had replaced the costly carpets, but the wood and stucco work, the paper and plaster, the carved grapes festooning the fireplaces, were mostly still there. As I followed the chatty manageress upstairs, only half-listening to her droning on about a murder in one of the bedrooms during the last century, "arsenic in her poor husband's lemonade," put there by a scandalous "American hussy" of a wife, I paused, letting my fingers linger caressingly over the banister and to admire the stained-glass waterbirds nesting amongst the reeds. It was all still there, just as I remembered it. In my heart, I was that young bride again, going up the stairs of her new home for the very first time. *Tempus Omnia Revelat,* I traced the familiar crest, the hawk perched upon a pile of golden bricks with a sprig of flowering may in his beak. *Time Reveals All.* I was very glad then of my veil; it hid the tears in my eyes, dripping down to give a salty tang to my sad little smile.

Chance, the Fool's name for Fate, led her to show me what had once been a part of my room, now a small, single, simple bed-sit with yellow-ivory walls and curtains of yellowed lace, coarse beige carpet, a single bed, white paint flaking from its iron frame, a table, scarred by cigarette burns and rings where someone had carelessly set glasses or beer or soda bottles without a coaster or napkin underneath, and a chest of drawers, one of which didn't seem to want to close completely. It had a stuck, lopsided look to it.

The fireplace drew my eye. The Fragonard reproduction and eighteenth-century beauties were long gone, but my little guardian angel, the Cupid medallion, set right in the center of it like a cameo on a lady's lace collar, was still there. I was *sure* he remembered me even though Lady Luck had forgotten all about me long ago. My fingers reached out to lovingly caress his little plump baby cheek and I remembered all those I had loved and lost. Their faces flickered past like a movie playing inside my mind, projected fleetingly upon the screen of memory, making me smile through my tears.

While the landlady was busy with her back to me, demonstrating that the window really did open—"it just sticks a bit, but you'll soon acquire the knack for opening it . . ."—I mouthed a silent good-bye to my little angel and quietly slipped out.

"The past is dead," I whispered as I swiftly descended the stairs. I lingered just a moment on the threshold, slowly, softly closing the front door, just saying good-bye. "The past is dead," I whispered, and never looked back.

When I finally stood before Jim's grave in Anfield Cemetery I was surprised at how little I felt. I thought I would feel more. I thought all the anger I had been carrying around inside me all these years would come bubbling right up and I'd push the cross from its pedestal, scream, and hurl myself onto the ground and rend and pummel the sacred earth like a madwoman. But I did nothing of the kind. I just stood there like any other ordinary mourner with a bunch of violets in my hand and let the truth sleep in its uneasy peace.

The Bible says that the truth will set you free. But would it? I've always wondered what would *really* have happened if I had revealed the diary and that candy box full of ghoulish souvenirs. Would it have *really* been as bad as I imagined? Would the wounds have never healed and remained raw and livid throughout all our lifetimes? Would I have been vindicated and acquitted? Or would my adultery still have cast too great a shadow? Would Judge Stephen, with his obsessive need to punish unchaste and misguided females, all those Delilahs, Salomes, and Jezebels, have still accounted my sins far greater than Jim's? Judge Stephen hadn't blinked an eye or cocked a brow at Jim's Mrs. Sarah and their five bastards. Would the murder of five prostitutes in Whitechapel have stirred any horror in his heart at all? Would it have all been for nothing? A daring act doomed to failure? Would I have been convicted and lost those fifteen years and my children anyway? Would they have scoffed at the whole story and said it was all a sham I had concocted? Would Michael's deep pockets have paid for experts to denounce the diary's authenticity? Experts are not infallible; sometimes they see only what they want to see or what they are paid to see. Maybe the diary and those macabre remembrances would have turned and rebounded against me like a boomerang. Maybe Michael, with the family's reputation, his career, and political ambitions to protect—he had given up the stage and become the Mayor of the Isle of Wight while I was in prison—

would have found some way to twist the truth and lay those crimes on my lap too. And, in a sense, they *really* were mine. Those women died standing proxy, for me. Maybe my fifteen lost years truly were a just punishment.

It's too late now. Wondering is as futile as walking a mile for exercise, then eating a pound of fudge as soon as you get home. I'll never know. I let the chance go by. The gambler in me wasn't brave enough to chance it and lay my cards down. I put my children first and foremost as a mother always should, and I can't really regret that in spite of the way things turned out. If I was going to do it, I should have done it *before* Jim died, but I made the decision to leave Jim in God's hands instead of surrendering him and the evidence against him to worldly justice of judge, jury, and hangman. *I* made the decision.

Did we *both* play God, each of us in our own way? Jim took lives; I kept his secret. I aided and abetted him in my own fashion. Yes, I *am* guilty of that. I put the powder in the meat juice, I *almost* did what he asked me to, but then I spilled it. Maybe that is enough to convict me of evil intentions, even though a change of heart, a change of mind, came, in the form of an accident or divine intervention at the last minute.

But the fact remains that I kept silent. I let the chance slip by when it might or might not have changed everything, for better or worse, in sickness and in health, just like the vows we make in marriage. And I *still* don't know if that was right or wrong. Did I keep a vow I should have broken? I know I broke some that I should have kept.

For years I've borne this terrible burden all alone. *I* made the sacrifice. *Willingly* I *chose* to carry that weight. In the end, I can blame no one but myself for what was and wasn't and what might have been. Maybe those do-gooders, philosophers, Bible-thumpers, and would-be saints are right—maybe everything really does happen for a reason, and that reason is often God's alone to know. *Ask and ye shall receive.* When we pray for it to be revealed, sometimes it is given. Sometimes the answer is *yes,* sometimes the answer is *no,* and sometimes it is *not yet.* Everything in God's own time. *Tempus Omnia Revelat; Time Reveals All.* In the end, we are all the murderers of our own dreams.

I knelt and laid my poor little paltry bunch of violets upon Jim's grave. Then I laid my head down where his shoulder would have been beneath the earth and waited for my anger to end. I closed my eyes and remembered the first time I saw him, smiling at me, mustachioed and dapper, with a diamond horseshoe twinkling in his tie. I think I knew then that we'd be together all our lives. I remembered walking with his hand in mine, dancing in his arms, the smiles and laughter and love we'd shared, the way our bodies fit hand in glove in passion, slick as silk, warm as velvet, every night ending and every morning beginning with my head on his shoulder and his arms around me, how good he'd been to me, the way he doted on and spoiled me—I was a wife and a little girl all at once, sensuous siren and naughty schoolgirl—and the way we both believed in luck, our fingers, his and mine, stroking the diamond horseshoe in his tie before each wager. Sometimes we won, sometimes we lost, and the worst thing we ever lost was each other. We let too many things come between us. I remembered how in happier days he'd come and lay his head in my lap and I'd playfully count his gray hairs and tease him that it was time for another application of Indian Princess Hair Blacking. Even when he was in his most murderous rages I never truly stopped believing that he loved me. I never stopped hoping that what was lost would again be found. I was always willing to give us another chance, to try again for a fresh start. There'd been so many and never enough. And the sins, the crimes, he committed . . . all for love. . . . Love diverted, love perverted, love had driven him mad and turned my gentle Jim into a fiend. Oh, Jim, oh, Jim . . .

I kissed the earth his cold lips lay beneath six feet deep, wishing with all my heart that I could feel their warmth again and his arms around me. I caressed the earth, imagining his hair beneath my hand and the diamond horseshoe sparkling in the close darkness of his coffin, a little glittering *U* to catch and hold my love, the way it had once held our luck.

"I *still* love you," I whispered fervently, "and here I renew my promise—I've come back and I forgive everything!" I kissed him again and my tears watered the earth over him. "The past is dead, but not my love for you! May you rest in peace and God forgive you for what you have done, as I have."

The past is dead, I said again to myself as I stood up with a clear conscience, to let it sleep in peace, restful or uneasy, and went home to America.

❧ 39 ❧

After a few more years of wandering, I finally found a home and a haven in Gaylordsville, Connecticut. I had recently read a novel someone had left behind in a bus station, *Show Boat* by Edna Ferber, and the gambler, the reckless wooer, Gaylord Ravenal, reminded me of Jim, and maybe I saw a little something of myself in Magnolia, the woman who loved her husband through thick and thin. I could just see Jim's smile lighting up his eyes and the diamond horseshoe twinkling in his tie again. I took it as a good omen, that I had finally found the place where I belonged.

I met a pair of ladies on the train, a Mrs. Clara Dutton and a Miss Amy Lyon, who were respectively the matron and nurse of a boys' school. Seeing that I had nothing, they offered to share their hamper of sandwiches and slices of lemon jelly cake with me. They were kind to me, and for the first time in many long years I told them something of my story, making it clear as the finest crystal that I didn't want notoriety, I longed only for peace.

"You poor soul, it *has* been a long and wearying journey for you; hasn't it?" Mrs. Dutton said. Then she shared a lengthy look with Miss Lyon, who smiled and nodded. "But I think it's over now," she clasped my hand.

They told me about a spot of land near the school that nobody wanted because it was too near a railroad track. "When the trains go by they would make any walls near there shake, and I'm sure they'd shake the thoughts out of anybody's head too," Mrs. Dutton said. But the land could be had very cheaply if I didn't mind the noise and a little discomfort. It turned out I had just enough money saved to buy it and build a little shack to call my home. There wasn't enough money for electricity or running water, but I had always preferred the kind, gentle glow of candles and lamps and there was a stream just a few steps outside my back door and the trees and blackberry brambles around it provided me enough privacy to bathe. I was no longer a pert-breasted blond beauty, so I couldn't imagine anybody braving those brambles to spy a glimpse of my nakedness.

To welcome me to my new home, Mrs. Dutton brought me a blanket she had crocheted in orange, pink, and white stripes, in remembrance of how that first conversation had begun when I admired the orange and pink taffy-colored clouds outside the window. Her sister-in-law, Mrs. Roberson, the wife of the school chaplain, sent me a loaf of the fresh-baked banana bread she was famous for. And Miss Lyon gave me several packets of vegetable and flower seeds. Some of the boys from the school—how sweet of them, since they hadn't even set eyes on me—painted me a little placard that said "Home, Sweet Home" in bright pink letters, with the sun smiling down on my little house and flowers springing up all around it, and Mrs. Dutton said that some of them had even volunteered to come hoe and weed the earth for me.

The "friendless lady" wasn't friendless anymore. For the rest of my life, I would bear the name I had been born to—Florence Chandler. They respected my wishes and kept my secret. No one ever asked me a single question about my former life or my guilt or innocence; they let those tired old ghosts rest.

I can't say there were no more dark moments to mar my new-found happiness—no one can say that—but, on the whole, I was content. Sometimes the demons would rear their ugly heads and pull me back into the sticky, sluggish black tar pool of depression, but I fought them back down into the pit of Hell as best I could and just got on with the business of living. From time to time, especially as I got older, the diary would beckon to me from the dark corner where it lay hidden, demanding that its story *must* be told now that there was no one who needed protecting anymore. But, following the philosophy of out of sight, out of mind, I just piled more of the magazines, old newspapers, and discarded books I endlessly collected on top of it, trying to stifle its evil whispers.

Mrs. Dutton, Mrs. Roberson, and Miss Lyon found me little jobs to do around the school, nothing too taxing, as I was getting on in years, but simple, pleasant things like helping in the library, decorating the chapel, and assisting Miss Lyon in the dispensary, helping to minister to and soothe her little patients who were trying so hard to be brave little men in the face of scrapes, burns, and the occasional dislocated shoulder or broken limb. It was just enough to make me feel that I had actually earned my nickels and dimes and the hot lunches I was provided.

Some of my benefactors still remembered me, and tiny bequests came in the mail from time to time, though these trickled off during the years of the Great Depression, when times were lean for almost everyone and many millionaires were feeling the hard pinch of poverty. Some even, I'm told, ended up selling apples on street corners or jumped out of windows when faced with the prospect of living without their fortunes.

Several stray cats found their way to my door, and I took them all in and loved every one of them as though it were my very own child. Tiny tins of fish-flavored food for them and my movie tickets became my greatest expenditure and joy. I had a little door cut into the bottom of my back door so they could come and go as they pleased and would never feel like prisoners of my love. Their warm, wiggly, soft bodies and contented purrs provided me with the comfort and affection I'd been missing all these years. Why hadn't I thought of that before? I'd finally found the love I'd been waiting for. Of course, it wasn't the same as holding or being embraced by a man or boy in lust carnal or maternal, but it was enough and in some ways it was better. Those cats certainly made better friends than anyone I ever met in the Currant Jelly Set.

I went to the movies several times a week, sometimes walking or hitching rides into adjoining towns to see different features or to follow a film I especially favored and wasn't ready to say good-bye to just yet. All the managers and ushers, even the candy counter boys and girls, knew me and were very kind to me; they seemed to understand how much the movies meant to me.

I was mesmerized by *Pandora's Box*. I watched entranced as the doomed Lulu, who had destroyed everyone who had ever loved her, unwittingly led Jack the Ripper to her room one lonely, foggy Christmas Eve. In my mind's eye, Louise Brooks's sleek black-helmet bob grew long and swirled into a mass of gilded curls and her shabby short skirt grew rich and sprouted lace and melted down to her feet and filled out to billow and bounce with a perky bow-bedecked bustle as she became me and her companion became Jim. She turned on the stairs and, smiling, reached out her hand to him as the audience gasped at the knife he was hiding behind his back. "I am she; she is me," I kept whispering as I watched her until the candle of her life went out. It was such a scandalous picture—*shocking, immoral, wanton, lurid*—everyone said, and Mrs. Dutton and Mrs. Roberson were simply *appalled* that I had seen it. It was quickly withdrawn, but I sat riveted to my seat through every showing. It made me wonder if someone else knew my and Jim's secret, but no, it could not be. Vivacious, impetuous Lulu's resemblance to the girl I used to be was merely a coincidence, and Jack the Ripper was only a melodramatic and morally convenient method for her demise; women like her had to be punished.

I was particularly partial to the costume pictures and those sparkling-witted comedies poking fun at the gay and giddy rich with their Pekingeses and protégés and scavenger hunts, with colorful casts of Champagne Charlies and madcap heiresses often falling for ordinary working-class Janes and Joes or even the butler or an absentminded scientist.

I watched the love goddesses of the modern world flit by fleetingly as butterflies. I saw the vamp Theda Bara become a living caricature; thankfully the real-life woman had the sense to gracefully retire when the public would not let her change with the times. I watched the fast-living redheaded "It Girl," Clara Bow, who replaced her crash and burn. And "the platinum blond" comet who was Jean Harlow, the tart with a heart both men and women took into their own, blaze briefly across the silver screen only to die, suddenly, at twenty-six. Why did no one ever notice that her eyes never smiled? She made sex seem like an alluring dress she could put on or take off at random; you just instinctively *knew* she was still a little girl inside only playing at dress-up in all that slinky white skintight satin, feathers, diamonds, and furs, and the sassy, tough cookie dialogue was all bravado.

I cried like a baby over *Stella Dallas*. When Barbara Stanwyck stood out in the rain watching her daughter's wedding through a window, I saw myself watching Gladys. And Madame X and Madelon Claudet sacrificing themselves for their sons' greater good; if only I had been so noble, if only I had stayed away from the Le Roi Gold Mine. And there I was embodied by Kay Francis as the happy, breathless young bride falling in love with the house on 56th Street, wanting to live and love there forever, just like the long-lost Florie the day she first set foot in Battlecrease House.

I lost myself in the musicals, now that the movies not only talked but sang, watching Fred and Ginger fall in love as they danced, tapping their way through all sorts of silly romantic complications to the inevitable happy ending, while Nelson and Jeanette made love in soaring operatic trills, like a pair of bittersweet warbling lovebirds. And I marveled at the Busby Berkeley spectacles, where the master deployed beautiful chorus girls in military-like maneuvers that his camera captured at clever angles. I loved to sing along with the musicals. Sometimes I'd get so carried away that despite my increasingly stiff joints and rheumatism, I'd get up and dance up and down the aisle, brandishing my Eskimo Pie ice-cream bar like an orchestra conductor's baton, spattering those seated nearest with droplets of melted chocolate and vanilla, as I sang until an usher inevitably came and escorted me back to my seat, explaining the manager was worried I might break a hip if I kept on and then I wouldn't be able to come watch movies anymore.

I sat and stared in unflinching fascination at the monsters—Dracula, Frankenstein, and the Mummy—and wondered who they were before and if love had been responsible for their sinister transformation, if it had done to them what it did to my husband. I pondered the allure of the sphinx-like Garbo as Mata Hari, Queen Christina, and Camille and sat torn between love and hate for the fast-talking, rum-running, gun-toting gangsters, wept over doomed romances, and quaked with laughter at the comedies.

It was a world where I found *everything* I was looking for, and I *never* wanted to leave it. Sometimes I was there when they opened the doors for the first show and the last to leave when the time came to lock them. Popcorn, candy, soda, and ice cream were like the nectar of the gods to me, and I wanted no other banquet. They fed my body as the flickering images on the silver screen fed my soul.

By lamplight late at night in my shack or sitting out on the steps in the bright light of day, I voraciously devoured all the fan magazines I found, fished out of rubbish bins, or was given or spent my scant coins on. I wondered how all these bright, beautiful young people who now filled my world never quite seemed to figure out that fame and fortune were not the answer. I charted the rise and fall of popularity, the slow fade into oblivion, or the sudden shock and abrupt departure ordained by death, and condoled and wept over their scandals. I'd felt the pinch of those shoes; I knew what it was like to fall.

It was in a movie theater in 1936 that God granted me my moment of grace, the greatest, most sweetest gift I never expected to receive. It was a cold, rainy day, so dreary, awful, and gloomy I'd almost stayed home. But I just couldn't settle, no book or magazine could hold my attention, and the rain tapping on the tin roof overhead, usually so soothing, only needled my nerves. I felt some compulsion calling me to the movie house, so I pulled on my galoshes and raincoat and went out.

I arrived just in time to see the tail end of the first showing of a costume picture called *Lloyd's of London,* sort of a frilly valentine about maritime insurance and thwarted love with lots of pretty people in even prettier costumes; I was *sure* I was going to like it. I was busy jostling my popcorn, soda, and candy and wiggling out of my raincoat when I happened to glance up at the screen. In that moment I *froze*. Every hair on the back of my head stood up, and my heart leapt into my throat when I glanced up and saw *that* face. It was a MIRACLE! Bobo was dead, but the movies, through the grace of God, had given him back to me, more beautiful than he had ever been in life, if that was possible.

In a dark dressing gown, he leaned weakly within a window, framed by heavy satin drapes trimmed with tassels, streaks of ludicrous, improbable silver painted into his black hair to give the suggestion of suffering and age to a boy barely past twenty. The most *beautiful* face I had ever seen rested its brow against the glass, lips parted, trembling, in grief and anguish, black-coffee-brown eyes shimmering, wet with tears, as he gazed down upon his childhood friend's funeral cortège solemnly passing. Slowly, the eyes dropped, the head bowed, the camera drawing caressingly closer, until that face fully filled the screen, then the lashes fell, the same magical double row, so long and thick they cast shadows upon his cheeks. His name, the credits soon revealed, was Tyrone Power.

My husband was right, words of wisdom scattered amongst the carnage of his diary like a single diamond-bright star lighting up the blackest night—the Lord sometimes sends the strangest angels to those who least deserve it.

I sat through that picture three times that day. I was back again the next morning, waiting when the theater opened, and every day after that until they changed films. I sat there, spellbound in darkness, leaning forward, feasting my soul, drinking that boy in with my eyes, feeling as though I had been touched by the divine.

I like to think we never really lose the ones we love; they just come back to us, if we're lucky and wait long enough, in different guises.

Bobo was dead. I *knew* that; he'd been moldering in his grave for twenty-five years. But with this beautiful long-lashed boy up there on the silver screen, I could pretend Bobo was still alive, eternally young and immortally beautiful, impervious to wrinkles and time, that he had become the matinée idol of my dreams after all, instead of a dull, serious-minded mining engineer. I could imagine that though we were still sadly estranged, he no longer denied me images of himself; instead he generously gave me leave to look my fill. I could paper my walls and fill my scrapbook with his pictures, as many as the magazines and movie studio I wrote to could provide. I could pore over the articles, gaining glimpses into his personality—I just *knew* he would be kind; young Mr. Power was just as sweet and sincere as my boy should have grown up to be if Michael hadn't gotten his wretched hands on him! I could discover Ty's likes and dislikes and, like any mother, scrutinize the girls who caught his fancy—Janet, who looked as though butter wouldn't melt in her mouth, and Sonja, that baby-faced blond Norwegian ice-skater. And I could visit the movie theater and see him from time to time, like being invited to a palace for a personal audience with a handsome young prince. I no longer looked at the faded photographs of my real son anymore, the boy whose frozen images had at fourteen vanished abruptly from my life, and the smudged and tear-blurred, now indistinct images that had accompanied newspaper notices of his passing; I had found something better.

My surrogate silver-screen son was more generous than my real son had ever been. He gave me presents three or four times a year: clever modern dress comedies, frothy meringue musicals, swashbucklers, and historical romances, the most beautiful of all being the sumptuous, costumed confection of *Marie Antoinette,* when he brought to life the gallant Count Fersen. When Norma Shearer stood before him, gazing at him with stars in her hair and love in her eyes, I knew just how she felt. That night when I laid my head down upon my pillow I was a young bride in my blue linen suit again waltzing through Versailles with Jim, so happy and so in love, living a dream I never wanted to end.

When young Mr. Power appeared in a feathered turban and brocaded tunic festooned with pearls and gems in *The Rains Came* I smiled and remembered Bobo in the little maharajah's costume he had worn on Gladys's sixth birthday, the day he cut his curls and made my tears fall like rain. And when Tyrone donned the Suit of Lights and played the matador in *Blood and Sand* I left before the end; I couldn't bear to stay and watch him die, even though it was only a film . . . not this time. I sat outside in the sun and ate an Eskimo Pie and fingered the rosary Mrs. Roberson had given me with tears in my eyes and thought of Bobo and Bobby, my lovely lost and found-too-late Biograph boy. I wasn't ready to watch Ty die, even if it was only in a movie.

But this young man I thought of affectionately as my surrogate silver-screen son was not the only boy in my life. On the contrary, my life was now *filled* with boys, and my heart was big enough to love *all* of them, not just the brunets. Living with my seventy-five cats in my little cluttered and untidy shack by the railroad tracks, wrinkled and withered, with no vanity or care for fashion anymore, I'd been afraid the boys would come to think of me like a witch in a fairy story, daring one another to knock upon the hag's door. But no . . . oh no! Some were of course timid and some were bold, but the boys of South Kent School never shied away from me or treated me with disrespect. They never played pranks on me at Halloween or threw stones or eggs at my tin roof and walls.

When they helped themselves to the blackberries that grew on the outskirts of my property, like the thorns surrounding Sleeping Beauty's castle, they always made sure to pick some for me. I'd come home and find a bucket or basket sitting on my steps, and of those they took home for their mothers to bake into pies, tarts, jellies, or cakes there would always be a sweet portion saved for me. They brought colorful pinwheels to spin in the breeze and little clay animals—squirrels, frogs, lizards, turtles, dinosaurs, and bunnies—they'd fashioned and fired in the kiln in their art classes to decorate my flower beds. And when they discovered how much I loved Tyrone Power, a boy would often approach me with one of the little colorful trading cards they found in packs of gum or candy or illicitly savored cigarettes and offer it to me, "since I know you like him."

Every Christmas Eve the boys never failed to bring me a tiny tree, with garlands of popcorn and red berries and little ornaments they made to adorn it. One year, when a manufacturer of the popular dainty vanilla ice-cream cups was putting assorted movie stars' pictures on their lids, the boys collected all the ones with Tyrone Power they could find, punched tiny holes in the tops, strung them with gold tinsel cord, and decorated them with red satin bows and hung them all over the tree they left on my front steps. They always shoveled the snow away from my doors and made sure I had enough firewood in winter and weeded my flower beds without my

ever needing to ask, and even erected a scarecrow in my little vegetable garden, amidst my paltry crop of tomatoes, squash, peas,
and pole beans. And one year, when they saw how weathered my
walls were looking, they painted my shack a cheerful bright sky
blue with rose-pink trim around the two windows to surprise me.
They were all *so* good to me, gallant young gentlemen all.

❧ 40 ❧

The story ends as it began, with me and the diary fated to be mated, like a convict and his ball and chain, to the finish.

He still reaches across time to touch me. The Jim I fell in love with caresses my heart, making me fall in love all over again, and then the murderer I never knew reveals himself and stabs it. If there's any lesson to be learned from all this, you, dear reader, must discover or divine it. I have no more stories to tell. It ends for me now—but it does *not* end in failure! I did what I set out to do, what even I doubted I could accomplish. I told the story, the truth as I know and lived it, start to finish. Yes, I faltered and laid down my head and cried from time to time, but I prevailed. I feel as though the final, tenacious lock has at long last been sprung and I am truly free at last.

I've given the beautiful candy box and the ugly burden it has carried so long a proper burial, with prayers from my heart and a rosary and sweet flowers laid within. I hope it will never be unearthed.

I had the strangest dream. I was standing on the staircase of Battlecrease House, a fetching young bride in her ice-white satin wedding gown and long veil, glowing and filled to near bursting with love. I turned and smiled and reached down my hand to Jim.

A smile lit up his eyes as he gave me his hand. I felt his love in every part of me. The diamond horseshoe twinkled in his tie. So did the knife in his other hand. I saw five women I never knew in life, only in death, as names and descriptions first in newspaper columns and then in my husband's diary. They were standing behind him with their throats gaping wide and weeping scarlet tears, wearing blood-stained rose-pink bridesmaids' dresses. A dark-haired young man with soulful brown eyes and a shy, sweet smile stood and gazed up at us from the foot of the stairs, beautiful as an angel, with an opalescent rosary clasped in his hands. He recited a prayer, tranquil as cool blue spring water, to purge us of all our demons and send them packing with their suitcases full of anger, hate, and evil.

> *"Lord, make me a channel of thy peace,*
> *That where there is hatred, I may bring love;*
> *That where there is wrong, I may bring the spirit of*
> *forgiveness;*
> *That where there is discord, I may bring harmony;*
> *That where there is error, I may bring truth;*
> *That where there is doubt, I may bring faith;*
> *That where there is despair, I may bring hope;*
> *That where there are shadows, I may bring light;*
> *That where there is sadness, I may bring joy.*
> *Lord, grant that I may seek rather to comfort than to be*
> *comforted;*
> *To understand, than to be understood;*
> *To love, than to be loved;*
> *For it is by self-forgetting that one finds,*
> *It is by forgiving that one is forgiven,*
> *It is by dying that one awakens to Eternal Life."*

The bloodstains vanished and all the wounds of soul and skin were healed. The knife fell from Jim's hand and disappeared, as though it had never been. All the wrongs were made right. And all that had been lost was at long last found. Jim took me in his arms and kissed me and I knew, this time, our love would last forever. There would be no more pain, suffering, or dying, waiting, or crying. There really was a new beginning waiting for me at the end.

That feeling of peace was still with me when I woke up. I lay in the gloaming gazing at the pictures arranged upon my windowsill: Jim and me—our wedding picture; Bobo and Gladys as children in their Easter finery, posing with baby bunnies and fluffy yellow butterball chicks; Mama in a black lace gown, big hat, feather boa, and diamonds looking as though she might have given busty, bawdy Mae West her inspiration for Diamond Lil; Edwin, dark haired and dashing as a Russian count in a black fur hat; Bobby, my sweet, shy, eternally young Biograph boy; and Ty, my surrogate silver-screen son, gazing at his own reflection in a mirror-topped table, making a sly, secret joke of the legend of Narcissus, because the handsomest man in Hollywood was devoid of personal vanity. It makes me wonder if Mr. Poe was correct when he said "all that we see or seem is but a dream within a dream."

EPILOGUE

On October 23, 1941, Florence Chandler Maybrick was found dead in her bed, surrounded by her beloved cats, old photographs, and yellowed newspaper clippings, on a mattress crawling with bedbugs. She was seventy-nine years old. A rosary was in her hand and her Bible was at her side. Tucked inside, folded away, faded, and long forgotten, was a prescription for a facial wash containing a minuscule amount of arsenic written by Dr. Greggs of New York in 1878.